THE
PRISONER OF
BRENDA

By Bateman

Belfast Confidential
Cycle of Violence
Empire State
Maid of the Mist
Wild About Harry
Mohammed Maguire
Chapter and Verse
I Predict A Riot
Orpheus Rising

Mystery Man novels
Mystery Man
The Day of the Jack Russell
Dr. Yes
The Prisoner of Brenda

Martin Murphy novels
Murphy's Law
Murphy's Revenge

Dan Starkey novels
Divorcing Jack
Of Wee Sweetie Mice and Men
Turbulent Priests
Shooting Sean
The Horse with My Name
Driving Big Davie

For Children
Reservoir Pups
Bring Me the Head of Oliver Plunkett
Titanic 2020: Cannibal City
The Seagulls Have Landed

THE PRISONER OF BRENDA

BATEMAN

headline

First published in 2012
by HEADLINE PUBLISHING GROUP

1

Cataloguing in Publication Data is available from the British Library

ISBN 9 780 7553 7867 8 (Hardback)
ISBN 9 780 7553 7868 5 (Trade paperback)

Typeset in Meridien by Palimpsest Book Production Limited,
Falkirk, Stirlingshire

Printed and bound in Great Britain by
CPI Group (UK) Ltd, Croydon CR0 4YY

Headline's policy is to use papers that are natural, renewable
and recyclable products and made from wood grown in sustainable
forests. The logging and manufacturing processes are expected
to conform to the environmental regulations of the
country of origin.

For Matthew

'No Alibis' is a real bookshop in Belfast. One or two other places also exist in real life. However, this book is a work of ficton. While the setting may be real, the plot and characters are made up. Nothing I have written should be taken to describe or reflect on real people. The fictional owner of 'No Alibis' bears no resemblance to the real owner of the shop.

Prologue

Alan Parker's exuberant gangster musical *Bugsy Malone* was released in 1977. From the moment it hit the fleapit Curzon cinema on the Ormeau Road, just around the corner from his gloomy terrace, Sam was doomed to be known forever as Fat Sam. And with a surname like Mahood, perhaps his destiny was also decided. At the time, Sam was neither *particularly* rotund nor possessed of an obvious criminal mentality, but with a sad inevitability, he grew into both roles. He ate, and he stole. His parents liked to see him eat. They fed him up like they were preparing him for slaughter. And in a way they were.

On a breezy September night some thirty-six years after being so christened, during which time he transformed himself from bullied to bully-er, Fat Sam Mahood lumbered into the bright and shiny new All Star Health Club, situated in a retail park just off the arterial Newtownards Road in East Belfast. There was a swimming pool on the ground floor and a gym on the glass-fronted first. If you toiled on an exercise bike upstairs, you were treated to a perfect view of the McDonald's opposite. It was like water torture, with burgers.

Fat Sam had never troubled the gym. His exercise regime amounted to fifty leisurely laps of the pool – after dinner, and before supper. He had an expensive tracksuit, cool trainers, a leather sports bag – and a Snickers before he got out of his car. He drove a Lexus, but only because the Porsche was in having its suspension checked.

He lumbered through the doors and grunted at Lesley, or Jackie, or Denise – he couldn't quite remember who was who – behind the counter and she buzzed him in; she'd only been there a few weeks but already knew better than to ask to see his membership card. A cleaner was pushing a mop around, and Fat Sam could have rounded the wet patch, but chose to walk straight across it. The cleaner looked across at Jackie and rolled her eyes; Jackie rolled them back.

Fat Sam did big and scary very well; he made a good living from it. He didn't like to exercise in front of other people, so there was an arrangement that he could turn up late at night after everyone was gone, and enjoy a swim in that twilight period between the official closing time and the management actually locking up for the night. Fat Sam was accorded this special treatment not because the manager of the All Star Health Club was sympathetic towards his body issues, but because he was frightened that he would send round the boys with the baseball bats to beat him to a pulp. Fat Sam was a gangster through and through. He had fingers in lots of pies. He loved pies.

The changing rooms were clean, towels were provided,

there was a water cooler, free bottles of shampoo and conditioner and moisturiser. There was piped Muzak. Just getting changed, Fat Sam was breathing heavily. He laboured into his budgie smugglers. He kept his gold chain on. When he put his belongings in the locker, he didn't bother to lock it. He ignored the rubber wristband he was supposed to wear. There were a few stragglers still getting dressed, but Fat Sam ignored them. Johnny, one of the fitness instructors, nodded across at him and Fat Sam nodded back. Johnny, not long in the job himself, had approached him once to offer his services and had been given short shrift.

In some ways, Fat Sam was the Van Morrison of gangsters – a grumpy sod, but a genius in his own way. Instead of a fortune from songwriting, he had one from protection. He was rich, he was powerful, and he took no prisoners. He liked to set the rules, and do things his way.

On the way to the water there was a sign that said *Please Shower Before Entering Pool*. Fat Sam ignored it. The pool was empty, the surface untroubled. Fat Sam slipped in, and sank down until only his nostrils and the top of his head were visible above the water. Then he pushed off. But instead of relaxing into the breast-stroke, as one might imagine a fat bloke would do, he immediately stretched out into a crawl, thrusting forward, his massive arms churning into the water, his face down for five strokes at a time before twisting left to suck in air. He was, actually, something of a force to behold, and he knew it. He imagined himself a dreadnought going to war.

The pool was not small, but Fat Sam completed his first length in no time. He collided with the far end like a bumper car and sprang back before twisting with surprising dexterity into his next length. He swam, and he swam and he swam. Fat Sam might even have become a formidable athlete, were it not for *Bugsy Malone*.

He was on his fourteenth lap when the fluorescent strip high above him went out; he hardly noticed with his head in the water; but then the other strips blinked out too, one after the other, until by the time he was approaching the turn the entire pool was in virtual darkness, and he stopped short, standing up and roaring out: 'HEY, I'M NOT FUCKING FINISHED HERE!'

Fat Sam stood there, his chest heaving, glaring towards the one source of light remaining, a rectangle around the closed door to the changing rooms.

'DO YOU HEAR ME? I'M STILL SWIMMING!'

His voice echoed, and it was the only response. He muttered under his breath, 'For Jesus . . .' before crossing to the side and hauling himself up the steps and out.

Fat Sam crashed into the changing rooms and yelled, 'I'm still swimming! You turned the bloody lights off!'

Still there was only silence. He spent a few moments dripping on the tiled floor while he decided what to do – whether to tramp the building looking for the idiot who'd blacked out his swim, or give it up for the night and tear their throats out in the morning. Fat Sam sighed and turned to his locker. He was out of the zone now. In the same way that one Minstrel can devastate a hardcore diet, someone flicking a switch had sucked the will to exercise from him. He grabbed one of the free towels and began to rub himself dry. He stepped out of his trunks and reached for his underwear.

4

Somewhere behind him a locker door was opened. In the silence, the sound echoed.

Fat Sam turned towards it. It had come from the other side of the bank of lockers facing him. He didn't like exercising with others, but he had no problem walking about naked. His huge bulk intimidated people even more without clothes. He rounded the corner, stomach first, cock lost.

There was a man standing at an open locker, at an angle, his back to him, his face hidden. He was in a black T-shirt, tracksuit bottoms.

'Hey,' said Fat Sam. 'They turned the fucking lights off.'

The man did not turn, or otherwise acknowledge him.

'Oi – I'm talking to you.'

Fat Sam was not a man you ignored. He looked about him in disbelief.

'Mate – did they turn the lights off on you too?'

Still nothing.

Fat Sam barrelled forward and poked the guy in the back. 'I'm fucking talking to you, deafo . . .'

At which point the man turned and Fat Sam saw that he was wearing a Hallowe'en mask, a fright mask, a Frankenstein's Monster mask with plastic bolts and a huge forehead, and he was struck dumb by it – and mesmerised and momentarily paralysed, so that even though he could now see that the Monster had a knife in his hand, there was nothing at all that Fat Sam could do. It took three thrusts of the blade, lightning fast, for him even to register what was happening.

Another man, with multiple stabs to the gut, would have gone down. But Fat Sam was carrying so much blubber that he hardly even felt them. And yet these were not slices;

these were going in up to the hilt. Fat Sam just stood there, shocked. He could – should – have grabbed the Monster by the throat, he was close enough. He could have throttled him. But instead he took a step back, and then turned and began to lumber away, his rolls of flab undulating as he crossed the tiles, blood streaming down his legs and leaving a crimson snail trail behind.

As he approached the changing-room door, Fat Sam glanced back, expecting the Monster to be right behind him, but he was still standing by the locker, the blade at his side, just watching him.

There was hope, there was hope, there was hope.

Fat Sam crashed through the door, back out to the pool.

And then before him: another figure, another mask. Dracula.

And another knife.

Straight into his stomach.

This time he felt it. Really felt it. Fat Sam lurched to his left.

Out of the darkness, a Werewolf.

Fat Sam stopped. 'No,' he said.

The Werewolf was barely a third of his size. He seemed to hesitate. The changing-room door opened. Frankenstein's Monster emerged. Dracula moved closer. Fat Sam had no power in his legs at all. The pain was starting. It was a nightmare – he was sure it was. He willed himself to wake up.

The Monster hissed at the Werewolf: 'Finish him.'

The Werewolf pulled his arm back. Fat Sam lowered his hands in a final useless attempt to protect his perforated stomach. There was blood everywhere.

The Werewolf ignored his gut and plunged the knife with considerable force into Fat Sam's neck, burying it up to the hilt. The shock of it sent Fat Sam staggering back, preventing the Werewolf from retrieving the blade; Fat Sam pawed at it for just a few moments, and then his legs finally gave way and he toppled backwards, over the edge and into the water, creating a meteoric splash and a tidal wave that swept away across the full length of the pool.

Fat Sam, for all the size of him, still floated. The Monster, Dracula and the Werewolf watched him for a little while, just to be certain that he was really dead. Then they nodded at each other. Their night's work was done.

But they were hardly getting started.

1

She came into No Alibis, the finest mystery bookshop in all of Belfast, bedraggled from the autumn wind and rain and sleet and hail, pulled her red hood down and spluttered *hello* and *long time no see* and *wouldn't this be a great wee country if we just had nice weather*, all in one puffy gasp, and I gave her the look I keep for idiots who deserve to be struck about the head with a hammer, but made sure to add a welcoming smile just to confuse her. Times were hard in the book trade, and one couldn't afford to look a horse-face in the gift-mouth.

I did in fact recognise her, because I never forget a long toothy gob, but I wasn't sure if she would remember me. She had been nice to me in the past, but that was no guarantee of anything. People change, or they have ulterior motives. You have to be on your guard at all times. I have been stabbed in the back thousands of times and have the mental scars to prove it, and one physical one where Mother caught me with a fish hook.

She stood there, dripping, and said, 'So how are you? How have you been?'

'Fine,' I said. There was a small sign hanging from the till that said *Ask About Our Christmas Club*. It was not aligned properly. I fixed it. Despite this, she did not ask. After a while I remembered to say, 'How are you?'

My on-off girlfriend Alison had lately been coaching me in the niceties, but I found them difficult, and ultimately, hypocritical. I didn't care how she was. I didn't care how anyone was. What was the point? We were all going to die.

'You do remember me, don't you?'

'Of course,' I said. 'Nurse Brenda.'

She smiled. 'Nurse Brenda,' she repeated.

'Nurse Brenda,' I said.

'You always called me that.'

'That was your name.'

She smiled. 'So this is what you do?'

It was a pointless question. It was clearly what I did. If this was not what I was doing, what was I doing there at all? People are stupid. Really, really, really stupid.

'Yes,' I said. 'This is me.'

'I've often passed, meaning to call in.'

'Do you read crime fiction?'

'No, I haven't the time.'

'I'm sure you do.'

Her brow furrowed, causing little drops of rain to scoot across her forehead like irrigation on a Chinese paddyfield.

I indicated the display of books directly behind her on my *Buy One Get One for Exactly the Same Price* table. 'There's the new Nesbo there, or Henning Mankell or a movie tie-in

Larsson. There's a whole world of Scandinavian crime fiction waiting to be discovered. Best summed up in the phrase, *the Viking done it.*'

'You're looking well,' said Nurse Brenda.

'I am well,' I said. 'Or if you prefer something closer to home, there's a whole range of medical thrillers. Robin Cook is a bit old hat, but he did manage a few classics. *Coma*? There's a Patricia Cornwell there that comes with a free sick bag . . .'

I glanced towards the front window, just to make sure there wasn't an ambulance outside. It was not beyond the bounds of possibility that Alison had reported me. Or that Mother had made more false accusations. I could not see an ambulance. That did not mean that it wasn't waiting around the corner. Or that they were in that Post Office van, lurking across the road, that it was some kind of Transformer that might at any moment morph into a vehicle with a padded inside and restraints adequate to transport me to a secure mental institution.

'Well, that's good. I like to see my boys doing well. Are you . . .?' And she raised an eyebrow.

'Am I . . .?'

'You know, doing well?'

'Exceptionally so,' I said.

'Married? Girlfriend? Boyfriend?'

I gave her a look. She was an equal opportunities nosy cow. 'Girlfriend,' I said.

'Aw, lovely. I'm so pleased for you.'

'She's not my first,' I said. It was on the tip of my tongue to tell her about all the sex I'd been having, even if it wasn't strictly true any more. 'In fact, I'm a father now.'

'You are? How wonderful.' She was beaming. She did appear to be genuinely happy for me. 'What is it?'

'What is what?'

'Your baby?'

'Oh. Yes. A little boy.'

'And he's okay?'

'Okay?'

'He's well?'

'Why shouldn't he be?'

'I didn't mean . . . I mean, I'm sure he's just gorgeous. And what's his name?'

'Page,' I said.

'Lovely. And you working in . . .'

'I don't work here. I own here.'

'Ah. Right. Very good. Page is a lovely name.'

'Some people think he's a girl, because of the name. But he's a boy. Called Page.'

I had chosen the name myself. Alison had wanted to call him Alan. We had compromised. His forenames were Page Alan. My mother refused to call him Page. For that matter she also refused to call him Alan. She did not call him by any name, in fact, but constantly referred to him as *It*. She gave him as much love as she had given to me. Alison and I cohabited on the ground and first floors of our house. Mother, newly returned from her nursing home, resided in the attic. Once, when Page was crying himself sick, and Alison had tried everything, she called up in desperation to Mother to see if she had any suggestions for old-fashioned remedies. Mother had shouted down, 'Yes, wrap It in a pillowcase and throw It in the river.'

12

People who did not know Mother well thought she had a very dark sense of humour. She did not. She had no sense of humour at all. She was evil.

'Well,' Nurse Brenda said, 'I'm glad that everything has turned out well for you.'

'My girlfriend says I'm a work in progress,' I said, and I smiled, and I immediately killed it, because I was confused as to why I had felt the need to say that, or to reveal anything at all about myself. And then I remembered that when I was *there*, Nurse Brenda was very good at getting me to talk, and that actually I had very much liked her.

'Anyway,' she said, and gave what could only be described as a nervous whistle.

It was most odd. She had clearly run out of inanities yet seemed disinclined to leave. I had asked her virtually nothing about herself, because I was not interested in whether she was married or had children or was otherwise happy or destitute, even though it was all pretty obvious. I saw that there was a circle of white flesh on her bare ring finger, and a small puncture scar where her wedding band had been snipped off because her marriage had gone to pot and she'd turned to food as a comfort and as a result her fingers had pudged up. I saw that she had her blue nurse's uniform on under her coat, but there was a flash of red there too, indicating that she'd been promoted. The whistle she had given invited me to focus on her lips; the lower one had a jagged black line across it – not a scar, but tissue dyed with tannin, indicating heavy recent consumption of red wine.

I could have characterised her as a fat old divorcée with a drink problem, had I so chosen, but I chose not to do so.

I knew then that she was not here by chance, or for old times' sake, or out of curiosity about my fate. She was here because she had heard that I was a crime-fighter and the champion of the underdog.

I said, 'You have a problem.'

She nodded. 'I do.'

'And you've heard that I'm a problem-solver.'

'I heard about you, before I realised it was you. You're like a private investigator.'

'People have said that.' It is what I do: it started as a hobby, but now dominates my life. Bookseller, always. Crime fighter, because there is no one else with my skill. Not in this city.'

'It's not a crime, my problem, it's more like a puzzle.'

'I like puzzles.'

'Or a mystery.'

'I'm a mystery man,' I said. I waved around the store. 'I have ten thousand books in here, and I've read them all. There's nothing I don't know about solving crimes.'

'It's not a crime,' said Nurse Brenda. 'It's a puzzle.'

Still she would not start. I prompted her with: 'A problem shared . . .'

'I shouldn't really be here, it's not official. And it's only a wee thing, but it has been nagging me. You know me – you know I care about all my boys and girls.'

Few of them were boys, and few of them were girls, but I knew what she meant. She had a heart of gold. I remembered that.

'It's just he breaks my heart every time I look at him. I just want to find out who he is. I want to get him home.'

I gave her an encouraging nod, and finally she began to

14

tell me about her problem. If I'd known then what I know now, I would have rammed a book into her mouth to stop her talking, I would have turned her round and taken hold of her raincoat and hurled her, face first, out of the shop and onto the pavement. But obviously I could not have known what I know now, so I listened, and was sucked into what would ultimately become *The Case of the Man in the White Suit*, the most perplexing, frustrating and dangerous case I have yet had the displeasure of being involved in.

2

Out of nowhere Jeff said, 'Who do you think invented butter?'

I said, 'What?'

We were in the Mystery Machine, on our way to my house. I was driving. I do not like to be distracted when I'm driving. I do not like the radio on, and I do not like small talk. Jeff was aware of this, yet persisted. I did not much like Jeff either, but he had been my part-time assistant in the shop for so long now that I had grown used to him. He was a student, and an aspiring poet, and he supported outmoded and pointless organisations like Amnesty International, and wittered on about them at every opportunity. It was like having a fly trapped in a small room with you. You could put up with the buzz for just so long and then you would have to open the window and let him out, or squish him mercilessly.

'Butter,' he said. 'Where did it come from? Who first thought it up?'

I sighed, for I knew that he would persist until I responded. I am the fount of some knowledge. 'We'll never really know,' I said, 'but it was probably an accident, like photography and penicillin and you.'

'I'm serious.'

I doubted that. The roads were, at least, relatively quiet, but I remained alert for danger. I kept the vehicle at a steady twenty-nine miles per hour. Behind me, cars pumped their horns impatiently. I ignored them. I was protecting them as well as myself.

'The more important question, Jeff, surely, is who invented cows?'

'God invented cows.'

'Then God invented butter too.'

'Not necessarily. He invented cows, and grass and stones, but He left it up to us to use what He created to create other things. He didn't invent butter. He facilitated its invention.'

'So who invented God?' I asked.

He didn't even give that any consideration. He was fixated on butter. 'No, really,' he said, 'who do you think was the first man or woman to take some milk and churn it up and produce what must have just looked like yellow gunk? And who was mad enough to even think of tasting it, let alone spreading it on their bap? For that matter, who was the first person to milk a cow? I mean, if you're the first person to do something, you usually get pilloried. Say, if way back when, in the Stone Age, there was a cow in a field and one guy catches another wanking it off, he would have been stoned to death for being a pervert.'

'You milk a cow, Jeff.'

'We know that *now*, but back then, if you just randomly went up to a cow and started pulling at its udder, it would have looked like—'

'Jeff, I worry about you.'

He nodded. 'My finals are coming up, and I'm not prepared.'

'Do they have anything at all to do with the invention of butter?'

'No.'

We drove on. The drivers behind were perplexed by my refusal to cross traffic-lights on amber. After a while I said, 'A far better question would be – who invented margarine?'

'Because?'

'Because that is answerable. In 1869 Emperor Napoleon the Third of France offered a prize to anyone who could make a satisfactory substitute for butter suitable for use by his army and the lower classes. And so a chemist called Hippolyte Mège-Mouriès invented margarine. But it didn't take off, so he sold the idea to a Dutch company called Jurgens, which is now part of Unilever.'

'I see.'

'And another interesting fact is that margarine was actually banned in Canada from 1885. To get round it, bootleg margarine was produced in neighbouring Newfoundland by the Newfoundland Butter Company, which, in fact, only ever produced margarine, and it was smuggled across the border where it was sold for half the price of butter. The Supreme Court of Canada only lifted the ban in 1948.'

Jeff nodded for a bit, before saying, 'I hope no one is taping this.'

* * *

Jeff knew that I had a case, but that was all. I was keeping it under my hat until I had the chance to sit down with Alison. I did not need her permission to take on a case, but I liked to include her in the discussions. It was just easier. But I would pay no attention to anything she said. I was my own man. She had enough on her plate. She had a baby to cope with. And whether she liked it or not, Mother too.

We sat at the kitchen table, Jeff and I, mesmerised, as Alison proceeded to breastfeed Page. I was mesmerised because it was my little baby, feeding on my little woman, with whom I had had sex on many occasions; a life I had created, the fruit of my loins, my son and heir. Jeff was mesmerised because he was seeing a breast, and quite possibly imagining what it would take to create human butter.

'So,' Alison said, 'a case.'

'Yes,' I said.

'I thought we had a No Case rule. That we were done with danger.'

'There is no danger in this.'

'That's what you always say.'

'This is different.'

'That's what you always say.'

'And this time it really is.'

I told her, and Jeff – and Page, for that matter – about Nurse Brenda coming into the store, and the nature of the case. Jeff yawned. He was young enough to still crave excitement. Alison nodded without enthusiasm. Page suckled contentedly.

'So there you have it,' I concluded. 'Absolutely no danger.'

'They start out like that, and then it all goes to pot.'

'There's no chance of that. It's just a puzzle. This poor man has lost his memory, and he doesn't speak or communicate, and nobody has come forward to claim him. He's been finger-printed and DNA'd till the cows come home, his picture has been in the papers and the police still haven't a baldy notion. All Nurse Brenda wants me to do is to try and help her find his loved ones. He's been convicted of nothing, yet the only place they can think to keep him is in a mental institution. That's not fair. That's not right. You wouldn't want me to be locked up like that, would you?'

There was a long pause.

Jeff said, 'Does it hurt?'

'Does what hurt?' Alison asked.

'Him sucking like that?'

'Jeff, stick to the programme,' I said.

'It can do,' said Alison. 'But there are creams I rub on my nipples.'

Jeff nodded. His cheeks had visibly reddened. So had mine.

'Sometimes,' said Alison, warming to her subject, 'the ducts get blocked and I can't feed him at all. I have to wear cabbage leaves in my bra. They help.'

'Why cabbage leaves?' Jeff asked.

'I've absolutely no idea. But they seem to work.'

I could feel Jeff looking at me. I sighed.

'If you must know, cabbages contain sinigrin rapine, mustard oil, magnesium, oxylate and sulphur,' I said. 'A combination of these ingredients helps the leaves to act like both an antibiotic and an anti-irritant. Meanwhile, the prisoner of Brenda remains incarcerated.'

'Could you use a lettuce?' Jeff asked.

'No,' I said. 'Now, I'm going to go to Purdysburn tonight, to check this guy out. Are you coming or not?'

'Yes,' said Jeff.

'I'm not talking to you. Alison?'

'I'm not sure it's appropriate, bringing a baby into a mental institution.'

'I'm not expecting you to. Leave him here.'

'With your mother? She'd eat him.'

'No, of course not.' I smiled at her. 'Why do you think I brought a babysitter?'

Jeff looked around the room for whoever he'd missed, until his gaze fell back on me, looking at him. His eyes widened.

'You've got to be fucking kidding,' he said.

'Watch your language,' Alison snapped, and then repeated the line to me. 'I've never left Page with *anyone*. Let alone . . .' She nodded at Jeff.

'He's not as big an idiot as he looks. He's the eldest of five – he's been around babies all his life.'

'I didn't come here to babysit,' said Jeff.

'Yes, you did,' I said.

'You never said a thing.'

'Would you have come if I had?'

'That's not the point. You gave me the impression we were going on a case.'

'No, you jumped to conclusions. If Alison doesn't come, you're welcome to tag along.'

21

'*Do* you have four brothers or sisters?' Alison asked.

'Yes, but—'

'And you're used to changing and looking after babies?'

'Yes, but—'

'Deal,' said Alison.

3

There was a lot of palaver to go through before we finally set out for Purdysburn. Most of it revolved around Alison refusing to let go of Page. I couldn't quite understand it. Even though he was my son and heir, ultimately he was still only a baby. There are billions of them. In India, you can't give them away. She hadn't left his side since he'd been born, which I considered rather odd. If something did happen to him, we could always bake another. Once, when he was in a cot in our room, and Alison needed to go to the toilet, she insisted on leaving both the bedroom and bathroom doors wide open so that she could keep an eye on him. Even at a distance of twelve metres, you never need to see your girlfriend having a poo. Hearing the splash would have put me off sex for almost fifteen minutes, if sex had been an option.

As we finally drove away, Alison, looking back at Jeff

waving Page's little hand from the front door, had tears in her eyes. 'He looks so sad,' she said.

'He'll be fine. I left him a box of books to sort out.'

'I'm talking about Page,' she said.

'I know that,' I said.

As we rounded the corner, she finally turned in her seat and slumped down. 'I feel like my right arm has been cut off,' she said.

'It hasn't,' I said. 'You're just used to the weight of him there – that's the side you hold him on. Muscle memory.'

Even though I was concentrating completely on the road and our safety, I could tell that she was looking at me.

'Sometimes,' she said, 'you're very cold.'

'It's the nature of me,' I said.

'Even that response. There's no *sorry* or *I don't mean to be* or *I'll try and do better*.'

'I'll try and do better.' Alison sighed. 'I don't mean to be. I'm sorry.'

'They're like the programmed responses of a robot.'

I nodded for a bit, and then once we were safely stopped at a red light I turned to her and spoke in what I hoped was a cold, robotic voice:

'We mean no harm to your planet.'

She just looked at me, then away.

'Weirdo,' she said.

Purdysburn is a place *and* a derogatory term. For a hundred years it was both a secure facility for the criminally insane and a day-care centre for those feeling a bit blue. Growing up, if you did anything daft, people would say you belonged in Purdysburn. School chums would hand you a piece of paper and say, 'Hey, you've dropped your bus ticket,' and you'd look on it and they'd have written *Purdysburn* on it, and sometimes, *one way*. It's a huge Victorian insanitorium, terrifying then and scarcely less so now even with a twenty-first-century make-over and a patient's charter. I was sweating by the time we stopped in the car park.

'Why put yourself through this?' Alison asked.

'I'm fine,' I said. I drummed my fingers on the steering wheel. We could both see the damp fingerprints they left.

'You never talk about it, even in the wee small hours.'

'There's nothing to talk about.'

'Right,' said Alison, and opened her door.

We crossed the car park. Alison mounted the steps and I took the disabled ramp. We met at the top and I put my hand out to take hers, and she kept hers to herself. Two could play at that game. When we got to the door, I refused to open it for her. We stood there. She looked at me, and I looked at her. She could outstare a statue, so eventually I caved in, but she was left in no doubt about how I felt. I was starting to think that she was suffering from post-natal depression. Certainly I was.

The reception desk was directly ahead. From previous experience, most notably during *The Case of the Musical Jews*, I knew that at night there was a security guard on reception rather than nursing staff, but on this drizzly, grim Belfast night there appeared to be nobody on duty at all. We stood at the desk and waited for someone to appear. There was a bell to ring, which Alison pressed. She screwed up her face and hunched her back and cried, 'The bells! The bells!' I gave her a look and she said, 'Lighten up.' Nurse Brenda was expecting us – and when I say *us*, I mean *me* – and although we were a little early, it still seemed odd that there was nobody around.

'She said she'd see you here? In reception?'

'*Yes*,' I said.

'There's no need to snap.'

'I wasn't snapping.'

'There you go again.'

Behind us the door opened again and we turned. I expected to see Nurse Brenda cantering towards us, but it wasn't her, it was a man in a grey raincoat, flanked by two police officers. I recognised the man and Alison recognised the man, and the man recognised us.

'What the hell are you pair doing here?' DI Robinson barked.

'Visiting,' I said.

He stopped before us. He studied me. And then Alison. He wasn't our nemesis, exactly, more like our competition. What irked him most was that we got to solve crimes free of paperwork and any kind of responsibility. Alison had once said that he probably had a kitemark on his arse. I didn't much like her thinking about his arse and sulked.

'Have your baby?' he asked.

'Obviously,' said Alison.

'Congratulations.' He looked at me again, but was still addressing Alison. 'Everything fine?'

'Absolutely. He's a bouncing—'

'I haven't time for this.'

DI Robinson stalked off and the two uniforms followed.

He stopped by the lift and prodded the button twice. He looked up at the lights above, then went for the stairs on his left with his comrades scrambling after him. As they disappeared, and their footsteps receded, Alison said, 'Fancy seeing him.'

'He always had an eye for you,' I said.

Alison shook her head. 'Your head's a marley,' she said.

'I notice these things.'

'Well, despite him having the hots for me, he didn't seem pleased to see us.'

'He did not.'

We pondered.

'What sort of cases does he normally investigate?' Alison asked after a while.

'Criminal ones,' I said. Alison raised an eyebrow. 'That tend to involve violence.'

We both looked towards the lift, and could see that the lights above were now rapidly descending.

'This is just a puzzle,' I said. 'There's no possible danger in it.'

Nurse Brenda appeared out of the lift, looking fraught and frazzled. There was a streak of blood on the shoulder of her uniform. She said, 'I'm awfully sorry, but I'm going to have to cancel.'

'What's happened?' I asked. 'We saw the police – they're not anything to do with . . .?'

'I'm afraid they are. The man you were coming to see, The Man in the White Suit, I'm afraid there's been a stabbing.'

'Is he . . .?'

'He's fine, but the man he stabbed is not. They've rushed him to the City but I don't think he'll make it. Stomach wounds are . . .' She let out a long sigh, and then focused in on Alison. 'Are you . . .?'

'His better half, yes.'

'And you just had a little one?' Alison nodded. 'Look at you, there's not a pick on you.' And then she looked at her hands, and saw that she had blood on them. 'I'm sorry, I'm such a mess. It was a bit of a shock.'

'Why did he . . .?' I began.

'Oh, there's no rhyme or reason for things in here, you know that. An argument over a piano, that's all. Next thing you know . . .' She moved as if to rub her hands on her uniform, then thought better of it. 'I'm sorry to have wasted your time. He's been transferred to the secure unit, and the police will be talking to him there. I'm sure they'll be half the night at that and they still won't get anything out of him. And I don't suppose it matters so much any more who he is or who has lost him, because he isn't going to be going anywhere for a very long time.'

Alison said, 'Anything we can do to help?'

'No, honestly, the police have it under control. I'd better get back up.'

She nodded at us – time to go. Alison gave her a sympathetic smile, took my hand and led me away. Just as we were going through the doors Nurse Brenda called out to us and we stopped and looked back.

'I just wanted to say – Page. It's such a lovely name.'

28

There was something very sad, I thought, about the way she said it. But I didn't know how to respond, so I just gave her a stupid grin and the thumbs-up, and went on out into the mizzled night.

4

I did not think much about *The Case of the Man in the White Suit* for the rest of the night, because that was taken up with Jeff's head wound.

We found him nursing Page in the crook of his left arm on the sofa in our lounge, while pressing a wad of kitchen roll to a nasty-looking gash above his right eye with his other hand. He said, 'Your mother attacked me.' We did not really need to ask why, because we knew Mother. Her motivations were often obscure and her actions rarely justified. But we asked all the same, and tended to him. I went up to see her. She was sitting up in bed reading James Hadley Chase's pulp romp *No Orchids for Miss Blandish*, with a cigarette in one hand and a glass of Harvey's Bristol Cream in the other. I had recently bought her a Kindle, and spent several hours lying about its virtues and downloading out-of-copyright books for her, and she was getting full use out of it by using it as an ashtray. The paperback in her hand was yellowed with age and had a cracked spine, but it was a thing of beauty.

I said, 'Mother, did you strike Jeff with a table lamp?'

She raised one eye, and kept the other on the book. Hadley Chase was a horny old misogynist, but he was difficult to put down. 'Jeff?' she said, somewhat laconically. 'I don't think so. I defended myself against a pervert. He tried to molest me in the bath.'

'He says you shouted down the stairs for a cup of tea, and he took it up to you and you clobbered him.'

'He barged in on me while I was in the nuddy. He could have been anyone.'

'It was Jeff. You know Jeff.'

'I didn't have my glasses on.'

'I told you he was here, looking after Page.'

'Who?'

I looked at her. She had had a stroke a while back, but she was now largely recovered. The doctors had said there might be some residual brain damage, and she had seized on this as a convenient cover for her more extreme acts. The truth was that she had always been barking.

'I get confused,' she said.

'Jeff is babysitting for free, you can't go abusing him.'

'He was trying to abuse *me*. I was in the bath.'

'Mother, there is no table lamp in the bathroom.'

'I brought one in with me.'

'Why?'

'In case somebody tried to molest me.'

'Mother . . .'

'I don't want to talk about it. I'm tired now. I'm going to sleep.'

She reached across to switch off her bedside lamp. Before the light winked off, I saw that there was a small pool of blood at its base. The room was now lit only by the dull glow from her half-melted Kindle, which she knocked over as she turned away from me, wrapping herself in her quilt, spilling ash and butts across the cover. I wasn't about to start cleaning them up, so I retreated to the doorway, but then lingered there for several moments, thinking.

Eventually I said, 'Are you enjoying the book, Mother?'

'No. It's a lot of shite.'

'Do you want me to take it away?'

'No, I want to see what happens.'

I recognised the Hadley Chase conundrum, although it was not exclusively his.

I said, ''Night, Mother. Love you.'

There was no response. I didn't mind that. I was lying.

I followed the drips of blood down the book-lined, carpet-free stairs back into the lounge, where Alison had repossessed Page and Jeff was struggling into his army surplus jacket while continuing to try and staunch the flow.

'It's going to need stitches,' he said. 'I'm going to be scarred for life. I should press charges.'

'She says you tried to molest her,' I said. 'It's your word against ours.'

'Ours?'

'Family always comes first, Jeff, you know that.'

He stared at me.

Alison said, 'Don't listen to him, Jeff, you know he'd sell

her and all of us down the river if there was a couple of quid in it. Even my little darling.' She juggled Page in her arm.

'That's not fair,' I said. 'Mother, you and Jeff – yes, obviously. But Page absolutely not. I would expect more than a couple of quid.'

I smiled. Alison smiled. Jeff did not.

'I'm serious,' he said.

I doubted that. He was a well-known whingy whinger. 'C'mon,' I said, 'I'll drive you to the hospital.'

Alison gave what I can only describe as a guffaw. She got up from her armchair. 'If you drive him to the hospital, he'll probably bleed to death by the time you get there. *I'll* take him. You look after our baby.' She pushed Page into my arms, and I'd no choice but to accept. 'It'll do you good. You don't spend enough time with him.'

'I . . .'

'Don't argue, just do it. He doesn't bite. Unless you intend to breastfeed him. C'mon you,' she said to Jeff, scooping up the keys to the Mystery Machine and quickly ushering the dripping Amnesty International apologist out of the living room and down the hall, leaving me speechless, with Page snuffling in my arms and gazing curiously up at me.

He looked like *Kojak*.

It was not a good look.

I tried to put Page in his cot, but he was having none of it. Alison had left expressed breast milk in the fridge, and I fed him that. For a while I thought about what it would be like to have enormously engorged nipples, one on each breast and a third in the middle of my forehead. I wasn't sure what the practical application of having a nipple in the middle of my forehead would be, but I was sure, given time, that I could have come up with something. I had plenty of time. Eight hours, if the National Health Service was up to its usual standard. I knew Alison well enough to know that she would not merely dump Jeff at Casualty the way I would have done. She would stay with him until he was stitched and infected with *clostridium difficile*. He'd be lucky if he came home with both legs.

Soon, Page started crying and would not stop. I whispered, and sang, and cuddled and cooed to zero effect. I even peered into his nappy to see if that was the source of the problem, and was relieved to find that it was not. He was just crying for the sake of it. I walked the floors with him. Up and down the stairs. I went out into the back garden, and then out with him in the stroller and up and down the street. I peered up at windows in the vain hope of seeing someone getting changed. I checked out cars for personalised numberplates and was relieved to find none in the immediate vicinity. It had been a while since I had scratched the paintwork of cars with personalised numberplates with my nail; mostly it was the recession that was making them rarer, but I liked to think that their absence had at least a little bit to do with my campaign of hate. While I pushed the stroller, I also toyed with the thought of just thrusting it out in front of the first lorry that came along, just to see how quickly it would stop, but it was late at night and there was little traffic.

Page had quietened down pretty quickly once we were outside, but the minute we went back through the door he started up again. I walked the house some more. It was a big house, with a lot of rooms, most of them stacked with books, and I walked them all, with the exception of Mother's room and next to it, what had been, in a bygone era, an old luggage room. At Alison's request I had recently allowed her to convert it into a small studio where she could pursue her hobby of drawing comics. She said she needed somewhere to escape to. I said, 'From the baby?' and she nodded, vaguely. It was a room I had not lately ventured into because I have no interest in her unfulfilled ambitions. Sometimes I pretend to be fascinated by her comics, but I'm really not. She should get a life. But now, desperate to try any change of surroundings that might quieten the mewling, I slipped into it, flipped on the light and stood blinking for a moment while my eyes grew used to the brightness, and then struggled to comprehend what they were seeing: taped to the walls, and indeed the ceiling, were dozens, possibly hundreds of drawings of a baldy-headed baby, but so distorted, so bloated, so disjointed and scaly-skinned, so monstrously mutant and hellish – and yet, still so recognisably Page – that my paper-thin heart almost imploded.

Page's cries turned to screams.

From the next room Mother yelled: 'Will you shut that child up! I'm trying to fucking sleep!'

5

I had a lot on my mind the next day in work. I always have a lot on my mind, very little of it to do with affairs here on earth, but this was different. I was very disturbed by what I had found in Alison's studio, but had not yet raised it with her. She had returned very late from the hospital, so late that I was already feigning sleep. Page had finally succumbed to the drugs I administered. I was up and away out before either of them woke in the morning. This was not unusual. I am an early riser. I do not sleep much, and haven't since the Falklands War, but I could have hung around to question her about the paintings and drawings. I chose not to because I do not like confrontations, or arguments, or contrary opinions, at least until I can get straight in my head what I think about something. It is easy to lose an argument if you haven't properly considered every possibility or explored every tangent. It is why lawyers often present ridiculous scenarios in court and then harry and bully a defendant to respond quickly, so that what he or she says is inevitably ill thought through and incoherent, thus underlining their guilt, when what he or she really needs is time and the opportunity to give a sober and considered response, possibly by e-mail.

There were no customers all morning. This was not unusual. The book trade was dying on its feet. There was plenty of time to ruminate, while also reading the most recent Dennis Lehane. I am a great multi-tasker. Since Parker died, Lehane is now Boston's finest living crime writer.

I was not only worried about Alison's paintings, but by Mother's sudden explosion of violence. Jeff was off studying for his finals, through one eye. The other had swollen closed and there were six stitches above it. I wasn't worried *for* Jeff, obviously, because he's a useless idiot, but for Mother. Not because she had lashed out – that had been her form since I was a nipper – but by the weapon she had chosen. She had wielded the lamp in the bathroom. There was not normally a lamp in there – it is already an extremely well-lit room. According to Jeff she had not only clobbered him with it, but swung it at him at the end of the electrical flex, the way a South American gaucho might swing a bolas. But the fact was that it had been plugged in from her bedroom, stretching to the edge of her bath via two adaptors. To go to that much effort for a little extra light – there's a shade on the lamp and a low-wattage bulb – didn't make any kind of sense. *Unless she was intending to plunge the lamp into the bath.* It now seemed obvious to me that she had only struck out at Jeff as a reaction to being interrupted in the act of committing suicide.

Which worried me, a little.

Mother had always been an evil old witch, but she was *my* evil old witch. If anyone was going to kill her, it should be me. Clearly she was depressed. But why? Was it my fault? She would be dead soon anyway, but I couldn't think of any reason for her to want to speed up her conclusion. She was old, decrepit, a brain-damaged harridan and a violent psychopath to boot, but she had always been as such. These were no reasons for her to want to top herself. If I have learned anything in life, it is that you should learn to embrace your deficiencies. And appreciate your situation: Mother was waited on hand and foot, she had access to an inexhaustible supply of sherry, she had her own dutiful son living with her and a lovely little baby bringing renewed life to her shabby old house. She should have been singing 'Roll Me Over in the Clover and Do It Again', yet she had chosen instead to try and kill herself using a lamp fitted with an energy-saving light bulb.

I couldn't settle my head, and turning my thoughts to Alison's bizarre paintings certainly did not help. Was she merely letting her imagination run wild, or were they some mad kind of manifestation brought about by the trauma of giving birth or living with Mother? Or what if she had *literally* become possessed? Was there some unspeakably evil force loose in the house, something intent on picking off the members of my family one after the other?

I needed to confront Alison. That much was clear. I needed to look into the eyes of the demon.

But first, lunch.

I don't normally close the shop at lunchtime because I send Jeff out for it, but with no alternative I locked up and sauntered across to Starbucks. I order from their menu in strict rotation, going through it from start to finish once a month, although this applies only to their beverages. I very rarely eat their sandwiches because I had found that I had to stand perusing the ingredients for so long that lunchtime was invariably over by the time I finally found something I was able to eat without putting my life at risk. I am allergic to many things, including ham, cheese, chives, oregano, molasses, pesto, Polo mints, leather thongs, Shredded Wheat, Romanian *Big Issue* sellers, humans, dogs, leopards and geese, but not, as far as I could determine, to anything in my eventual choice that day, a Roasted Vegetable Panini, containing 350 calories and 25 mgs of cholesterol.

I was just about to take my first bite, when the chair opposite me was pulled out and a man said, 'Do you mind if I sit down?' and then sat before I could protest. I don't like to eat in front of people because generally they make me sick, and Detective Inspector Robinson was no exception.

I set down my Panini and pulled my Caramel Frappuccino closer. I looked warily at him. I had absolutely no doubt that this was not a coincidence, and also I knew from sad past experience that it was never a good sign when DI Robinson came looking for you. Here, in Starbucks, we did not even need to go through our regular charade, which involved him asking me to recommend collectible books while I tried to avoid giving him any discount. Today he looked grey, and there were bags under his eyes.

'So,' I said.

He was studying me. He said, 'I still haven't quite worked you out.'

'I'm unworkoutable,' I said.

'You're either as mad as a bag of spiders, or it's all an act.'

'I'm allergic to spiders,' I said.

He nodded. He had a plain black coffee. He stirred sugar into it. I waited, patiently.

Eventually he said, 'What were you doing at Purdysburn last night?'

'You don't know?'

'Yes, I know. It was a rhetorical question.'

'Ah.' I took a Frap sip. 'You know,' I said, 'in the sixteenth century, an English printer called Henry Denham invented a rhetorical question mark. It was the reverse of an ordinary question mark. It didn't catch on, but I think it could have been very useful.'

'Really?'

'Is that also a rhetorical question? And if it is, see how useful it would be?'

He thought about it. After a bit he gave a shrug and said, 'Sure, if we were writing this down. But we're not. We're just enjoying a coffee.'

'How do you solve a problem like Maria?' I asked.

'Excuse me?'

'How do you solve a problem like Maria? From *West Side Story*. It's a rhetorical question. And one that is repeatedly answered with another question throughout the song, suggesting that actually the problem of Maria cannot be solved or does not require an answer.'

DI Robinson leaned forward over his coffee. 'Tell me, Mystery Man, does a bear shit in the woods?'

'Are you being rhetorical?'

'Yes. And no. You have a habit of interfering in my investigations.'

'I'm sorry, am I the bear or the shit, in this scenario?'

'You're both. You were at Purdysburn last night trying to see The Man in the White Suit.'

'Everyone seems to be calling him that. I'll be very disappointed if he doesn't have one. And *trying* is the word.'

'How did you find out about him?'

'I haven't found out about him.'

'I mean, who called you in?'

'I'm not at liberty to say.'

'Management?'

'They just wanted me to find out who he was. And by *they* I mean whoever it was who called me in, be they a he, she or a goat.'

'And are you finding out?'

'No. Once he stabbed someone, he, she or the goat didn't seem so keen. I suppose they, he, she or the goat hoped the police would take a keener interest. Incidentally, how's the guy who got stabbed?'

'He died in the early hours,' DI Robinson said wearily.

I lifted the Frap. It was very good. Starbucks has a famously high standard in its beverages. I wasn't sure if this store was owned directly by Starbucks or was part of a franchise operation. Franchise operators can be hit or miss.

'Yes, indeed,' said DI Robinson. 'So it's a murder investigation.' He nodded at me. 'Although fairly open and shut.'

He raised an eyebrow.

I raised one back.

We were at something of an impasse, while my Panini,

41

which they had thoughtfully heated for me, was getting cold. I still couldn't bring myself to take a bite. Instead I sipped Frap again. I dabbed my lips with a napkin and said, 'I have to get the shop open again.'

I began to get up.

'Hold your horses,' said DI Robinson, and made a waving-down motion with his hands.

I am, in fact, also allergic to horses. But I did not mention this. I settled back down. I did not need to get the shop open. It was a device for cutting to the chase.

'This is a murder investigation,' he said. 'But it's not just one murder.'

He let that sit in the air for several moments.

Eventually I said, 'In the hospital, last night?'

'No. Beyond that, I'm not prepared to say.' He leaned on the table, his shoulders forward. If he meant it to be intimidating, then it was. 'All I know,' he said, his voice slightly deeper, 'is that somehow you're attempting to become involved in this, and although we have collaborated successfully in the past . . .'

'Well, if by collaboration you mean that I've solved cases and you have taken the credit, then yes, we—'

'This time I don't want you sticking your nose in. I'm not warning you off, exactly, I'm just saying – you are now a family man with responsibilities. Don't put your loved ones in danger, because if I'm right, this Man in the White Suit is not only a psychopath who deserves to spend the rest of his life locked up exactly where he is, in the nut house, he's also going to be a target for some very nasty individuals who will be looking for revenge – and you don't want to put yourself or your family in the way of that, do you?'

'Obviously not,' I said.

'I mean it.'

'So do I.'

'I *really* mean it.'

'So do *I.*'

DI Robinson nodded. 'Okay,' he said. He gave another hand signal, palm out, towards the door.

I got up, clutching my Panini.

'How're you getting on with that girl of yours anyway?' he asked.

'Fine,' I said. 'Although I think she may well be possessed by the Devil.'

DI Robinson shook his head wistfully. 'Tell me about it,' he said.

6

I stood by the window, watching.

I take copious amounts of sleeping pills, but they never seem to work. They are properly prescribed, though sometimes I had the notion that Dr Watt, one of my current GPs, had been supplying me with sugar-coated placebos. In fact, it is probably the sugar that was keeping me awake. He believed that I was taking too many tablets, and that was without me letting on how many herbal remedies, pick-me-ups and potions I was also purchasing from the health-food store downtown. Though, it has to be said, I had recently cut back on these.

The store was run by a nice Indian gentleman who wooed me by joining my Christmas Club. It was kind of a quid pro quo – an 'I scratch your suppurating back and you rub my engorged stomach' kind of a deal. We became so pally that he gave me first dabs on whatever new wonder medicine came into the store. He called me his little guinea pig,

44

although coming from a devout Muslim I wasn't sure if this was a compliment or an insult. I pulled him on this and he went off to consult the Koran, but before he could report back he suffered a massive coronary thrombosis which killed him stone dead. So he left me in the lurch on that one. It wasn't much of an advert for the benefits of his health-food store either. His son took over the running of the store, but refused to honour his father's commitments to my Christmas Club, so I had lately taken my business elsewhere, mostly onto the internet. Alison, for her part, was pleased that I'd apparently cut down on the pills. She believed that 99 per cent of herbal remedies were 'pish'.

That night, however, I could not sleep mainly because I was thinking about The Man in the White Suit and why DI Robinson had given me a warning-off which he claimed was not a warning-off, but which *was* a warning-off. I had simply been asked to identify a lost soul, and he would have it that my baby's life, my girlfriend's life and more importantly, my own life would be in danger if I chose to pursue the case. He had also said, on the pavement outside my beloved Starbucks, that this was not some kind of a double bluff and that by trying to dissuade me he was not actually really trying to encourage me because he had come to a dead end and realised it was time to call on my superior investigative skills and to take advantage of the fact that I was unfettered by the need for warrants or permissions or respect for consti-tutional rights, and that, furthermore, he believed I could not only successfully identify The Man in the White Suit but also expose those who were plotting revenge against him while bravely ignoring what would surely be a desire on their part to exact bloody retribution against my family for daring to stick my nose in. He was saying that this was definitely not what he was suggesting.

I said, 'That's what you call a bluff, not a double bluff.'

'Are you sure? I mean about it being singular?'

'Fairly,' I said.

'Either way, I don't want you involved.'

'Does that make it a double bluff, now that you've warned me twice in thirty seconds? Or if it's the same bluff, does it count as double? Or does saying either way negate the . . . Never mind, these are rhetorical questions.' I made the sign of the reverse question mark, to emphasise the point.

He said, 'Alison was right. You are a fucking space cadet.'

'When did she say that?' I not only didn't like that she was talking about me behind my back with someone who clearly fancied her and wanted to have sex with her, but also that she was getting so close to the truth.

DI Robinson, for his part, ignored my question. 'Just take this on board, Mystery Man: keep your big nose out of it. Okay?'

'Okay,' I had said.

Alison joined me at the window. There was a steely greyness to the sky, which was as close as we ever got to the sun coming up. This high up in the house, the view was reasonable. Most nights I get to see people getting changed for bed across the road, and some mornings as well, when they forget themselves and open their bedroom curtains before they've thought to put many clothes on. I also like to keep an eye out for unfamiliar cars, gypsies and mother ships.

Alison slipped an arm around my waist and nestled her head into my pigeon chest. 'What's wrong, baby?'

'Nothing. I was just thinking.'

'Usual shit?'

'No.' And then: 'I was thinking that nose cartilage continues to grow your whole life. In ten years' time I'm going to need scaffolding.'

She gave me a squeeze. 'Oh, love, don't be daft. With all your ailments? In ten years' time you'll be eight years dead.'

'I'm serious, it just keeps growing.'

'I know you are. You wouldn't be you if you didn't have something to worry about. But the length of your nose is the least of your worries.' Before I could react properly to *that* she kissed the side of my head. '*Joking*,' she said. 'I've never met a healthier man, at least physically.'

'And what's *that* supposed to mean?'

'I mean, you have great empathy with people who suffer from severe mental illness.'

I studied her. 'Elucidate,' I said.

'I know you, I know what you're thinking about. That poor man in Purdysburn.'

'I am not,' I said. She raised an eyebrow. 'Well, not much. I'm just curious.'

'I know you are.'

'Why do you say, *poor man*?'

'Because if you don't know who you are, it must be very confusing. It would be very easy to lash out.' I nodded. 'Or he might even have multiple personalities. You can relate to that.'

'I . . .'

'I'm *joking*. I just think that if anyone was able to tease something out of him, it's you. Being locked up in there, no friends or relatives to turn to, he could probably do with a friendly face, and you have a lovely friendly face.'

'I was never locked up,' I said. 'What do you think I am?'

'I know exactly what you are.' She gave me another squeeze. 'You're my Love Bug.'

'I'm allergic to—'

'Don't spoil it,' she said. She let go of me and sauntered back to our bed and crawled under the quilt. She reappeared at the headboard end and threw the corner of the quilt back to reveal her topless self. 'Our offspring has not yet awoken, we should make hay while the sun shines.'

Hay and *sunshine*.

She was trying to kill me with kindness.

So we had the sex and it was good. I told her as much. 'That was good,' I said.

'Don't damn me with faint praise,' she replied.

'No really, it was nice.'

'Jeez.'

'It was fine.'

'Never say fine. Girls hate *fine*.'

'Fine is a fine word. It's wonderful.'

'Then say wonderful. Don't say fine.'

'But it was fine. A *fine wine* is a great compliment.'

'You're saying I'm old, now. *Vintage*.'

'No, I'm—'

She put a finger to my lips. 'Stop.'

I stopped. I had been contemplating raising the subject of her devil pictures. I decided not to. It did not feel like the right time. Instead, I would keep her under observation.

After a while, she said. 'Did you ever have a nickname at school? I'm sure you did.'

'Where did that come from?' I asked. She gave a little shrug against me. I said, 'Why, did you?'

'Briefly, yeah. They called me Frida. After Frida Kahlo. She was a Mexican painter who—'

'I know who she was. Was it because you have a moustache like hers?'

She dug me in the ribs, which was a dangerous thing to do with someone who suffers from Brittle Bone Disease.

After a bit she said, 'I don't have a moustache, do I?'

I studied her face for a long time. Eventually I said, 'N . . . ooo.'

She giggled. It was nice to see.

She said, 'It was because I loved art so much, and was briefly infatuated with her. I was *fourteen*.'

'And that was it? Your only nickname?'

She nodded against me. 'You? More than one?'

'A couple, yes.' I thought for a moment. They were never far from the surface. 'Well, they called me Snorky. And SpeccyFourEyes. And Gormless. And Thickfuck. Snout Honker. Beaker. Spine. Spineless. Spinefree. Sickboy. Mentalboy.'

'God, you—'

'Biafran, Bostik-head, Joey Deacon, Moron, Maggot, Gayboy, Fruitcake, Shirtlifter, Albino, Sambo, Space Cadet . . .'

'You—'

'Shit-kicker, Ballet Scrotum, Barnacle Arse and Spastic.'

She nestled closer and stroked the single red hair on my chest. 'God. Love.'

'Yes, that first day at school was difficult. But you know what they say, sticks and stones will break my bones, but names will smooth my passage to a secure mental institution.'

'Is that what happened? Why you ended up . . .?'

'Amongst other things.'

'And your mother wasn't any . . .?'

'My mother was amongst the other things. Why do you ask, about the nicknames?'

'I was just wondering how you felt about Love Bug.'

I shrugged. 'In the grand scale of things it's fine.'

'*Fine*!?'

'It's good.'

I smiled. We smiled. Her palm was now flat against my chest. If she'd wanted, she could have poked a finger through my waxy skin and speared my paper heart. She looked me in the eye. I looked away. She guided my chin back towards her until our eyes locked. She said, 'You are a good man, and getting better all the time. And I love you. If you want to check on The Man in the White Suit, you just do that. You have my blessing. I mean, what harm can come of it? He's behind bars already.'

Somehow I had neglected to tell her about DI Robinson's dire warning of impending doom if I pursued the case. I would have, but there was no point in ruining a nice morning.

And then I let out a sudden yell as Alison yanked that single red hair from my chest.

'Got it!' she guldered. 'That fucker has been annoying me for months!'

7

I arrived at the hospital unannounced. Although I am always one for order, and planning, and have twice been nominated for the OCD Hall of Fame, when I am involved in a case it is best not to alert people to an impending visit; it only gives them an opportunity to say no or hide behind a sofa. Nurse Brenda had not actually told me that I was no longer required to solve *The Case of the Man in the White Suit* – and I didn't see why the fact that he had been charged with murder should have changed anything. He was still unidentified. I was only interested in revealing who he was, not in the details of his murder or the concerns of those who apparently held a grudge against him. I wished to study him, and deduce. That was all.

I sat outside in the Mystery Machine for a while, waiting for my heart to slow. Partly it was to recover from my fear of traffic, and signals, and pedestrians, and the possibility of asteroids, but mostly it was the terror of once again being in Purdysburn, and the memories it stirred. I should have been asking myself why I was there at all, if this was how it was going to affect me, but I did not, because if I started asking myself questions I would be there all day, sitting behind the wheel, talking to myself. I'd done it before. Once for eight hours. And that was me debating whether to order a sandwich or to drive home and make one. There are infinite possibilities and variations and tangents. Having an intellect superior to most humans is no easy burden to carry.

Eventually I got out. I approached the hospital. It was no less foreboding in daylight. As I entered and crossed from the door to reception, I found myself studying the tiles underfoot. Every third one featured a series of hieroglyphics. Most people cannot read hieroglyphics. I can. I suspected that these hieroglyphics did not actually mean anything, which only served to make them more cryptic. If I let myself, I would start looking for a code, and then the key to it. Months might pass before I got to the reception desk.

I forced myself to look up. I asked for Nurse Brenda. I said I was there to see her on a private matter, that I wasn't a patient. The woman behind the desk said she would phone and check. She did not ask for my name. When she spoke to whoever she spoke to, however, she said my name. This was surprising. Either word of my crime-fighting exploits had spread, or she recognised me from No Alibis – or she recalled me from my time as a patient in Purdysburn. She looked old enough. I'm not great at remembering faces, unless they are bizarre. This woman had a plain, unmemorable face. There was nothing distinctive about it at all. It was bland, dull, insipid and weak. It lacked personality, distinctive angles or anything other than coherence. She had a medium-sized mouth and adequate teeth. Her hair was a mousy brown and her eyes were exactly the same distance apart.

She said, 'She'll be down in a minute.'

Her vowels were flat and her accent middle-class, middle-of-the-road and from somewhere in the middle of the Province. I had a tremendous urge to hit her with a hammer. Instead, I said, 'Thank you.'

She smiled. She said, 'Do you not remember me?' I shook my head. 'I remember you. You were very sweet. And I remember your mother.' We nodded. 'Is she . . .?'

'Dead, yes,' I said.

'Sorry,' she said. 'She was certainly a force of nature.' I nodded. 'A law unto herself,' she added. 'And you're well?'

'Perfectly,' I said.

We nodded some more. Then I shuffled to one side, and to take my mind off my suicidal mother and the tiles that wanted to talk to me, I studied a small noticeboard. There was a poster advertising the Friends of Purdysburn's fund-raising production of *One Flew Over the Cuckoo's Nest*. I supposed it was to be an ironic production, and liberating, and inspirational. I would not be attending. Not after the last charity event I'd been persuaded to buy tickets for, when the Brittle Bone Society's production of *Seven Brides for Seven Brothers* had ended in bloody carnage.

There were footsteps on the stairs and Nurse Brenda appeared, smiling. She glanced across at the woman behind the desk and raised her eyebrows at her, which I did not much like. I was interpreting it as her saying, 'Thanks for calling me down to see a nutter,' but I could have been mistaken. She could have been saying thank you. I am a glass half-empty kind of a guy. I know that. Alison has told me often enough. She says I often take offence where no offence is intended. I took offence at her for pointing this out to me. She said I was too judgmental. I rest my case.

Nurse Brenda said, 'You're getting to be quite the regular. Next you'll be wanting a wee bed for the night.'

It was supposed to be funny, and out of respect for our past relationship, I gave her a smile. But I didn't like it. She put a hand on my arm and guided me away from the desk, then made sure to position herself so that her back was to the receptionist.

'Sorry,' she said quietly, 'but that one's a nosy cow. How're you doing? Wasn't that a dreadful thing the other night?' Without waiting for my response she went on, 'I was going to call you as soon as I saw daylight, but I've been on duty ever since with just a couple of hours of a lie-down upstairs to keep me going. I didn't sleep, of course, for worrying. There's been people coming and going all day.'

'The Man in the White Suit – has he said anything?' I asked.

'Not a dickeybird. They sent a solicitor up to represent him, but he got nothing either. He just sits there looking vacant. I mean, my boy. I feel so dreadfully sorry for him.'

'Even though he's a murderer?'

Nurse Brenda took a deep breath. She looked at me, and glanced back at the receptionist, and then moved me a little further away. 'There is absolutely no doubt about it that he *did* commit murder. Half a dozen people saw him.'

She hesitated.

'*But*?'

'Those half a dozen, they were all patients. Well – you know what it's like up there. That copper fella was tearing his hair out after he took their statements. They all agreed that our boy did the murder, but they've all given wildly different accounts of it. One of them was in rhyming couplets. That copper said he wouldn't even consider submitting the statements or bringing the witnesses to court.'

'But The Man in the White Suit is still being charged?'

'I don't know. The copper said because there was so much blood, and everyone tramped through it before the police got here, and one patient actually rolled in it, that the usual forensics were going to be very complicated. They all seemed to have had a bit of a play with the murder weapon before it was handed in as well.'

'There's many been put away with less,' I said.

Nurse Brenda blew air out of her cheeks. She put a hand to her chest. When she had finally composed herself, she continued: 'What he seemed to be suggesting was that our man might be brought before a court, but only so that they can lock him away somewhere without him actually having to stand a proper trial and with no possibility of ever getting out. We have a secure facility here, but it's not peopled with murderers and psychopaths, it's really just to protect patients from themselves and add an extra layer of protection for the staff. You know that.'

'I was never in the secure unit.'

'No . . .?' She looked at me doubtfully. She did not seem convinced. This served to make me doubt myself. I was virtually certain I had never been in the secure unit. But there were gaps. 1994 was a bit of a blur. She said, 'But you see what my concern is? That nice, placid, peaceful boy up there, who might have murdered someone, is quite possibly going to be locked up somewhere really horrible for the rest of his life. Irrespective of whether he's guilty or not, he deserves to have someone in his corner, and it isn't going to be that idiot Legal Aid solicitor they sent, and it isn't going to be me because they'll be sending him somewhere else pretty sharpish. It has to be his family, and until we know who he is and who they are, there's nothing can be done for him. He'll just be swallowed up by the system. He has no one.'

'No one but me,' I said.

She appeared to glow. 'Exactly,' she said.

'I'm his last best hope,' I added.

We were interrupted by the elevator doors opening behind us and several nurses coming out. Nurse Brenda had a brief banter with them, and then waited until they were out of earshot before returning her attention to me.

'Sorry,' she said. She moved a little closer. 'But you have to understand, if this wasn't official before, now it has to be even less so. I was going to sneak you in to see him, but I can't do that now. I'll have to work out another way.' She put a hand on my arm. 'You're a good man. You care. I always knew you had a good heart.'

She meant metaphorically, because my literal heart could explode at any time.

Also, she was completely and utterly wrong.

Neither she nor Alison seemed to understand that really I *did not care* about this mysterious man. He was nothing more than a curiosity to me, a puzzle wrapped up in an enigma. I like to know the answers to questions. Once I had worked him out, it would make no difference to me if he was banged up for life or sliced up by his enemies. I have to admit, however, that although I didn't care one jot about him, there was a very small part of me that rather liked the idea of being someone's last best hope. Usually I was the last person someone would choose to turn to in a crisis.

I said, 'There's no chance of me seeing him now?'

'No.'

'For five minutes. If I can just get a picture of how he—'

'No. Honestly. I will work out a way for you to see him, trust me, but it's going to take a while. This is still the NHS – there are levels of bureaucracy here you wouldn't believe.'

'It's absolutely vital,' I said. 'Please, just two minutes, I can be in and—'

'Nurse Brenda says no.'

I nodded and studied my feet.

Involuntarily.

I had forgotten how powerful she could be. She was well-used to using trigger words with which you had no choice but to comply. She had never been a force for evil, but she was very definitely one for order. You needed something like that and someone like that to keep a lid on the mental wards. But it was still a little too close to *The Manchurian Candidate* for comfort.

She said, 'I will call you as soon as I have a plan. It may be later today, tonight maybe.'

She took my numbers, and with the important stuff out of the way asked some inane questions about Page and how I was coping, and then said she'd better get back upstairs. She gave me a wide smile and hurried away, but something had been niggling at me so I called after her and she stopped and turned.

I moved closer and said, 'Nurse Brenda? This concern for The Man in the White Suit. I was just wondering.'

'*Yes*?'

'You don't seem overly concerned for the victim here – the man he stabbed.'

She had been on the third step up. But now she came back down and drew close to me. 'I'm a nurse,' she said, 'and I have to concern myself with the living. Also, the man he stabbed was new on the ward, and uncooperative, and a bit of a shit. I'm sorry, but we're only human, and we have our favourites. Once, you were my favourite. Now it's him. I just feel that there's something special about him. I know this will sound ridiculous, but once you see him, you'll understand. He's naïve and innocent. You know what I call him sometimes? My little angel. Daft, I know, considering what they say he did, but he's just so placid and lovely and . . .' She sighed. 'Well, that's how I think of him. My little angel. Yes. Can you understand that at all?'

'Absolutely,' I said.

I could not only understand it, I could relate to it.

8

Nurse Brenda had always worn a small silver cross around her neck, so I could see how she might even be open to the idea of The Man in the White Suit *literally* being an angel. If you're into God, you have to swallow the whole kit bag and caboodle. You can't be *a bit* religious. Over many years of looking after the mental wards she had been exposed to the extremes of human behaviour – to all of the sordid, disgusting corruptions of which men and several women are capable – so it probably helped to have some sort of over-riding faith. But I had presumed that she was long enough in the tooth to understand that you really couldn't judge a book by its cover; yet The Man in the White Suit, a man accused of a bloody murder, had somehow managed to win her over. Perhaps she had just been on the front line for too long.

I returned to No Alibis and waited and pondered. There wasn't much else to do. Between the hours of 2 and 4 p.m.

I had precisely one customer. I should qualify that. *Customer* suggests that there was even the remote possibility of him buying something, but he was really just keeping out of the rain. He entered the shop, did a few circuits, and left. He did not make eye-contact.

Alison had suggested that I should try and be more welcoming and perhaps offer customers a cup of coffee and engage them in conversation. But Jeff was still away doing his exams, so there was nobody to make the coffee, and small talk has never been my forte. I can talk about books forever, I can guide you to precisely the right volume despite only having known you for a few minutes, but I need an opening, an *in*. I have a horror of shops where sales assistants put you under pressure to buy with their obsequious wheedling and hand-wringing and their, 'Is there anything I can help you with today, sir?'

Mother, when she worked the till, didn't have my reticence, and while I didn't condone her lamentable attempts at customer relations, I at least understood them. She had once cried: 'Either buy a book or get the fuck out,' to a customer. The tearful child, searching for a birthday present for her father, was absolutely distraught. The father came raging into the store after Mother had finished her shift and would have decked me if I hadn't suffered a timely epileptic fit. He ended up putting me in the recovery position and telling me about his passion for the works of Elmore Leonard, even the crap Westerns.

I had suffered from epilepsy since the age of eight. It came on after I cracked my skull by becoming the boy who really did run out from behind an ice-cream van without checking for oncoming traffic. The ice-cream vendor was very concerned by all the blood, and instead of waiting for an ambulance, he bundled me into his van and rushed me to hospital. Or at least, he tried to rush me, but the traffic slowed him down. Vehicles don't pull over to the side of the road for a Mr Whippy in the way that they do for an ambulance when it sounds its alarm. On the plus side, he was knowledgeable enough to jam my broken head between two large tubs of mint chocolate chip ice cream for the journey, thus lessening the eventual brain damage.

But I digress.

During my long afternoon in the shop during which this 'customer' was my only disturbance, I had ample time to think. Denied immediate access to The Man in the White Suit, I began to wonder if I might approach the case in another way, by trying to discover exactly why he had so suddenly turned to violence. That knowledge might lead me back to the original point of the investigation – his identity. To this end I turned to the internet to consult the newspaper reports of the murder. There were not many and the details they contained were sketchy at best. The man The Man in the White Suit had murdered was called Francis Delaney. He was a thirty-one-year-old mechanic from North Belfast who had been admitted to Purdysburn suffering from depression. The police said that a man had been arrested at the scene but that no further information was being released while their investigations were ongoing. The *Belfast Telegraph* carried a single death notice which stated that Francis Delaney would be deeply missed by his wife Sonya, and that a funeral service would take place at St Malachy's on the Shore Road at 11 a.m. the next day.

I checked Directory Enquiries and found a number for a Francis Delaney in Mount Vernon Park, which was close enough to the church on the Shore Road to convince me I had the right late man. Before I called the number I got a Twix and a can of Pepsi Max from the fridge in the kitchen. I positioned myself with my feet up on the counter and devoured one leg of the Twix. I took a drink. I was about to interrogate someone who had recently lost her husband. It was important to be relaxed. I don't like using phones at the best of times, but I prefer them to actual interaction with real breathing humans. Alison says I have difficulty empathising with people. I say that I don't consider it a difficulty.

I phoned and a man answered in a rough Belfast accent. I asked if I could speak to Sonya Delaney and he asked who was calling and I told him my name was Sergeant Cuff from CID and he said it was an appropriate name for a cop and I agreed it was. He probably didn't know that Sergeant Cuff was one of the first and greatest of fictional detectives, appearing in 1868 in Wilkie Collins's *The Moonstone* – a book, incidentally, hailed by Dorothy L. Sayers as probably the very finest detective story ever written. Dorothy was no slouch herself, if a bit of a dry old tart. I used Cuff's name rather than my own because I have a business and its reputation to protect and it is best not to confuse my parallel careers. And I suspected that the denizens of the Shore Road might not be familiar with the works of Wilkie Collins or books in general.

The man on the phone said he would go and get Sonya. A few moments later she said hello. Her voice was as rough as his. She said, 'Youse have more questions? I said everything to the other guy.'

'Detective Inspector Robinson?'

'Aye, him.'

'He's quite a disagreeable fellow, isn't he?'

'A what what?'

'Never mind,' I said. 'This will only take a minute.'

'Aye, all right, fire away. It's just, I've people here. You know, for a drink, to see the . . .' and she faltered, and she sniffed up. 'You know, the . . .'

'Corpse,' I said.

'Don't say that,' she said.

'I'm sorry. I meant – the *deceased*.'

'Don't say that. It's so . . . final.' There were many things I could have said to that, including *Precisely*. But I held back. I waited for her to gather herself. 'I'm sorry,' she said after a bit. 'It's just been such a shock.'

'I understand.'

'You must deal with murders all the time.'

'Frequently,' I said. 'They're like water off a duck's back.' She let out another little cry. 'Mrs Delaney, I won't detain you too long. Your husband, did he ever mention this man who is accused of murdering him? I know he was only in Purdysburn for a few days, but if you were visiting him, did he ever say he'd had a run-in with him or anything like that?'

'No, no, nothing like that.'

'Did he mention him at all?'

'No.'

'He suffered from depression, your husband?'

'That's right. I told all this to the other mister.'

'I understand that. Sometimes we have to double-check these things. I won't take up much more of your time. He was clinically depressed?'

'He was depressed, yes.'

'Had he been hospitalised before?'

'No. And what difference would it make if he was?'

'In case he had run into this man, the man accused of his murder, on a previous occasion.'

'Accused? He killed my husband.'

'Yes, quite. Do you mind me asking what your husband's behaviour was like before he was admitted?'

'He was depressed.'

'But how did his depression manifest itself?'

'Manifest?'

'Was he violent? Uncontrollable?'

'No. He was depressed. Listless. Didn't want to go out, or go to work.'

'Okay. Listless, didn't want to go out. Did he talk to you, or relatives or friends about it?'

'No, he didn't really talk to anyone. He was *depressed*. He sat in the corner and stared at a wall. Why do you need to know this?'

'It's helpful to us in building up a picture of what might actually have prompted this attack. If your husband had been violent, then you could see how a fight might occur; but if he was quiet and unobtrusive, then that is so much more unlikely.'

'Can't you get this from his doctor or psychiatrist?'

'Yes, of course, and we will, but quite often they only get

to see patients under specific, clinical conditions, they don't see what they're like in their day-to-day lives, what their behavioural patterns are like away from the spotlight, or stethoscope, or microscope of medical observation. So it's good to talk to the widow as well.'

'Don't call me that.'

'Call you what? Oh, you mean widow?'

'Yes, I don't like that. It's a horrible word.'

'I understand. It's a dark word indeed. Unless you add Twankey.'

'Excuse . . .?'

'Sorry. I'm just saying, it's the only way to lighten a word like widow. Its connotations are otherwise usually always dark . . .'

'I really—'

'Like the Black Widow Spider. Or the Black Widows themselves.'

'The Black—'

'Widows of Liverpool, sisters – were hanged for murder in 1884.'

'Please stop saying widow.'

'Absolutely. I apologise.'

'I really need to get back to my family, Sergeant Cuff.'

'Yes, quite,' I said. 'I fully understand. But just one more thing. Your husband, did he go voluntarily to the hospital, or was he sectioned?'

'He was . . . persuaded to go.'

'By his doctor?'

She sighed. 'By his family, by *me*. But through his doctor.'

'Okay, and just one more thing, as Columbo would—'

'You said the last thing was—'

'What medication was your husband on, Mrs Delaney?'

'What do you think?' she snapped. 'He was *depressed*. He was on *anti-depressants*. Okay? All right? Jesus!'

And with that she hung up.

I drummed my fingers on the counter. I didn't know what the widow was getting so het up about. It was a perfectly reasonable question. Different medications can affect you in different ways. Some can make you aggressive or violent, they can increase your libido or put you into a vegetative state or bring you out in boils or inflate your testicles to the size of balloons. God knows, I'd tried them all. It wasn't important to know exactly *what* had set The Man in the White Suit to murder, because my focus was still mainly on identifying him, but all information is relevant and stored away. It might be required the next day, or thirty years down the line – although, of course, the very notion of me being alive thirty years down the line was ludicrous.

I examined the second leg of Twix, which I had coura-geously resisted during my interrogation of the widow. I found it to be exactly as a leg of Twix should be. Satisfied, I then tried to slip it into my left nostril.

I knew from past experience that it should not fit, but if my nose cartilage really was continuing to grow then it might indeed have widened sufficiently to admit the Twix. It was a pleasant relief, therefore, to find that it was still too large. Content, I returned to the business of Twix consumption and the pondering of *The Case of the Man in the White Suit*.

9

Jeff turned up for work the following morning looking ragged, depressed and sporting an eye-patch.

'Take off that eye-patch,' I said. 'You look like a spoon.'

He said, 'My exam today did not go well. I am a disaster and a failure.'

'Take off that eye-patch,' I repeated. 'You look like a spoon.'

'I have no future. Or my future is here. Working alongside you. Partners in the solving of crimes.'

'You don't work alongside me, you're my employee,' I said, 'and we are not partners in the solving of crimes. You occasionally give me a hand, though you're as much of a hindrance as a help. And take off that eye-patch. You look like a spoon.'

He sighed and took off the eye-patch.

'Put it back on again,' I said. 'I can't have you facing customers like that.'

His wound was infected and weeping; his eye was still

puffed up and half-closed over. It would have been perfect for discouraging charity collectors or people seeking directions, but as I was already in the midst of surfing for more information on my case, I needed him to be at least partially presentable so that in the unlikely event of someone actually wanting to spend some money, he wouldn't frighten them away to hell or Waterstones.

Jeff replaced the patch and slipped off his jacket. He leaned his elbows on the counter and supported his head on his bunched fists. He looked down, down, deeper than down, but that wasn't my problem.

I turned back to the computer. DI Robinson had told me that the 'other' murder had not taken place in the hospital, therefore it had to have taken place before The Man in the White Suit was admitted; it seemed reasonable to assume that he wasn't talking about something that had happened in the distant past, but much more recently. In days gone by, it might have been difficult for a mere mortal to track down a particular murder in Belfast, because there were so many of them, but we live in a post-Troubles society, and although Ordinary Decent Criminals have emerged en masse since the ceasefires, we are still relatively free of major crimes. Murders, in particular, are rare. The Man in the White Suit had been a guest of Purdysburn for three months; his date of admission was 28 July; it had taken me just a few clicks to discover that on 27 July, barely eleven hours before he entered the hospital, the gangster known as Fat Sam Mahood was stabbed to death at a health club in East Belfast. Instinctively, and also because it was bloody obvious, I knew that this was not a coincidence.

From behind, Jeff said: 'The life of a poet is not an easy one.'

'Do you know any poets, Jeff?' I asked.

'Just because you don't understand something, you don't have to belittle it.'

'I'm not belittling *it*, Jeff. I'm belittling you.'

'You have the disadvantage of not having read my poems.'

'I would not consider it as such. Jeff, poetry is not the answer, not for you. We know poets. They are shits.'

'As opposed to crime writers?'

'Crime writers reflect our society, and they pay their own way. Poets are blood-sucking leeches.'

Jeff sighed. 'Maybe you're right,' he said. 'But at the moment, poetry is all I have.'

'Don't forget where you are, Jeff,' I said. 'You have work here. You have Alison, you have me. We're your family.'

'Do you mean that?' I glanced back at his hopeful, bloated face. He saw the look on mine and his jaw sagged. He looked beyond me to the computer screen. 'Is that *The Case of the Man in the White Suit*? Can I help?'

Normally I would have told him to get on with some book stacking or box openings, but his gob was miserable enough without me adding to it, and so, finally recalling Alison's advice on empathy, I reluctantly nodded and told him precisely where I was with the case, and what I had discovered.

'Fat Sam Mahood? Who's he?'

'Fat Sam Mahood is – *was* – a loan shark who ran protection rackets. He was an enforcer for the paramilitaries, a dealer, a gangster, he was—'

'Fat?' Jeff ventured.

'Fat, and he was murdered *here*.' I had Google Maps up on screen, and indicated the location of the All Star Health Club on the Newtownards Road. 'While our Man in a White Suit was discovered *here*, on Seaforde Street, which is just off the Newtownards Road, but about a mile away from the health club.'

'Discovered?'

'The family that lives there were away for the night. They came home in the morning and discovered him asleep in their bed. He'd climbed in through an open window. They called the police, who immediately put two and two together.'

'Based on what?'

'Exactly. Based on a man who can't say who he is, who has no history, who can't defend himself. The word "convenient" springs to mind.'

'As in "scapegoat",' said Jeff.

'Or "patsy",' I said. 'Or "chump, fall guy, soft touch, sucker, mug, mark, dupe" . . . yes, indeed. We don't have access to the police, so we don't know if they have anything else on him. But we have to presume it doesn't amount to much or they would have charged him. He's been in Purdysburn for three months.'

'Maybe they're waiting until he emerges from whatever funk he's in so that they can question him properly.'

'Funk, Jeff?'

Jeff shrugged. 'You know what I mean.'

'That may be. But our concern, Jeff, is not whether he murdered Fat Sam Mahood or indeed his fellow patient, Francis Delaney, but who exactly he is. That is what we

– and when I say *we*, I mean *I* – have been engaged to discover.'

'But if he's innocent and—'

'That is not our brief.'

'But—'

'Jeff?'

'Okay. I understand.' He nodded 'But—'

'But nothing.' I clasped my hands. 'So, where do we go now? Denied immediate access to our man, and without police cooperation, how do we find out more about him? What would you do if you were in my orthopaedic shoes?' I gave him the eye.

'Is this some sort of a test?'

'Yes.'

'I've just failed my exams. I don't need another test.'

'Jeff. *Jeff.* Please. Try and excel at something. Just *think.*'

He sighed. He moved a little closer to the screen and studied it. His eyes flitted up to me. I gave him an encouraging nod.

'Right,' he said. 'First off – he's not from here. I mean, from Belfast, Northern Ireland, is he?' I raised an eyebrow, meaning for him to continue. 'Because . . . we are a very small country, and people don't stay unidentified for very long. If the police are right, and he did murder this Fat Sam, then you would think normally that it must be related to the business Fat Sam was in – something ganglandy, right? But the police here would know most everyone involved in those kinds of shenanigans, wouldn't they, because either they've been arrested or questioned or observed before. So I don't think he's involved in local criminal circles. He might have had some kind of personal grudge against Fat Sam, but then we're back to how come nobody else knows about it or recognises him.'

'Very good,' I said. 'So?'

'So he's from outside of Northern Ireland, and most probably the rest of the United Kingdom, or Dublin or anywhere in the south because he'd be on the radar. Fat Sam was a drug dealer?'

'Yes.'

'So, for instance, The Man in the White Suit could easily be someone from, say, somewhere in Europe, who came here to do a deal, got involved in a row, and Fat Sam was murdered.'

'Possibly. So how then did he end up in Purdysburn?'

'The trauma of the murder caused some kind of a break-down.'

'Or . . .?'

'It's all an act. Is that what you think too?'

'It's a definite possibility.' I smiled at Jeff. 'Not bad, not bad at all. I might make something of you yet.'

'Do you mean that?'

It was almost pathetic, his need for approval. Obviously, I ignored his question. Instead I stood up and began to pull on my coat.

'If we cannot speak to The Man in the White Suit,' I said, 'and the police in general and DI Robinson in particular do not want us involved and are denying us access to their files, how might we further advance our case?'

'We would go somewhere that involves wearing a coat?'

'Exactly. The All Star Health Club is the one crime scene we do have access to. Agreed?'

'Absolutely.'

Jeff reached for his own coat. It was like having a seeing-out-of-one-eye dog, enthusiastic but mostly useless. I said, 'I appreciate your help in this, Jeff. And the best way for you to help, is to stay here and man the till.'

'But—'

'*Stay*,' I commanded.

10

Obviously, I had never previously darkened the doors of a health club. The very *idea* of exercising for pleasure *literally* brought me out in a rash, which, luckily for the young woman showing me around the All Star gym on the Newtownards Road, was largely confined to my nether regions. Jackie was petite, but trim and toned and tanned, with gleaming white teeth. She somehow managed to smile widely as she spoke. She was giving me a tour of the equipment and the pool, and several times asked if I wanted to try out the elliptical trainers, the exercise bikes, the treadmill, the rowing machines, the weights or if I was interested in the range of supplements they had on sale. This latter was the only offer that piqued my interest. I have an interest in pills of all kinds.

I said, 'You mean like those steroids that body-builders take and they get huge but psychotic?'

I nodded across the floor of the gym. The weights were

in one corner. There was also a punch bag, which was being punched. There were a lot of big men pumping iron. They were good evidence of the new poverty gripping our nation – unemployed and unemployable, but with enough money to enjoy the benefits of a gym. They were sleek with sweat and oozing testosterone.

'No, I mean vitamins,' said Jackie. She studied me. 'Are you okay? You're . . .' And she indicated my brow, which was streaming with sweat.

'I'm fine,' I said. 'I have the flu.'

She starting talking about spin classes. The gym was busy enough, there were housewives with ponytails on the tread-mills and bespectacled men with big earphones whose physiques were not hugely different from my own pushing up bars set at the lowest possible resistance, but my eyes kept being drawn back to the guys in the corner. It was almost as if they were members of a different club, standing posing and swapping jokes. I did not envy them at all. They were huge, but prisoners of their regime. A few weeks off the weights and they would all droop into fat and flab.

Jackie said, 'I've loved my time here, and I wouldn't hesi-tate to recommend it. I don't think I could sell something I didn't believe in one hundred per cent.'

I said, 'You sound like you're leaving.'

She said, 'It's my last day. And I'm really going to miss it.'

I said, 'It's not a very good advertisement, trying to get me to join, when you're leaving.'

She laughed. It was a very attractive laugh. 'I know – but I swear to God, you'll love it here. The only reason I'm leaving is my health hasn't been the best, and I've gotten another job that isn't quite so physical. I'm *really* annoyed about it.'

She appeared to be the picture of health. If I'd been on a mission from my home planet to take a well-nigh perfect specimen of womanly humanity back for experimentation, she is exactly whom I would have taken. Luckily for her, that was not currently my mission.

I said, 'I'm not even a member, and I'm missing you already.'

'Aw,' she said, 'that's really nice. Well, what do you think?'

'About?'

'Membership!'

'Oh. Yes. I'm definitely interested. But I'm a little concerned.'

'Concerned?'

'Well, you know – about what happened. I mean, this area, I live here, it's rough enough, but you want to feel safe when you're in your shorts, you want to feel relaxed when you're trying to give it everything . . .'

'Well, I can assure you—'

'He was stabbed, wasn't he? Fat Sam. Were you here? Did you see the body? What was it like? Was there blood everywhere?'

'No, I—'

'It must have been bad for business. Did you know him? What was he like? Did he have any enemies? Did he ever threaten anyone?'

'I'm not—'

'You understand my concerns? I'd like to join, I'd really like to join, but not if there's a possibility I'm going to be in danger, not if someone is going to burst through the doors with a machine gun and start shooting. You never know these days, you just never know. There's a different gym I could join on the Lisburn Road. It's further away, but no one has ever been murdered there or stabbed repeatedly.'

Jackie was working hard to maintain her smile. I had not meant to suddenly assail her with questions, but it had all come flowing out. It was amateurish in the extreme. The only mitigating circumstances were that I had swallowed thirty-six ProPlus in the car park outside. They were only caffeine pills, but I had definitely exceeded the recommended intake by thirty-four. I was in the midst of an experiment. I wanted to know how many I could take before they killed me. It's always good to know your limits. There was probably some caffeine in the Starbucks coffee as well. I was enjoying my own private spin classes. I was, as they say, fucking flying.

Jackie said, 'It was an unfortunate incident, but it was three months ago now, and there's been nothing since.'

'But I'm just not sure that I'd want to be a member of any club that would have Fat Sam Mahood as a member.'

The smile assumed the dynamics of resignation.

'We are offering a significant discount on our membership,' she said.

'Well, that might help. I'm sorry to go on about the murder, but I presume everyone's the same. It is fascinating.'

'Yes, they are – and yes, it is fascinating,' she said. 'But there's really nothing I can do but reassure you. It *was* three months ago. So – c'mon: let me introduce you to Gary, our manager. He's in charge of dotting the i's and crossing the t's. If you'll just follow me.'

She led me down the stairs. I had to grip the handrail.

My eyes felt like they were out on stalks. The pool was visible through glass. There were half a dozen people swimming. I shuddered. It was mostly the caffeine and partly my allergy to chlorine. I do not like swimming pools at the best of times, not to mention the worst of times. The single worst *worst* of times occurred when I was nine. For a joke, I put inflated armbands onto the feet of my best friend, and then encouraged him to jump into our local pool. Obviously, as soon as he entered the water, his feet rose to the surface but his head sank towards the bottom, and there was nothing he could do about it. It was very funny right up to the point where he drowned. He should have known better. He was a fool. When I say drowned, I do mean drowned. He was clinically dead for eight minutes. He was, eventually, resuscitated, but had to attend remedial classes, although really, seriously, he wasn't that bright to start with. I have avoided swimming pools ever since. They bring back bad memories of me being blamed for something I did.

Jackie showed me into a tidy office, with certificates on the wall and a buff man in a shirt and tie behind a desk. There were shelves with various trophies on them. Gary stood up and extended his hand and introduced himself and I hesitantly took it, because with my brittle bones I have to be wary of big manly handshakes. His grasp, however, was surprisingly light. His teeth were very bright. He said, 'Hello, how are you? Welcome to All Star. Can I get you a coffee?'

'No!' I said with a little too much passion, and he glanced at Jackie who probably would have rolled her eyes if I hadn't been staring at her, unblinking. She backed out of the room.

I smiled at Gary, who indicated for me to take a seat and

said, 'So, you're interested in joining our little family here at All Star?'

'No,' I said.

'*No*?'

My head was buzzing too much for me to keep up the pretence. I said, 'I'm sorry, things have become a little confused. Jackie, who is lovely by the way, and a credit to your business, and it's a shame that you're losing her – she thought I was here for a guided tour of the facilities with a view to membership, but actually I'm here to ask a lot of questions about Fat Sam Mahood and what happened to him.'

Gary's mouth dropped open slightly. He started to say, 'I'm afraid—'

But I cut him off with: 'I represent the man who has been accused of Fat Sam Mahood's murder. He's going to be put on trial for his very life. You have to help him. All I need is some background information. It won't take long.'

He said, 'Really you'd need to speak to—'

'You were manager here when he was murdered?'

'Yes, but—'

'Then it's you I want to talk to.'

'Do you have some form of identification?'

'Yes,' I said. But I did not proffer any.

'Can I see it?'

'Do you really want to go down that road?' I asked.

'What road?'

'Being awkward,' I said. 'Gary, you've cooperated with the police, I know that. They speak highly of you. Detective Inspector Robinson in particular. He is very keen that you extend that cooperation to me. The alternative? Well, for a

79

start, we would have to take your computers, and your paper records . . .'

'What possible relevance . . .?'

'That's not for you to ask, Gary,' I said. 'We're talking about a murder – *everything* may be considered relevant. Background checks on all the staff, your financial records would be forensically analysed, and anything from minor CV inflation to major fraud might be uncovered. You sell a lot of supplements.'

'Vitamins, yes.'

I nodded. And said nothing.

'What exactly do you want to know?' Gary asked.

'What do you want to tell me?'

His brow furrowed. I nodded some more. He swallowed. I looked around the room. 'These certificates and trophies, they're all yours?'

'Yes. Jiu-Jitsu. I've competed all over the world.'

'You've done well.'

He said, 'Would this be off the record?'

'Yes, it can be. It's really just background information.'

He got up from his desk and moved behind me and closed the door. He then stepped back to his chair and sat down; putting a finger to his lips, he chewed briefly at a nail.

I smiled and pointed at the lowest shelf. It was bare apart from a small, flat square of what looked like lead sitting on top of a pile of magazines. 'Is that a trophy as well?'

'No, that's a paperweight.'

I said, 'Relax.'

He said, 'This is a good club, everything's above board,

but it's in a dodgy area and sometimes you have to accept what goes with that. I told the police everything. Fat Sam hung out here more than I liked, but there was nothing I could do about it. He was like the Kray Twins, but there was only one of him.'

'Protection money, blackmail, extortion . . .'

'Yes, all that.'

'And he practised it here?'

'Sort of. He walked around like he owned the place. We stayed open late to facilitate him, he never had to put his hand in his pocket for anything and he certainly didn't figure in our membership data. I was told, by the owners, that anything Mr Mahood wants, Mr Mahood gets. The staff knew that as well. He was no trouble, exactly, just unpleasant, but you get that, Mr . . .'

'Thompson, Jim Thompson.' It was not my real name, for I had a business and its reputation to protect. 'As in the crime writer,' I added.

He gave a slight shrug. He wasn't a reader. He was a fighter. He might be able to beat me up, but I would slaughter him in a literary quiz.

'Mr Thompson, these are challenging times to be running a business, especially a leisure business, and particularly in an area like this. East Belfast.' He waved his hand around him. 'There are a lot of hard men with time on their hands. The owners felt that paying a relatively small amount for protection was preferable to constant harassment and vandalism. So we paid, and we didn't have any trouble.'

'Until Fat Sam was stabbed to death.'

'Exactly.'

'And now where does the money go?'

'It doesn't. Nobody has asked for it.'

'And the harassment?'

'Has not recurred. Maybe they haven't realised he's . . .'

'No,' I said. 'I think you'll find that Fat Sam was probably responsible for the intimidation in the first place. That he was the problem *and* the solution. That's how protection usually works.' Gary blew air out of his cheeks. 'Ironic though, that Fat Sam spends his life threatening the well-being of others, yet he ends up dead in a health club.'

'Is that what irony is? I've never really understood what it meant.'

I said, 'In the seventies the US Product Safety Commission had to recall 80,000 of its own lapel badges promoting toy safety, because they had sharp edges, used lead paint, and had small clips that could be broken off and swallowed. That's another example.'

He cleared his throat. 'Well, that's good to know.'

'Were you working here the night it happened?'

'What? No, I don't usually hang around that late.'

'So who was?'

'A couple of cleaners, and two staff to lock up. There was some confusion: they thought Sam was finished and had already changed and gone home – that was his way, he didn't linger. Anyway, somehow they missed him and switched off and locked up and went home, only he was still here and . . .'

'Here with the killer?'

'Yes.'

'So how did the killer get in?'

'I don't know. No locks were damaged. He may have hidden out until he had the opportunity to . . . do it.'

'Then how did he get out, if it was all locked up?'

'I don't know.'

'Because if he was leaving, he would have set off an alarm. Or if he was breaking in, he would have set off an alarm. Surely.'

'You would think that.' He nodded.

'There's no footage?'

'Of the reception desk, yes. You can't be having cameras in the changing rooms. There are some in the gym, but none covering the pool. Whatever there is, the police took away.'

'You've seen what there is?'

'I had a quick trawl through. I didn't see anything that showed anything.'

'Was there much money on the premises? Maybe he interrupted someone . . .?'

'No, very little. A float for the café, that was about it. We're not really a money business. It's mostly direct debits.'

'Who discovered the body?'

'Two different members of our gym team, and one from the café, found the body in the morning when they opened up. The police have their full statements.'

'Good,' I said. 'They can tell me as well. You know about the man they've arrested for this?'

'I'm aware they arrested someone. I saw his photo in the paper.'

'And you didn't recognise him? He wasn't known to any of the staff?'

'Nope, no one had ever seen him before. I hear he's in the nut house.'

'That's my client you're talking about.'

Gary cleared his throat and looked away. 'Sorry,' he said. 'But that's what people said at the time. I don't know. I just want it forgotten about, you know? Times are hard enough without this *still* scaring people away.'

He was right. Times were hard everywhere. Yet, from my observations, he already had more customers in one day than I had in a calendar month, and he probably didn't even enjoy the benefits of a Christmas Club.

'What sort of a discount are you offering if I join?' I asked.

'If you . . .? Well, it's normally thirty quid a month. I can offer twenty.'

'Would you do ten?'

'No.'

'Fifteen.'

'If you sign up for twenty-four months.'

'Would it not be easier to say two years?'

'Sorry. It's the way we're trained.'

'Can I cancel at any time?'

'No, of course not.'

'Ah,' I said, 'that's the deal breaker.'

He did not look too disappointed. I told him that what I needed now were contact details for his staff who were not currently on the premises and also for his former staff and he said yes, that wouldn't be a problem, and he got up to get them from his secretary. I sat there for a couple of minutes, but with my head and heart pounding to the ProPlus beat I got up and began to pace the floor, counting, counting, counting, and then when I got bored with that after twenty seconds I began to study Gary's numerous certificates and awards, and found that he had travelled widely and enjoyed many victories in far-flung places, and I wondered if he was the greatest success to come out of East Belfast since Van or the *Titanic*.

My eyes wandered to the paperweight, which I tried lifting but barely could, given the state of my wasting muscles. I set it back where it was but not before I turned it in my hands and found that there was an inscription on the reverse side, in Latin, and it puzzled me, not because I couldn't read the Latin, because I could, but because of what it said. In fact, I took out my phone, and took a photo of it. I heard Gary come back into the office. Without turning I said, 'Where exactly did you get this from?'

When he didn't respond, I glanced around and saw that he was standing inside the doorway, but not alone. Two of the muscle squad from the weights corner were with him. They did not look friendly.

'I called Detective Inspector Robinson,' said Gary. 'He's never heard of a solicitor by the name of Jim Thompson. He asked me to describe you, so I did. He knew exactly who you were. He says you're a useless retard who has nothing to do with the investigation into Fat Sam's murder. You're a time-waster and a refugee from a mental hospital. He says I should throw you the fuck out.'

I said, 'I don't suppose that discount is still available.'

He snorted, and sent the muscle boys forward.

'Don't hurt me,' I said, 'I have Brittle Bone Disease.'

They ignored me.

*   *   *

It wasn't exactly *Goodfellas*. I had grazed knees. There was a hole in my trousers. The palms of my hands were also scratched. Falling on gravel will do that. They didn't even throw me down, they just gave me a bit of a shove and my dodgy ankles gave way. One of them helped me up. I thanked him.

I limped into McDonald's. I hate McDonald's but I went nevertheless, so that they wouldn't see me get into the Mystery Machine, which would have given my identity completely away. DI Robinson, as far as I could tell, had not actually told them who I was. He had merely described me as a retard and a refugee from a mental institution.

I ordered a strawberry milkshake and took a window seat and watched the All Star until the muscle boys disappeared back inside. I opened my wallet and took out an antiseptic wipe and rolled up my trousers and carefully began to clean the grazes on my knees, extracting as much gravel as I could, and grimacing, and wiping the tears from my eyes with the back of my hand. I knew I could never get all of it, and that some was already in my system and that it would make its way to my kidneys or liver or spleen or stomach or brain and kill me. Also, with my haemophilia, I was undoubtedly already bleeding internally. It would go undetected for hours, or possibly days, but it would get me in the end. I was a ticking time bomb. My only hope was that I would survive for long enough to exploit the potentially vital piece of evidence my visit to the health club had uncovered, evidence that would undoubtedly put me on track to solve *The Case of the Man in the White Suit*.

11

Jeff was huffing because I'd left him behind. I told him to grow up. He told me to grow up. I told him to grow up and not be so childish. He told me to grow up and not be so childish. I told him to grow up and not be so childish. It went on for about half an hour. He was refusing to empty boxes, stack shelves, order books or deal with the customer.

The customer was after 'anything Scandinavian' in complete defiance of my current promotion of Irish crime fiction. I rolled off the names of the current best-selling Scandos, including Mankell, Larsson, Nesbo, Hellstrom, Läckberg and Fossum, just to show her my expertise, but then steered her towards the best-kept secret of Nordic crime fiction – Astrid Lindgren and her savage, visceral debut, *Pippi Longstocking*. I explained that it was like *The Curious Incident of the Dog in the Night-time*, written from the point of view of a child, but was actually aimed at adults and was really 'fucked up'. I said it was exceedingly rare and this was the only copy of it I had, and possibly the only one in the UK. And she fell for it all. She was just handing over the money when I cracked and said I was only joking, that it really was a children's novel I had acquired as an investment for my son, but she didn't believe me, wrested it from my damaged hands and paid over the odds for it and was away out of the shop clutching it to her flat chest before I could tell her it was in the original Swedish.

Jeff said, 'Well done, another customer lost for ever. You are a despicable human being.'

'I never claimed to be human,' I said.

Jeff shook his head. 'If I had another job to go to, I would go.'

'If you had another job to go to, I would be very surprised.'

He thought about that for a moment. 'I suppose,' he said.

He really was a half-wit. To ease him back into being my willing slave labourer I told him about my visit to the All Star, and what I had learned from Gary, the manager. Then I indicated the screen of my PC and said, 'Why don't you come over here and see what I found at the health club? Give me the benefit of your wisdom.'

He fell for that one too. He moved beside me.

'What is it?' he asked. I was displaying the photo I had taken in Gary's office.

'That, my young friend, is a *defixio*.'

'A . . .?'

'*Defixio*. It's Latin. For *curse tablet*. In Roman times, if you wanted revenge on someone, you made one of these, and you put an inscription on it asking the gods to do harm to your enemy either in this life or the next. Then you would bury it next to where he lived or worked.'

'And the relevance of this is?'

'It was sitting on a shelf in the manager's office. The inscription, for verily I do know Latin, reads: *In the name of Hermes, curse for all eternity the murderer Samuel Mahood.*' I nodded at the screen.

Jeff said, 'You're serious?'

'Always,' I said.

'That's what it really says? It's like something out of a movie. Or Roald Dahl. *Tales of the . . .*'

'. . . *Unexpected* – yes.'

Jeff reached forward and traced the outline of the *defixio*. 'And it was just sitting on his shelf?'

'Sitting there minding its own business.'

'And he didn't know?'

'He knew it was there, obviously. But unless he was being remarkably blasé, he didn't have a clue what it was or what it said.'

'The number of people who speak Latin in East Belfast must be pretty small.'

'You don't *speak* Latin, Jeff. It's not a conversational language.'

'What do they do in Latin America?'

'Are you making a joke, Jeff?'

His face remained blank. 'Obviously,' he said finally.

I pointed at the screen. 'Tell me what you think this does for our case.'

Jeff raised his hand to his mouth and nibbled on his thumbnail. 'Well,' he said, 'are we presuming it's not someone just messing around?'

'We're presuming nothing.'

'*Okay*. If it *is* a joke, it would seem like a lot of trouble to go to, making something like this, having it inscribed in Latin and then putting it on display, and nobody spotting it until you came along.'

'People have been reading Patterson for years and still haven't gotten the joke. It happens.'

'It's made of . . .?'

'Lead.'

'Lead, okay. And we don't know how it came to be in the office?'

'No, but . . .' I ran my finger around the edges of the image. 'Here, in the grooves where the lead has been folded, there's soil, which suggests it was in the ground, which fits with the traditional methodology for laying the curse. The All Star is in the middle of a retail park. There's no open ground, but there are a number of concrete flower boxes immediately outside the club. I sneezed on the way past them – you know what my allergies are like. The flowers were in bloom, but had not been picked or otherwise vandalised, and the soil wasn't peppered with cigarette butts – which suggests that it was either turned over fairly recently or replaced. The soil on the edge of the *defixio* is dark, suggesting recent contact with water and that it hadn't had time to dry out since it was washed, which could mean that it was only discovered in the past few days.'

'Uhuh,' said Jeff.

'You're probably wondering how long it had been there?'

'Indeed,' said Jeff.

I clicked on the screen and brought up an article from the

Belfast Telegraph about the murder which was accompanied by single column photograph of Fat Sam, and a larger one of the All Star itself.

'Notice anything?' I asked.

'He's no oil painting.' I raised an eyebrow. 'Uhm, right . . . no.'

'Flower boxes,' I said. Jeff nodded. I then clicked onto the next article I had saved. It was a copy of an advertising feature from the same newspaper, but dated a month before the murder. 'Look – more or less the same photo, but see?'

'No flower boxes,' said Jeff.

'Exactly. They were only put in place in the few weeks between the advertising feature appearing and Fat Sam being murdered, so we at least know that the *defixio* could have been buried there.'

Jeff shook his head. 'I get what you're saying, but I don't get why anyone would be arsed doing it. If they wanted to kill Fat Sam, why not just do it instead of going through all this palaver?'

'Well, who knows? Crazy people will find a reason to do things in a particular way.'

We looked at the screen for a little bit without saying anything.

Eventually Jeff cleared his throat and said, 'This isn't just about finding out who The Man in the White Suit is any more, is it?' When I did not immediately respond he folded his arms across his chest and said with some considerable resignation: 'It always starts like this, with something small and uncompli-cated, but pretty soon there are bodies all over the place and I get beaten up. Does Alison know you're pursuing this?'

'Up to a point,' I said.

Jeff blew air out of his cheeks. 'I only ever wanted to be a poet,' he said. 'Not to be involved in murder and mayhem.'

'You chose to work in the book business, Jeff,' I said. 'Murder and mayhem go with the territory.'

He nodded, because he knew it was the truth.

12

I had decided that in future the man we had come to know as The Man in the White Suit would be rechristened as Gabriel. It was too cumbersome to refer to him as The Man in the White Suit, and his new name was more appropriate, I thought, what with Nurse Brenda considering him to be such an angel.

While he, Gabriel, remained out of bounds, and the mystery book business remained flaccid, I had little else to do with my time but to contemplate the business of murder, and in so doing acknowledge what Jeff had already correctly surmised, that solving the mystery of Gabriel's identity would be a mere footnote to proving who was responsible for Fat Sam's murder. That would be the real challenge. The murder of Francis Delaney did not interest me so much. I was pretty sure Gabriel was guilty of that. It was the puzzle that was important, always the puzzle, and there was no real puzzle with Delaney. Fat Sam's death was the mystery. It wasn't particularly about proving whether Gabriel was innocent or guilty of it, more about showing the world once again how talented I was.

'I know how talented you are,' said Alison, from the doorway.

'Did I say that out loud?'

'Yes, you did. You were a million miles away. I could have given you a hand job under the counter and you wouldn't have noticed.'

I did not much like her talking dirty, particularly with Page in a sling on her chest. I said as much.

'He's too young to understand.'

'Well, Jeff isn't,' and I nodded down at Jeff, sitting cross-legged beneath the counter, sorting through a box of receipts.

Alison peered over the counter at him. 'Hi Jeff,' she said.

'Hello Alison,' said Jeff.

'You'd notice me giving you a hand job, wouldn't you?'

'Yes, I would.'

They both should have been red-faced, but it was only me, and Page, who was teething.

By way of deflecting their focus from my coloured cheeks I said to Alison: 'Perfect timing, I need your help.'

'There's a first,' she said.

'No really,' I said.

I explained what I had in mind: that she, and Page, should accompany me to Fat Sam Mahood's home, so that I could interview his widow. She was, according to the newspaper accounts, a formidable, fiercely loyal woman who, via the judicious use of an elbow, had broken the nose of a reporter who had been hassling her following Sam's murder.

'You mean you want us to hang around and say nothing.'

'No, I value your—'

'And you think she won't abuse you because you're with your wife and child.'

'You're not my wife,' I said.

'Yet,' said Alison.

It was a statement, and a challenge. Obviously, I ignored it. I said, 'Are you coming or not?'

She said, 'There's a first time for everything,' and sniggered, and Jeff sniggered too, and my cheeks got redder. 'I suppose I will come with you then, just out of curiosity. I'll just sit around and smile – I'll be your little bit of eye-candy.'

'If you really don't want to go,' said Jeff, 'I can be your eye-candy.' He said this with the pus leaking out of his eye and drying in a yellow streak down one side of his face.

'You mind the till,' I said, 'there's a good boy.'

We took the Mystery Machine. There was a child seat in the back. Alison strapped Page in, and then sat beside him. As we pulled out I said, 'I feel like your chauffeur.'

In the mirror, Alison nodded.

After a while she said, 'Do you not want to get married?'

'Yes, I do,' I said.

'I mean to me.'

'Yes. Maybe.'

'What kind of an answer is *maybe*?'

I shrugged.

She said, 'Do not shrug. I'm serious.'

'I'm just trying to concentrate on the driving.' I was, as well. You have to be careful. Page was asleep. Alison stared out of the window. 'Anyway,' I said, 'how are you? How's your mental state generally?'

Our eyes met in the mirror.

She said, 'You're asking me how *my* mental state is?'

I said, 'I was thinking that maybe you have a wee touch of post-traumatic stress disorder?'

'Do you mean post-natal depression?'

'No, I was *there*. There was blood everywhere.' We stopped at lights. There was an old woman crossing the road. I had an urge to crush her. She smiled at me and mouthed *thank you*. 'How's the painting coming on? I haven't been in the studio in a while.'

'It's hardly a studio. It's a luggage room.'

'Well, how's it going?'

'It's going fine.'

'Are you working on anything in particular?'

'Not really.'

'Do you find it therapeutic?'

She shook her head. 'I'm not the one with the problem,' she said.

Gloria Mahood lived in a large detached house off the Holywood Road in East Belfast. There was a Porsche and a Lexus in the driveway. There were two trees in the garden, bare for autumn but boasting fairy-lights, waiting for a Christmas turn-on which was still three months away. As we walked towards the front door, Alison said, 'I do believe you're getting more human. Normally you prefer to use the phone.'

'She's ex-directory,' I said.

Alison had managed to get Page out of his chair and into her sling without waking him. Now she stroked his brow. 'If he wakes up, he'll want fed, and I've no bottles.'

'You're not breastfeeding him while I interrogate someone,' I said.

Alison snorted. 'The very notion of you interrogating someone.'

The inner door opened, and Mrs Mahood, whom I recognised from her photo in the paper which appeared after the nose-breaking incident, stood before the sliding outer door, which she did not slide. She was a thin woman, with an angular face; she had on a lot of eyeliner and a black dress – lots of jewellery.

'Yes?' she barked.

I explained that my name was Stan Dalone, and that I was a private investigator working for the man accused of murdering her husband, and that I would like to ask her some questions. She slid the outer door open and snapped, 'And why the fuck would I want to answer your questions?'

'Because I don't believe my client is guilty, and I *do* believe it is in both of our interests to find out who really is. I'm sure you wouldn't want an innocent man to go to prison, any more than you would like your husband's killer to be out there walking the streets.'

Her eyes had been flitting back and forth from me to Alison. Now they fixed on her.

'And who are you with a baby in a sling?'

'I'm his sidekick, and this,' she said, patting Page's head, 'is *my* sidekick.'

'Are youse a pair of jokers or what?'

'No,' I said, 'we're deadly serious.'

'I'm slightly less serious,' said Alison, 'and he,' she added, patting Page's head again, 'doesn't contribute much.'

Gloria's eyes narrowed. She pointed at me. 'You, I don't like much. But you,' she said to Alison, 'I have more time for. And this one,' she reached out and touched Page's cheek, 'I could just cuddle all day. You may as well come in. My life couldn't be any more fucked up than it is already. I'll help you if I can.'

She turned back into the house. Alison smirked at me and stepped in after her.

Her lounge was large, neat, modern, with a massive TV and a glass-fronted cabinet with several shelves full of small trophies. She saw me looking at them as she brought in a tray with three mugs of tea on it. She hadn't asked if I wanted tea. I despise tea. But I said nothing. I was being professional.

She said, 'I used to play a lot of darts. That's where I met Sam, in the Harland and Wolff Welders Club. I was captain of the ladies' team. He was captain of the men's. It was quite romantic.'

'Aw,' said Alison.

Gloria smiled at the memory of it. 'Yeah, Sam – he had his moments. Though he wasn't beyond a knee-trembler up the back alley either. And by back alley, I mean behind the club.' She cackled suddenly. 'Oh, we had a laugh, Sam and I. He could be such a sweetheart. Oh, he could put the fear of God into people as well. But I like that in a man.'

'So do I,' said Alison.

I said, 'How aware were you of your husband's . . . activities?'

'The illegal ones?'

'Were there legitimate ones?'

'Of course. Listen, he was always a scallywag, but in recent years, not so much. He kept his hand in, but we had property too – rental mostly. He was pretty good at it. That's where our money came from.'

'I imagine he didn't have a problem with overdue rent.'

'He had his business, and he saw to it. He looked after his family, and when he came home at night, he left the business behind him. We were not blessed with children, but we had a good life together. Marrying him was the best thing that ever happened to me.'

Alison said, 'Good for you. My man, over there, is trying to avoid marrying me. He has a commitment phobia, amongst other things.'

'And you with a bairn?'

'And me with a bairn.'

Gloria studied me. 'What's the problem?'

'There's no problem,' I said.

Alison raised an eyebrow.

'*Sam*,' I said, 'is alleged to have been involved not only in protection, but in drugs as well.'

'*Alleged*? No. He absolutely was involved, though God knows he wasn't very good at it. Seriously. I've seen all those articles about what a big dealer he was, but really, he was out of his depth. Honestly? He did some coke in his time, some dope, but once all those new designer drugs hit the market, he didn't really get them – understand them, you know? I mean, seriously, one day he came home and told me he'd scored a shipment of MBNA and I had to explain to him that MBNA was a credit card, and that he probably meant MDMA. And I only knew that because I read the *Daily Mail*.'

'What about steroids?' I asked.

'What about them? Oh – because he was murdered in a gym? I get you. But no. I don't think so. They weren't his thing.' She picked up her mug for the first time and took a sip and then cradled it in her hands. She let out a long sigh. 'I miss him. I really do. I know what people thought of him, and they weren't always wrong, but he was different with me, different when that front door closed. He was just a normal bloke then. And sensitive. I know he did things, but that doesn't mean he deserved to die the way he did. This man they have for it – you really don't think it was him? When I spoke to the police, they seemed absolutely certain.'

'Well,' I said, 'it's quite possible that he is guilty. The problem is that since the day and hour he was arrested he hasn't spoken, he hasn't been identified and nobody knows anything about him. Because of his mental condition he may not ever stand trial for your husband's death, which means we might never get to see or hear the evidence against him. So the chances are we will never know for sure, and that has to be worrying for you, because it means your husband's killer could still be out there walking around. I mean, Sam is bound to have made a few enemies over the years.'

Gloria set her mug down. Instead of directly answering the question, she nodded at the coffee table. 'Do you see that telephone directory? You could open that at random, and whatever page you're on you could probably find the names of half a dozen people who would happily have done Sam in. He wasn't in a business where you made friends. So if you don't think it was this nut job in the loony bin, then I'm afraid you may be looking for a needle in a haystack.'

I nodded gravely at her. But inside I was smiling, for they were *exactly* the kind of odds I loved.

13

I stopped outside the house to drop Alison and Page off. I
did not get out of the Mystery Machine, or cut the engine.
I had work to go to. It wasn't good to leave Jeff alone in
the shop for longer than strictly necessary. He might start
offering advice or worse, discounts. But Alison showed no
inclination to get out. She looked at the house, at the steps
leading up to it, at the split and splintered wooden barrel
that had once, many years ago, hosted flowers, at the front
door with the light bulb above it that only occasionally
worked, the lock that rattled in a slight breeze, and the floors
above, the windows where columns of books were clearly
visible and the attic where Mother now dwelled, and she
shivered.

'I don't like this house,' she said. 'It's creepy.'

'It's just an old house.'

'It creaks, and it never really gets warm, there's no natural
light, and it disturbs me.'

'We can discuss double glazing.'

'And your mother hates me.'

'She is what she is. I can't help that.'

'She's never liked me, and she despises Page.'

'She just has a funny way with her. She likes you well enough. If she didn't, she'd probably slit your throat while you slept.'

'That's good to know. Now I can relax.'

'And she's just not good with kids. She has no patience, never has had. None of us are perfect.'

She chewed on her bottom lip. 'Do you think she tried to kill herself?'

'I don't know. Yes. Probably.'

'What if I go in there and she's hanging from the banister?'

'The banister is riddled with woodworm, it wouldn't support a body.'

'We need a place of our own.'

'We have a place of our own.'

'With your mother.'

'She won't be around for ever. Maybe you should look into insurance policies yourself.'

I gave her a theatrical wink. She responded with a thoughtful nod.

I returned to No Alibis. Jeff looked distinctly uncomfortable as I came through the door. He nodded down the shop. We had a customer. Or, rather, we had DI Robinson. He was a customer insofar as he occasionally bought books from me, but I wasn't convinced that he had a genuine interest in them. I believed he bought them as a way of paying me for my advice on the cases he found too difficult to solve himself.

DI Robinson glanced at me, but immediately returned his attention to the books. He was wearing a grey overcoat, with a leather man-bag slung over one shoulder. I raised an eyebrow at Jeff.

'I didn't tell him anything,' he whispered, 'about anything.'

DI Robinson turned and moved towards the counter, behind which I had taken up a defensive position. He had in his hand, I saw, a mint condition copy of Chandler's *The Big Sleep*. It was a paperback edition published by Avon Books in 1943 with a cover price of 25 cents. I kept it in a plastic jacket, and on a high shelf. When I was in the shop, I rarely let it out of my sight. It was worth a small fortune.

'I'm aware of what cops get paid,' I said, 'and that's out of your league.'

'How much are we talking about?'

'If you have to ask, you can't afford it.'

He said, 'I hope it's insured then. In case something happens to it.' He tapped the book on the counter. 'You've been busy.'

'I'm always busy.'

'Do you want to talk about this in front of Cyclops or do you want to go somewhere private?'

'I keep nothing from Jeff,' I said.

Jeff glowed. He also seeped, which was less endearing.

'Okay, Clouseau,' said DI Robinson, 'I want to nip this one in the bud once and for all. I warned you there was nothing for you in this, but that it could get dangerous. I can't always be looking out for you. I know you were thrown out of the gym. I know you've just been to see Gloria. I know you're trying to figure out who bumped off Fat Sam Mahood, and who killed his sidekick in the mental ward . . .'

Jeff started to say something. I kneed him, surreptitiously.

'Did you just kick him?' DI Robinson asked.

'No,' Jeff and I said together.

'You two are . . .' He stopped and shook his head at us. 'And I've had enough of it. You're representing the man in Purdysburn?'

'Gideon,' said Jeff.

'Gabriel,' I corrected.

DI Robinson studied me.

'It's a codename,' I said.

'Whatever the hell you want to call him, he's as guilty as sin. Here, I brought you something. Stick this in your machine.'

He opened his bag and took out a DVD and waved towards my computer. He was one of perhaps only three people in the world who still called a computer a *machine*. I obediently took it and slipped it in.

'Security-camera footage from the All Star Health Club,' he said.

We are conditioned to expect CCTV footage to be grainy, indistinct, sometimes only in black and white. This was in HD colour. Perfect. It showed the reception area, it showed well-lit corridors, it showed the car park outside and glimpses of the McDonald's opposite. After about five minutes of watching it I was about to say it also showed nothing whatsoever of interest. Then DI Robinson said, 'Slow it down here.'

The time showed it to be 10.15 p.m., a quarter of an hour after I knew the staff had locked up for the night, when Fat Sam Mahood was most likely labouring through the last lengths of his life. The point of view of the camera was from behind and above the reception desk, looking down on the counter and the customer side of it; it showed enough of the staff side for us to see that there was a figure hiding there, hunched over, wearing white. Then he moved out of shot. I was about to say something but DI Robinson stopped me and a few moments later the man's face was back, right up close to the lens, and then he was beating furiously at it, his face contorted and sweat lashed, and then the lens cracked, and the picture died, but it left us with a very clear impression of a man who was not in the least bit angelic.

14

'*Now* will you stay out of it?' DI Robinson asked.

'Absolutely,' I said. 'He's as guilty as sin.'

He nodded. 'You know, sometimes I appreciate your help. You have a way of looking at things that they don't – *can't* – teach at college. Off-kilter. Sometimes I think you're from a different planet, the way you go at things.'

I raised my hand and gave him the 'live long and prosper' salute. He blinked at me.

'Kepler 22,' I added by way of clarification.

He gave a kind of half-laugh and said: 'It's him, it's your Gabriel. We also have footprints down by the pool which match his shoes. He *is* as guilty as sin, but you'd be amazed how much someone acting dumb can mess up the system.'

DI Robinson rubbed at his chin, as if he was thinking, or debating. It was quite theatrical. And that made me think that it was staged, and that his purpose in visiting No Alibis was probably not only to reveal the evidence of

Gabriel's guilt, but actually to seek my counsel, as he had in the past.

'So,' he said, 'we can close the book on this, can we?'

'It is shut and slipped into a protective plastic jacket.'

'Because even though we have our man, and he's not going to be killing anyone else, there's still an investigation going on into Fat Sam and how he operated and who he was connected to and where all his money went. If you're sticking your nose in upsetting people, then those people we're trying to keep an eye on will be on the alert, they'll clam up or just go to ground. So, much as I understand why you're involved, and asking questions, I really do need you to be stopping. That's why I came and showed you this. Your Gabriel is guilty, can that just be the end of it?'

I said, 'I was never really interested in Fat Sam anyway, I just wanted to know who Gabriel was. I suppose it doesn't matter now.'

'Okay, good, excellent. Now what about this book?'

The Chandler was back in play.

I'm sure DI Robinson was quite adequately remunerated for his crime-fighting work, but by the time he walked out of the shop, without the book, I managed to make him feel like a poverty-stricken hobo with delusions of grandeur. It is good to take people down a peg or two. I enjoy the confusion it sows when condescending types realise that while they might be proficient in one field, when it comes to another, they are hopelessly at sea; books are my business, and I excel at them. DI Robinson left a £300 deposit on the Chandler, which he would forfeit if he didn't come up with the other £1,200 in ten days, and tramped out of the shop with a look that suggested he knew he had been scammed but was quite incapable of doing anything about it.

'I was just looking at the Chandler yesterday,' Jeff said. 'You'd written the price in pencil inside the front cover. It was £200.'

'Your point?'

'You made him pay a deposit which is greater than the value of the book.'

'I didn't *make* him do anything. He kept upping his offer. That's business. Besides, don't you know, beauty is in the eye of the beholder?'

He looked at me doubtfully, which was understandable, given the state of his face. 'Well,' he said, 'at least we can forget about *The Case of the Man in the White Suit* and concentrate on *The Case of Making Ends Meet*.' He gave me a big, stupid grin.

'Don't be ridiculous,' I said, and took up position in front of the computer. For good measure I added: 'Don't you even *listen*?'

'To what? I don't under—'

'Francis Delaney, the man whom Gabriel murdered, was Fat Sam's sidekick. Do you think Robinson just dropped that into the conversation by mistake? He doesn't want us to drop the case – the very opposite: he wants us all over it.'

'I didn't get that impr—'

'No, Jeff, *you* wouldn't. But we've been down this road before. He can't just come out and say he's stuck and needs our help, but he's saying it all the same. That's why I played him for so much on the Chandler. He paid the deposit on the book, but needs approval from above to go to £1,200. I've absolutely no doubt he'll get it, and I've absolutely no doubt he either knows the true value of the book or will find out very shortly. And he won't care, because it's not about the book, it's about securing my services, and to get them he knows he has to throw out the budget and pay me what I'm worth.'

'Right,' said Jeff.

I began to type. I could feel him watching me. 'What?' I asked.

'But if Gideon – Gabriel – *is* guilty, why are we . . .?'

'Who says he's guilty? Jeff, there is much, much more to this than meets the eye. Now, I am putting out an appeal to my lovely database of Christmas Club members, Facebook friends and Tweeters, seeking information on the staff of the All Star, whom I need to talk to, and then I will be trawling for more information on Fat Sam, on Francis Delaney and what might possibly connect them to Gabriel. And I want you to go home and get your suit on.'

'My suit? Why?'

'Because Jeff, you're going to Francis Delaney's funeral. Which kicks off in,' I glanced at the time in the bottom corner of the screen, '. . . about half an hour, at Roselawn, so you'd better get your skates on.'

'Why am I . . . What am I supposed to . . .?'

'You're to use your initiative, even though it usually gets me into trouble and you beaten up. But if you were to mingle, and surreptitiously take photographs, that would be good. I want to know who's there, who his friends and colleagues were. I want to know about his connections and why he might have felt compelled to enter Purdysburn to try and kill Gideon.'

'Gabriel.'

'I know that.'

'Who says he tried to kill him?'

'*I* do. I know it. Now you'd better get moving.' But he stood there. '*What?*'

'Can't you come with me? You're so clear about what you want, and I'm really not . . .'

'Jeff, I don't do funerals. Not after last time. Do you remember what happened last time, Jeff?'

'There was a fire in the crematorium.'

'Exactly.'

'And you were nearly lynched.'

'See? Now will you please go?' I pulled his jacket off the back of his chair and pressed it into his chest. 'Jeff, you were whining about not being taken to the All Star, you whined about not going to Gloria Mahood's, and now that I'm actually giving you something to do, you're starting to whine about that too. What the hell is going on with you?'

'I just thought – you know, we could do it together.'

'Together, Jeff?'

'Like partners. You know – buddies.'

'Jeff, as wonderful as that sounds, you know I can't go to the funeral. And who's going to run the shop?'

'I don't know. Alison?'

'Alison is busy with Page. You need to do this by yourself, you need to own it. It's not really about me going, is it, Jeff? You're depressed about your exams, and you're suffering a crisis of confidence. But you can do this, you know you can.

Get out there, Jeff, and just do it, show me what you're made of. I'll be with you, in spirit. Go. Go.'

I guided him to the door and ushered him out. He looked back at me and nodded and gave me a bit of a smile.

'I'll do my best,' he said.

I gave him the thumbs-up and he walked off.

I had always thought of my faithful young friend as being rather gormless, but now I absolutely knew that he was also needy, clingy and pathetic. He fitted right in at No Alibis.

15

I called Alison. I had not heard from her. I had an inkling that Mother might indeed have hung herself from the banister, which would perhaps just about have held her frame, at least until the front door opened and that tiniest little draught was all that was required to sway the body enough to cause the banister to finally snap and her dead weight to hurtle down three flights to land on top of Alison, who had either been killed outright by the impact or was, even now, pinned under the corpse, quite unable to move, due to multiple fractures and a damaged spleen. I wasn't sure how disappointed I was when she answered her phone.

Nevertheless I said, 'Good, you're alive,' and added: 'How is the light of my life?'

'I'm fine.'

She waited. I waited. She waited some more, and could have continued to wait until the Rapture, so I said, 'I meant Page.'

'I knew you did, and he's grand.'

'And how's my other little woman?'

'You know, hanging around. Or do you mean me?'

'You know who I mean.'

'I'm afraid I do. She's fine too. I was hardly through the door before she was yelling down for a hot water bottle.'

'And you . . .?'

'Told her to go fuck herself.'

'I suspect you did not.'

'Only because I'm a lady.'

I said nothing. She said nothing. With the Rapture getting closer, I said: 'So you're okay?'

'I *am* okay. I'm just surprised that you're phoning me. You hardly ever phone me. Not that I'm complaining. Are you coming home for tea?'

'No. I'm on a case – I may be late.'

'Developments?'

'Mmm, yes.'

I told her about DI Robinson and the DVD I'd played in the *machine* and how he was actually appealing for my help by trying to prove there was no case for me to pursue, and Alison *hmmm-hmmmed* through that, but then perked up when I mentioned Francis Delaney being Fat Sam's sidekick and explained how I'd grabbed the bull by the horns by sending Jeff to the funeral to act as my eyes and ears, seeing as how my own eyes are myopic and my ears have a variety of tinnitus which instead of emitting a high-pitched shriek plays the soundtrack from the original London stage production of *Les Misérables* on a constant loop.

She said, 'So Gabriel being caught at the scene doesn't deter you?'

'Au contraire.'

'Do you think, my Mystery Man, that there's a possibility that DI Robinson doesn't have as many sides to him as you seem to think? That he really, genuinely doesn't want you involved in this?'

'He would have said.'

'As far as I can understand, he *did* say.'

'No,' I said. 'He realises his own shortcomings, and turns to me for help. We know this.' Alison said nothing. 'I'm going to wait for Jeff to come back from the funeral, and then I need to go through what he's discovered. I will probably be late.'

'When you get started, you're like a dog with a bone.'

'It's why you love me,' I said, and then hung up before she could respond. But I knew she would be smiling.

I tried to concentrate on ordering stock, but I found it dispiriting. There are very few good, new writers out there now. Most crime novels, if you ripped the cover off and gave them to a reader without identifying the author, they wouldn't be able to tell one writer from the next. There is a template, a style, which 90 per cent of crime writers adhere to, and they are killing the genre. Crime writing is like a rogue Great White shark. It has to keep moving forward all the time, while taking care to kill plenty of people along the way. There are few stylists, few innovators, and fewer wits. If Chandler were alive today, he'd be very old indeed.

I ignored the stock, and lifted the phone.

'I think that's a *lovely* name,' Nurse Brenda said as soon as I told her. 'Gabriel. My angel. *Gabriel*. The *Archangel* Gabriel.

Yes. Lovely. So, if I'm doing the paperwork, how long do you think you're going to need?'

'An hour. Tops.'

'Really? Is that all? That might be a problem.'

'How so?'

'Well, the only way I can get you in upstairs is if I check you in as a patient. Visitors are strictly monitored, and since the murder Gabriel has been kept in solitary confinement, so the only way you're going to be able to even observe him is by seizing whatever chance you can. But I doubt that will come around within a specific hour. You would need to come in for assessment, and the *minimum* assessment period is twenty-four hours. There's no real way round it. But at least you'll have a longer window during which to grab your opportunity to get a look at him.'

My throat immediately felt a little drier than normal. 'You mean to stay overnight?'

'Yes. It allows any drugs you may be on to get out of your system.'

'I'm not on any drugs.'

'I didn't say you were, but I'm afraid it's standard procedure.'

I rubbed at my chest. It was definitely tightening. 'But this is just for the paperwork, surely?' I said. 'It can show that I'm in for twenty-four hours, but actually I'll just be nipping in for an hour, and you'll whip me out of there as soon as my job is done.'

There was a pause. And then: 'I told you, this doesn't have the approval of my superiors. This is totally between you and me. If my bosses found out about this, I'd be for the chop. It's not done, it's just not done. I'm doing this for Gabriel. You and I are the only chance he has. The only way I can get you into the unit is if I write here on this form that you have had a psychotic incident and require urgent assessment under secure conditions. That will require a twenty-four-hour stay. You will be assessed by a team I have no say over or access to. There is no way round it. There will be no slipping out when you're done. There are safeguards in place to prevent any one person being able to override the system, so as far as everyone is concerned, you will be a patient, and a fairly dangerous one at that. I'm sorry, it's the only way I can work it. Nobody can know about this. Nobody.'

I said, 'I can't do that. I have a shop to run. And a child.'

'Gabriel needs you.'

'I understand that, but—'

'And *I* need you.' She was doing it again. That voice. It could probably control the tides. 'I'm asking for twenty-four hours to save a man's life. And I'm not exaggerating. We run a secure unit here, but it's nothing compared to where he'll be sent as soon as they sort out *his* paperwork. I've seen a lot of terrible things in my time in mental health, but those places, they scare the pants off me. My Gabriel would not last in one of them for more than a few days. He would be torn to shreds. Do you understand?'

'*Yes*, but—'

'I'm risking my entire career for this, and all I'm asking for is a night and a day to save Gabriel. You're not going to let me down, are you?'

'No, but—'

'Good. Now I want you to swear to me that you won't tell anyone else what you're doing.'

'I can't, I have a—'

'I want you to swear to me. People talk – people *always* talk. It's human nature, it's the human condition. If this gets out, I will be ruined, I will never work in the health service again, and I could not live with that. It would kill me. So I want you to promise that you won't tell anyone. Anyone.'

I rubbed at my brow. 'Just my girlfr—'

'*No.*'

'You can trust her.'

'*No.* You have to understand. She may swear never to tell a living soul, and that's fine for today or tomorrow – but what about the day after? What about the day where you have a row and she shouts something out in anger, or she runs away and she meets someone and she tells them?'

'Why would she do that?'

'Because that's what people do. If it's a secret they cannot resist telling someone. Secrets are burdens. Secrets are worms that burrow into your core, and they might stay there for years but eventually they work their way out again. So I need you to promise me that you will tell no one. Promise me.'

'*Okay.* I'll work something out.'

'Say it. Say you promise.'

'I promise.'

'You promise what?'

'I promise that I won't tell anyone I'm going undercover into a secure mental ward.'

'You promise that you won't tell anyone that you're going into a secure mental ward *what*?'

'What?'

'You promise that you won't tell anyone that you're going into a secure mental ward *what*?'

I owed her nothing, yet somehow I owed her everything as well. I wanted to solve *The Case of the Man in the White Suit* but I most definitely did not want to spend any more time than I needed to in Purdysburn. I had a deep-rooted horror of the place and its denizens. I liked my new life in No Alibis, I liked the fact that I had a girlfriend I could parade around and show people that I had a girlfriend, and I especially liked it when she was pregnant so that people would know that I had had sex and was no longer a virgin, and I adored the fact that I had a baby I could wheel around so that people would know for sure that I had had the sex, and to be doubly sure I always added whenever people stopped to admire Page that he definitely wasn't adopted. And I had a terrible gnawing feeling that if I was admitted to Purdysburn, even in the cause of good, and did adhere to Nurse Brenda's conditions, that something would happen, that my incarceration and renewed exposure to the extremes of mental illness would somehow conspire to destroy a life I had so painfully rescued from the abyss. And yet, I had no choice.

'I'm waiting.'

I took a deep breath.

'I promise that I won't tell anyone that I'm going undercover into a secure mental ward, *Nurse Brenda*.'

'That's more like it,' said Nurse Brenda. 'You always were a *very* good boy.'

And with that the die was cast.

119

16

It was cold and damp, and that was just in the shop. The weather outside had taken another turn for the worse, and I had a cold which was a sniffle short of pneumonia and a body temperature that was a degree north of hypothermia. Jeff was standing there in his T-shirt. 'It's boiling in here,' he said, and went to open a window. I prevented him by telling him he would be sacked if he did. I was quite serious. 'It's barely autumn,' he said. 'You get like this every year. It's balmy out there. In here, it's like the black hole of Kolkata.'

'Of where?'

'Kolkata.'

'Of where?'

'*Kolkata.*'

'Of where?'

Jeff sighed. Brendan Coyle also sighed. He was in the shop with us; he had removed his sports jacket and was standing in a short-sleeved shirt. And trousers and shoes and socks, but they are hardly relevant. Brendan Coyle is a literary novelist who sometimes moonlights as a crime writer. He also teaches a creative writing class in No Alibis on a Saturday morning. I despise most humans, but I reserve a special despiction for Brendan, because he is a know-all, and a snob, and a hypocrite, and successful. The audience he attracts to his class is responsible for one third of my weekly book sales. This does not amount to a huge number of books, but it can mean the difference between profit and loss, so I could not afford to poison him, bludgeon him, have him iced by my gangland connections or otherwise piss him off because I wanted to keep my baby in Pampers.

As if it needed saying, I said: 'Calcutta.'

'The name has changed,' said Jeff.

'But the expression has not. Now let me concentrate.'

I was hunched over the computer, examining the photographs Jeff had taken at Francis Delaney's funeral. Thus far, the only face I recognised was that of DI Robinson.

'Did he see you?' I asked.

'I am a master of disguise. I move like a shadow. As stealthy as a midnight cat, as—'

'He saw you then.'

'Yes. He said, "Hello, Jeff, what're you doing here?" I said I was a friend of the deceased's sister.'

'Did he believe you?'

'He made no comment.'

'I'll take that as a no, then. Well attended, I see.'

'The church was packed. I wasn't really able to take pictures – it would have been . . .' He struggled for the right word.

'Indelicate,' said Brendan.

'Too much trouble,' I suggested.

'Indelicate,' Jeff agreed. 'But most of them continued on to the graveside, and it was a bit easier there. I pretended I had a phone call and wore my apologetic face.' He made it. It did not look very apologetic to me.

Brendan Coyle leaned over me and examined the photo I had up. 'This is the case you're working on, eh?'

'Clearly,' I said. He smelled of pipe tobacco. He did not actually smoke a pipe. There was a spray on the market which gave the same effect. It was called *Pipe Delight*. It cost a lot of money. Brendan was not literally an idiot, but he had idiot tendencies. I pointed at a small group of burly men bunched together. 'These guys look like the weightlifters from the gym, but I can't be sure with their clothes on. Beyond that . . .' I flicked onto the next photo, another wide shot taken at the cemetery. 'Who did you get speaking to?'

'Well, no one at the church, or the cemetery for that matter. It was all very quiet and respectful. But they all went back to the Stormont Inn afterwards. People were more forthcoming once the drink got flowing. That said, they were very complimentary about the deceased.'

'Did they talk about the hospital, why he was in there?'

'No. I tried asking, but it was kind of ignored – as if being murdered wasn't the dreadful thing, but being in the mental hospital was.'

'That's the way of it,' I said. 'Was there talk of Gabriel, or Fat Sam?'

'Just that Gideon was the c word, and Fat Sam was a good employer.'

'Was there a connection made between Fat Sam and Francis's murder?'

'Nope.'

'No knowing nods or winks or looks?'

'Not that I was aware of, though my vision is impaired because of what your mother did to me, so I'm not the best person to ask.'

Chortle isn't a word that is used very often these days, but it is the right one to describe the sound coming from Brendan Coyle.

'You sent a partially-sighted man to be your eyes at a funeral?'

'His eyesight is better than mine, Brendan, even though he has one closed over.'

'But clearly not good enough to recognise these gentlemen.' Brendan reached out and tapped the screen. 'The Brothers Karamazov.'

He was indicating two men, in middle age, in better suits than most of those around them. One was bald, and one, if I wasn't mistaken, had gone the way of wig.

'The . . .?'

'Forgive me – it's how they're often referred to in the circles in which I move, that is to say, the cultured circles. It's a little bit of an in-joke.'

'Clearly I don't move in such circles,' I said, 'otherwise I would get it.'

'Me neither,' said Jeff.

Brendan waved a hand loosely around the shop. 'Crime fiction, my dear boys. Much better to be on the outside, looking in.' He moved a little closer to the screen. 'Yes, indeed, that is certainly two of them. They're actually from Donegal originally; the name of their firm is O'Dromodery Construction. You've heard of them, surely? They've built half of Belfast these past few years.'

I had, but vaguely. 'I don't get the Karamazov.'

'There was a bit of a stink about them a few years ago because they were just about the first to bring in cheap Eastern European labour. It didn't go down awfully well with the local chaps, but the O'Dromoderys made their fortune from it. And they seem to quite enjoy throwing some of it at the arts. They believe, and rightly, that people of influence, people who matter, often move in artistic circles, and so they have attempted to curry favour by way of sponsorship – but everyone knows they are *total* philistines. As the story goes, they thought *The Brothers Karamazov* was a rival construction firm. The story may be apocryphal, but it has rather stuck. They are not supposed to be the most pleasant people in the world, but show me a rich businessman who is. They haven't been around town much this last year, but I suppose that's understandable, after what happened to the brother.'

He nodded to himself, and he waited.

Finally, Jeff said, 'The brother?'

'Yes, indeed. Poor Fergus. I met him a few times, and he was – how shall I say? – less *coarse* than the other two. Actually, he was quite nice and decent and sensitive – over-sensitive, as it turns out. Some deal or other went wrong, and he threw himself off the company building. Poor bugger.'

'And what would the O'Dromodery Brothers be doing at the funeral of Francis Delaney?' I asked.

'Haven't the foggiest,' said Brendan.

I have a certain sympathy for anyone who is desperate enough to throw themselves off a tall building. It was never an option for me, being afraid of heights, but then, given my brittle bones, height was never a requirement. I could have achieved the same result by throwing myself off a modestly constructed Lego house. But I understood the process, and the desire, and the only reason I hadn't killed myself was my certain knowledge that the world would be a poorer place without me, and that murderers would remain free, and that Belfast would be left without a guide to the greats of mystery fiction, and that Page would be deprived of a father, and that Alison would be left without a lover, at least for a few days, and that Mother . . . well, she would probably only notice when I wasn't around to empty her ashtray and give her luxurious massages in the bath.

Although it could not possibly last, I had a *purpose*, and for the moment that *purpose* was *The Case of the Man in the White Suit*, which had now led me to the death of one of the Karamazov Brothers. I was as intrigued by this as I was by the brothers' presence at Francis Delaney's funeral, and then by Francis Delaney's presence in Purdysburn Hospital, and his ultimate death, presumably at the hands of Gabriel. By their very physical presence in each other's lives and deaths, I could plot them on a Venn diagram, and would – yet their connection was as knotted and confusing as a tangled ball of Christmas-tree lights. But I love the process of unravelling. Also, I was intending to do everything in my power to solve *The Case of the Man in the White Suit* before I had to do my sleepover in the mental hospital, the dread of which was already well lodged in my gut.

After a very long while, during which he made many cruel and cutting remarks about crime fiction, Brendan Coyle finally departed, and a little after that Jeff went off into the stormy night as well. I locked up the shop and turned off the lights and sat as I like to do, in the darkness, before my computer, with a Twix in one hand, and the heating switched off to save the pennies, and I began to search for the key that would unlock *The Case of the Man in the White Suit*.

Ninety minutes later, I was arrested for criminal damage to a hydrangea bush.

17

Sometimes, when I have accumulated a lot of information, I need time to let it marinate. On these occasions I like to walk, even in my condition. I love the cover of darkness, though my night vision is poor and I am scared of cats. I always take my Nail for the Scratching of Cars with Personalised Numberplates with me in case I get lucky. On this night my walk deliberately took me past a Pound Shop, where I purchased a small trowel and a set of surgical gloves. I placed them in the pocket of my parka. I was already thinking of the implement as the Trowel of Hope. The gloves were to protect my hands from soil, mud, dirt, bugs and plants. I was also wearing a black woollen hat which could fold down into a balaclava if required. If by some chance I was spotted before I could do what I intended to do, the worst the police could charge me with was going equipped for gardening. I knew I would have to be quick, not just to avoid being spotted, but also to avoid the extreme reaction

I suffer when I'm exposed to rubber gloves for more than five minutes.

I walked through the rain, fingering the Trowel of Hope and occasionally scratching cars, until I came to the Holywood Road. To get there I had to pass the All Star Health Club, which I now knew had been built three years earlier by the Brothers Karamazov who, following the suicide of Fergus, now comprised of Bernard and Sean O'Dromodery. My research told me that they had once been regarded as one of the richest families in Ireland, but that they had only just hung on by their fingernails during the recent property crash. Instead of dozens of building projects employing thousands of builders, they now appeared to be concentrating on just one, a major new shopping centre build on surplus land they had purchased from St Mary's High School for Girls on the Falls Road in West Belfast, which they hoped would restore their fortune.

The O'Dromodery Brothers' headquarters were a quarter of a mile away from the health club, set back from the main road and overlooking sports grounds opposite, with the twin cranes of the Harland & Wolff shipyard only visible beyond because of their sporting red lights to stop planes crashing into them at night. There was a tarmac forecourt set out in parking spaces, and between them and the main building were four concrete boxes. These were now filled with soil and plants, and would originally have been used to prevent terrorists from parking car bombs too close. The building itself was four storeys high, and not much of an advert for innovative design. It was just a bigger concrete box.

There were three vehicles in the car park, a light in

reception but nobody behind the desk, and there were lights on the top floor, but no one was visible at the windows. I sheltered under a tree overhanging the pavement across the road for nine minutes, checking for signs of movement. When I saw none I lowered the balaclava and crossed the road. I pulled on the surgical gloves. I then exposed the Trowel of Hope and approached the first of the concrete flower boxes and began to dig.

I had a theory. I often do.

The hydrangeas were not in flower. The soil was moist thanks to the rain and easy to penetrate. It was with considerable relief that I discovered that the concrete boxes were mostly solid, with only about two feet of earth to sift through. I dug around the roots of the plant and widened my search in an expanding circle until I hit the edges of the first box without finding what I was looking for. I moved onto the second box. This hydrangea seemed to be younger – its roots were shallower and less tangled. It was easier to actually remove the plant with its roots intact so that I could work more swiftly through the soil. I had just completed this action when my face, and the scene in general, was illuminated by the beam of a flashlight.

'And what the bloody hell do you think you're doing?' a gruff voice demanded. I turned towards it and could just about make out a rotund figure in some kind of a uniform. 'Put down your weapon.'

'It's not a weapon,' I said. 'It's a trowel.'

'Drop it!'

He did not himself appear to be armed. He was just a security guard. If I'd been a better man I would have taken him down. I had read ten thousand crime novels and knew as many ways to kill a man. But I lacked the physical strength, and a backbone, so I dropped the trowel and blinked at him.

'I'm not doing anything,' I said by way of explanation.

'Yes, you are – you're stealing our flowers.'

'No, I'm not,' I said, 'and it's a shrub.'

'Right,' he said, 'you're coming with me.'

He had the confidence of bulk, but he would have no speed. I could have attempted to run away, but I knew that my arthritic knees and calcified joints would let me down. It would be a fat bloke chasing a cripple, and the result would be too close to call. Besides, I was keen to see the inside of the O'Dromodery building, so I did as he indicated and walked ahead of him towards the reception. As I set off he stooped to retrieve the trowel. He held it carefully so as not to smudge any fingerprints. He had clearly been watching too many cop shows. I smiled to myself. This was probably the highlight of his month. With his other hand he reached down and lifted the hydrangea. When we got to the front door, I had to open it for him.

We entered the reception. He told me to take a seat. He moved behind the desk and set the plant down on top. He opened a drawer and took out a bag containing elastic bands. He emptied these out and slipped the trowel into it instead. He took a Post-it note, wrote something on it and then stuck it to the bag and slipped it back into the drawer. I believe he was trying to intimidate me with efficiency. But he had no idea who he was dealing with. I ate the likes of him for breakfast. Once, literally.

He said, 'Things are bad when you steal the very flowers.'

'Shrubs,' I said.

He shook his head. 'I'll be needing some ID.' I took out my business card and slipped it across. It was the one that said *Murder is Our Business*, amongst other things. I had nothing to hide. He studied it intently. His eyes flitted up. 'Odd name,' he said.

I shrugged.

He said, 'You can take off the gloves.' I took off the gloves and handed them to him. He bagged them.

He said, 'What do you want to tell me about the . . . shrub?'

'It's a hydrangea.'

'Right. What do you want to tell me about the hydrangea.'

'The *hydrangea macrophylla*.'

'*Yes.*'

'It's deciduous.' He blinked at me. 'That means it sheds its leaves.'

'I know what deciduous is. Don't be smart. You were caught red-handed.'

'I was just doing a little pruning. It's essential.'

'We have people who do that.'

'Well, clearly they're not doing it.'

'You were stealing our hydrangea. It was on the ground.'

'Only until I could clear out debris from its bedding. It has been used as an ash-tray. That's not good for it.'

'Why would you do that?'

'I'm a Midnight Gardener,' I said, and then we both sat silently for quite a while, as we both tried to work out what I meant. Finally it came to me. 'We are urban guerrillas,' I said. 'We protect the rights of potted plants and shrubbery. Perhaps you've heard of us?'

'Are you on some kind of drugs?'

'I'm high on life,' I said.

'I'm going to phone the police now.' He reached for the phone.

'They know all about the Midnight Gardeners. They have a special unit that deals with us. Ask for Special Branch.'

He hesitated. His swollen cheeks were reddening. 'You're fucking with me, right?'

I smiled. I reached out and plucked a leaf off the shrub. I held it up to my nose and breathed in. 'Do you know there are over six hundred variations of hydrangea? I could probably name you two hundred of them.' I rolled the leaf into a ball and held it up. 'And do you see this?' He nodded warily. 'Every part of the hydrangea plant contains *cyanogenic glycosides*, or as you might know it – cyanide.'

'Cy . . .?'

'How would you handle a death in custody, on your watch? I can tie you up in paperwork for the rest of your life. I'll become a cause celeb and a conspiracy theory.' I popped the leaf into my mouth and began to chew. 'Long live the Midnight Gardeners,' I said. 'Let me go or I'll swallow and then you'll have the blood of a dead man on your hands, amongst other excretions.'

I grinned at him. I really was fucking with him. There was sweat on his brow, a rapid, engorged pulse at the side of his head and his eyes were blinking like a punch-drunk boxer's. I had introduced a virus of doubt and panic into his system:

and he was just about self-aware enough to know that he was out of his depth.

When I turn it on, I turn it *on*.

I was flushed with my own sense of power.

And then I was just flushed. In fact, *sweating*. My heart was thundering. My leg began to shake. My mouth grew moist, and then sweet, and then bitter, and I felt the bile rise and then the room began to rotate and my security guard began to grow an extra head. I toppled forward and everything grew vague and all I was aware of was a vague, distant voice saying:

'I need Special Branch . . . and an ambulance.'

18

I wasn't *wrong*. I didn't make a *mistake*. But science is not an exact science. There *was* cyanide in the hydrangea leaf. I am an *expert* on cyanide. It has long been a favourite of Nazis and crime writers. Agatha used it in *And Then There Were None* and *Yellow Iris*. Chandler poisoned Philip Marlowe with it in *The Little Sister*. It is true that I had not expected such an extreme reaction, one that led to me hurtling and hurling in a screaming ambulance through Belfast's dank streets and then being smashed through hospital doors en route to a waiting trauma team. I had *not* miscalculated the amount of cyanide in the hydrangea leaf, but without actually testing it in advance I had taken a reasoned gamble on what the content might be in a randomly plucked leaf. It *should not* have been present in such quantities as to endanger life if ingested. Otherwise thousands of little children, who eat everything, would die every year. Hydrangeas would be outlawed. There would be Hydrangea Police employed to root them out. Either the leaf I chose had an unusually high concentration of *cyanogenic glycosides* or my body had over-reacted to the intrusion. I am, after all, one of the most sensitive people on the planet. Alison maintains that I should live in a bubble.

Meanwhile, I was dying.

I was not aware of fighting for my life, which apparently I did. I have never been much of a fighter. I *always* prefer flight. Given the option, I might have taken my battle for life to arbitration. There was no out-of-body experience, though it would have been such a relief to escape for however brief a time from the pain and misery I endure on a daily basis. I was reliably informed later that the trauma team worked hard to save me, but that there was really little to be done for cyanide poisoning. They applied oxygen and performed artificial respiration using a bag and mask, as mouth-to-mouth resuscitation can be lethal to the person applying it. Then they made me inhale amyl nitrate to speed up my heart. And then they left me to see if I would wake up.

In the morning, I came round and asked for a Twix. I was not actually hungry. But it was my default setting.

The doctor, Dr Winter, who came to check on me, tried to take a complete medical history but called a halt around 1992 suffering from fatigue. He asked me if I had suicidal tendencies and why I had eaten the flower, and I informed him that I had no desire to kill myself, and also that it was a shrub. I was lying in bed, and a little groggy and weak, but that was not far removed from my normal condition.

Dr Winter said, 'We tried to notify your next-of-kin. There

was a number in your wallet for a shop – No Alibis? But there was only an answer machine. Then there was just the one number on your mobile phone.' He checked his clipboard and read it out. It was my home number. I do not have a wide circle of friends. 'We called it and an older-sounding woman answered but said we had a wrong number.'

I was not surprised. Mother frequently denied my existence. She wavered between me being a mistake and an abomination.

'Anyway,' he said, 'I think you will be right as rain. But it was a close call.' He looked at me for a bit, and then said: 'The Midnight Gardeners. I've heard of them. I have to say, I'm right with you.'

'Good,' I said.

He waved around the ward. 'In this business you get a lot of do-gooders. They don't actually care about the patients, they just want to be seen to be doing good. But you, the Gardeners, you do it in the dark, in secret. You just do it because it needs to be done, not for the glory. I think, actually, that the police were quite sympathetic, although obviously they couldn't say that.'

'The police?'

'Oh yes. They came in with you. And some kind of a security guard. He was determined that you be charged with theft or criminal damage or something like that, but once he explained what had happened, you could tell they really weren't interested. They took notes and sent the guard on his way, but as soon as he was gone they were laughing and joking about it. They said they'd file a report, but that nothing would come of it. They said if they arrested every nutter out there they'd never have time to catch any real criminals.'

'I'm not a nutter,' I said. 'Would a nutter know the chemical make-up of a hydrangea leaf?'

'You're not helping your case,' said Dr Winter.

He wheeled me down to the doors himself. He seemed like a decent sort. Overworked, underpaid, but enough about me. He said I should go home and rest. I said there would be plenty of time to rest when I was dead.

'Well,' he said, 'you came pretty close.'

He asked how one might go about joining the Midnight Gardeners. He said he had a lot of downtime and was rapidly going off humans. He gave me his mobile phone number. I told him to expect a call. I got out of the chair and walked out of the City Hospital and onto the Lisburn Road. He was still standing there watching me when I glanced back. He gave me a salute. I quite liked it, and would encourage Jeff to do the same.

I walked to No Alibis. It was only around the corner, literally a hop, skip and a jump to a healthy person, but any one of them would break my spine. It was already after nine, but there was no queue of customers anxious as to why I hadn't opened up on time. I unlocked the many, many locks that keep my precious books secure. I entered the shop, and the first thing I did was check my messages, and sure enough, there was one there from the hospital, and, also, sixteen from Alison. They began chirpy and became more concerned before descending into panicked desperation.

It is nice that she worries about me.

I sat at the computer and began to check my e-mails. There were plenty relating to the book business, but none yet in response to the plea I had sent out to my database appealing for information on various aspects of *The Case of the Man in the White Suit*. I did not, of course, specify that this was the name of the case or go into details about the specifics of it, but I did ask for details about various characters who were figuring in it.

After about an hour, and there still being no sign of a customer, and my not expecting Jeff until the afternoon, I closed the shop up again and crossed to Starbucks, where I found my place on their menu and ordered. After prevaricating for some while, because I do not like daylight or passers-by, I took the only available table, which was by the window. I sipped my Espresso Frappuccino and thought some more about the case, but was distracted after ten minutes by my view of the shop, which I had locked but not shuttered, and where I could now see Alison with her face pressed against the glass door peering in. Page was strapped to her chest, like a suicide bomb.

I sipped some more, and thought some more, and when I looked up again Alison was just passing by the coffee-shop window. Our eyes met and I looked away and then I looked back and she was just standing there, with her mouth half-open, her cheeks puffy and her eyes red. And then she came storming in and stood over me and yelled, 'Where the fuck have you been?'

'I . . .'

'I've been going out of my mind with worry!'

'I . . .'

'I thought you were dead or injured or lying in a coma!'

I said, 'Sorry, I should have called. I was working on the case, lost track of time.'

'I left you hundreds of messages! Why didn't you pick up?'

'I was out for a walk and must have missed them. Sorry.'

She was still glaring at me, but nevertheless she pulled out the other chair and sat down. 'Where were you? Where were you exactly?'

'Here, there, everywhere. You know how I am.'

Her eyes narrowed. 'Your hair, what there is of it, is all over the place. Your clothes are rumpled.' She reached across and took my hand, but not lovingly. She raised it to her nose and smelled it, and then the arm of the jacket I was wearing. 'You smell of antiseptic. And flowers.'

'Shrubs,' I said.

'What?'

'I'm *fine*. Don't worry about me.'

'Of course I worry about you!'

'You shouldn't. There's nothing to worry about.'

'There's everything to worry about!'

'Like what?'

'Like who you are and what you get up to and the people you get involved with. I worry *all the time*. Don't you know that?'

'There's nothing to worry about,' I repeated. 'Chill.'

'Don't tell me to chill! Christ!'

I sipped. It was very good coffee. 'Do you want one?'

'No!'

'I'm not sure if you're allowed to sit here if you don't—'

'Will you shut up? I was out of my mind with worry! What *happened*?'

I looked at her. They say that some people are beautiful when they're angry. Alison was not. She looked revolting. But still, I had a certain soft spot for her. She was not normally such unpleasant company, and there was always the prospect of sex. I had chosen not to tell her about the hospital because if it got out that I was someone who randomly consumed shrubbery, people would no longer bring their business to me.

'There's nothing to tell,' I said.

'Are you seeing someone else?'

'Excuse me?'

'Are you having sex with someone else?'

'No, and keep your voice down.'

'I want to know. Are you? I can handle it. I'm a big girl. Are you? Is that what's going on here?'

I said, 'Don't be ridiculous, I love you.'

And her mouth dropped open again, and I realised my mistake immediately.

'You've never told me that.'

'I'm sure I have.'

'No, never, ever. Really? You did tell me once before, not long after we met, but you were very, very drunk.'

'I'm allergic to alcohol,' I said.

She said, 'You really love me?'

'Yes, I do.'

There were tears in her eyes and a smile on her face.

'What do you want for dinner?' she asked.

'Rissoles,' I said.

*   *   *

On the way back to the shop she hooked her arm through mine, which I didn't like one bit. At the door she said, 'I love you more than all the tea in China.'

I nodded. I do not like tea. China remains the largest producer of tea in the world. It makes one and a quarter million tonnes of it every year. India is not far behind. Tea, like love, stays freshest when stored in a dry, cool, dark place in an airtight container.

Alison had things to do. She kissed me goodbye. It was good that people saw that. She went on her way and I opened the shop and after a while Jeff came in and asked how the case was going and I said it was going well. He took up position behind the till while I paced and thought. It was dark outside by four thirty. People say that Scandinavian crime fiction is so gritty, depressive and malevolent because those countries have such harsh winters and they spend many months in virtual darkness. I believe that is rubbish. If there was any truth in it, they would also have conquered the world with their happy-clappy twenty-four-hours-of-daylight summer novels, but to date, the best they had managed were Moomintrolls, which would drive you to suicide.

Because I knew that the vogue for Scandinavian crime fiction was over, and that my attempts to foist Irish crime fiction on the world were failing miserably, I was now preoccupied with finding what other region of the world might be open to ruthless exploitation. I was thinking deeply about this when the shop door opened and a large man in a black jacket and blacker polo-neck came in. He glanced at Jeff, and then further down the shop at me.

Jeff said, 'Welcome to No Alibis, is there anything I can help you with?'

The man shook his head, and then walked the full length of the shop, passing me on the way. He came to the store room at the back, entered it and disappeared from view. Jeff looked at me, and I looked at him. There was a machete I kept beneath the counter for maniacs and Jehovah's Witnesses, but I was frozen to the spot, and my tongue to the roof of my mouth. Jeff knew about it, but did not have the wit or gumption to reach for it before the man reappeared and walked back across the shop to the front door, which had remained open. He gave a thumbs-up sign in the direction of a grey people-carrier parked outside. A door on the vehicle slid back and a man in a pin-striped suit stepped out and hurried across the pavement. He carried a briefcase at his side. He slipped past the man in the doorway, who then took up a position that would block anybody else from entering, as unlikely as that might be.

This new man was short, balding, and vaguely familiar. He faced Jeff across the counter. He reached into his inside jacket pocket and felt around for something. With the feeling coming back into my legs, I took a step towards the exit at the back of the store. Before I could take another one, the man found what he was looking for and slapped it down on the counter.

'You left this behind.'

Jeff was studying what, even with my eyesight, appeared to be one of my own business cards.

'Do you know who I am?' the man asked.

Jeff's eyes didn't even flit in my direction, but he said out

142

of the side of his mouth: 'Can you help this man? He doesn't appear to know who he is.'

It was a joke, but a Jeff joke. Nobody was laughing. Not I, not Jeff, not the big bloke blocking the door or the man whose intense gaze was holding steady on my trusted assistant. He was a man I now recognised as one of the Karamazovs. He clearly believed Jeff was me. I did nothing to disabuse him of this belief until I determined if there was danger involved.

'I am Bernard O'Dromodery,' he said gravely, 'and I believe I have something you've been looking for.'

He set his briefcase down on the counter and unlocked it. He raised the lid, and before he spun it round to show Jeff the contents, I saw what he was about to reveal.

A second *defixio*.

19

I moved forward to examine it. I could not help myself. It was instinct, with a dash of bravery. Bernard O'Dromodery gave a nod, as if to say, *Ah, now it makes sense. This seeping idiot could not be the famous Mystery Man, the private detective who has solved numerous murder cases, unmasked spies, saved governments and rescued several cats, despite a very serious allergy.*

I made a 'Do you mind?' gesture towards him and he stepped back to allow me to remove the curse tablet from his briefcase. I set it on the counter. Like the first one I had seen in the All Star Health Club it was written on a sheet of black lead, the curse scratched out in Latin which, for Jeff's benefit and to impress the Karamazov brother, I immediately translated:

> *This curse on the House of O'Dromodery*
> *Let them suffer, let them boil*
> *Bring fear and death down upon*
> *The forever-cursed House of O'Dromodery.*

Jeff said: 'It doesn't even scan.'

'It's not a poem, Jeff,' I said. 'It's a curse.'

'You read it like a poem, and it's set out like a poem.'

I sighed. I looked at Bernard O'Dromodery and said, 'This is from the hydrangea pots outside your headquarters.'

He nodded. 'We found it about a month after my brother Fergus fell to his death. I heard about that business with the flowers last night, and once I saw the business card I knew what you were after.'

It was on the tip of my tongue to say *shrubs*, but I held off. I was curious, and although it has never been a motivating factor, I also sensed money.

Bernard O'Dromodery tapped the curse tablet. 'This is a *defixio*, but I'm sure you know that. I had you checked out, so I know what you do. I know you're very good. I want to hire you. I have very deep pockets. I want to know who created this *defixio* and why. I want to know who murdered Fergus.'

Jeff was dispatched to the kitchen for coffee, and I ushered Bernard O'Dromodery towards our couch. Alison insisted on there being one to encourage customers to sit and browse. She also insisted that I offer them coffee and engage them in conversation and give reading advice, so as to make them feel connected to the store and part of our community and other shit. When she wasn't around I took the springs out of the sofa to make it particularly uncomfortable to sit on. Coffee was indeed on offer, but it was always bitter and lukewarm. No Alibis was a crime bookshop with an edge. We didn't do cosy.

Bernard O'Dromodery sat, awkwardly. 'You make a living from this?'

'Yes,' I said, defiantly.

'You own the property or do you rent?'

'I own it.'

'Much of a mortgage?' I raised an eyebrow. He said, 'Sorry, *sorry*. Old habits. But I hope it's not too big, since this is going to get worse before it gets better.'

I said, 'Why do you think your brother was murdered?'

He rubbed at his brow while he searched for the right words. 'I'm sorry,' he said again, 'but I'm not used to this. Usually I snap my fingers and things get done. But this, this is out of my control. So – yes, my brother was murdered. I am certain of it. I know what people think – they see that we were struggling, and that he was our chief financial officer. The banks were calling in our loans and everywhere we turned there was doom and gloom and we were going to lose everything we worked our whole lives for . . . but if they knew anything about us, about Fergus, they would know that whatever might drive another man to throw himself off a tall building would have inspired our Fergus to fight back. Fergus saw saving our company as a challenge, not as a reason to kill himself.'

'But the police . . .'

'The police are idiots. The inquest was a nonsense.'

'And you suspected it wasn't a suicide immediately?'

'Yes. And no. When these things happen, even if you have doubts, you tend to listen to the experts. As it turns out, my brother Sean had similar misgivings, but we didn't realise we were all thinking the same thing until someone else was killed.'

'Francis Delaney.'

He blinked at me for a moment. 'No – I mean yes. Francis Delaney worked for us on and off as a casual labourer. I was just at his funeral yesterday, in fact.'

'I know you were.'

'But I'm talking about Sam Mahood.'

'Ah,' I said.

'Yes. He was working for us. I understand you're investigating his murder already.'

'Not really – but it's connected to a case I'm working on.'

'The mental case in Purdysburn.'

Jeff emerged from the kitchen with the coffee for Bernard. He knew better than to make one for me. He handed the mug to him and he took it, turning it slightly so as to better examine the *No Alibis* logo and *Murder is Our Business* legend on the side.

'You have been doing your homework,' I said. 'Although I would hesitate to call him a mental case.'

He took a sip of his coffee, but did not look impressed. He set the mug on the floor. 'Tell me,' he said, 'who are you working for then? Who's paying you? It can't be him, because as far as I understand, he doesn't speak or can't speak or communicate.'

'Nobody is paying me,' I said.

'Then why would you do it?'

'Curiosity. I heard about the case and found it interesting.'

'But you're *really* not being paid?'

'It has its own rewards.'

'Well, I'm going to pay you to find out what happened to Fergus.'

'Okay,' I said.

*   *   *

'Fat Sam was . . . necessary,' said Bernard O'Dromodery. 'He did things we . . . could not.'

'Muscle,' said Jeff.

'We're in the property business – millions of pounds are involved. People always want a cut of millions. Sometimes you need to deter them. Fat Sam did that. But he was not unnecessarily crude with it. Sometimes a hard stare was all he needed to deliver his message.'

'Well, he seems to have lost the staring match.'

'Yes. Indeed.' Bernard O'Dromodery was in late middle age. His face was saggy and his complexion grey. He took a second sip from the *No Alibis* mug, and immediately his lip curled up. 'This coffee is disgusting,' he said.

'We're in the disgusting business,' said Jeff.

We both looked at him, and Jeff decided it was time for him to return to the counter.

Bernard nodded at me. 'You know, you don't do your business any favours by hiring idiots. We discovered that a long time ago.'

'He's not an idiot,' I said loyally, 'he's a poet.' Though in truth, they were one and the same thing. 'You built the All Star Health Club on the Newtownards Road.'

'Yes, several years ago.'

'Did you maintain a financial interest in it?'

'Yes, but we sold up when the recession hit.'

'Fat Sam was hitting them for protection.'

'I didn't know that till after.'

'You know about their *defixio*?'

'I do, although only recently, which has prompted this. They were looking for an extension to the building, and we

148

were pitching for it. Not something we would normally do, but times are hard. Went there myself, and spotted it, and it spooked me, and I'm not one who spooks easily. We only found our own one by accident. One of our lorries backed into the flower boxes and it crumbled. Driver spotted it and it was brought to me. I kind of laughed it off till the other one turned up at the All Star.'

'They didn't appear to know what it was.'

He shook his head. He raised his mug again, and then thought better of it and set it back down, possibly for the final time. '*Defixio*. A curse tablet. It's just . . . bizarre. All of it is. I know Fat Sam was murdered and that Francis Delaney followed not that long after, but I don't know if the two are connected by anything other than coincidence. If this was London – I'd say the chances were ten million to one. But Belfast is an incredibly small city – God knows, we built half of it – and you bump into people all the time. So Francis Delaney could just have ended up in the wrong place at the wrong time. Fat Sam was not on staff, he was freelance, maybe one or two days a month; he had no shares in our company, was not privy to our plans nor had he access to our financial information. He was, as your one-eyed friend so eloquently put it, the muscle. As for my brother Fergus, I would be very surprised if he'd even met Fat Sam. Fergus was creative, had a great eye for detail, but he wasn't exactly hands on. He would have been *aware* of Fat Sam, and would have realised the necessity of there having to be a Fat Sam, but he would have kept his distance. I honestly cannot think of anything that they had in common, apart from the fact of Fat Sam's occasional employment.'

'Murderers,' I said, 'can make links that aren't always apparent. What's interesting to me, and I suspect it's the reason you're here, is that the curse on the *defixio* isn't specifically against Fergus. It's a family curse. That's what's keeping you awake nights.'

Bernard O'Dromodery swallowed. 'That's exactly it. I am, frankly, terrified and have been ever since this turned up. And also . . . I believe I'm being watched. There's no evidence of this, no specific instances or places where I can say definitely that there was someone there, I just . . . know it. It's like that feeling your mother would say was someone walking over your grave.'

He did not know my mother, but he had her desires down pat.

I said, 'We can all feel a little paranoid.'

From the counter, Jeff snorted.

'That may be,' said Bernard O'Dromodery, 'but I cannot shake it. I once spoke to Fat Sam about how best to protect against attack, and he said if someone wants to get you, they'll find a way. President Kennedy had all the resources in the world, but nobody thought to check the Book Suppository.'

I decided not to correct him. Life was too short, as his might be and mine definitely would be. The Karamazov stood up, and buttoned his coat.

'We haven't discussed a fee,' I said.

He suggested one. I said that would be fine. 'Plus VAT,' I added.

'I'll need your VAT number.' When I did not immediately respond he said, 'Maybe we can work around that.'

He said he would have the first instalment dropped off. He asked if cash would be okay and I said if he insisted. He nodded and held out his hand. Even though I was loath to do it, what with my brittle bones, we shook. He moved to the door where his bodyguard had stood undisturbed by mystery fans or assassins throughout our meeting. He looked at Jeff, and then at me, and said, 'Good luck.'

I nodded my thanks, and added, purely to reinforce the paranoia and to keep the pay days coming: 'Keep your bodyguard close until I sort this out.'

'He's not my bodyguard,' said Bernard O'Dromodery, 'he's my husband.'

'Okay,' I said. 'Good one.'

20

Of course, nothing had changed beyond the fact that I was now being paid to do what I was already doing. I would feel no loyalty or allegiance to Bernard O'Dromodery, just a mild appreciation for the manila envelope stuffed with cash which his husband Martin Brady dropped into the shop later that afternoon.

Martin was a large man, confident, rather intense. As I counted the money I subtly interrogated him and learned that he had been married to Bernard O'Dromodery for eighteen months. They lived off the Antrim Road in a large, old house they had lovingly refurbished. They holidayed in Mauritius – 'Delicious,' he added. He had dark stubble and a receding hairline, and his high brow was damp with a moisturiser I recognised as Nivea For Men. I do not use moisturiser myself, because of my allergies, but I have made a study of them. He showed no interest at all in our Christmas Club.

I had asked if the marital home had a garden, and he said

a small one at the front, larger at the rear. I asked if they employed a gardener, and they did not. I suggested that they do so immediately and that he be instructed to thoroughly dig over every softish surface front or back of their property to determine if a *defixio* had been buried there. If there wasn't one, then the available evidence on the modus operandi of the killer or killers suggested that Bernard O'Dromodery would at least remain safe while he was in the marital home.

'I'll do it myself,' said Martin. 'I'm ex-SAS. I've dug for mines before. In Afghanistan. If someone comes for my husband, I will take him down.'

'I'm ex-Army too,' I said. He looked at me doubtfully. 'Salvation,' I added.

His expression did not change. 'That's not a proper army,' he said.

'Well, they put the fear of God into most people,' I said.

Still nothing. He placed his hands on the counter and leaned a little closer. He voice deepened as he said, 'I've killed six people. Two of them with my bare hands.'

I nodded. He nodded. I could never kill anyone with my poor brittle bare hands, but I could do a lot of damage with a tambourine.

His business done and his interrogation over, Martin turned for the door. As he walked past the window, I made sure he wasn't looking before I gave him a salute. I did not like him. He had no sense of humour, and he was too confident by half. And also, he was a thief.

'How do you work that out?' Jeff asked.

'I counted the money. There's nine hundred and eighty pounds here in brand new Northern Bank notes.'

'So?'

'That means there's twenty quid missing. Nobody counts out nine hundred and eighty pounds, you would always round it up to a thousand.'

'You know that for a fact?'

'Yes. There have been studies done.'

'Of that?'

'Of something very much like it.'

'Maybe he borrowed twenty for car parking or a kebab.'

'Hardly the point. The fact that he took it suggests he's untrustworthy. Also, he informed us of how many people he had killed with just a little too much relish. He was warning us as much as whoever's after his husband.'

'You read an awful lot into quite a little.'

'That's why I'm Belfast's most successful private detective.'

'Definitely. And also Belfast's *only* private detective.'

I mulled that over. There would probably come a day when there would be another private eye working the sordid back alleys of Ireland's grandest city. We would vie to be the first to solve whatever heinous crime was outfoxing the police, and when that day came I would prove that I was the best. But for now I had a case to solve, one that was continuing to throw up new and suspicious characters, if not quite suspects.

I did not trust Martin Brady. For that matter I did not trust his husband. I suspected Bernard O'Dromodery's motives for employing me. He also worried me because he had had no qualms at all about hiring a thug like Fat Sam. He did not strike me as someone who was fearful for his life, but rather as one who could and would throw money

The Prisoner of Brenda

at a problem in order to make it go away. For that matter, I did not trust the manager of the All Star Health Club either. He had been paying off Fat Sam and was possibly involved in the supply of steroids. I did not trust Fat Sam's wife, the dart-throwing Gloria, with her cheap jewellery and casual acceptance of his violent ways. I did not believe what Francis Delaney's wife had told me about her husband's depression and admittance into Purdysburn, though I was reasonably sure that she did. And I certainly did not believe Detective Inspector Robinson's repeated assertions that he already had his man.

I had previously trusted Nurse Brenda, but now I didn't quite know what to make of her. She was a strong, independent, opinionated woman, yet she was showing such blind faith in Gabriel that I was beginning to wonder if she had an ulterior motive for wanting his identity established. Indeed, of all the players, the only one I had no negative views about at all was currently being held in the high security wing of a mental hospital, accused of two savage murders.

'Well, my mother used to say, "if you've nothing good to say, say nothing". Maybe Gabriel is keeping quiet because he knows he's as guilty as sin.'

Alison was in the bath, covered in bubbles. She was drinking a glass of wine. She had two different devices sitting on the rim – a baby monitor, and an iPhone set into a small amplifier. She was listening to our baby's snuffles in the next room and Bachman Turner Overdrive from a selection of *Hits of the Seventies*, while at the same time giving her views on recent developments. She could multi-task. I was updating her on those recent events, while at the same time wondering how badly she would be electrocuted if I pushed both devices into the water at the same time. I could multi-task too.

I said, 'I've been around mental-health facilities all my life. They can pretty much tell if you're faking it.'

'Did *you* fake it?'

'Fake what?'

'Is that a trick question?'

'Is *that* a trick question?'

She smiled. 'We're meant to be discussing the case, but you're mostly studying my breasts.'

I reddened. I had several times made love to her, but mostly in the dark. I had an excessive amount of freckles and other spiny body issues and didn't like to parade myself. Although I had seen her naked on other occasions, and played with her favoured left breast, I still found it fascinating to observe her without clothes while she was unaware of it. The bubbles only partially covered her. I could not help but look.

'You are as odd as begot,' Alison said. She raised her hand out of the water and casually blew along her fingernails. 'And *so* easy. Now tell me when you're going to go and see Gabriel – that's what you really need to do, isn't it? He's the key.'

'Yes,' I said. 'And I don't know. I'm waiting to hear.'

'You are keeping me up to scratch on this, aren't you? Just because I've had a baby and I'm feeling a bit under the weather, it doesn't mean I'm disabled, and you're still looking at my breasts.'

'You're still displaying them.'

'I'm in the *bath*, trying to relax.'

'I thought you wanted to discuss the case?'

'I wanted to have a chat about it. But you're being evasive.'

'I'm not being . . .'

'If they're that fascinating, why don't you climb in here with me and we'll see what comes up?'

'I would love to,' I said, 'but I'm allergic to dead skin.'

Satisfied with my explanation, I turned and left the bathroom.

Behind me I heard her say, 'There he goes, the last of the great romantics.'

I was in Page's bedroom. He was fast asleep. The baby monitor was on and I could hear Alison singing a nursery rhyme. I knelt beside it, and lowering my voice and distorting it through the end of an empty toilet roll, I hissed: 'The Devil will sacrifice this child for His eternal glory.'

Alison stopped singing. She said: 'Would you ever wise up? And put the kettle on, I'll be out in a minute.'

'Okay,' I said.

21

I sat in the darkness of the front room and worked on my laptop. Alison was in bed. She always went up early. I like sitting in the darkness and looking out. Mother occasionally joins me. Several times we have frightened Alison half to death when she has breezed into the lounge and put the light on and found the two of us just sitting there, watching. But this night I was not much bothered with what was going on outside. I was engrossed in the *Belfast Telegraph* on-line archive again, rereading the story about Fat Sam's murder at the All Star. When nothing new jumped out at me, I returned to the original advertising feature on the health club. There were three other photographs in addition to the one of the exterior of the club, which showed groups of staff members smiling for the camera in their crisp new uniforms. Jackie was there, beaming, and Gary, showing a client a piece of equipment.

Outside, there was a noise.

Sometimes it is difficult to tell, with the tinnitus, and the voices, what is real, and what is not. But something disturbed my concentration enough to make me glance up at the window, and down at the street, our window being elevated. There was nothing moving. I do not wear a watch, as I do not trust the Swiss. But the time on the laptop showed that it was 3.12 a.m. I returned my attention to the screen, and thought some more; and found myself worrying, so I set the machine down and moved to the window for a closer look. It came to me that this was exactly how Bernard O'Dromodery must have felt when he supposed he was being watched. I could see nothing, but that didn't mean there was nobody there.

I stood there, stock still, for forty-five minutes. Three cars passed, two cats – and one drunk, sobbing woman.

At 4 a.m., I slipped out of the house, down the steps, and removed a dessert spoon from one trouser pocket and a small torch from the other. I was no longer in possession of the Trowel of Hope. We do not have a garden, but we do have a small enclosed front yard which is haphazardly concreted and which features a neglected wooden barrel, which is rotten and split, with the soil spilling out of it and the dead husk of an unidentified plant sticking up. I flicked on the torch and examined the barrel for signs that it had recently been worked upon. Its degraded state, however, made that impossible. So I began to sift through the damp soil with the Spoon of Hopefulness.

I had been working at it for just a few minutes when I heard a noise above me, and I looked up to see Mother staring down from her attic window. She was leaning out a little too far. Her hair was all over the place and she had a cigarette hanging out of the corner of her mouth. She was backlit by her bedroom lamp, and looked like the Gorgon.

She said: 'What the hell are you doing down there?'

I straightened, shone the torch on my face and called up: 'It's me, Mother.'

'I can see that, you half-wit. What the hell are you doing at this hour?'

'Gardening,' I said. 'Now go back to bed.'

'Weirdo,' Mother called down, lovingly, and closed the window.

I returned to my task. Just a few moments later, the Spoon of Hopefulness scraped across something metallic. I hesitated, and then glanced up at the distant barking of a dog. I checked the street, and the doorways, and the walls and the trees; there were so many different shades of dark – but nothing. I carefully traced the outline of what was rapidly revealed as a small box. I dug down a couple of inches around it until I reached its base, and then extracted it. The box was just about large enough to contain a *defixio*, but although metallic, it lacked the weight of lead. I carried it back into the house, and set it down on the kitchen table. I cleaned the soil off it using a damp green sponge purchased in a five-pack for £1.99 in Poundstretcher. The box had a faded yet intricate pattern, in which the soil was deeply ingrained. There were hinges on one side and a small latch on the other.

I studied the box from all angles, including the base, which had a maker's mark which would help me trace its origin, if required. I took a deep breath. I carefully pushed up the latch, and then jumped back as the lid unexpectedly sprang up.

It took several moments for me to recover my composure. Then I cautiously leaned forward to examine the contents.

Inside, there was a tiny, tiny skeleton.

It was less than three inches long, and definitely not human.

It came to me that in 1978 I had buried my pet gerbil in such a box, with full pomp and ceremony, and placed it in the then robust wooden barrel in the front yard.

I had not thought about Lightning, as I had called him, in many, many years. I loved him very much. I used to let him out of his cage to run around our front room. We had great fun and games.

One day, Mother knelt on him.

She broke his neck.

She said it was an accident.

I did not believe her.

I screamed and yelled at her and she put me in a cupboard.

She opened the door five hours later and asked if I was still accusing her of gerbil murder and I said no, but at the very least she should be charged with gerbilslaughter. She said I might be precocious for an eight year old, but that *gerbilslaughter* wasn't a word. I said if I said it, it became a word. She closed the cupboard again.

I always kept a small torch in that cupboard, because I was frequently in it. I used it to locate a tattered copy of *Moonfleet* by J. Meade Falkner which I had begun reading during previous imprisonments. It was a children's adventure story about smuggling, set in 1757. I remember it being very exciting. A feature of the narrative was the continuing reference to the game of backgammon, which was played by the leading characters on an antique board bearing a Latin inscription. I remember it to this day because it was my first encounter with the language and I found it fascinating: *Ita in vita ut in lusu alae pessima jactura arte corrigenda es*, which was translated thus – *As in life, so in a game of hazard, skill will make something of the worst of throws.* The inscription provided a moralistic metaphor to the story of the orphan boy who in the end overcame his travails. I could relate to it, and often had, since.

I sat in my kitchen, with my baby upstairs, and my girl-friend asleep, and my mother smoking in bed, and I stared at the skeleton of Lightning, who was not quick enough to escape my mother's knee, and I cried for him.

Although, given the state of my tear ducts, they were dry tears.

Once I started crying, I found that I could not stop. The dry heaves rocked my brain, and became so intense that whatever *had* been blocking my tear ducts suddenly gave way and the dammed-up tears burst forth and tore down my cheeks until they splashed onto the kitchen table and spread across the surface in a lake of sorrow around Lightning's open casket. My whole body began to convulse and I let out howls of despair and rage and anger and loss until the kitchen door burst open and Alison stood there horrified. 'Baby . . . baby . . . baby . . .' she cried, 'what is it? What is it?!' and she threw herself upon me, and held me, and squeezed me.

'What is it? What's wrong?' while from upstairs there came more howls from Page and further up still there was Mother screeching, 'What in the good name of Christ is going on down there?!' And still I howled against her and she crushed me tight until I couldn't take it any more and I pushed her away but she came back towards me and I yelled at her to leave me alone, and she stood there shocked and frightened while I picked up Lightning's box and hurled it against the wall where it shattered on the framed picture of Mother with Mussolini which I had once Photoshopped as a joke and given to her as a Christmas present and she had unwrapped it and stared at it in disbelief because she couldn't ever remember meeting Kojak, and all the while mites of desiccated straw and bone from the box were filling the air while I collapsed down onto my chair again and buried my head in my hands.

Alison moved back to me and put her arm around my shoulders and said, 'Baby, tell me, what can I do? What's happened? Has something happened? Please, baby?' And I collapsed against her for a moment before slithering off the seat onto the kitchen floor where I curled into a hedgehog with spikes erect and she stood over me, wringing her hands – and then Mother was in the doorway tutting and telling Alison she'd made her bed so she could lie in it and Alison came off with a mouthful no lady should be proud of and Mother went quiet and crouched beside me and stroked my brow and then Alison was going through my phone looking for the name of my doctor and there was only that of Dr Winter at the City and anyway all of my regular doctors are Mexicans who are lax about issuing prescriptions.

She phoned and explained, and Dr Winter asked if Alison was a Midnight Gardener as well and she denied it and he asked if I had soil on my hands and she examined me and yes, indeed I had, and he said the fate of the planet had become too much for me and it was important that I received the proper psychiatric care – but that provision in Northern Ireland was shockingly poor and there was a very long waiting list but that he knew someone he could call and within an hour, with me lying on the floor all that time in the essence of Lightning, there was a knock on the door and then paramedics were kneeling beside me reassuring me that I was going to be okay and quietly asking Alison if I'd been violent and she said *ish* and then they were strapping me to a chair and telling me they were taking me somewhere I could be looked after and made to feel better and I cried and mewed as they wheeled me out and loaded me up, and I had the briefest glimpse of a distraught Alison on the bottom step outside the house with Page in her arms and Mother just behind her and Mother's bony arm snaking out and curling around her in what was meant to be a reassuring squeeze but which was just like the Devil claiming her for her own . . . and then the ambulance doors were shut and I lay there burbling while we zipped through the dawn-damp streets with lights flashing and alarm sounding towards Purdysburn.

22

'You're much calmer now,' Dr Richardson said.

'I feel much calmer. Thank you. The horse tranquilliser worked.'

'It was mild sedation. Do you know why you're here?'

'To be assessed as to my mental condition, health, or well-being.'

'Can you tell me your name?'

I drew myself up and said grandly: 'Count Leopold of Prussia.'

He began to write it down.

I said, 'I'm only joking,' and gave him my name.

'Yes, we knew that,' he said. 'Just checking. We have had some difficulty accessing your full medical records. Bits and pieces, mostly.'

'That's because they are spread far and wide, under different names and political systems.'

He made a note.

He was a tall, wan man in wire spectacles who was, I believe, striving to appear older than he was. He wore a plain white shirt and green tie. To be any sort of a psychiatrist, you need to look wise, and that only comes with age. He couldn't have been more than thirty-two. There was a certificate on the wall behind him. It was probably from the Royal College of Psychiatry, but with my eyesight it could just as easily have been confirmation that he had passed his cycling proficiency test. His office was plain, and lacked personal effects, which suggested that either it was used by several members of staff, or that he didn't want to give his patients ammunition to use against him, literally or figuratively. There was a buffed linoleum floor and a large double-glazed window overlooking the grounds, an internal window gave a view of the corridor outside, although there were Venetian blinds if privacy was required. The office door was closed. There was probably a panic button, purposefully concealed.

Everything was going according to plan – apart, obviously, from the bits which weren't. I was secure in the secure wing at Purdysburn, but instead of spending my time exploring and investigating, interviewing and observing, I had spent the best part of twenty-four hours in a drug-fuelled sleep in a locked room. They had taken the laces from my shoes and both My Nail for the Scratching of Cars with Personalised Numberplates and the Dessert Spoon of Hopefulness. I had been woken by a male nurse at 6 a.m. and given breakfast on a tray. My head felt woozy. The coffee was lukewarm and the porridge milky and cool. My clothes had been removed and there were hospital-issue pyjamas, dressing-gown and slippers. I was, for the first time in many years, without my pills and potions. My hands were already shaking. The rest of me would shortly follow. It was as inevitable as loathing follows lust.

Dr Richardson said, 'Why don't you tell me how you've been feeling?'

'You go first.'

'I understand you own a bookshop? Must be difficult times for a bookseller, what with downloads and Amazon and whatnot.'

'Yes,' I said. 'But come the revolution . . .'

'Yes?'

'Trading conditions are difficult. Yes. But we will endure.'

'We?'

'The shop, and I. And my staff.'

'But depressing, all the same.'

'Yes.'

'Are you depressed?'

'I'd be a fool not to be.'

'You've been a patient here before.'

'A very long time ago.'

He looked down at a file on his desk. 'And then there's a very considerable gap, which we are seeking to fill in, until . . . just a few days ago, when you were admitted to Belfast City Hospital following a suicide attempt.'

'It wasn't a suicide attempt.'

'According to this report you were behaving bizarrely and you ate flowers containing a potentially fatal amount of cyanide.'

'Shrubs,' I corrected, and he made a note.

'The doctor who referred you to us and signed you in has noted that you have an obsession with gardening.'

'No,' I said.

'Midnight Gardening.' He raised an eyebrow. And then lowered it. 'Your partner, to whom I have also spoken, reports that you destroyed a flower pot and were throwing soil and other sediments around your house.'

'I just lost my temper. I'm fine.'

'Did you have a garden when you were growing up?' I nodded. 'Did you ever have any unpleasant experiences in that garden?'

'Yes. No. No more than anyone else.'

'Do you hear voices?'

'Often.'

'I mean, inside your head.'

'That's where you would usually hear them.'

'Do you believe sometimes that you are the Devil, and imagine sacrificing your son?'

I sighed. 'You shouldn't listen to my partner, *she's* the looper.'

He nodded, sagely, and made another note. Then he reached into his pocket and removed a set of keys. He found the small one he was looking for and inserted it in his desk drawer. He lifted out a see-through plastic bag.

'Your partner, she brought us this. Do you recognise it?'

'The contents? Yes.'

'Yes, this is indeed the medication that you currently take, or at least as much of it as your partner could find. She says she is always turning up packets and bottles and syringes hidden around your house.'

'Not very well hidden, clearly.'

Dr Richardson rattled the bag. 'I am, quite frankly, bewildered as to how you managed to obtain all of this, and then also, how you manage to still be alive. This lot would kill a herd of elephants.'

'I'm allergic to elephants,' I said.

He set the bag back in the drawer and locked it.

'I imagine you've seen a lot of psychiatrists in your time.'

'You have a good imagination.'

'And I also imagine that you are very used to dealing with them. Psychiatrists almost always are convinced by their own powers of observation; their decisions as to your future are usually based on one short meeting, because they haven't time to take the weeks or months or perhaps years that they would really need in order to make an accurate diagnosis. It is repeatedly drilled into us as students that patients are adept at showing the side of their personality or personalities that they want us to see, that they are often very accomplished actors. Even though we know this, we are so very reluctant to take on board second- or third-hand reports because they do not come from a trained medical professional. And yet who is best placed to monitor a patient's behaviour – a partner who spends the greater part of each day at their sides, or a psychiatrist who has to decide in a matter of minutes what the best course of treatment actually is?'

'If it's all the same to you,' I said, 'I'll go with the snap judgement.'

'Your partner, Alison, loves you very much.'

'So she says.'

169

'But she is increasingly disturbed by your behaviour.'

'She's one to talk.'

'And she very much wants us to get to the bottom of this.'

I folded my arms. 'Go for it,' I said.

'She never quite knows whether you're acting it out or you're genuinely suffering, if you're playing a game or you're seriously disturbed. She was very upset when she saw the state of you at your home, and when you were admitted.'

'She followed me to hospital?'

'Of course. You didn't think she would?' I shrugged. 'And your mother came too. She was very upset. Everyone cares for you a lot.'

If there was a stick to be had, he had clearly gotten hold of the wrong end of it.

'I have to warn you, that if any part of this *is* an act, then you are in for a very serious wake-up call. If you don't treat the doctors here with respect, then they, we – *I* – have the power to keep you here for a very long time. And if you don't treat your fellow patients with respect then . . . well. You are in here because of your behaviour, some of it violent – it's at the lower end of the spectrum, to be sure, but still we have to err on the side of caution. That's why you are in this secure unit. It is fair to say that this unit also contains many at the *other* end of that spectrum – so it's only right that I warn you to be on your guard at all times. Although we have adequate staff, when it happens, violence can be very, very quick and very, very savage.'

'I read you had a murder here a few days ago.'

Dr Richardson made a note. 'Yes. Indeed. It was a very unpleasant business. But it should not worry you unduly, since the man responsible is being kept well offside. It's the others that you should be watchful for, the ones who are still free to roam, the ones who are placid for ninety-nine point nine per cent of the time and then they just explode. In fact, in just the way that you exploded with your partner.'

'She said that? I was only violent to some shrubbery and a dead gerbil.'

'Well,' said Dr Richardson, 'there's nothing that can't be sorted out. I want you to have faith in me, and what we can achieve here. Although, before we can even start to address what is clearly distressing you, we need to get you off all of this . . . junk,' and he indicated the drawer where he had returned my medications.

'It is not *junk*,' I said. 'Some of the finest chemists in Nigeria developed those pills.'

'And it isn't going to be easy or pleasant.'

'I'm sure there's a pill for that too.'

'If you are not experiencing them already, then very soon you are going to start having withdrawal symptoms. There will be sweats, vomiting, convulsions. It will be deeply unpleasant. But it is only when this vicious concoction is out of your system that we are going to be able to assess you properly, really get to the bottom of what is wrong and why you are behaving in this manner. It may take several days, perhaps a week to get you fully detoxed . . .'

'I can't do a week. Twenty-four hours, max. Just sluice me out, let me have a bit of a doze and a relax, and then I'll be right as rain. The shop can wait for a day, but tomorrow, absolutely, I have to be open. It's our busy time of year.'

Dr Richardson shook his head. 'You're not quite getting

this, are you? The shop is being looked after by your staff. Don't you worry about it. You, on the other hand, are being looked after by me, and my staff. And Rome wasn't built in a day.'

'It's just not possible for me to—'

He cut me off, and sternly. 'I'm trying to make this as clear and straightforward for you as I can,' he said. 'You have been sectioned. Do you understand what that means? You have been judged by your closest relatives, a referring doctor and the admitting staff here to be no longer capable of looking after yourself or of making a reasoned judgement. In other words, you are considered to be a danger to yourself and to others. You are here, sir, until we decide if you are safe to be let out on the streets again.'

23

Dr Richardson walked me back to the security gate. An orderly hovered just behind us. When I felt dizzy and staggered, he grabbed me and guided me forward. The doctor told me to go back to my room and lie down and a nurse would look in on me and give me something if the withdrawal got too bad. And then I was through the gate like a child, flying alone, escorted off a plane by a caring hostess, only to be hurled into the heaving maelstrom of an international airport. Odd, distorted faces leered at me, crooked hands pushed and prodded and fondled me. The corridor along which I was attempting to make my way became tubular and I began to cycle up the walls of some mad kind of velodrome which I knew was being conjured by my fever but about which I was quite unable to do anything other than to compete with the other racers. We were twelve retards on Choppers shepherded by tracksuited Nazis screaming at us to go faster, faster, faster . . .

I slept; I tossed; I sweated. I was vaguely aware of voices – the prick of a needle – Devil babies and being trapped in a cage with cannibal gerbils. And then I was in the kitchen and Mother and Alison were preparing dinner and they brought the roast out of the oven and it was Page, ready for carving, just a little crisp on top and I screamed and screamed and screamed and an orderly was in the doorway telling me to shut up and I sat up and yelled at him and he Tasered me – or did I dream that? There was night, and then there was day and I was lying on my back, on top of the bed, and I felt like I had been knocked down by a bus but the fever had broken and the same orderly was in the door with a breakfast cart and he being perfectly pleasant. He asked if I wanted eggs and I said yes even though I was allergic to them and I knew my head would swell up to the size of a Spacehopper but I ate them anyway and was surprised when it did not, not even a little bit, and I lay there some more and then I heard a piano playing in the distance and I knew it was The Man in the White Suit and then suddenly I was back to thinking about the case and whether I'd fooled them all or whether they had, in fact, fooled me.

This much was clear: or, indeed, unclear. I had created a pattern of unhinged behaviour and allied it with my acting skills to ensure that I was carted off to Purdysburn, thus keeping to the bargain I had struck with Nurse Brenda not to reveal to anyone that I was going undercover, even her. But now there was the unexpected irony of being outfoxed by the very people I was trying to fox.

The more I thought about it, the further back I could trace it, and the more people I could figure into a back-stabbing plot. Perhaps it had begun on the very day that Alison first walked into No Alibis claiming to be interested in Brendan Coyle's creative writing class. I had stood up and fought for her to be allowed to join, even though it was oversubscribed, and Brendan had acquiesced – after what now appeared to be a token show of defiance. What I had thought was a bond between *us* could in fact be an alliance between *them* and *others* designed to seize control of No Alibis and to gain influence over the future direction of mystery fiction, which was, after all, a billion-dollar business, or multi-million if you subtracted Stieg.

I held my head and tried to stop it from spinning. But I could not. Someone had removed the bolt from my neck, and now it just kept going round, and round, and round, and round, and round, and round, and round, and round, and round, and round, and round – and then I was thinking that somehow Alison had found out about the influence Nurse Brenda had had on me as a teenager, and met up with her, and they had hatched this scheme to have me locked up. Alison had repeatedly scorned my medication and constantly belittled my illnesses and doubted my allergies, and when we fought over important issues like patterns in tiles and the dangers of spice racks, she often cried that I was as mad as a box of frogs, and now I knew that *this* was all a result of *that*.

Nurse Brenda had used Gabriel as the bait to draw me in. Jeff was involved as well, he had to be. He'd always fancied Alison, and she could wrap him round her little finger. They were probably having the sex, and had been all along. Page was Jeff's baby. Or DI Robinson's. The only reason *he* kept hanging around the shop was to see Alison. He didn't want between *my* covers, he wanted between hers. He had played along with the Gabriel story. He knew that by warning me off, it would only encourage me to get in deeper. And between them all they knew that the frustration of being denied direct access to Gabriel would drive me to take matters into my own hands by going in undercover, and now they had me exactly where they wanted me.

Quite possibly, Francis Delaney's death had nothing to do with Gabriel at all. The only evidence of Gabriel's involvement came from DI Robinson himself, and from Nurse Brenda. Perhaps Gabriel wasn't even suspected of Fat Sam's murder; he was just some poor sap who didn't know who he was, and because of that, he could become anyone; perhaps he didn't even exist, and the newspaper articles had been fabricated, or he had been identified months ago and quietly released, but the plotters had perpetuated his story so that they might gain the ultimate prize: control of No Alibis. And the little sideshow to that was that Alison was having sex with Jeff and DI Robinson, probably at the same time, one at either end, while Page, the experimental baby, was relentlessly probed by scientists looking for evidence of ancient alien civilisations.

A very tall man at the door said, 'You don't have to be mad to work here, but it helps.'

I said, 'Do you work here?'

'No,' he said.

He was middle-aged and paunchy and unshaven and he had bags under his eyes the size of teabags. I am allergic to tea. I was not allergic to him, *per se*, but I was prepared to be. He was wearing blue jeans that hung low because belts weren't allowed; he had on a grey sweatshirt and blue canvas slip-on boating shoes.

I said, 'I'm new.'

He said, 'I know that. JMJ said I should give you the tour. Ready?' My gown was soaked through with sweat and dribble. I peeled it out from my body and made a face. 'Your clothes will be in your drawer there. When you come in they delouse them. They'll be a bit starchy. I'll give you five.'

He ducked back out of the room. I pulled the covers back and sat up. My head was numb. My legs and arms were sore, but somehow a different sore to what I was used to with my arthritis and rickets and fibromyalgia. I stood up and tested my weight and then stumbled across to the small bathroom which came with the room. There was a shower. I prefer a bath. It is next to impossible to drown yourself in a shower, and God knows I've tried. There wasn't even a plug in the sink. There was an electric shaver, already plugged in. Apparently safety razors were not deemed safe enough. I showered, holding onto the walls for support. The water was lukewarm. I found my clothes, neatly pressed, even my days of the week underpants. I sat and stared at them. The single pair I had with me was for a Tuesday. I had no idea what day it now was, apart from the fact that it was no longer Tuesday. Normally, if I wore the wrong day it would mess with the space-time continuum and I would not have been able to leave home until the crisis had passed or the correct underpants were produced. But now, I pulled them on with only a little hesitation. I slipped into my shirt and trousers. I pulled on my trainers, although without the laces they were too loose to do anything other than shuffle along in; when I stepped out into the corridor I discovered I was not alone, that we were a community of shufflers.

The tall man was waiting.

'I was just coming to get you,' he said. He pushed a hand out towards me. I hesitated, and he saw it, and withdrew. 'Name's Bertie, and I've been in here fifteen years, so there's nothing I don't know about this place. Walk this way.' His voice had the haggard rasp of cigarettes. I fell in beside him. He asked me my name and I told him. He asked what I was in for and I said assessment. He said, 'No, what did you *do?*'

'Nothing,' I said.

'Pedo?' he asked.

'No,' I said.

'Well, watch yourself, this place is full of them. *He's* one.' He pointed at a short, balding man in his thirties, with glasses perched on the end of his nose, sitting on a stool reading a Kindle. I nodded. 'Morning, Jock,' said Bertie, and introduced me. Jock grunted back without looking up. Bertie rolled his eyes at me and we continued on.

'This is the corridor,' he said needlessly, 'and it continues on down here and then in a loop right back to the entrance, though of course it's not a loop, it's a straight corridor, with junctions and angles, if you get my drift. These are the toilets – you're lucky, you have one in your room, not all of us have though. I don't for example. I have to go in here, with the pedos. Have to be constantly on my guard.'

'Why?'

'Because they're pedos.'

'But surely they'd only be interested in—'

'Just along here, this is the recreation room. The *rec* room.'

It was large, open-plan, well-windowed (and barred) with a widescreen television, three computers, a pool table, a small library of paperback books and a dozen chairs set out in a circle, with one in the middle. There were four other men in the rec room. Two were playing pool, one was sitting typing at a computer, and the other was staring at the TV, which wasn't switched on.

Bertie stood in the middle of the room and cleared his throat. When nobody paid any attention he barked: 'Listen up!' and told them my name. 'He's the new chap, here to replace poor Francis. Back up to the round dozen!'

He indicated the men at the pool table. 'Fella with the bandana there, that's Raymond.' Raymond nodded at me. He had a Village People moustache and a capless white T-shirt. '*Pedo*,' Bertie whispered under his breath. 'Fella he's whipping is Morris.' Morris was a skinhead with bulging eyeballs. He also nodded. '*Pedo*,' added Bertie.

We moved along to the computers. A much younger man, looking no more than eighteen, with floppy hair and big, square glasses, was typing furiously.

'Patrick, say hello,' said Bertie. 'He's writing the great Irish novel.' Patrick raised a hand, but didn't look round. Beside me, Bertie mouthed, '*Pedo*.'

Trying to be friendly, I said to the back of Patrick's head, 'What's it about?' and moved a little closer to look.

He immediately covered the screen with his hands and snarled, 'Fuck *off*.'

I stepped back.

Bertie said, 'They take a little bit of time to get used to strangers.' He indicated the man sitting staring at the TV. 'Andy's been here longest of us all, pushing twenty years. That right, Andy?'

Andy didn't respond, but kept on watching the TV. He looked to be in his sixties – with sallow skin, hanging off him. He was the only one of my fellow patients I'd met so far who was wearing the dressing-gown and slippers ensemble.

Bertie turned and began to lead me out of the rec room.

'Andy is . . .?'

'Pedo,' nodded Bertie.

'If you don't mind me saying,' I said as we moved on down the corridor, 'that's a very high proportion of pedos.'

Bertie ignored me as he pushed through two sets of swing doors and then sturdier ones which took us outside and onto a flat roof, which was used as an exercise area and was set out with a running track, a small five-a-side football pitch and a basketball hoop. It was surrounded by a high fence with a wire net across the top to prevent the balls, and presumably the patients, from falling to the car park below. There were four more men kicking a ball around, with another in nets. One of them, rounder than the others, took a shot and scored and then took off in celebration, his arms raised and yelling in joy.

'Look at them,' Bertie growled. 'They think they've got a great little team, but they're never going to play anyone else, unless there's some kind of Pedo League.'

I sighed.

Bertie called out to them, several times, and they eventually stopped their game and we went through more introductions.

'I had a trial at Leeds,' said Joe, the rotund goal-scorer, soaked in sweat.

'In the High Court,' Bertie whispered.

Malachy was in nets. When Joe had shot, Malachy had turned his back while simultaneously covering his head with his arms to avoid being struck by the ball. He was wearing a pair of mittens so thick that they looked as if a pair of oven gloves had been cut in half. Later I discovered that they had been.

The third player was Scott. He was the only one wearing a full football kit, with expensive-looking trainers. He was lanky, with dank, sandy hair and a hooked nose. He avoided eye-contact.

'Scott would play footie all day every day, if he could,' said Bertie. 'JMJ has to order him off the pitch at lunchtimes.'

The fourth player was Michael. He was wearing a baseball cap pulled down low and an enormous pair of earphones which didn't seem to be doing much to confine the sound of heavy bass and beats. He couldn't have heard my name, but he gave me the thumbs-up anyway.

The fifth was Pedro.

'He's Spanish,' said Bertie.

'*Sí*,' said Pedro. He ran to rescue the ball from the back of the net.

'He's not really,' said Bertie, 'he's from Portadown, but he was in a car accident. Brain damage. He thinks he's Spanish and we play along. The only word of Spanish he knows is *sí*. He speaks English, but with a Spanish accent. He runs around like a headless chicken and never passes. Last week, they tried to murder him.'

Joe, the goal-scorer, called over: 'Hey – you any good? You want a game?'

'No,' I said.

'C'mon,' he continued, waving me over. 'You can't be any worse than these spastics.'

'No, really,' I said, 'I have Brittle Bone Disease. It could kill me.'

He looked at me doubtfully. 'I had a trial at Leeds,' he said.

Bertie ushered me back inside. It was nice to be back in the heat. We moved down the corridor again. He pointed out the canteen, which was just a small room with a table set for twelve. 'We eat lunch and dinner here. Don't be late. JMJ doesn't like it and won't let anyone eat until we're all there. Once she kept us sitting there for an hour and a half until Scott could be persuaded in from football. Our potatoes got cold.'

We arrived back in the rec room. Raymond and Morris were still playing pool. I observed that there was no white ball. It did not seem to be hindering them.

A female voice behind me said, 'There is no white ball because it causes dissension.' I turned to find a nurse, a Sister, in a blue uniform with red epaulettes, similar to what Nurse Brenda wore. 'And dissension is the enemy of placidity. You must be . . .' And she looked at her clipboard and read out my name. 'I am Sister Mary, and I heard you screaming last night, and had to administer an injection, though I don't suppose you remember that.'

'No,' I said.

'Well, you were crying like a baby. But you're up now, right as rain. Our job is to make you as comfortable here as possible.' She moved closer to me. She was small, with a short, flat nose and a crinkled brow. Her skin was very white, and her eyes confident. 'As you may have gathered, most of our patients here are longterm. We are hoping that you will be in and out in a matter of weeks. Good discipline, manners and the right attitude will speed things along nicely for you. Is that clear?'

'Yes, absolutely,' I said.

Behind me, Raymond suddenly let out a screech, leaped around the table and grabbed Morris by the throat. He pushed him back against the wall, while continuing to throttle him.

Sister Mary raised a hand and clicked her fingers and two orderlies appeared from a side room. She pointed at the struggling pair and the orderlies dragged them apart. She then moved forward to examine the pool table. There was a long tear in the green baize.

'Jesus, Mary and Joseph,' said the Sister. 'Would you look at that, and it was only repaired the week before last. Right – you two, to your rooms and not a peep or there'll be no lunch for either of you.'

'But he . . . !' Morris began to cry.

Sister Mary turned to him, and he immediately fell silent. The orderly waited for the nod from the nurse before releasing him, and Morris then tramped unhappily away.

'You too, Raymond, and please don't let me down again.'

'Yes, Sister Mary,' said Raymond, and he was also released.

There was another shout, and then pained screaming, but

from further away, and the orderlies were suddenly charging towards the swing doors.

'Jesus, Mary and Joseph!' cried Sister Mary, taking off after them. 'There's no rest for the wicked!'

'JMJ,' I said.

'JMJ,' said Bertie. 'C'mon, I'll show you the—'

'*Shhh.*'

I stood in the middle of the rec room, with my eyes closed and my arms spread. I could hear raised voices from the football field; I could hear the clatter of plates being set out for lunch; I could hear the subtle hum of the air conditioning; the ping of the elevator as it stopped outside; the tap-tap-tapping of Patrick's typing as he composed the Great Irish Novel; even the harsh suck and blow of Bertie's ravaged lungs. But what I could not hear was the original cast recording of *Les Misérables*.

'What?' said Bertie.

'Do you hear that?' I asked.

'Hear what?'

'The sound of *nothing*.'

My tinnitus was gone.

24

I had not felt so healthy for a long, long time, possibly ever, and it worried me greatly. I knew that, quite often, before people die, they suddenly feel better, maybe just for one night, or a few hours. Now, not only was my tinnitus gone, but the relentless pain in my limbs had subsided, the gagging reflex I usually suffered when I swallowed or encountered a Presbyterian had eased, and as for the voices, the voices had *vanished*. But I had seen *Zulu* – and I knew they would be back, and in greater numbers. It was important to strike now, while the iron was hot, and before I suffered a cataclysmic final break-down and death.

JMJ supervised the lunch at least until the food was served and everyone was seated, with the exception of Raymond, who hadn't been able to stop whining about the pool table. She said Grace. Everyone closed their eyes. Mine remained open until I realized JMJ was staring at me. We had mash and sausages and beans. Everyone but Andy seemed to be enjoying it. He sat there staring at his plate with the same concentration he employed when watching the TV, but he made no effort to eat. After five minutes JMJ departed, leaving two orderlies to oversee us. Immediately forks reached across the table and scooped up Andy's mash and beans and speared his sausages. When JMJ checked in on us again, she patted Andy on the back and said, 'Good man, finished first again!' before ducking out again.

Andy got a round of applause. The orderlies, relaxing back against the wall, just nodded and smiled. Bertie said Andy hadn't eaten since Christmas.

Morris, the skinhead, reached across the table with his fork and speared one of Patrick's sausages. The young writer grabbed it back and swore at him.

I said, 'I keep hearing snatches of piano, can anyone else?'

'*Sí*,' said Pedro.

'I keep hearing snatches of piano,' Malachy the goalkeeper repeated. 'Can anyone else?'

'I can hear an oboe,' said Patrick.

'I love the sound of breaking glass,' said Jock, the small fat one who'd been reading a Kindle, 'especially when I'm lonely.'

'I had a trial at Leeds,' said Joe.

I looked at Bertie. '*Pedo*,' he mouthed.

'No, really, is anyone hearing a piano?'

At the end of the table, Jock raised his hand.

'You've heard it too?'

'No. But do you want your sausages? You haven't touched them.'

I glanced around. The two orderlies had moved to the

doorway, and were chatting to each other. I lowered my voice a little. 'Whoever can tell me most about the piano, and who's playing it, is welcome to them.'

Immediately every hand but Andy's went up. I pointed at Pedro. He smiled widely.

'It's a Steinway,' he said, his accent thick. 'They've been making the world's finest pianos for over a hundred and fifty years.'

'Yes, okay,' I said. 'Not so much the origin of—'

'Sometimes we used to stand around it and sing,' he said, 'But JMJ took it away after Franno got killed.'

'Who's Franno?' I asked innocently.

'Franno,' said Bertie, 'was a disagreeable little oik.'

'Franno was okay,' said Scott, 'and he had a lethal left foot.'

'What happened to him?' I asked.

'He was knifed,' said Jock, 'with a knife.'

'Big fucking knife,' said Michael, lowering his earphones for the first time. The beats boomed out.

'Who knifed him?' I asked. 'One of you?'

There was an immediate chorus of *no*'s and denials and excuses and confessions. Joe and Michael raised their knives and began making stabbing motions. They were plastic knives, for good reason. Bertie shouted at them to quieten down. Michael reached across and tried to steal one of Joe's sausages. Joe slapped his hand away. Patrick, the writer, used the distraction to grab one of Michael's. The orderlies stepped back into the room and warned everyone to quieten down. There was a chorus of *'it wasn't me.'*

When the orderlies had returned to their conversation

I said, 'Who then? Who stabbed him? Who *really* stabbed him?'

Bertie leaned forward. He looked around the table. He said quietly, 'We never knew his real name, but we called him The Man from Del Monte.'

'*Why?*'

'Because he was a fruit,' said Pedro.

'Or looked like one,' said Michael, 'in his white suit.'

'A white suit?'

'He always wore a white suit,' said Bertie.

'They were the only clothes he had,' said Joe.

'He was offered others,' said Patrick. 'He chose to wear the white suit.'

'It made him look like a fruit,' said Michael.

'And that's why we called him The Man from Del Monte,' said Jock.

'I never knew why we called him that,' said Patrick. 'I don't know where Del Monte is.'

'It's in America,' said Bertie, 'but it's not a place, it's a company, which makes tins of fruit. It's based in San Fransisco.'

'Home of the fruit,' said Jock.

'Anyway,' said Bertie, 'The Man from Del Monte is what we called him, because we didn't know his name and he never spoke. All he ever did was play that piano. Can I have my sausages now?'

He made a move. I blocked him. 'Not so fast. Where is he now, The Man from Del Monte?'

'They dragged him away after he killed Franno,' said Pedro, 'and we haven't seen him since. Day after, the piano went too. But we hear it from time to time.'

'So you think he's playing it? That he's still here?' I asked.

'Maybe. Thing is, they're not supposed to lock us in our rooms at night, 'cos of health and safety.'

'Damn right,' said Michael.

'But they do it all the same. The other night I heard noises and looked through the keyhole and I just had this wee glimpse of the orderlies walking Del Monte past.'

'They were taking him away?'

'No. About half an hour later they walked him back.'

'So what do you think they were doing?'

'Well, either they had him out in the exercise yard, or he was bound for the shock corridor.'

As if they'd planned it in advance, they all raised their hands, and spread their fingers and touched the tips of them together across the table and made a *bzzz bzzz bzzz* sound and shuddered.

I looked around them in disbelief. 'You're *serious*? I thought electric shock went out with the Ark.'

'Nope,' said Bertie, 'it's back in fashion. JMJ swears by it.'

I looked at him. 'What's it got to do with her? She's only a nurse.'

They all had a good laugh at that.

Malachy slowly raised his hand, and I nodded at him.

'It wasn't electric shock he was getting,' he said, 'not if he walked back. It must have been the exercise yard.'

There was a general agreement and, it seemed to me, a little disappointment with that.

'If they'd shocked him,' Patrick observed, 'maybe we wouldn't have to put up with that fucking piano. It drove us all up the wall when he was in here, and it's still doing it even though they have him locked upstairs somewhere.'

'So you *can* hear it?'

'Of course we can,' said Patrick. 'We're mad, not deaf.'

And that got them all laughing again.

When they had quietened a little, Pedro stretched out his hands in front of him. 'Always the same tune,' he said, and began to mimic playing it. Beside me, Bertie joined in. Then Michael, and pretty soon the whole table, with the exception of Andy, was following suit. Including me. I have never had any musical talent, but playing the invisible piano proved to be quite easy.

After a bit, I asked if anyone had actually seen him stab Franno.

'I did,' said Patrick. 'Cut him straight across the belly. His guts were spilling out all over the place.'

'Don't listen to him,' said Scott. 'He makes shit up all the time.'

'I had a trial for Leeds,' said Joe.

'How'd that work out for you?' Jock asked.

'I would have made it,' said Joe, 'if my knee hadn't given out.'

'Pedo,' whispered Bertie in my ear.

I prodded my fork into my sausage, and raised it, together with my voice. 'I'm *serious*,' I said. 'Did anyone *actually* see what happened?'

But they were no longer looking at me. Their attention had been diverted to the doorway, where JMJ was standing, with her hands on her hips and a black banana of a scowl on her lips.

'I've told you all,' she growled, 'you're not to be talking about that *stuff*. It's not good for you.' She clapped her hands together. 'So no more – no more! Now, if you've finished your lunch, get outside and enjoy the fresh air before your activities begin. Come on – out with you, and let's hear no more about it!'

They all jumped up, with the exception of Andy, and me, and began to file out. Bertie moved around the table and helped Andy to his feet. As he guided him towards the door, Bertie looked longingly at my sausage.

And then it was just me, and Sister Mary.

She said, 'New fella, you've hardly touched your lunch.'

I said, 'I was distracted.'

'You'll get used to it,' she said.

'I hope not,' I replied, and pushed back from the table. 'When does my assessment begin?' I asked.

'It began the moment you were carried through these doors screaming and crying like a little girl.'

She meant it to sting, but it did not. I had lived with Mother for too long.

'Little girls,' I said, 'would certainly be popular around here.'

Her brow furrowed.

As I approached the door, which she was partially blocking, she gave me a long look before stepping to one side. But as I passed her she brought a hand down hard on my shoulder to stop me. Her grip was firm.

'We all rub along quite nicely here,' she said. 'I do hope you're not going to be a disruptive influence.'

'I hope so too,' I replied.

25

Dr Richardson was wearing the same suit as the day before but a different tie. There was some sort of crest on it, and a tiny figure of a golfer. He asked me what he thought were pertinent questions about my childhood, my parents, my friends, relationships with girls and women, my arrests, my probations and why I liked to look in people's windows at night. I gave him the truth, variations of the truth, and lies. He took a list of the medications I had been officially prescribed, and then those I had picked up by nefarious means, mostly the internet or from little Chinese men in herbal shops who were both inscrutable and unscrupulous. He asked about the various diagnoses I'd been saddled with over the years, which included me being a manic depressive, having a personality disorder, having multiple personality disorders, being schizophrenic, paranoid, having delusions of grandeur, delusions of inadequacy and just generally being delusional. He noted that one doctor had accused me of suffering from hypochondria and I said the important word there was *suffering*.

He said, '*Do* you think you're dying?'

I said, 'We're all dying.'

He made a note. I yawned. He said that the treatment of mental illness had come on in leaps and bounds in recent years.

'Like Tigger,' I said.

He made another note and said, 'And the medications have improved vastly. I might want to try you on something new.'

'Really,' I said.

'You appear dismissive.'

'Different circus, same old clown.'

He made another note. 'You think I'm a clown?'

'Am I laughing?'

'Tell me about the attraction to crime fiction.'

'I'm not attracted to it. It's what I enjoy reading, and turning other people on to.'

'Turning them on to it?'

I sighed. 'Do you read it?' I asked.

'A little. If I was to ask you for your favourite authors, who would you say?'

'How long have you got?' He smiled, and opened his hands to me. I smiled too, and nodded at them. '*Knights of the Open Palm.*'

'Excuse me?'

'*Knights of the Open Palm* is thought to have been the first hard-boiled detective story. Carroll John Daly wrote it for *Black Mask* magazine in 1923.'

'I see. And he or she would be your favourite writer?'

'No, but your hands made me think of it. He's kind of obscure, but he certainly kick-started it. Hard-boiled would be my preferred style of crime fiction. You'd probably be more familiar with Dashiell Hammett or Raymond Chandler or James M. Cain or Cornell Woolrich, or Dorothy Hughes, or Jim Thompson or Dave Goodis or Charles Williams or Elmore Leonard or—'

The palms were up again. I stopped.

Dr Richardson said, 'Explain to me what you mean by *hard-boiled.*'

'It has to do with the writing style – lean, direct, gritty. The unsentimental portrayal of violence and sex.'

'And what then is *noir* fiction?'

'That's like a sub-section of hard-boiled. The main character isn't usually a detective, but may be a suspect or the criminal himself. Usually he's involved in the crime in some way, so he's not someone who's called in to solve it.'

'Is there much sex in *noir*?'

'Yes, usually. It's used to advance the plot and highlight the self-destructive qualities of the characters.'

He began to read out some of the notes he had made. 'So, let me see, we have . . . unsentimental violence and sex, self-destructive characters . . .'

'It would be a mistake,' I said, 'to read *me* into what I read.'

'Really? And why would that be?'

'Your profession is mental illness. Does that make you someone with a mental illness?'

He pursed his lips. 'Okay. Fair point. Yet, I understand that you have taken this fascination with the darker side of life one step further than reading about it, since you've set yourself up as some kind of private detective. You investigate crimes. You get involved in them. You expose yourself to danger.'

'Not if I can help it,' I said.

'Nevertheless. What do you think that says about you?'

'I don't think it says anything other than I like to help humans, and I like a good mystery.'

'Humans? You like to help humans?'

'Yes.'

'It makes it sound almost as if you didn't consider yourself human.' I looked at him. 'Are you human?'

'As opposed to . . .?'

'You tell me.'

'Like a giraffe?'

'You're not a giraffe.'

'Are you sure about that? I might be a giraffe in disguise.' I raised my head, and stretched out my neck. He made another note.

'I'm interested – why did you choose giraffe?'

'I chose it at random. I might as easily have chosen a barn owl.'

'A barn owl. Interesting.'

'Why?'

'Both a barn owl and a giraffe could look through your windows at night. You like to look through windows at night.'

'I have an insatiable curiosity.'

'Insatiable. You know, your reading and your language is littered with sex words.'

'So you think this is all about sex?'

'Most things are. Repression of, depression about, resistance to, no resistance to, premature, immature, ligature. It all comes back.'

'I do believe you're the only one bringing everything back to sex. In crime-fiction terms, you've been leading the witness, and swaying the jury, and you're also the judge, who'll be delivering the verdict. It doesn't really matter what I say, you'll interpret it your own way, and I'll swing for it.'

'Do you see everything in terms of punishment?'

'No, just sex, apparently.'

'And do you really think you're on trial here?'

'Am I not?'

'We're just having a friendly chat, getting to know each other.'

'Are you married?'

'Excuse me?'

'Do you have a wife?'

'Yes, I do.'

'Tell me about her.'

'That's not really—'

'I thought we were getting to know each other?'

'Well, there have to be boundaries, otherwise—'

'Do you have a lot of sex?'

'I'm not—'

'Do you play golf?'

'What? Yes, yes I do.'

'Often?'

'Twice a week. Why, do you?'

'This isn't about me.'

'I . . .'

'Are you good at putting?'

'As it happens, I'm not bad at—'

'Do you like to see balls going into a hole?'

'I'm not sure I—'

'Do you use those big golf sticks with the heavy bits on the end?'

'You mean drivers?'

'Yes. Drivers. Do you like to get a good firm grip of the shaft?'

'I'm not sure I—'

'What do you call that when you bring the stick back?'

'You mean when I swing the club?'

'Yes. Do you do that?'

'Do I swing? Yes, I swing, of course I—'

'You swing. Interesting.' I made a note. An imaginary one. He watched me write it. He almost leaned across the table to see what I was writing. 'Well,' I said, 'I like to think we've gotten to know each other a little better. I'm going to write you a prescription here for the latest – and I mean *latest* – drug on the market that I really think will work wonders for you.'

I peeled off the script and set it on the desk and pushed it across to him. He pretended to pick it up and read it. He nodded. Then he mimed balling it and throwing it across the room towards a metal bin in the corner. I studied the trajectory.

'Missed,' I said.

He clasped his hands and nodded slowly. 'When you get started, you're very good. Attack as a form of defence. You know, I've made quite a lot of notes, but do you know what I'm going to do?'

He showed me his notebook, and then tore the top sheet off. He repeated the process for three more sheets before aligning all four neatly together. Then he crumpled them into a single ball and threw it across the room. It landed perfectly in the bin.

'Why would you do that?' I asked.

'Because I think they're worthless. I think you've been flim-flamming me. I don't think I'm going to get anything that is at all useful until either you let your guard down, or I find a way to climb over this wall you've put up. You know, I'm not your enemy.'

'I'm being kept here against my will.'

'*No*. Well, yes. But for your own good. I'm trying to help you, and I'm trying to be your friend.' I raised an eyebrow. 'Okay, not your *friend* friend, but I do have your best interests at heart. We all do. All we're doing is assessing you. It's like getting you ready for an MOT. If a car's not running properly, you get it checked out; you think it might take an hour, but the mechanic discovers the problem's bigger than you thought it was, and he has to keep it a few days and you have to make alternative transport arrangements. It's a bit of a pain, but it won't last for ever and you'll get your car back all shiny and running efficiently. And you know, compared to how you were when you first came in and the first morning we spoke, there really has been a remarkable improvement. It's amazing what can be achieved in a week.'

'A *week*?'

'Yes, normally it takes—'

'A *week*? I've been here a *week*?!'

'Yes. Didn't you know?'

'Jesus, Mary and Joseph?! How could I have been here a week?!'

He raised his hands in a calming gesture. It did not help.

'It's okay,' he said, 'it's nothing to worry about. You were unconscious for most of it, at least when you weren't vomiting and screaming. But it has done you a world of good, and certainly the electro-convulsive therapy has helped to return you to factory settings. I'm really—'

'You . . . *what*?'

'I'm sorry?'

'Electro . . . you *gave me* electric-shock treatment?'

'Yes, it's one of the procedures we—'

'Jesus! I mean – Jesus.' I jumped up. My whole body was trembling. I began to hyperventilate. I needed a pill. Any pill. 'You gave me . . . while I was unconscious, you gave me . . . without so much as a . . .'

'Your family agreed.' I stood there, *staggered*. 'Please. Sit down.' I *did not*. 'It was all discussed. You had so many drugs in your body, all working against each other, the medical staff here were frankly surprised that you didn't expire years ago. I saw the toxicology reports myself, and they were mindboggling. The consensus . . .'

'My family *agreed*?'

'Yes, of course. Although it was our preference, we wouldn't have done it without family approval. Your partner – Alison? – we went through it all with her and she took some considerable time to decide, but she agreed in the end. Legally, it's a bit of a grey area, you not being married to her, so it was also put to your mother, and she saw the wisdom of it straight away. She was very approving. So . . .' He showed me the palms again.

I stood there. He opened a drawer and took out a brown paper bag.

'Breathe into it,' he said, reaching it across. 'You're having a panic attack.'

I took it, and crushed it into a ball, using all my strength, and hurled it behind me without looking.

'Close,' said Dr Robertson, 'but ultimately off-target.' He smiled benevolently. 'Look, I can see that this has been a bit of a shock – no pun intended – but honestly, it was for your own good, and I can see the benefits already. And please understand – you're thinking about *old* electric-shock treatment. That's the problem we have with it to this day: the public see it as barbaric and inhumane, mostly because of *One Flew Over the Cuckoo's Nest*. *That* was basically torture. That was shock therapy, delivered without an anaesthetic. *This* is *entirely* different. You're unconscious, there's no pain at all, and it's just a nice, gentle pulse. Honestly, it's been showing wonderful results, and by the time you get to the end of the treatment, you'll be an entirely new man.'

'The end of . . .?'

'Yes, every other day for two weeks. At the end of that I'm quite certain you'll be back to work and happy as Larry. In a good way. Honestly. Please. Trust me. By the time this is finished, you won't know yourself. And nobody else will either.'

26

I was in my room, in my bed, with the covers over my head; and then I jumped as something that felt like a hand was brought down on my thigh and I threw it off and Bertie was standing there, looking concerned.

'Don't *touch* me!' I hissed, and he stepped back and apologised but said he'd spoken to me three times and I hadn't responded and he was just checking I wasn't dead and I said no such luck.

He said, 'Don't say that. Life is a gift.'

'It should be returned unopened.'

He smiled. 'I like that. *Returned unopened.* As long as you have the receipt.'

'What do you *want*?'

'JMJ sent me to get you. We're having a session.'

'You can tell JMJ to *fuck off.*'

'Don't say that.'

'I just did. And you can fuck off too.'

He blew air out of his cheeks. 'Please. You really have

to come,' he said. 'JMJ won't start without you. If you don't come, your privileges will be revoked.'

'Privileges? In this place? That's a laugh.'

'*All* of our privileges. And we'll just sit there, till you come.'

'Well, I'm not coming.'

I pulled the covers back up. I had been electrocuted. They had burned part of my brain away. I would never know what information had gone with it. Johnny Cash had once sung 'I Forgot to Remember to Forget', or at least, I thought it was him. I had allowed Bertie to sneak up on me where once my Spider sense would have alerted me to his presence. I jammed my eyes tight closed and tried to remember as many classics as I could: Patricia Highsmith's *Strangers on a Train*, William McGivern's *The Big Heat*, Geoffrey Household's *Rogue Male*, Edward Anderson's *Thieves Like Us*, Derek Raymond's *I Was Dora Suarez*, Donald Westlake's *The Ax*, Dorothy Hughes's *In A Lonely Place* . . . and then, and then I had the title – *Too Many Cooks* – but I couldn't remember the author; it was there but I couldn't quite grasp it and I knew that the reason I couldn't was because Dr Richardson and JMJ and my girlfriend and Mother had conspired to fry my brain. If I couldn't remember the author of *Too Many Cooks*, what was the point of me?

'Please,' said Bertie. 'She'll keep us there till midnight. And we'll miss visiting time.'

I lowered the cover, slightly, just enough for my eyes to peek out. 'Visiting time?' Bertie nodded. 'How do you know if someone's coming to see you?'

'You don't. Please come? Please?'

*   *   *

JMJ said, 'So glad that you could join us.'

There were six of us loopers on chairs in a circle that began and ended with JMJ. Bertie said that the whole twelve was too many to manage. Besides Bertie and me there was young Patrick, the writer, and Andy, the silent one, and Joe, the footballer who had once, apparently, had a trial for Leeds, and Pedro, the unlikely Spaniard. JMJ introduced me and asked if I'd like to tell them all something about myself and I said no, and she coaxed me and I said no, so to encourage me she turned it round and asked the others to talk a little about themselves and Joe went down the Leeds route before JMJ cut him off and suggested that he might want to talk about why he liked setting fire to things and he just sniggered and stared at the carpet.

JMJ said, 'Yes, Joe, and the supermarket you burned down most recently, was that funny? Was that a bit of a laugh?' Joe shook his head. JMJ looked at me. 'Three firemen fell through the roof, one of them died. No, not funny, Joe.'

Pedro said, 'I have brain damage.'

'Tell us how you got that, Pedro,' said JMJ.

'In the Civil War.'

Bertie rolled his eyes. 'The Civil War in Ballymena.'

'The Spanish Civil War. I was shot in the head when we took Seville.'

'Your milk-float crashed, you cretin,' said Bertie.

'That's enough, Bertie,' JMJ said firmly. 'Why don't *you* tell us about your own predilections?'

'I don't know what you're talking about.'

'Why are you here, Bertie?'

'I've been depressed. I'll be back to school in no time.'

Patrick said, 'Yeah, right, Bertie. Good luck with that.'

'I'm on a sabbatical,' said Bertie.

Patrick nodded at me. 'He was caught . . .' and he made the international sign for wanking '. . . a fourteen year old.'

'That's enough, Patrick,' said JMJ, 'we're all of us here for a reason.' She regarded me anew. 'Perhaps now, you're ready to tell us what . . .?'

'I like to garden,' I said. 'In the middle of the night.'

'In the dark?' Joe asked.

'I use a torch.'

'But not your own garden,' said JMJ, 'other people's gardens.'

'Why would you do that?' Patrick asked.

'Because they need prunning,' I said.

'Right,' said Patrick. 'So why are you locked up with the rest of us and not downstairs with the volunteers?'

'There's been a conspiracy.'

'Involving . . .?' JMJ prompted.

'Everyone.'

'You think the whole world is against you?'

'Pretty much.'

'Do you think *I'm* against you?'

'Absolutely.'

'And what about Andy, who wouldn't say boo to a goose, is he against you?'

I looked at Andy, who was staring at his hands.

'It's the quiet ones you've got to watch,' I said.

'Do you not find,' JMJ asked, 'that that sense of paranoia is fading a little, now that you're here, and your treatment has begun?' She smiled around our group. 'Do you not find the atmosphere . . . convivial?'

'No,' I said.

'Well, tell us how you do find it.'

'Electric,' I said.

Patrick stood in my doorway. I was perusing a *Reader's Digest* compendium. It was the only type of book allowed on the ward. He said, '*Electric*. I saw what you were doing there, but she didn't get it. She's stupid.'

'I doubt that,' I said. 'She just lacks humour.'

'If I ran into her outside,' said Patrick, 'I'd fuck her up.'

I nodded. I studied the book. I had to remember where I was. These were not normal people.

I said, 'How's the novel coming along?'

'Why do you want to know?'

'I'm just interested, I see you working hard at it.'

'Are you trying to steal my ideas?'

'No, of course not. I own a bookshop. I've met a lot of writers. I might be able to help you with—'

'I don't need your help.'

'Okay.'

'I've written one hundred and seventy thousand words.'

'That's a lot of words.'

'I'm nearly done. It's going to win the Booker Prize.'

'Excellent. Good luck with that.'

'I don't need luck.'

'Okay. That's good.'

'It's going to win the Booker Prize.'

'So I understand.'

'It'll be the first crime novel to win the Booker.'

I sat up. And then I sat down again. And then I sat up again. I said, nonchalantly, 'It's a crime novel?'

'Yes. Do you have a problem with that?'

'No, I . . . it's just, my bookshop is a crime-fiction bookshop. I am a world-renowned expert on crime fiction. Really, seriously, if you want me to read your book and give you my opinion, I'd be more than happy to.'

'Do you know what I'm in here for?'

'In Purdysburn? Yes, kind of.'

'Kind of?'

'Yes – whatchamacallit . . .'

'Whatchama . . .?'

'Kiddyfiddlin,' I said.

He laughed. 'Who the fuck told you that?'

'Bertie.'

'Aw, fuck, Bertie thinks everyone's at it, but he's the only one. No, I was done for stabbing someone.'

'Oh,' I said.

'The last person who tried to read my book, in fact.' He pointed a finger at me. 'So consider yourself fucking warned.'

He turned on his heel.

I lay back on the bed. Then I sat up again.

Rex Stout.

Author of *Too Many Cooks*.

27

I was in the rec room with lanky Scott. He was no longer wearing his Barcelona football strip and had changed into what was apparently known as a West Ham outfit.

'Well,' I said, 'looks like it's you and me are the only ones not getting visitors.'

They had called them, one by one, the orderlies standing at the door to the rec room and barking out the names. Bertie and Raymond and Patrick had gone together, then Jock, reading his Kindle as he went. Joe went. Then Malachy and Michael. Andy was called but was nowhere to be found. Morris the skinhead paced and paced and muttered and muttered and looked miserable until his name finally came up and his whole face beamed. Pedro was the last to go, mumbling in Spanish and glancing at his watch.

Scott said, 'I don't have anyone. My parents are dead. I don't have friends. Nobody ever comes.'

I patted his arm gently.

The orderly said, 'Scott, your wife's here.'

Scott bounced up and away.

I rolled the balls across the pool table. It had not yet been repaired. I have never played a game of pool in my life. It is a little too energetic. But now I picked up a cue and tried to pot a ball. I missed, and tore another hole in the baize. I glanced around, but there was nobody to notice. I wandered out of the rec room and along the corridor, past JMJ's office to the security doors that led to the other parts of the hospital. Andy was standing close to them, peering out.

I said, 'They're looking for you, you have visitors.' He did not react. He was an older man, with bedraggled hair and many, many laughter lines, and I thought that once, he might have been the life and soul of a party, the way I had never been. I said, 'You seem to spend a lot of time watching a TV that isn't on. You should try audio books. I run a Christmas Club. There are many fine crime authors you could listen to. Call in one day. I will give you a discount.' He just kept staring out.

I moved closer to the door. I had not yet observed the access code being keyed in, but when I did I knew it would not be hard to memorise. I have a photographic memory – or *had*, before the electric shock. The jury was still out on that. The difficult bit would be the card that had to be swiped as well. It would have to be purloined. I told Andy I would let the orderlies know where he was and patted him on the shoulder before retracing my steps along the corridor.

JMJ was in her small office; the door was open – there was another woman with her. She was large, in upper middle age, with a green jacket over a blouse and long skirt; she had on a hat, and looked as if she was on her way to church. As I lingered, they both got up and moved into the corridor. JMJ saw me and asked what I was doing and I said nothing. She told me to go and do it somewhere else.

As I nodded and wandered on, JMJ said to her companion: 'I don't know how you have the patience. He never says a word. He hardly even blinks.'

'I feel there's a good soul in there,' said the woman, 'it just needs a little encouragement.'

They moved away, back the way I'd come. I followed at a discreet distance. They got to the security doors and JMJ swiped her card and then punched in her code. As the door opened, JMJ said: 'God bless you, Nicola, and if you've five minutes on the way back, let me know how you got on.'

Nicola smiled and departed. JMJ made sure the door was secure again and then turned back to find me immediately behind her. She looked startled.

'Jesus, Mary and Joseph! What're you doing sneaking around like that?!'

'Nothing, I—'

'You're not supposed to be down here. Now back up to the rec room with you.' I turned, but before I could even move she said, 'Hold on. Turn around.' I did as I was told. She studied my face. She said, 'Have you been crying?'

'No.'

'You are tear-stained, and your eyes are bloodshot. Is there anything you want to tell me?'

'No,' I said, 'I'm perfectly fine. I'm allergic to perfume. Your friend was wearing Chanel No. 6.'

'Chanel only does No. 5.'

'That's just what they want you to think.'

Her mouth opened slightly. Then she seemed to shake herself. 'Oh, I don't know why I listen. Go on, away with you!' She added a wave of her hand to confirm her dismissal.

I wandered back to the rec room, thinking about the large woman who was clearly going off to see Gabriel and what I would have given to be a bag of boiled sweets in her handbag. When I got to the rec room one of the orderlies was standing on the far side, looking exasperated. Then he spotted me and said, 'There you are! Visitors!' and I involuntarily lit up.

I had it under control by the time I was ushered into the visiting lounge for I really was not happy to see Alison. For that matter, I was not happy to see Jeff either. She was a coward and he was a spoon. They looked scared, and embarrassed, and like the guilty dogs they were.

I pulled out a chair and sat down. They were on the other side of a freshly wiped table. It smelled of Mr Muscle Toilet Cleaner, which was a criminal misuse of the product. The other tables were all taken. Everyone was chatting away, with the exception of Andy, who was staring at his own table and ignoring the good-looking twins opposite him. Michael had his earphones on, and I could hear the beat. His parents were talking away, and he was nodding, but their voices were not loud. Patrick was holding hands with a Goth girl.

I brought my eyes back to Alison and snapped: 'Where's Page?'

'Page is at home with your mother.'

'With my . . .?!'

'She's had a change of heart. She's like a new woman.'

'Because I'm in here?'

'No. Yes. I don't know. It's all very confusing. Look, I'm sorry if—'

'So how are you, Jeff?' I asked.

'I'm okay, thanks. How are you?'

'I'm okay, thanks. Thanks for asking. Okay as anyone can be who's just been stabbed in the back!'

'Really? Who . . .?' He looked at me, then suddenly went, 'Oh. I really didn't know until—'

'Shut up, Jeff.' I studied Alison. 'All you ever say to me is don't be so paranoid. And now fucking look at me!' My fellow patients, and their loved ones, looked across. 'You *conspired* against me, you and him and Mother and Nurse Brenda and DI Robinson and—'

'What are you *talking* about?'

'I've been here a week!'

'I know, they wouldn't let us see you until you were well enough to have visitors.'

'They stopped my medication!'

'They said it was the best course of action.'

'They gave me *electric shock*!'

'They said it was hardly enough to power a Hornby train round a track.'

'That's easy for you to say!'

One of the orderlies had been lurking unnoticed against the far wall. Now he came forward and leaned on the table; he gave me big eyes and warned me to quieten down or the visit would be curtailed – but as he pushed himself back up he winked at Alison. They were all in it together.

I said, 'Why did you bring this half-wit with you anyway? Jesus, it's not like he's family. He stacks shelves.'

'I do more than that!'

'Really? Do you? What else do you do Jeff?'

'I . . . open boxes. And I man the till. You know I man the till. And I help with your investigations.'

'Really? *Really*? Help or hinder? Does any of that explain why you're here, with my so-called girlfriend and mother of my so-called child? What exactly has it got to do with you?'

Jeff glanced at Alison. She gave a slight nod. My stomach lurched. They were about to confirm what I already knew. They had been having the sex. They were much better matched. Jeff was a student and a poet and had a career pushing a pen in the Civil Service ahead of him; he was a safe bet. I was locked up in a mental institution and had the life expectancy of a newt – which, incidentally, is twelve years – and I'd already used thirty-five of those up. It was a *coup d'état* with orderlies and electricity on tap to restrain me if I reacted badly. I would have strangled her and decapitated him if I'd had one ounce of strength in my wasting muscles. And then I thought that, actually, for once in my life, my muscles didn't feel too bad, that those idiots might have been too ambitious in getting me locked up, and forced into a regime that removed the drugs that had been holding me back from my body, that I might actually emerge stronger, and more able to cause them some actual real physical damage. I despised them, despised these maggots who were having the sex with each other and plotting to steal No Alibis and my baby who probably wasn't even my baby; poor sap Jeff had been sucked into it not knowing that he wasn't the father either, but the fall guy, while DI Robinson was laughing in the shadows. I wondered if Jeff was getting any kind of reward, a kiss or a grope; but the more I looked at him the more I knew that he was just a gormless big chump being ruthlessly exploited by the prospect of a real human girlfriend.

I looked at them, staring at me, and became aware that I'd said all of it out loud, and that they weren't the only ones who'd been exposed to it, that the visitors, and my fellow patients, and the orderlies had all been listening. I laughed suddenly, and gave them all the thumbs-up and said, 'Gotcha!' and they looked awkwardly at me, and the orderlies started to move towards me and I looked at Alison and burst into tears and she held up her hand to stop my restraint or removal and she got up and came round the table and put her arms around me and said, 'It's okay, you're going to be okay,' and I thanked her, and hugged her and told her how much I missed her and baby Page, and then Jeff came round the table and put his arm round me too and I told him to bugger off and he did and I loved the fact that I could now turn the tears on like a tap or a woman, it was a great talent to have.

'You're bound to be fragile,' said Alison.

'I am, but I'm feeling better – stronger, thank you.'

'We're not having an affair,' said Jeff, 'though I'm open to offers.'

'That's right, Jeff,' said Alison, 'just you keep yourself on stand-by there.'

They smiled at each other. It was good that they got on. They were my family.

I rubbed at my eyes and said, 'What were you going to tell me?'

The weight in my stomach was still there. My heart was pounding, driving the blood round my system at just under the speed of light. I felt high and low simultaneously. And they couldn't tell because I am an *acting God*. I was *allowing* them to continue their charade. I had been convicted of no crime, so eventually I would be released. *Then* I could dismember them.

'I'm not sure if we should say,' Alison began.

'I'm fine,' I said, 'please, just tell me.'

I wanted the ground to open up and consume them. Or at least for them to be involved in a serious road accident and to have forgotten to have renewed their insurance or for them to have named me as the beneficiary of their estates, even though I knew neither of them had much in the way of money. From Alison I might inherit some of her weirdo paintings and comics nobody else was interested in, and possibly Page; from Jeff, a lot of bad poetry – and worse, Amnesty International pamphlets. I have always liked the word pamphlet and enjoy repeating it endlessly. Pamphlet, pamphlet, pamphlet, pamphlet, pamphlet, pamphlet, pamphlet, pamphlet, pamphlet, pamphlet, pamphlet, but not necessarily out loud, as I now clearly was.

'Sorry,' I said, 'it's just one of the words they teach you here – repetition calms the mind. Pamphlet. Yes. That's better. Now, you were saying – if you're not here to shaft me further, what're you here for?'

'Darling,' said Alison, 'we didn't shaft you. You were out of control and needed help.'

'You think?'

'I *know*. And I also know you're never going to agree with me. So can we just park it for now? Because we have different fish to fry.'

'Bigger,' I said.

'*Different*,' said Alison.

She sucked in her breath, then gave Jeff a nod. From within his parka he removed a folded newspaper. He straightened it and smoothed down the front page with his hand before setting it down on the table and spinning it round to face me.

He tapped it. 'This—'

'I can read,' I snapped.

The headline said: *Bernard O'Dromodery Murder: Police Seek Two*.

'Jesus, Mary and Joseph,' I said.

28

Bernard O'Dromodery and his husband Martin Brady had eaten at the five-star Shipyard restaurant downtown and then parked their Aston Martin V12 Vantage in the driveway of their Antrim Road home and briefly argued about who had left one of their bedroom lights on. As it turned out, it was neither of them, but one or other of the two men in Hallowe'en masks who jumped them as soon as they entered. Martin was decommissioned immediately: for all his self-proclaimed SAS prowess he was Tasered from behind and could only watch helplessly while his husband was forced upstairs; he could only listen to the horrific screams as Bernard was repeatedly stabbed; and he could only claw pathetically after them as the killers stepped over him as they exited the house.

The words *cold-blooded* were used three times in the article. Police had appealed for information. There were tributes to Bernard from business leaders and politicians.

The only remaining brother, Sean, released a statement saying that there would be no statement. Martin Brady was too distraught to talk to the press. The *Belfast Telegraph* went out of its way to avoid calling him Bernard's husband, but referred to him as his partner, as if they ran a painting and decorating business together.

I said, 'This is three days' old.'

'It's the first time we've been allowed to visit,' said Alison. 'They have a strict regime here and you were mostly unconscious.'

'*Three days.*'

'There's been nothing new since, they just regurgitate the same facts in slightly smaller articles.'

I bit at my fingernail and reread the article. The police officer quoted in the story was DI Robinson. There was mention of the recent suicide of Fergus O'Dromodery, but nothing to suggest that the two deaths were in any way linked. There was a photograph of Bernard O'Dromodery at the helm of a speedboat with a caption that included the words *in better times*. A photograph of the house was shown, with a police car in the foreground. The front garden looked neat and well tended.

'Don't bite your nails,' said Alison.

'I'll . . .' I began. I took a deep breath.

'We thought you should know,' said Jeff, 'but we don't want you to worry about it. You're in here to get better. Alison and I have been handling the investigation.'

'You *what*?'

'It's business as usual,' said Alison, now smiling broadly.

'We were engaged by Bernard O'Dromodery to find out

who murdered his brother, weren't we? The case remains active, and enlarged. Like your heart, apparently.'

'You *what*?'

'You what to what? Your heart? Yes, they say it was twice the size of a human heart, or something to that effect, due to all the medication you were on. It could have exploded at—'

'Forget about the heart, what about this?'

'You forget about biting your nails, and then I'll continue.'

'Don't tell me what to do!'

'It's easier just to do what she says,' said Jeff.

'If I want your opinion, I'll ask for it!'

'That's what *she* says. You're like two peas in a pod.'

I shook my head. 'I don't believe you two. You lock me up in here, you take over my bookshop *and* my business.'

'You're half-right,' said Alison. 'The shop's been more or less closed all week. We tried your mother back behind the till, but it didn't work out. She kept setting the smoke alarm off.'

'The shop is *closed*?'

'Temporarily. We can't do everything.'

'It's our busiest time of the year!'

'That's not true. There *is* no busy time of year. The money Bernard O'Dromodery paid us is four times what you earn in a month. It's a simple matter of economics.'

I drummed my fingers on the table. I steadied my breathing. I pointed at Alison.

'Don't point at me like that,' she said.

I gave an exasperated sigh and lowered my hand. 'Right. First of all, the shop is the cornerstone of everything. I don't care how you do it, but until I'm out of here, you have to work out a way to open it up. You cannot leave people without a bookshop, I don't care if there's only a tenner coming over the counter . . .

'Some days,' Jeff began.

'*It stays open.* Okay?'

'I don't know how we're supposed . . .' Alison began.

I brought my fist down on the table. 'Okay?'

After a bit she said, 'Okay.'

I looked at Jeff.

'What?'

'*Okay?*'

'Oh. Yes. Okay. I just do what I'm told.'

'Open the shop,' I said. 'I don't care if it's Page behind the counter or if Mother burns it down, make sure it's open. Once people start to think we've closed down, they'll presume we've gone. Now – the case. Yes, the money is handy. But that's not why I take cases. It's the puzzle. The puzzle remains the same. Gabriel – I'm here to identify him. That's the only reason. There's nothing wrong with me. Pamphlet. I'm here for Gabriel. Understood?'

'Understood,' said Jeff.

'Go on,' said Alison.

'I haven't gotten to him yet, but I will. Now you've taken on the mantle, show me what you have. I presume there's another *defixio*?'

'It's still a crime scene,' said Jeff, 'we haven't been able to get to see it.'

'Just do it, Jeff. Find a way. Midnight gardening is usually a safe bet. Have you spoken to the husband?'

'He's not answering his phone,' said Alison. 'I took flowers round, but had to leave them at the door, as nobody answered. The funeral is tomorrow. I was going to go to that, try and have a word and take some pictures, see if any of the usual suspects turn up.'

'Good,' I said. 'What else?'

'You left your laptop on before you were sectioned . . .'

'Before you *had* me sectioned.'

'. . . At the All Star Health Club pages, and that, together with a few phone calls, led us to three staff memebers who left in the wake of Fat Sam's killing. Their names are . . .' Alison slipped a small notebook out of her pocket. It had a girly pink cover and a sparkly binding. She flipped the cover back and read from the top page: 'Andrea Moffatt, Peter McDaid and Jackie McQuiston. Andrea Moffatt is working in a dental surgery, while Peter McDaid and Jackie McQuiston are both out of the fitness business and are working for some catering company.'

'I already spoke with Jackie.'

'Yes, I know that, so I spoke to Peter McDaid, and I sent Jeff to work his charm on Andrea.'

'You didn't send me, it was a joint decision.'

'You just keep thinking that, Jeff,' said Alison. 'Anyhoo – Jackie McQuiston was off sick when I called in. I wondered how they both ended up joining the same company. Peter McDaid said he couldn't get out of All Star quick enough – and he was only there for a few weeks before the murder. He hated the clientele, said there was always a bad atmosphere, knew there was a trade in performance-enhancers, was there on the night Fat Sam died and has been kicking himself ever since for not doing a final check to make sure the man was gone. He said security was pretty lax anyway, and the alarm had a habit of short-circuiting. Everything was done on the cheap, the equipment was crap and the swimming pool chemicals messed with his eyes – this made it difficult to work there. The pay wasn't great but he still had to work insane hours. He didn't have a good word to say about it. Anyway, he said Jackie felt the same way, and first thing they always did on a Thursday was get the *Telegraph* – it's jobs night – and they both spotted the same ad during their tea break and jumped at it. They'd a bit of a competition together to see who would get out of the All Star first, and as it turned out, they both got a job in catering. It's not their dream job, but money in hand till they find what they really want.'

A bell sounded. The orderly, relaxing against the back wall, straightened. Families began to gather up their belongings.

'And he just volunteered all this?'

'No, it was mostly pillow-talk.' Alison studied my face, and then added: 'God, I'd forgotten how gullible you are. He was just glad to be out of there – he was letting off steam.'

'Did you mention Gabriel?'

'I did. He claimed not to have heard about the arrest or seen his picture.'

'Why do you say *claimed*?'

Alison shrugged. She glanced at the relatives as they began to move past our table. She smiled at one. She leaned a little closer to me across the table. 'I don't know really. I mean, it just seemed odd, if someone was murdered in the place you worked, that you wouldn't watch the news or read the

221

papers and know that someone had been arrested. But then, I suppose, some people are very self-centred.'

She gave me the eye. I gave it to her back and then shifted to the spoon.

'Okay, Casanova, what about you?'

'I suffer for my art, that's what I do. The only way to get at Andrea Moffatt was to call into her dental practice for an emergency appointment. I told her I'd been doing a Hot Yoga class at the All Star when this pain shot through one of my wisdom teeth. She said they had a cancellation and sent me straight through and I had an X-ray with attendant radiation and three injections and my mouth swelled up like a bap.'

'Did you actually have toothache?'

'No! It's a scandal, we should investigate the dental industry, charging for . . .'

'Talk about self-centred. What'd *she* say?'

Before he could start, the orderly said from the doorway: 'Okay, folks, time to wrap it up.'

I gave him the thumbs-up, and leaned closer to Jeff. 'Go on.'

'Well, I got talking to her a bit more on the way out, though with the blood and the hamster cheeks she could hardly make out what I was saying. But she told me pretty much what the other guy said – shady characters and practices, and she jumped at the chance to get out. She's had some health issues, kidney transplant, so she's only working part-time now, so it suited her to—'

'Fat Sam, shady characters, any sightings of Gabriel?'

'Didn't like Fat Sam, was working on the night he was killed, but it wasn't her job to close the place up. She saw Gabriel's picture in the paper and thought he looked kind of cute.'

'*Cute*?' I said.

'He is kind of cute,' said Alison.

The orderly cleared his throat. Alison smiled apologetically at him and pushed her chair back. As she stood up, Jeff joined her. She leaned forward to kiss me. I moved my head to one side so that her lips caressed my cheek. She looked surprised. And a little hurt.

'Traitor,' I hissed.

I nodded at Jeff. 'I want you on Martin Brady. I want you on Sean O'Dromodery and the shopping centre the company was working on. See if there's anything dodgy there. There's something we're not seeing.'

'And what do you want *me* to do?' Alison asked.

I studied her.

'Time, gentlemen, please,' the orderly said from the door, and we looked at his grin and ignored him.

Then I took her in my arms and pulled her close. I whispered: 'I despise do-gooding cows.'

'*I'm . . . !*'

'Shhh. When you're in the mental ward and you've got no friends or visitors, they send them in to cheer you up, but all they ever do is try to convert you to Jesus. There's one went upstairs to Gabriel about twenty minutes ago. If you're lucky you'll catch her on the way out. She has on a green coat and a green hat and her first name is Nicola. She might be our way into him. Go get her.' I stepped out of her arms. 'Let me know how you get on tomorrow.'

Alison shook her head. 'We can't tomorrow. There's only visiting once a week.'

'I can't wait a week!'

'I don't make the rules!'

'Right! Okay. Okay. There has to be some way . . .'

She gave me a helpless look. Jeff was at the door. She joined him.

'You're going to get better,' she said.

'Pamphlet,' I said.

29

I lay on my bed and tried to think it through. It was an odd experience. I was used to thinking about a million things at once: the drugs, and the caffeine and my zest for life allowed me to do that. But I was off the drugs and denied caffeine, which only left the zest, which had never existed. But now there was *definitely* something strange going on: my mind wasn't whizzing along disconnected tangents, there was even a certain amount of clarity. I was able to focus on *The Case of the Man in the White Suit*, and put the feelings of betrayal and rage and the problem of pirated downloads of e-books and the likelihood of life on Kepler 26B to one side, with the full knowledge that I could get back to them later. It was like parking them in a pay and display: they were there, I knew they were there, and I would do my level best to get back to them before my time was up.

I was already, after just a week, becoming a new man,

physically and mentally. And I kind of liked it, but it also scared the pants off me. I had in the past devoted so much of my energy to appearing lethargic, but now I was beginning to feel I had an excess of it, as if I could almost do anything. I could run more than the length of myself and swim like a turtle or make love to a woman for more than a minute without fearing that my elbows would collapse. But what if all my many ailments and hang-ups were actually my strengths, were what made me the greatest detective of my age? What if, when the dust settled, all that was left of me was merely ordinary or unremarkable? What if I was *dull*? I was starting to feel as if I was in at least partial control of myself for the first time in years. I felt *sane*. But what was going to sustain me, and energise me, in the long months after the case was solved and I had murdered Alison, Mother and Jeff for their betrayal? I was going to be very alone.

And then I thought, *No*, there is always Jesus.

There had thus far been four deaths: three of them certain murders, and the other one more than likely. There were *defixios* for two of the dead for sure, but none for Francis Delaney, which suggested that that murder was separate. Francis Delaney was connected to Fat Sam, who was an enforcer for the O'Dromoderys. Bernard O'Dromodery had employed me to find out who was behind the *defixios*, so it wasn't stretching the bounds of possibility that he had also sent Francis Delaney into this hospital to interrogate Gabriel using methods which perhaps the police were prevented from employing. The O'Dromodery Brothers' presence at his funeral certainly suggested a strong connection. Bernard O'Dromodery was now dead, but he could not have been murdered by Gabriel. With two O'Dromoderys already dead, it wasn't hard to predict that the surviving brother, Sean, might need to start looking over his shoulder.

I had asked Alison and Jeff to find out what they could, but I knew better than to rely on them. I was the only one really capable of solving this case, and I was in the best place to do it, because I knew that Gabriel was still the key to it. But I would have to do it sooner rather than later if Sean O'Dromodery was to survive. I had to get to Gabriel; I had to *break* him.

'Do you really own a bookshop?' Patrick said from the door.

I sat up. 'I do. I specialise in crime fiction. Mystery fiction.'

'So you know something about writing.'

'I know a lot about the writing of crime fiction.' Patrick nodded. He kicked his heel against the doorframe and avoided eye-contact. I didn't mind that. Eye-contact is overrated. 'Do you want to talk about your book?' He gave a little shrug. 'Is it crime fiction?'

He shook his head. 'But there's a murder in it. I don't know. Maybe it is.'

'As long as the murder isn't solved by a cat, I'm more than happy to talk to you about it.'

'What do you have against cats?'

'Nothing. They just don't make for great detectives.'

'Macavity was a mystery cat,' said Patrick.

I liked him.

*   *   *

We sat on my bed and talked books and writing for an hour. I surprised myself. Normally I have no time for unpublished writers, mostly because of having had to endure an endless parade of poor deluded idiots through Brendan Coyle's creative writing class in my store on a Saturday morning; the only reason I tolerated them at all was my desire to sell them books. But as I was talking to Patrick I was thinking to myself that perhaps I had been unjustly negative about the class, and not really listened to what Brendan was teaching or what his students were writing. Writers had to come from somewhere, and while many arrived fully formed, others could benefit from nurture and trelliswork.

Patrick was probably about thirty years old, but he had the sullen/ecstatic demeanour of a teenager. When I eventually got him to open up a bit he proved to be smart and well read, but despite his earlier Booker bravado, lacking in confidence about his own writing. He was still well short of letting me read his book, but I didn't mind that. It was good to have an intelligent conversation with someone, and also I didn't want to discover that he had merely typed *All work and no play makes Jack a dull boy* one hundred and fifty thousand times. I was, after all, in a nuthouse. I could call it that, now that I was sane again.

I said, 'How long have you been in here?'

'Here? About a month. I have a history of burglary and suicide attempts.'

'That's an unusual combination,' I said.

'Yes, well. I almost instantly regret breaking in to people's houses, so I try to top myself there and then. It's just my thing. I'm not very good at it. I mean, the suicide. I'm good at the burglary, I can break into anything, but when it comes to the suicide I just don't seem to have it. Been close, a couple of times, but generally I wake up having my stomach pumped or being stitched back together. I don't even steal anything, I just like the challenge. I was downstairs before, voluntary.'

'And then you stabbed someone.'

'No. I was only joking about that.'

'I can relax then.'

'I beat them half to death with the leg of a chair.'

'O*kay*,' I said. 'Really?'

He nodded. 'But I prefer it up here. I can get on with my work. It's like a writer's retreat. More writers should be locked up, it concentrates the mind.'

'I'm with you on that,' I said, 'especially Scandinavians.'

He looked at me for several long moments, and I began to worry about how detachable the legs of my bed were, but then he began to laugh, and he lay back on the bed as it took a greater hold of him, and his whole body began to shake. It wasn't that funny, but I appreciated his appreciation. He sat up suddenly, without a trace of a smile and said, 'Who were they who came to visit you?'

'My girlfriend, and a guy who works for me.'

'Is she any good in bed?'

'Yes,' I said.

'What does she do that makes her so good?'

'That's none of your business.'

He nodded. 'And the fella, he works in the bookshop?'

'Yep. And also he helps out with . . .' and I weighed it up, and thought yes, this could work for me '. . . with my other work.'

'Like what?'

I got off the bed and pushed the door closed. I came back and sat down. 'Can you keep a secret?'

'Yes, of course.'

'Seriously?'

'Yes. Honestly. Ask anyone.'

'Okay. Well – you told me about your book. In my spare time, I'm a private detective. I take on all sorts of cases, from a missing dog to murder most foul. And that's really why I'm in here. I deliberately had myself sectioned. I'm on a case right now.'

'You are fucking not.'

'I really am. Did you not notice me asking all those questions at lunchtime about The Man from Del Monte?'

'You did ask a lot. He's your case?'

'He's being accused of a murder I'm pretty sure he did not commit.'

'I don't want to burst your bubble, but I seen him kill Franno, there's no doubt about it.'

'Yes, I'm sure he did, but it's the murder that got him in here in the first place that concerns me. A guy called Sam Mahood, he had the nickname of—'

'Fat Sam. Yes. Downstairs, we were allowed newspapers and the internet, and everyone was dead curious when Monte was brought in wearing his nice white suit. They wouldn't tell us why he was in, but we found out soon enough.'

'And he was then as he is presumably now – quiet?'

'Not a word. He just sat and played the piano.'

'They have one downstairs too?'

'Yes, but it's not in as good nick. More people pass through downstairs, so it gets more of a pounding, including from a lot of people who like to bang their heads against things. We don't have so much of that up here. We're more from the violent psychotic end of the spectrum.'

I cleared my throat and said, 'What about mealtimes? Did he attend lunches or eat in his room?'

'Bit of both. He ate, okay, but no eye-contact, no reaction to sounds, just in his own world, y'know? The Sister down there, Sister Brenda, she would spoonfeed him. She always has a soft spot for the waifs and strays – all of us really. She ruled us with a rod of sponge.'

I smiled. 'And when he was here, did JMJ spoonfood him?'

'Are you joking? She had him down the road for electro as soon as he arrived, and if he didn't show for lunch, none of us ate. Got to the point where if he didn't show the inclination, we dragged him along – and I mean dragged.' His eyes narrowed suddenly, and he pointed at me. 'You're interviewing me! I'm like a witness!'

'That's *exactly* what you are.' He grinned, and stuck his chest out. 'So, Patrick – and this is important – what happened when this· guy Franno came in? You've been around the mentally challenged, you recognise the signs the same as I do, would you say he was unwell? He was supposed to be in the black hole of depression.'

Patrick thought for a moment. 'Well, he wasn't exactly a barrel of laughs. And he had no patience with any of us, always snapping, and Sister Brenda didn't like him one bit because he was also a bully and seemed to be giving Monte a hard time about the piano. Sending him for electro didn't seem to cheer him up much either.'

'Did he *need* electro?'

'Does it matter? It's the JMJ way. I can't say it did him much good. He was angry when he went in, even angrier when he came out, and slightly singed.'

'Singed?'

Patrick smiled. 'No, of course not. But he was certainly furious once the drugs had worn off. Depressed? I don't know. It was his temper more than anything. You would get out of his way. And The Man from Del Monte didn't.' His eyes flitted up to me, just for a moment. Then he stared back at the floor.

'Patrick,' I said, 'I think you're going to be a very fine writer.'

'You haven't read anything.'

'It doesn't matter. Sometimes you can just tell from listening to someone, the way they tell a story. A great writer, yes. What you do is – you reflect real life, but you also embellish it, right?'

'Yes, I suppose.'

'But they're different things. There's real life and there's fiction, and it's important to know the difference.'

'Of course. I'm not an idiot.'

'I know that. You're the opposite of an idiot. But I'm investigating a murder, two murders involving Monte and several others which may be connected to it – so it's absolutely vital that you tell me the truth, not a version of it, which would be your inclination, the same as any great writer. Do you get me?'

'Sure.'

'Okay. So I need to concentrate on just the facts. At lunch, you were talking about how you saw Franno with his tummy cut open – did you really see that?'

'Yes, of course. His guts were hanging out.'

'Where was this?

'In the rec room.'

'And did everyone see this?'

'No. Just me. They were all out in the exercise yard, compulsory five-a-side.'

'And how come you weren't?'

'I just had a session with Dr Richardson. It overran a bit and by the time I came out they were already started.'

'And Monte?'

'He was at the piano. They tried to make him play footie, JMJ thought it might spark something off. They even managed to get him out of his suit and were trying to put a Liverpool top on him when they found all these stitches on him like he'd had major surgery, and when the doctors saw that they called a halt – health and safety and all that crap.'

'Stitches? Where?'

'Ahm . . . *here*. What's that, kidneys?'

'Yeah, I think so. Okay, okay. So he didn't do sports, and you were too late to play – how come Franno was there?'

'He wasn't long out of electro and still a bit woozy. Again, health and safety wouldn't let him out there in case he fell over and cracked his head.'

'So it was just the three of you in the rec?'

'No, I went to my room for a lie-down. Then I heard raised voices, and then – like a crash, glass smashing. I went out to see what it was, and there was the two of them on the ground; they'd landed on a table and the glass in it had smashed and the legs had given way so they were lying in all these shards and Franno had his hand round Monte's throat and I yelled at him to get off but he wouldn't . . .'

He trailed off and gave a little shrug. He studied the floor some more.

'Okay. That's good, Patrick. And the orderlies or JMJ, they didn't come to see what was going on?'

'I don't know where JMJ was, but the orderlies were outside at the footie. When there's a proper game it gets frantic and there's a lot of screaming and crying goes on – gets so loud a bomb could go off in here and they wouldn't hear it.'

'So there was just you, and Franno and Monte on the ground, and Franno has his hands like *this* . . .'

'No, just one hand. He was a big guy, strong guy – like a body-builder, you could tell.'

'And Monte was . . .?'

'He was pinned, and his face was going purple and I yelled at Franno again to get off him but he wouldn't, and . . .' Patrick rubbed at his jaw. He examined his fingernails. 'And then there was blood everywhere, just shooting out. Arterial blood, isn't that what they call it? His whole stomach was just split open, side to side. Gross. One minute he was throttling Monte, the next he was on his back, gutted.'

'The glass? Monte used a shard of glass?'

'Right across the tummy. Yeah. Yeah.'

'Even though he was pinned down by a body-builder.'

'He must have worked an arm free.'

'You saw that?'

'I . . . it all happened very fast.'

'And when you yelled at Franno and he wouldn't get off, what did you do? Go for help or stand there or . . .?'

'I don't know. It just – it's just a bit of a blur.'

'Did you not try and pull him off?'

'Yeah, sort of, but he was big and strong and he wouldn't budge.'

'And what did he say to you? Did he swear at you or threaten you?'

'Yeah, yeah, he yelled at me.'

'What did he yell, Patrick?'

'He just – yelled.'

'Like to eff off or something?'

'Yeah – that was it.'

'Patrick, this is great, really useful – you're a *brilliant* witness – but remember, I wasn't there. I can only go on what you're telling me – and the clues to what really happened might be in what you saw, in the detail you maybe haven't even thought about or you're not telling me because you don't think it's relevant . . . but it could be, it really could be. Just, just . . . create the scene for me again. You hear raised voices, right?'

'Yeah, yeah, absolutely.'

'Whose voices? Franno's?'

'Yes, of course.'

'And who else? You said there was nobody else there. Did you hear Monte's voice?'

'It must have been. Yeah.'

'But Monte doesn't speak. He hasn't said a word since he was brought in.'

'Well, he must have. Good point. Hadn't thought about that.'

'Can you remember what they were shouting?'

'No. Just . . . I don't know. Words. Yelling.'

'You recognised Franno's voice?'

'Yes, definitely.'

'And the other voice: what did it sound like?'

'I don't know.'

'Like Franno's?'

'No. Different. Franno's like broad Belfast, Monte's was different.'

'Different how?'

'I don't know.'

'Not so broad, a different part of Belfast?'

'No, more . . . I don't know. Foreign, maybe?'

'Any words at all you can remember?'

'No, honestly.'

'But possibly foreign.'

'Yeah, possibly.'

'And it was definitely his voice?'

'I don't know. There was no one else there, but by the time I got to the rec room he wasn't saying anything because he was being strangled.'

'Okay, so you come in, and Franno's on top of him, pinning him to the ground, one hand round his throat?'

'Yes. Like *this*. Throttling him.'

'And his face is purple?'

'Yes. Or, what's that word? Puce. His face was puce.'

'So he's being choked by this guy who's so strong he only needs one hand to do it, and his face is puce – he must have been nearly dead by the time you arrived?'

'Yes, yes, he was.'

'And you yelled at Franno to get off him. What did you yell?'

'I don't remember.'

'Like, "get off him"? "Get the fuck off him"?'

'Yes, like that.'

'And what did he do? He was nearly killing Monte – he ignored you or yelled back at you?'

'Yes, he yelled at me to get off.'

'So you had your hands on him?'

'I was trying to get him off Monte. I pulled at him and pulled at him, but he was a big shithouse . . . and he was shouting at me to get off him.' Patrick scrunched his eyes up and spat out the words. '"Fuck off, get the fuck off me, you fucking retard".'

'But you didn't.'

'He was killing him! I stuck my fingers in his eyes and tried to wrench his head back, but he just kept squeezing and squeezing, and then I . . .'

His eyes opened again and properly fixed on mine for the first time. He was breathing hard, gasping and grasping for words. I put a hand on his arm.

'It's okay,' I said. 'It's all right. This goes no further, okay? Just tell me. Monte was helpless, he was *dying*. On a good day he wouldn't have had the strength to shift Franno off him; you neither. You were trying to save his life. They were lying in shattered glass, the only way you could possibly have . . .'

Patrick let out a long sigh. And then slowly he opened his left hand and I saw a long cut across the palm, so fresh that it hadn't even begun to knit. He closed his fingers over it, into a fist, yet as if he was holding something. And then he slowly dragged it sideways across his stomach in a slicing motion, nodding at the same time, and his eyes not leaving me for one moment.

30

Patrick pulled up his sleeves and showed me his bare arms. They were criss-crossed with old scars.

'Ironic, isn't it?' he said. 'I've spent half my life cutting myself with every sharp object I can get my hands on, and the one time I do it properly, someone else gets the benefit.'

'Ironic,' I agreed.

'Anyway,' he said, 'it's getting late. I always have a shower before dinner. It's pizza tonight. Catch you later.'

He strolled out of my room. Before he showed me his scarred arms I'd asked him how Monte or Gabriel or Gideon had reacted to being saved, and Patrick shrugged and said, 'He didn't, he just lay there with Franno on top of him, and all his guts spilling out over him.'

'You didn't help him up?'

'Nope. I could hear the others coming in from footie, thought it better to get off-side.' He hesitated for a moment before laughing. 'Off-side – that's a pun.'

I agreed that it was. 'You weren't covered in blood then?'

'Nope. See . . .' And he acted it out before me. 'I got him from behind and sliced him, and the guts fell out and down, and the blood sprayed down too. Maybe a wee dribble on my hands, but I washed that off quick enough.'

I said, 'Patrick? The murder in your book – is it anything like what happened to Franno?'

'It's *exactly* . . . Yes, good point. I should change it.'

'No – really, leave it as it is. It sounds edgy, realistic. People like that. Critics love it.'

I sat and pondered. He had become a little animated while relating his story, but he didn't appear to be overwhelmed by guilt or remorse. He had killed Francis Delaney by ripping a shard of glass across his stomach, and then he had walked away in the same casual manner with which he had just left my room. There was, of course, the strong possibility that he had just made it all up. He was, after all, not only a writer of fiction, but a long-term resident in the secure wing at Purdysburn. Yet he hadn't volunteered any of it, rather it had been my incisive and gently insistent line of questioning that had wrung it out of him. I had what The Clash had called a 'bullshit detector', but Patrick hadn't set any of my alarm bells ringing. So either he was telling the truth or my powers had been diminished by the lack of powerful opiates in my system or devastated by my being hooked up to the national grid. If he was telling the truth, then Gabriel was an innocent man, a victim both of extreme violence and a potential miscarriage of justice. *Proving* it would be difficult, but getting hold of Patrick's book would be a start: it might give me enough leverage to force DI

Robinson or someone more senior or sensible to take a second look at the murder.

Somewhere in the background, I heard the piano. I had been hearing it off and on all day. I recognised but could not identify the music. It was very frustrating.

I have never had a great appetite. Mother mostly fed me on gruel and sticks. In my teenage years I had a bad experience with hot cheese, and had not attempted pizza since, but now the prospect of it had my juices flowing. When I arrived at the dining room, I found that I was thirteen minutes early. It was open, but unattended. There was a cutlery drawer with plastic knives and forks. To kill some time, I busted all the forks.

On my way out, an orderly was coming in. He said, 'You must be hungry.'

I said, 'Famished.'

I entered the rec room. Patrick was at his computer. When I approached, he shielded the screen so I couldn't read his book. I noted a red memory stick in one of the ports. Stealing it would not be a problem. I said, 'I enjoyed our conversation.'

'Fuck off,' he said.

Raymond and Morris were back at the pool table, this time playing harmoniously. Andy was before the TV. Now it was switched on to a news channel. He was staring at it with the same intensity, but his eyes did not appear to be focused on the pictures.

I wandered out of the rec and along the hall. JMJ's door was open and she was behind her desk, talking to another nurse. I wandered on towards the security doors to take another look at the keypad, but stopped short of it and retraced my steps and looked through JMJ's door again, and then knocked on it and the nurse turned and yes, sure enough, it was Nurse Brenda and her eyes widened in surprise and her cheeks flushed and for a moment she looked panicked and then I said that I thought I recognised that face even though it had been turned away from me, and I came in with my hand outstretched and JMJ too looked briefly panicked until I reassured her that Nurse Brenda and I were old friends from downstairs many, many years ago and sure she didn't look a day older. I was doing great, I said, and had a shop and a girlfriend and a baby and I was only in here for a check-up and because I'd tried to commit suicide by eating a hydrangea bush – not the whole bush, I corrected, but some of the leaves that turned out to be more than averagely full of cyanide – but apart from that life was grand and we were having pizza for dinner.

Nurse Brenda recovered herself and beamed at me. 'Oh, you were such a grand boy! It's so lovely to see you!'

She got out of her chair and hugged me close and her voluminous bosoms squished against me. I do not like humans close to me at the best of times, not even during the sex, but I did not find this unpleasant and even experienced a carnal thought, which was understandable now that I was free of sex-suppressing drugs but incarcerated in a single-sex environment.

I saw JMJ over Nurse Brenda's shoulder and she did not look impressed, but nevertheless she got up and said, 'I've things to be doing, why don't you two have a catch-up?' and slipped past us. And as soon as she was gone, Nurse

Brenda let me go and gasped out: 'Where *were* you? I was so worried!' as if she hadn't conspired with Alison at all.

'I—'

'What are you even doing here? How did you get in? I had the paperwork all ready and then I couldn't find you. The only number I had was for the shop and there was only ever the answer machine and I couldn't leave a message in case someone else got it! And I went round twice. It was all closed up the first time, and then this old woman claimed never to have heard of you and chased me away, and I got so paranoid that our secret was out! Thank God you're okay – but what are you doing here?'

'I'm—'

'They're moving him tomorrow! You have to do something – you have to do something right now!'

'I'm doing my—'

She caught me by my shoulders. She gave me the eyes. 'If they take him away tomorrow, he will never see the light of day again. They will put him in with dangerous people who will tear him to shreds. You promised me. I'm depending on you. My boy is depending on you. I can't even go up and see him, I've no reason to and Sister Mary guards her territory like, like . . .'

'A Spartan,' I suggested.

Nurse Brenda nodded and mouthed *Spartan*. 'You've gotten this far without my help. I need you to go the extra few yards.' She glanced at her watch. 'It's five thirty now. They're due to move him tomorrow morning. They always do it early. You have to get to him tonight. I know you can do it.

243

I've heard about how you solve the most complicated cases. Solve this one. Save him.'

JMJ passed by the open door, glancing in, but carrying on. She did not smile.

'What's up there?' I asked. 'Where *exactly* are they holding him?'

Nurse Brenda's eyes flitted to the ceiling. 'The rooms are built into the roof. The old attic was used for storage when I first started here, and then converted when we needed more secure accommodation. They always had plans to run the lifts up to that extra floor, but there was never the money – so there's just the stairs up. An orderly sits at the top, checks you're supposed to be there and then buzzes you in. He has the keys to all the rooms.'

'There's no security code?'

'Not up there. The security code is for down here, and it's mainly to keep you from escaping. But you don't need to worry about that. Your concern isn't getting out, it's getting in to see him and finding out who he is. Can you do that?'

'I'll do my best,' I said.

'Don't do your best,' said Nurse Brenda, taking me by the shoulders again and squeezing. 'Just *do it*.'

'O*kay*,' I said.

I had serious concerns that I'd missed the pizza. But when I entered the rec room everyone was standing shouting at each other and the orderlies were dragging Patrick and Morris apart. Joe, Scott and Malachy were chanting, 'Big fight, big fight!' and Bertie had his hands over his ears and was crying, 'I can't stand the noise, I can't stand it, I tell you!'

As I drew closer, JMJ appeared from the other side, clapping her hands together and shouting for quiet. As the voices faded, she stood between Patrick and Morris and waved her finger around the circle. 'This will not do, this just will not do! All of you! Now what's this all about?'

'These two were tearing chunks out of each other,' said one of the orderlies.

'He stole my memory stick!' cried Patrick.

'He stole *my* memory stick!' Morris responded.

'You don't have a memory stick, you fucking half-wit!' Patrick yelled.

'Jesus, Mary and Joseph! Enough!' JMJ turned to Patrick. 'Now you tell me – what happened?'

'I went for a shower and forgot to take my memory stick out of the computer. I came back to get it and that wanker was sitting reading my book and I told him to get off and he told me to fuck off and grabbed the memory stick and tried to run away but I grabbed him and he won't give it back. Make him give it back.'

JMJ swivelled to Morris. 'Is this true?'

'No! *I've* been writing a novel, it's *my* memory stick!'

'Morris – have you really been writing a novel?'

'Yes! Ask anyone!'

'That's bullshit!' Patrick spat. 'What's your novel about? Go on, what's it about, Morris?!'

'Yeah, yeah? I'll tell you what it's about – it's about a man who's in a car crash and wakes up thinking he's God and tries to raise the money to build his own church and ends up murdering someone and—'

'That's my book! You just read it off the fucking computer!'

'It's mine! It's mine! *I* wrote it! Ask anyone!'

'Morris – are you telling the truth?' JMJ asked.

'Yes!'

'And where's the memory stick now?'

Morris opened his left hand to show her. JMJ nodded. 'Patrick? Is that your memory stick?'

'Yes! Of course it is!'

'Morris – did you steal Patrick's memory stick?'

'No! It's mine! Ask anyone!'

'Give me the memory stick.' JMJ put her hand out. When Morris hesitated, she clicked her fingers. '*Now.*'

Morris reluctantly stepped forward and pressed it into JMJ's palm. As he did, Patrick stepped forward to collect it.

'Stay where you are!' JMJ snapped.

Patrick stopped. 'But it's my—'

'*Quiet.* Now, Morris. I want the truth. Is this your memory stick!'

'Yes. Ask anyone!'

'Patrick – are you sure this is yours?'

'Yes, of course it is! You know I've been working on my book.'

JMJ shook her head, not just at Patrick, but around the assembled patients. 'This is my ward. I believe in harmony. I don't believe in violence, and I cherish honesty. If we cannot agree, then the only solution is to take whatever is causing the disruption out of the equation. Therefore . . .' She held up the memory stick. Then she bent it.

'Jesus fuck no!'

Patrick lunged forward, but the orderly grabbed him and hauled him back. Morris just giggled. JMJ continued pulling at the stick, trying to make a clean break, but there were wires keeping the two parts together. She gave up when it was bent almost double, and dropped it on the floor.

'Why would you even fucking do that?' Patrick cried. 'I've been writing . . .'

'And you will write again, Patrick. You have plenty of time. But we all have to learn to get on together. Let this be a lesson to you all – caring is sharing. Now, I happen to know that the pizza has arrived, and it's getting cold. Enough of this nonsense – let's go and get our dinner, eh?'

'Yeh!' shouted Morris, and everyone else joined in.

She led them away, except for Patrick who slumped to his knees and burst into tears. I crouched beside him and put my arm around his shoulders and he cried against me. 'I hate her,' he whimpered as I used my free hand to scoop the broken memory stick up and into my pocket, 'I fucking *hate* her.'

31

Revenge, I convinced him, was a dish best served cold. If I had not been there to discourage him, then he might have surged after JMJ and did for her as he had done for Franno, but I soothed him and promised him that his day would come, if he would help me, and I whispered what I needed from him and he nodded against me and slipped away, and I fingered the memory stick in my pocket and smiled to myself because I was very good. I sauntered towards the dining room fully expecting and mostly prepared for what was coming.

They were all around the table, with JMJ at its head and half a dozen pizzas sitting untouched in the middle with various side dishes between them, including coleslaw and potato salad. There was not the usual hubbub. My fellow patients, at least those who weren't staring into space, eyed me with anticipation. As I entered the room, an orderly stepped up beside me.

I said, 'You should have started without me.'

JMJ said, 'We don't do that. Where's Patrick?'

'He went to the toilet. He'll be here in a minute.'

JMJ said, 'Is there anything you want to tell us?'

'About Patrick? He's quite upset. You just destroyed his novel.'

'*My* novel,' said Morris. 'Ask anyone.'

'Be quiet, Morris,' said JMJ. 'I'm not talking about the novel.' She nodded down at the table before her. I could see the broken forks spread out, and the cutlery drawer open behind. 'Is there anything you wish to say about this . . .' her hand hovered over them '. . . wanton vandalism.'

'Nope,' I said.

'Did you break these forks?' she asked.

'Has someone said I broke those forks?'

'That is not what I asked. My colleague,' and she indicated the orderly, 'only recently placed these forks in the cutlery drawer. He spoke to you as you left the room. He discovered the forks all broken when he returned.'

'The evidence, I contend, is circumstantial. He may have done it himself.'

'*Why* would he do that?'

'You don't have to be mad to work here . . .'

'Good one,' said Bertie.

'Did you break these forks?'

'As it happens, yes I did.'

'Why would you do that?'

'They were there to be broken.'

'What do you mean?'

'They were left unsecured, and I had the opportunity to break them, so I did.'

'But why would you do that other than for badness?'

'You've hit the nail right on the head.'

JMJ's hands moved to her hips; it was the naval equivalent of taking battle formation.

'Are you *deliberately* trying to provoke me?'

'It's a distinct possibility,' I said.

'You do know that there can only be one winner here?'

'It's better to have loved and lost than never to have loved at all.'

'*What?*'

'A bird in the hand is—'

'Enough! Jesus, Mary and Joseph! I've had you down as a troublemaker from the moment you were carried in here, and now it's right out in the open for everyone to see! Well, you listen to me, *mister*, we live by harmony here, not anarchy! These pizzas have been brought in from outside at not inconsiderable expense, as a special treat, but they'll bloody well go in the bin if you continue with this outright . . . *defiance* – yes, that's exactly what it is – defiance! Do you think *I'm* going to go without dinner tonight? No, but these poor souls, they certainly will if you do not see the error of your ways and apologise for your attitude and your behaviour. *Immediately.*'

Her stare was intense.

Michael slipped off his earphones. 'Apologise, man, you're not going to win.'

Joe said, 'Do it, I'm starving.'

Malachy pointed a finger at me. 'Say you're sorry. We get pizza once a month if we're lucky. Don't fuck it up.'

Andy stared at the pizzas.

JMJ raised an eyebrow. '*Well*?'

Yes, her eyes were good, but she was no Nurse Brenda – or Alison, for that matter – and I knew my plan was good, and for every moment I held my silence I knew that it was drawing closer to fruition.

'Okay,' she said, 'have it your—'

I spoke. *Muttered.*

'What was that?' JMJ snapped. 'If you're going to apologise, speak up, let everyone hear you.'

I said, a little louder, 'Food fight.'

She screwed up her eyes and leaned a little closer. 'What was that?'

'I said . . . FOOD FIGHT!'

I reached down and picked up one of the pizzas. It was cold and as firm as a discus. The orderly looked from the pizza to me to JMJ and back, utterly confused and seeking direction.

JMJ began to say, 'Put that d—' but then had to duck as I Frisbeed it across the dining room towards her. It smeared off her left shoulder and hit the wall behind her, leaving a snail trail of cheese as it slipped to the floor.

'C'mon!' I yelled, urging the others to join in, 'Food fight!' I lunged at another pizza just as the orderly jumped at me, knocking me forwards and across the table. 'Food fight!' I screeched. He had me by the neck, pressing down. I screwed my head to one side and spat out: 'C'mon, you half-wits! Food fight! This is your chance! C'mon!'

But they sat there, looking blankly at me. I managed to grab another pizza but a second orderly came rushing in and caught my hand and bent my fingers back until I let go and then they

251

pulled me up and back and JMJ came round the table and put her face in mine and raised her hand and grabbed my cheek and pinched it between her fingers and twisted it and snarled, 'Anything you want to say *now*?'

'Yes . . . *yes*!'

'Well?'

'You don't eat pizza with forks, you fucking witch!'

'Pathetic!' And she twisted my cheek even harder and it brought tears to my eyes and she smiled and said, 'Take him to his room and lock him in, and I don't want to see him until breakfast. You can have a long hard think about your behaviour and I expect a full and sincere apology or I swear to God . . . !'

Patrick appeared in the doorway as they began to pull me through it. He gave me a wink and I gave it to him back and then I cackled and kicked back against the orderly's shins and one of them let go my arm just long enough for me to grab JMJ's lizard neck and she screamed and both orderlies pounced and one chopped my hand from her throat and they pinned me to the floor and started raining blows upon me and JMJ was coughing and spluttering and everyone at the table was laughing or crying with the exception of Andy who continued to stare at the pizza and probably wasn't even aware that I was face down and JMJ was on her hands and knees and hissing in my face that I was going upstairs to solitary and that in the morning she was going to fill me so full of electric that I wouldn't know my own name when I woke up and I begged her please no even though inside I was laughing my head off because I was so good.

252

32

I was talking to Jesus and comparing scars in the palms of our hands, and He was saying that I had a persecution complex and I was saying that He had a crucifixion complex and that in any paintings or stained-glass pictures of Him I'd ever seen He seemed to have a pretty fit body and wondered if He ever played sports at all, and how I always remembered from growing up even though I despised football that Jesus Saved but Best Nets the Rebound – and He didn't smile at all but said instead that He preferred cricket.

And then He slapped my face and I turned the other cheek but He slapped that too and then I opened my eyes and it wasn't Jesus but Patrick looming over me and I covered my face and begged him not to kill me and he told me to wise up and that they'd given me something to calm me down and it was the early hours and it was the first chance he'd had to get up and I had to strike now if I was going to strike at all.

For a little bit I had no idea what he was talking about but slowly my form of clarity returned and I remembered that he had used his burglary and thieving expertise to steal keys from the orderlies' desk when they went off on their circuit downstairs and he'd made it upstairs, knowing that the orderly up there did his circuit at exactly the same time but that it only took a couple of minutes for him to check all the doors and that the prisoners or patients, call them what you will, were sleeping and that if I wanted in to Monte's cell I'd have to move *now* and so I did and he opened the door and we slipped along the corridor and three doors up he fumbled for the key and we heard the footsteps on the tiled floor as the guard came back our way and he found it just in time and pushed me through the door and then charged back to my cell where he rolled himself into my quilt with his face to the wall so that when the guard looked through the spy-hole he would see someone sleeping there and when he looked through Monte's he would see that lunatic sitting at his piano still playing and not see me crouching beneath the spy-hole knowing that I had only an hour to find out what I had to find out before the sun came up and the staff arrived and we were caught and I was doomed to be lit up like a Belisha beacon, the first of which was erected in Wigan in 1935.

Monte was playing that tune, and he did not look at me as I entered, or pay any attention as I slithered down beneath the spy-hole and held my breath until I heard the footsteps recede. And then I stayed where I was, and just studied him as his fingers roved along the keyboard with his eyes fixed on a point on the exposed brick, painted-white wall in front of him. He wasn't as handsome as his newspaper photos showed, and he was badly in need of a shave, while his white linen suit was as threadbare as an impoverished missionary's. And, as I listened to his playing without the filtering effect of floor and walls and the hubbub of mentalists, I realised that it wasn't actually that competent; that there were bum notes and missed notes which the constant repetition should have ironed out.

I stood up and moved to the piano, leaned on it, smiled at him and said, 'Hi,' and there was no reaction. I introduced myself and told him that I was a private detective masquerading as an insane bookseller and that my only purpose was to get in to see him because he was about to be sent away to a *really* high security mental hospital for the rest of his life for a murder or murders I was convinced he had not committed. All I needed from him, I said, was a sign that he understood his predicament and some indication that he was prepared to help me be his champion, but he just kept playing that stupid tune.

I said, 'Give me something. *Anything.* General knowledge. The capital of Peru or the square root of a twenty-two thousand and fifty-six? No?'

No.

I stood behind him and listened to him play. After a couple of minutes he came to the end of the piece, and his hands dropped briefly to his sides. I cautiously took hold of his left hand and raised it; he did not resist or otherwise react when I turned it and examined his fingers and palm, and then repeated this with the other hand. I let them go, and they each fell back onto the keyboard and he immediately began playing again. Up close, I could also see that there was scarring on his neck and under his chin; I had been told that there was also evidence of a recent operation in the area of his kidneys. I did not check. Although I believed him innocent, I wasn't about to get that intimate with him in case he murdered me.

I talked to him some more, about Nurse Brenda and how wonderful she was and how she had put her whole career on the line to employ me to come in and see him, and told him how much his fellow patients downstairs really liked him even if he never did say anything and annoyed them all with his piano-playing.

I said, 'I had you all worked out – all this piano-playing had to mean you were a concert pianist gone doo-lally or at the very least you tinkled the ivories in a hotel cabaret, and that one tune is the key to who or what you are.' I showed him my own hands, palms down. 'See these knuckles? The way they're out of shape? Mother used to beat me if I didn't play my scales right. I still can't play for toffee, but I'm at least as good as you.' I sighed. 'That piece? It's one of the Russians, isn't it? It's on the tip of my tongue but I just can't get it.'

I was sure I would have known it but for the electro. JMJ had burned the knowledge out of me.

Gabriel played on. I stood over his shoulder and peeled back his suit jacket and read the label within, hoping for something Moldovan or Slovakian that might lead me to an obscure store in a dusty backstreet of an obscure city where an old tailor would remember selling a white suit to a nice young man who thought he could play the piano and that he came from a well-to-do family who just lived up that hill, the one with the vineyard. But instead I got Blue Harbour, a label sold exclusively through Marks & Spencer. I crouched down to examine his shoes, a badly scuffed pair of black Oxfords, checking the heel for a secret compartment in case he was a spy. It was not such an outlandish idea: I had a pair of Clarks Commandos as a boy, with a compass in the heel in case you ever got lost or kidnapped by a paedophile, though of course that was before paedophiles were invented. But there was nothing within the well-worn heel.

I examined him from every angle. When I stood directly in front of him, I might as well not have been there; his eyes bore through me, to the wall and through it to infinity and beyond. I knew that look. I had seen it before, in the mirror, staring back. It was a look of fear, of trauma, of terror.

I was not aware of footsteps or what must have been the very subtle turn of the key in the door, and in fact only realised that Patrick had returned when I found him standing beside me.

'Well? Did you get what you want?'

'I need more time. I told you I needed at least an hour.'

'You've *had* an hour. And we don't have more time. It's coming up to the end of their shift. The new staff will be coming on, they'll be doing breakfast and we'll be trapped. If we're going to get going, we need to get going now.'

'I can't. I haven't been able to . . . I can't get my head around it . . . I just need to be able to . . .'

'No! We have to go! You *promised*! My *book*!'

I had in fact promised that if he broke me in to see Gabriel, and then broke me out of the hospital, that I would be able to save his book, and more than that, get it read by one of the most respected authors of our times, one Brendan Coyle, who was sure to recognise its genius.

'I will still do your book, Patrick. Just give me half an hour, there's something I'm just on the verge of—'

He grabbed my lapels and stuck his face up close to mine. 'No, we have to go now.'

'Let me go, Patrick. You have the skill to get me out anytime, later today, tonight, tomorrow. Just give me fifteen minutes more.'

'No! We need to get out of this hospital before JMJ arrives!'

'What're you talking about – we – Patrick?'

'I'm going with you!'

'Patrick . . .'

'I have to go! There's no point in my book being out there if I'm not with it!'

My grand plan did not include him coming with me. Apart from the fact that I'd no idea if his book was salvageable from the broken memory stick, I had no wish to associate myself with him outside of the confines of a secure mental institution.

'That's not we agreed, Patrick. You can't go changing—'

'I *have* to go. I left a note for JMJ when I broke into her office. I called her all the names of the day.'

'You were angry – she'll understand.'

'I also had a dump on her desk, and in her top drawer. She will have me fried alive. You know she will. I have to get out *now*.'

I looked at Gabriel, playing away, not paying any attention

to us at all, and knew that I had not even scratched his surface, and that in a matter of hours, or perhaps minutes, he would be spirited away to somewhere I would never have any access to him and where he might spend the rest of his life drugged up in a padded room or be torn asunder by lunatics as soon as he arrived. I had no doubt *at all* that I could solve the case, but it was the time that was killing me.

'Right,' I said, 'then he's coming with us.'

33

We made it through the swing doors onto the stairs with moments to spare. The orderly passed above us. If he had glanced through the glass he would have seen us pressed against the wall, but he did not, and continued on to his desk at the head of the corridor. We waited a few more seconds until he was settled, then I nodded at Patrick and he gently peeled Gabriel away from the paintwork and guided him on down the stairs. We were then in the hands of fate. If the orderly on the floor below was keeping to his schedule as well as his colleague above and had returned to his desk, then we would be too late to make it through the security doors and out into the wider hospital and freedom.

We arrived at the doors at the bottom of the stairs. Patrick peered through the glass at the nurses' station where the night orderly usually sat: the desk was empty. He nodded to me, and pushed through, pulling Gabriel after him. The ward was quiet, with the only light coming from a reading lamp on the desk. We approached the security doors. Patrick reached into his back pocket and removed the card he had liberated from JMJ's desk and swiped it through the security panel, which immediately lit up. He then punched in the code. It immediately flashed up: *Code Error*.

'*Shit*,' Patrick whispered. He tried the numbers again. *Code Error*.

'What's up?'

'What do you think?!' He shook his head and tried them for a third time. 'This doesn't make sense. I've watched her – she always writes the numbers down on a pad. I memorised them, these *have to* be right.'

'Go back and check.' He remained staring at the panel. 'Patrick, go and check, you might have got them wrong.'

'I *didn't*! These are correct. They *have* to be.'

Close at hand, a toilet flushed. Someone was whistling. The orderly was on his way. Patrick keyed in the numbers again.

'It's not going to change its mind,' I hissed. 'Hide – we have to hide until . . .'

I caught Gabriel by the arm and began to turn with him, but my way was suddenly blocked and I let out an involuntary shout. But it wasn't the orderly, it was poor dumb Andy wandering in the darkness, and I whispered the name of the Lord and followed it with a sorry and went to move past him, but as I did Andy put his hand to my chest to stop me. And then he raised his other hand and deliberately picked out four numbers on the security panel and the locks shifted and the door opened just as wide as my mouth did and Andy smiled and said, 'Audio books, good idea,' and gave me the thumbs-up and I was so surprised that I just stood there grinning until Patrick grabbed my arm and pulled me through the doors and I still had a grip on Gabriel and he got dragged along with me, and before I could say anything to Andy we were racing down the flights of stairs to freedom.

Or, at least, the reception area downstairs. It was still very early, but day staff had begun to arrive, the lifts were going up and down and the main desk was now manned by white-collar staff rather than security. I sat Patrick and Gabriel by a small refreshment kiosk close to the doors which was not yet open. None of us looked like staff, but I hoped we would be mistaken for voluntary patients, perhaps just waiting for our fix of non-NHS coffee. Meanwhile I searched for and located a pay-phone and made a reverse charges call to someone I knew I could depend on in my time of need.

'Whhhaaat?'

'It's me,' I said.

'Whhhaaat?'

'Jeff. It's me. Your employer. I need you to get up. I need you to come and get me.'

'Whhhaaat?'

'JEFF! Wake *up*!'

I glanced around me; I smiled at a nurse. My eyes wandered to the hospital entrance. JMJ was just coming through the doors. Her path would take her straight past Patrick and Gabriel.

Jeff said, 'Who . . . what . . . what time is it?'

Patrick saw her. His mouth dropped open.

She walked straight past him. I turned my back and bent into the phone.

'Hello? What the fuh . . .?' Jeff moaned.

She went past me too, and joined a small group waiting for the lift. I allowed myself to breathe again and said, 'Don't curse at me, Jeff, I'm your boss.'

'You're . . . what? Wait – who is . . .?'

'Jeff, get a grip. Is your mum's car outside?'

'Wha . . .? Mum's? The . . . yes, it's outside. Why? What are you . . .?'

'I'm at the hospital. I need you to come and pick me up. I've been released.'

'Now? It's only – Jesus – six in the morning.'

'Jeff, just do it.'

'Can Alison not—'

'*Jeff.*'

'She didn't say anything about—'

'*Jeff.* Come now. If you're not here in fifteen minutes, you're fired.'

I hung up. The elevator was gone, and JMJ with it. In a matter of seconds she would reach her floor. She might stop to chat to the night staff or her colleagues, but she would very definitely go to her office within the next couple of minutes. She might not notice that Patrick was gone, that I was gone, or that the double murder suspect in the White Suit was gone, but she would very definitely notice that someone had taken a dump on her desk. And very soon after that, our absence.

I rejoined my fellow escapees. Patrick's knee was going ninety to the dozen. Gabriel sat placidly. The kiosk was open now, and the aroma of fresh coffee was beginning to waft across. I never drink coffee apart from Starbucks, but the smell was getting to me. I glanced at Patrick: his eyes were glued to the girl serving in the kiosk.

I said, 'Our ride is on its way. We'll be out of here in a minute.'

He said, 'I could kill a double espresso.'

'Where we're going, there's a Starbucks just across the road. It's wonderful.'

'That smell is killing me. I haven't had a double espresso in months.'

'Soon enough,' I said.

Nurse Brenda entered reception from the car park. She saw us immediately and her eyes fixed on Gabriel and she got that panicky look again. She didn't know whether to stop or walk on, and she hesitated where she was just inside the doors, and someone bumped into her from behind and she flushed and said sorry and looked to me for guidance and I shook my head and she nodded and walked on.

'It's okay,' I whispered to Patrick. 'Just a few minutes . . .'

But he stood up. 'I need an espresso,' he said.

I took a panicked gulp of air and said, 'Have you money?'

He shook his head and moved forward and I jumped up and grabbed his arm and said, 'None of us have. It's not free, Patrick – just sit down and you can have as many as you want as soon as—'

He brushed me off and stepped up to the kiosk and said, 'Double espresso, please.'

The girl was only about eighteen. She smiled and said, 'You're up early,' and turned to prepare the coffee.

264

'Patrick, *please*.'

He shook his head again. 'Espresso,' he said.

The girl glanced behind her, and smiled a little more hesi-tantly. I looked to the doors and to the car park beyond for some sign of Jeff, and then back to our seat and saw that Gabriel was gone and my heart jumped – and then I saw him over at the elevators and I sprinted across and took his arm and turned him round and he didn't resist as I sat him down again. I turned back to the kiosk and the girl was telling Patrick it would be £2.50. She hadn't yet handed over the coffee and I knew then that she had been down this road before with patients. Patrick had his hand out and was clicking his fingers and saying, 'Espresso, espresso, give me the espresso.'

And then there was an alarm sounding, and a door opened behind the reception desk and two security guards came running out and towards the elevators and I knew that JMJ had discovered not just the Patrick poo but that he and I were missing and quite possibly Gabriel too, and that it would only be minutes or seconds before they began a lockdown because a couple of nuts on the loose was one thing but an escaped murderer was something else entirely. There wouldn't just be hospital security, there would be police, and many of them.

Patrick clapped his hands together, and it cracked across the reception area.

'Espresso!' he shouted. 'Give me the fucking espresso!'

I pulled Gabriel up and dragged him across to Patrick. I got a grip on Patrick's arm with my free hand and turned him towards me and said, 'We have to go now. This is our last chance, come on, come on now.'

'Espresso,' he said, 'I need espresso!'

I tugged at him but he would not budge and I looked to the doors and there was Jeff in his mum's Volkswagen Golf pulling up and then the elevator doors opened and there was JMJ and two security guards and the alarm was still blasting and the girl was pulling down the shutter on the kiosk to protect herself from attack and I tried one more time with Patrick but he just stared at me and I could see in his eyes that it had nothing to do with the espresso but that he was terrified of leaving the hospital and I let him go and he stood there while I dragged Gabriel through the doors and across the car park with the security guards now charging after us and I pulled open the rear door and pushed Gabriel in and hurled myself in after him without even a moment to consider that I had run and tumbled and did action-type things when I was a man well known to have Brittle Bone Disease and collapsible lungs, yet I seemed to have plenty of flexibility and breath, more than enough to yell, 'Drive! Just drive!' at Jeff and he took a moment to put the Golf into gear and then indicated that he was pulling out.

He *indicated*.

Who ever did that in a getaway?

Who ever, ever, *ever* did that in a getaway?

Jeff did.

And I loved him for it.

34

Jeff got us to the gates at speed, but then, under advisement, proceeded at a leisurely, unremarkable pace along the Queen's highway. Several police cars passed us almost immediately, lights flashing, sirens sounding on their way in to Purdysburn. I noted that they were *not* indicating. I told Jeff to keep his eyes on the road and away from the mirror, but he couldn't help himself.

'Is that Gab . . .? Is that . . .? Is that . . .?' And back to the road for a moment before returning to the mirror. 'That's – that's – that's –'

'Yes, it is,' I said.

'You haven't been released, you've escaped. With *him*.'

'That would be correct. Now concentrate on the road.'

'But you called *me* in our time of need.'

'Yes, I did.'

He glowed. He was easily flattered. Jeff was dependable. You could depend on him to do what he was told. You could depend on him not to think things through properly and to only put up the most token resistance. He also did not have a backbone. In Nazi Germany, he would have been one of the many only following orders. He had a quisling mentality allied with cowardliness. I had phoned him mostly because I knew he had access to his mum's car and that it would not be as obvious or immediately traceable as the Mystery Machine. Also, Alison would have understood immediately that I was making a bid for freedom, and that Gabriel being with me would make her equally liable to be charged with aiding and abetting the escape of a murder suspect. She had already had me committed once. If I had told her of my escape plan she would have informed the authorities, and now that I was out, if I contacted her she would undoubtedly attempt to lure Gabriel into a trap.

Gabriel, meanwhile, had closed his eyes and appeared to have fallen asleep almost instantly. Playing the same tune over and over again for twenty-three hours a day will do that for you.

Jeff glanced back at him again and asked if I'd managed to crack him and I said no.

'And are you okay?'

'Yes,' I said.

'You would say that.'

'How're your exams going?'

'Not well.'

'Your eye has cleared up nicely.'

He used his cleared-up eye to eye me suspiciously.

'Where are we going?' he asked.

'We're going to the shop, via the wasteland behind Botanic station they use as a car park.'

'Okay. Why there?'

'You'll see. Does your mother still keep that spare container of petrol?'

'Yes, she does. How do you know about that?'

I shrugged. I watch people at night and sometimes poke around. I had checked out Jeff's mum's car several times. She never seemed to lock it. I knew she kept spare petrol in the boot, and a quarter of Mint Imperials in the glove compartment. Once I sucked one of the Mint Imperials down to about half size and left it stuck to the passenger seat. I never knew if she noticed it, or had ever mentioned it to Jeff. It wasn't the sort of thing I could bring up in casual conversation without it looking suspicious.

I said, 'We're a little low, good to have some insurance in case we're caught short.'

'We've plenty,' said Jeff, 'unless we're making for Rio.'

I rolled down the window and breathed in. The air had a cold bite to it, but it was refreshing after so long sucking in the antiseptic fumes in the hospital. Jeff shook his head. I said, 'What?' and he said, 'Nothing.'

I looked again at Gabriel. He was snoring lightly. I leaned forward and tapped Jeff on the shoulder.

'So tell me what you have on Martin Brady?' I asked quietly.

'*Have*? Nothing, beyond a nice series of wedding photos from an old issue of *Belfast Confidential*. They looked very much in love.'

'*Was* he in the SAS?'

'I don't know. The SAS don't seem to publish a yearbook.'

'Is that sarcasm, Jeff?'

'No one I spoke to had a bad word to say about him.'

'And who did you speak to?'

He looked a bit shifty, and admitted that he had only spoken to the guy who had taken the photographs for *Belfast Confidential*, which had ceased publication two years previously, and a corner shop where Martin Brady occasionally stopped for groceries.

'It was only yesterday you asked me, and I had revision.'

'What, then, on Sean O'Dromodery and the shopping centre they're building?'

'Likewise.'

'Revision?'

'I'm sorry, I have a limited amount of time to devote to this. I'm only human.'

I said, 'Okay. Don't worry about it. Your exams are important.'

'Is *that* sarcasm?'

'No. I mean it.'

We stopped at traffic-lights. He used the opportunity to look back at me. 'What did they *do* to you in there?'

I laughed. I rolled the window up. The wasteland car park was to our right. Jeff pulled in. He took a ticket at the machine. There were only three other cars. I directed him to park at the far side, well away from them. He switched off the ignition. He turned in his seat and looked back at Gabriel.

'Okay, wakey-wakey,' he said and squeezed his knee.

Gabriel's eyes blazed open and his hand shot up and grabbed Jeff by the throat. Jeff's hands flapped helplessly as Gabriel tightened his grip. It shocked me so much that it was a few moments before I shook myself into action. I grabbed Gabriel's wrist with one hand and then tried to peel back his fingers with the other.

'It's okay,' I said as soothingly as I could, 'it's okay, it's *okay*. Let go, you're okay, let *go*!'

But I was making no impression on him, and all the time Jeff was getting bluer and bluer in the face. It is a universally accepted fact that I have no strength, and if it had been left entirely to me to save him, then my occasional assistant would have departed this mortal coil unpublished – but in the end it was Gabriel himself who loosened his grip; some kind of realisation that Jeff was not a threat must have permeated his shutdown mind, for he abruptly let go and sat back as if nothing was amiss, leaving Jeff to collapse into his own seat gasping and coughing.

'What the . . .' he wheezed out. 'What the *fuck*!' Gabriel was now quite placidly staring out of the window. 'He's a *lunatic*! What the *fuck* are you doing helping him escape?'

As he was wracked by another fit of coughing, Jeff opened the car door and rolled out onto his hands and knees in the gravel. 'Lunatic,' he growled, between gasps. '*Lunatic.*'

I got out and knelt beside him and patted his back and said, 'You just took him by surprise. He's been in a psych ward for months – who knows what's been done to him? He's just like a porcupine, putting his spikes up.'

'Fucking prick, more like,' Jeff spat. 'He needs locked up. Locked *back* up.'

I helped Jeff up. I dusted him down and said, 'Please don't think the worst of him. He's innocent, I know he is. And together, Jeff, we're going to prove it. Okay?'

He shook his head. 'You've got to be joking.'

'Jeff . . . *Jeff* – come on: you spend half your life championing innocent victims for Amnesty International, but they're always in some foreign hell-hole like Iran or Wales. Here's one right on your doorstep.'

'I champion political—'

'Who's to say this isn't political? It's a travesty of justice, Jeff, that's for sure, and it could lead *anywhere*. Yes, he attacked you, but you attacked him first, at least, that's how he interpreted it. Come on now – I need your help on this, Jeff. Please?'

I had never knowingly laid the P-word on him before. He blew air out of his cheeks and gave me the big eyes. '*Okay*, but just remember . . .'

'*Later*. I need you to go on up to the shop and make sure it's all clear. Do you have the keys on you?'

'No, Alison won't let—'

'Doesn't matter. You know the secret hiding-place for the spare one for the back door?'

'Under the bin?'

'That's it. Keep your eyes peeled. If anything looks dodgy just walk on past and loop back round. If it's all clear, get into the shop, go upstairs and put a light on in the front store room. I'll bring Gabriel up as soon as I see it.'

Jeff nodded warily. He reached into the car and took the keys, and then said, 'Do you want to get him out so I can lock up?'

'That might take a wee while. Sure, leave me the keys.'

'I'd really rather . . .'

'Jeff, leave me the keys. I'm a big boy, I'll do it.'

'It's my mum's . . .'

'*Jeff.*'

I put my hand out and snapped my fingers. He bit on his lip for a moment before pressing them into my palm. 'Make sure it's properly locked and the windows are up,' he said, 'and don't be too long, I only put an hour on the pay and display – and I have to get it back to her.'

'I hear you. Don't worry. I'll be right behind you. I just don't want to walk into an ambush, and I need a word with Gabriel so he doesn't react like that again. Okay?'

Jeff nodded and gave his assailant a final glance before trudging off, still rubbing at his throat. I waited until he had disappeared round the corner onto Botanic Avenue before I opened the back door and gently encouraged Gabriel out of the car. He came without any bother. I guided him a dozen metres away, and then patted his arm and told him to wait there. I moved back to the car and opened the boot. The plastic container of spare petrol was exactly where I remembered it. I took it out, removed the top, and liberally splashed the inside of the vehicle with it. I put the key in the ignition and turned it enough to switch on the cigarette-lighter but not enough to start the engine. When it had heated sufficiently I removed it, stepped back out of the car and pressed the lighter into a sponge Jeff's mum kept in the driver's side pocket to help with the demisting of the windscreen. It began to burn and melt simultaneously. I then tossed it into the back seat and stepped back sharply as Jeff's mum's car went up with a *whoosh*.

Afterwards, I wasn't quite sure why I did it, but it seemed like the right thing to do at the time.

35

There is a reading lamp I have by the computer which I use when I'm working late ordering stock or surfing for information about badgers; Jeff got hold of it and moved it to the counter and twisted it so that it was shining directly into Gabriel's eyes. He was a breath away from saying, 'We have ways of making you talk,' when I took hold of the flexible stem and turned the brightness away from our guest. 'Would you catch a grip?' I said.

'We have to do something,' said Jeff. 'He's just staring into space like a gormless big idiot.'

I studied Gabriel, nodding slowly. 'Like *Tommy*,' I said.

'Tommy who?'

'No, *Tommy* by The Who.'

'The *what*?'

'It's a rock opera. About a deaf, dumb and blind kid, by The Who?'

'The *who*? I don't know what you're—'

274

'Are you trying to wind me up? Everyone has heard of The Who.'

'The . . .?'

'Jeff? Just be quiet.' We studied Gabriel some more. And then I said, 'You've really never heard of The Who? Or *Tommy*? It went double platinum in the States in 1969.'

'My *parents* weren't even born in 1969,' said Jeff.

'What were they, like twelve when they conceived you? On second thoughts, it doesn't matter. It doesn't matter how old you are, you should know of The Who.'

'Well, I don't. And also, you can't say that he's deaf, dumb and blind. I've done a course.'

'Okay, Jeff, whatever you say. I'm sure being politically correct will help us solve our case. Gabriel, you aren't deaf or dumb or blind, you're hearing impaired, vocally challenged and visually skew-whiff. Feel better now? Oh, I forgot, you're deaf, dumb and blind and you can't hear me, or see me or feel me.'

Gabriel did not react.

Jeff, on the other hand, cast a nervous glance towards the shutters. 'I don't know what we're even doing here. We've just heard about his escape on the radio and they've advised people to approach him with caution and I'm bloody locked in here with him. As soon as they know it's you, they'll be thinking of this place, and as soon as they spot the car round the corner, they'll know for sure and then they're going to come blasting their way in, shooting first and asking questions later. It'll be like Placido Domingo all over again.'

'Jean Charles de Menezes,' I corrected.

'That's who I meant. *Christ*.' He rubbed at his brow. 'You

see what you're doing to me? I'm losing it. I've hardly slept with all the revision, and that's what I should be doing, not being here with this . . . this *vegetable*.'

'This *vegetable*, Jeff, nearly throttled you.'

'What*ever*. I need to get going, Mum will be waiting for the car. She goes to St George's Market on Wednesday mornings. She likes to get there early. Really, seriously, I need to go. Why bring him here *at all*?'

'Because these,' and I waved my hand around the books, 'they inspire me. This is my nerve centre, Jeff. It's like Quantico. Quantico crossed with Fort Knox.'

'Is Quantico not like Poundstretcher?'

'No, Jeff. Quantico is the FBI Academy in Virginia. And relax, the police couldn't shoot their way in here with anything short of a heavy artillery: those shutters are reinforced steel.'

'You mean unless they cared to check under the bin for the back-door key?'

'You replaced it?'

'Yes, *of course*, as you're always telling me to.' He gave a long, low moan. 'I really have to go. I don't like this. I don't like it one bit.'

'Jeff, you're always complaining that I don't treat you like my partner, that I favour Alison when it comes to investigations. Well, this is your chance to contribute something.'

'I always contrib—'

'Something *meaningful*.'

'I came to the hospital, I—'

'I know, and that was great. But this, this is the real meat and potatoes. Crack this and we crack the case. Okay? Never worry about your mum's car, it's safe, it's fine, and I knew this would take a bit of time so I put an extra couple of quid on the pay and display. So relax. The police are not that smart. They are not going to find their way here that quickly. And I just need a bit of time on this, with you, and then we can announce to the world that he is innocent and you will be carried shoulder-high through the streets by Amnesty International's top worriers. Stick with me, Jeff, and share the glory.'

He made a face. 'It's just my mum . . .'

'I'm sure your mum can make her own way to market. Okay? Are you with me on this?'

He looked genuinely pained. Maybe the stress of his exams really was getting to him. Or he was an utter wimp. 'Yes . . . *mostly.*'

'And tell you what, I will personally coach you through whatever revision you need to do. You know how smart I am, Jeff, I'm borderline genius. By the time I'm through with you, your exams will be a walkover.'

'Really? Seriously? You would do that?'

'Absolutely. You have my word.'

'You've promised me things before and you always manage to wriggle out.'

'Jeff – look at me. I'm a changed man. I'm off all those bloody pills and potions. You can see I'm different; all I'm asking you to do is trust me on this.'

He ummed and aahed a bit more, and I gave him the encouragement of raised eyebrows and eventually he succumbed and promised to stay with me while we took on the enigmatic stranger now sitting on a bar stool on the customer side of the counter. Alison had brought it into the store while she was pregnant and due to be working the till, saying she didn't want to get varicose veins by standing about all day. I suspected that it had as much to do with her being lazy.

Apart from when he was involved in a life or death struggle with Francis Delaney or was trying to strangle Jeff, Gabriel seemed like a gentle soul. I was convinced by his violent reaction to Jeff's knee squeezing that the solution, the fix, lay very close to the surface with him and that the key to it was still the music he'd been playing relentlessly in Purdysburn. If there'd been a keyboard in the shop he would have been playing it, but as there was not, I half-expected him to be picking out imaginary notes on the counter but his hands were resting palm down on his legs, without a hint of movement. The only sounds came from my pacemaker and the growing rumble outside as rush hour approached. In amongst the snorts and coughs of the traffic, I detected a distant Fire Brigade siren. I turned to Jeff.

'You heard the music at the hospital when you came to visit. Did it ring any bells?'

'The piano stuff? I thought that was just like Muzak, piped in.'

'No, it was Gabriel. All day, and all night.'

'I remember it being really annoying. And . . .' His brow furrowed; he waved a finger in the air as if he was conducting an orchestra. 'It was kind of familiar. I remember thinking, What is that? It reminded me of something. Yes, it did.'

'Of *what*?'

'I don't know. That's the thing, it's one of those really annoying tunes you can't remember. It was . . .' He clicked his fingers. 'Hum it for me.'

I made a couple of false starts before I got to my best approximation of it. As I did, I studied Gabriel for some reaction, but there was none, just that same vacant look. In *Tommy*, Tommy was rendered *dd* and *b* because as a child he discovered his mother having passionate sex with a stranger, which he mistook for her being attacked. Given what I now knew of the intimacies of sexual congress, what with the fitting in of various parts to various holes, I understood how that would have been incredibly traumatic for any child. It was a situation I could well relate to, having once discovered my mother *in flagrante delicto* with two sailors and a dwarf; but I was clearly made of sterner stuff and it hadn't affected me at all. If Gabriel had indeed been traumatised, I was thinking that it must have something to do with the murder of Fat Sam.

As I hummed his theme tune, Jeff wagged his finger in time and said, 'I do know it, I do, but I just can't get it.'

'*Think*, Jeff.'

'Your telling me to think doesn't help. It's like when I lose the shop keys, you always say. "Well, where did you leave them?" It's no help at all. Just . . . hum it. Hum it again.'

I hummed, and I hummed, and Jeff began to hum along with me and we were just reaching a harmonious climax when there was a hammering on the shutters outside and we both let out a shout of fear. I was halfway to the rear exit, leaving Jeff in my wake and Gabriel in his daze before I recognised a distant, shrill voice demanding to be let in and I knew that we had been rumbled by Alison.

*   *   *

I said, through the shutter, 'Not today, thanks,' and Alison said something that included an expletive, so I told her to go round the back and a few moments later Jeff sheepishly unlocked the door and ushered her in before quickly securing it again.

Alison came down the shop, with her eyes fixed the whole way on Gabriel, nodding to herself and going *uh-huh, uh-huh, uh-huh* and then stopping in front of him and looking into his face and giving a last *uh-huh* before finally looking at me and snapping out, 'Do you mind telling me what the bloody hell you think you're playing at?' So I told her and she said, 'Bloody hell, you half-wit, you know everyone and their police dog is out looking for him – and you, for that matter? And it's only a matter of time before they search here?'

'I thought the shutters being closed might throw them off the trail,' I said.

'Sure, Mystery Man, for about twenty minutes. What were you *thinking* of? And why didn't you call me instead of *that* lummox?'

'I think we both know the answer to that.'

'Jesus, get over yourself. You're my partner and the father of my child, I'm not going to turn you in.'

'You had me committed, Alison.'

'I had to, and I was just getting round to thinking that you were much improved. Now I'm not so sure. I can't believe you called this *idiot* instead!'

She nodded at Jeff, who gave her a helpless gesture in return.

'He was the only idiot I thought would come and get me at that time of the morning,' I said.

'And I did,' said Jeff. 'But listen, I'm sure you two have

plenty to talk about, and I have revision to do.' He made a move for his keys, which were sitting on the counter, but I scooped them up first and held them at arm's length.

'Hold on to your horses,' I said. 'We're not done here.' I indicated Gabriel.

Jeff sighed and said, 'We're getting nowhere. Humming is getting us nowhere.'

'Humming?' Alison asked.

Pretty soon our little gathering, comprising one murder suspect and three-quarters of a barbershop quartet, was humming the theme from Gabriel, but getting no closer to identifying it. Alison said she recognised the melody, but couldn't place it. Jeff invited her to join the club.

'It's like from a TV advert or something?' she suggested.

'Exactly,' said Jeff. 'And yet . . . not. It's on the tip of my tongue.'

'It's *really* annoying,' said Alison. She moved closer to the unblinking Gabriel. 'Look at him, he doesn't look like he'd harm a fly.' She reached out to touch him.

Both Jeff and I made a grab for her arm.

Jeff got there first, because he has the reactions of a human.

I said, 'Don't do that. He has a tendency to overreact.'

'He nearly killed me,' said Jeff, 'yet I'm shouted down if I dare suggest he might still be capable of murder.'

'I didn't shout,' I said. 'I used reason and logic.'

'Look at my throat,' said Jeff. 'It's going the colour of my eye.'

Alison said, 'Well, at least the jury is still out on *him*, because it won't be out for long when they try you two for helping him escape.'

'I was only following orders,' said Jeff.

Alison gave him an exasperated look, before transferring it to me. 'You didn't call me.'

'Because I knew you would hear about the escape on the news, and you'd guess we'd be here. I didn't want there to be any record of me calling you because you are, as you so rightly point out, the mother of a child.'

'*Your* child,' she said, poking me, 'and *your* partner.'

'If you say so.' I took hold of her hand and cupped it in mine. 'I just wanted to keep you out of trouble, okay?'

'What about *me*?' Jeff asked.

'What about you?' Alison and I said at the same time.

We smiled at each other. It was good to be in a loving relationship. I put my arm round her and gave her a squeeze. Together we scowled at Jeff for a bit. Eventually she smiled up at me. 'I'm just glad you're safe. DI Robinson was convinced you'd end up in a skip with your guts hanging out. He said you were easily led, and I have to agree.'

I unhooked my arm. It was good while it lasted.

'I – he – when were you speaking to him?'

'About half an hour ago. Darling, I didn't know you were on the news. I'm too knackered being up all hours with Page to be bothered with the TV or radio. I found out because DI Robinson banged on our door at seven this morning looking for you and Laughing Boy here.' She poked a finger at Gabriel. 'And he didn't believe me when I said I knew nothing about it. It took me ages to get rid of him. He checked the whole house out. He woke Page and your mum, and they both screamed blue murder. He said if I heard from you, you were to turn Gabriel in, though he didn't call him Gabriel.

He said Gabriel was a nut who would chop anyone up who crossed him. He said he knew you were up to your neck in this, but this time it had gone too far. He said interfering and meddling is one thing . . .'

'Two, technically,' I said.

'. . . but a psychopath on the run from a mental hospital is another thing entirely. And I'm not convinced he wasn't talking about you.' I made a face. She made it back. 'When I left the house, he followed me.'

'Here?'

'Do I *look* that stupid?'

'The jury's still . . .' Jeff began, but then stopped when Alison looked at him.

'I gave him the slip. It was easy enough. He got caught at the lights, we turned the corner. I jumped out and hid behind a car, he came round the corner and cruised right on after the Mystery Machine.'

She looked pleased with herself. Jeff and I looked at each other, confused.

To make it clearer, I said, 'I'm confused. Who exactly was driving if you got out?'

'Who do you think? Your mother.'

'No, I mean, seriously. Who was driving?'

'I *am* serious. She takes Page out for a spin once in a while to help get him to sleep.'

I stared at her. 'What . . . what the fuh . . . no, I mean, really. Really who—'

'Your mother! She's fine! And leading Robinson on a wild-goose chase as we speak.'

'Alison,' I said, *'please* tell me you're joking. Mother has not had control of a vehicle since she drove a tank during the Prague Spring. And also she has recently had a stroke. Tell me you didn't leave her behind the wheel of the Mystery Machine with my son and heir on board at the same time.'

'Yes, I did, and she's perfectly fine.'

'Jesus! What is happening to the world? Did someone turn it upside down?'

'That's what I was thinking,' said Jeff.

'Your mother is a new, new woman these last few days. Friendly, charming, and desperate to help out. It's a pleasure having her around.'

'Have you taken leave of your senses?! She's a fucking monster!'

'*No.*' She looked stern now – *hard*, even. 'What *has* become clear is that there was another monster in the house all along. But you're getting better now.'

'That – that – that – that – is just *ridiculous*. I love my mother, but she has *bewitched* you.'

She glared, and I glared back.

'Well,' she said eventually, 'time will tell, won't it? Now do you want to know what I managed to find out about the case, while *you* were busy escaping, and *you* were busy aiding and abetting, and why I haven't called the police myself to let them know where you are?'

36

First, there was coffee from Starbucks to be had. We sent Jeff, on the grounds that if DI Robinson spotted him he would dismiss him as being unimportant, irrelevant and an idiot, or for shorthand purposes, a poet. While he was gone I said, 'You seemed pretty certain I'd be here.'

'Where else would you go?'

'The shutters down didn't fool you?'

'Nope. And leaving a light on upstairs, when I knew I'd switched everything off didn't help your cause much either. Actually, I thought you'd already been caught. I was walking up Botanic and there were police cars and the Fire Brigade and I expected to find you under siege, but it was just some old car burning on that wasteground round the corner.' She shook her head and clutched my hand and said, 'What am I going to do with you?'

I said, 'More to the point, what are we going to do with *him*?'

Alison regarded Gabriel and laughed. 'God, we'd be better off opening up the shop and putting him behind the till. He'd talk to the customers more than you do.'

'That's not fair,' I said.

'It's fair and it's accurate.' She raised an eyebrow. 'Do you want to hear what happened, or do you want to wait till Igor gets back?'

'Wait,' I said. 'His input is occasionally useful.'

She raised the other eyebrow. She was talented like that. Jeff returned fairly quickly. We gathered anew around the counter. I sipped at my Caramel Macchiato while they drank filter Americano. He had bought a salmon bagel for Gabriel. He handed it to me and I handed it to Alison and she very, very carefully pressed it into his hand and curled his fingers around it. When he didn't immediately raise it to his mouth, she gingerly lifted his hand and brushed his lips with the edge of the bread, but he didn't open up or otherwise react. She set his hand back on his leg, still clutching the bagel.

'You can lead a horse to water,' she said.

'Or a whore to culture,' I added.

She studied me and then decided not to make an issue of it.

'What did I miss?' Jeff asked.

'Nothing,' I said. 'We were waiting for you.'

Jeff beamed. Alison snorted.

'Well,' she said, 'if you're all sitting comfortably? If I remember correctly, your instructions to me were to follow Nicola, the woman in the green hat and coat. You said, "Go get her", which I interpreted as "Find out who she is and what she's managed to get out of Gabriel", and then report back to you.'

'The problem was our lack of access,' said Jeff, 'so is it not pretty irrelevant now he's here?'

'No, as it turns out,' said Alison. 'Listen – her full name is Nicola Sheridan, she is a history teacher at Methody . . .'

'Methodist College,' I said.

'Do you mind? She is a history teacher at *Methody* – in fact, she runs the history department. I didn't quite manage to talk to her as she left the hospital, but I was able to follow her. She has a house on the Castlereagh Road, a big detached place, a bit ramshackle. I gave her ten minutes to get in and settled, and then I knocked on the door. Remember how she was dressed, like a Sunday School teacher? And you said she was a do-gooding cow? Well, by the time she answered the door – what a transformation. Hair all down and straggly, designer jeans, cigarette in one hand and heavy metal blasting out of the front room. Before I could say anything she apologised and went to turn it down. She came back out and I showed her your card . . .'

'*My* card?'

'Well, I have no other. And I said I was a private investigator and that I understood that she was a regular visitor to Purdysburn Hospital, delivering much-needed pastoral care to the patients there. I said I was working on behalf of one patient in particular, in the secure wing, the unidentified man in the white suit, and would she mind answering some questions about him, and she invited me in and sat me down in the lounge and offered me a cup of tea and I said, "Yes, black with two sugars".'

'Great detail,' I said.

Alison made a sarcastic face, and said, 'I followed her into the kitchen, dishes everywhere. She put the kettle on and studied your card and read out the Murder is Our Business bit and seemed impressed by that but said she wasn't sure how she could help me or even if she was allowed to, but that anyway The Man in the White Suit never said anything and all she did with him was recite a few verses from the good book and say a prayer – so how could that be of any use to us? I asked if he *never* said anything and she said, "No, he just sits there and I pray for him," and I said, "You must have the patience of a saint and a heart of gold, to go in there with all those dangerous men," and she said she felt it was her calling, and I asked if she'd been doing it long and she said about six months, and I asked how she got into it in the first place and she said her husband had died quite recently and that left a big hole in her life and she was really just looking for something challenging, and rewarding, and then she looked at the card again and said she'd heard of No Alibis before, wasn't it a bookshop and she saw the address and said, "Yes. No Alibis, I've been past it a few times and always meant to call in," and I said, "Yes, everyone says that but they never do, that's why the business is in crisis".'

'Did you really need to tell her that?'

'I was ingratiating myself,' said Alison.

'By doing me down?'

'I wasn't doing you down, I was getting her onside because I didn't know if you were going to get access and she might have been our only means of getting to him, and this all happened while the kettle was boiling, so she made the tea and put it on a tray with Jaffa Cakes and carried it into the lounge, and I got the impression that she was keen to talk. I asked her how long she'd been at Methody and she said too long and laughed, and that's when she said she taught history and that she loved it, and I asked about her husband and what happened and she said they'd only been married five years but he had died suddenly but that it was God's will. I remarked on the heavy metal blasting out and she said it was Christian rock and that it did her head good and I said I was more into hip-hop and she made a face and we laughed, but really, I wasn't laughing because you know something?'

'Lots,' I said.

'It wasn't Christian rock. I grew up with heavy metal. My sister . . .'

'You have a sister?' Jeff asked.

'*Yes*. My sister . . .'

'Is she single?' Jeff asked.

'As far as you're concerned, no. My sister was – *is* – a heavy metal nut. I hate it, but at the same time I know an awful lot about it, I couldn't help it. Nicola Sheridan wasn't playing Christian rock, she was playing "Children of the Grave" by Black Sabbath.'

'Maybe she played it by mistake,' I suggested.

'*Nobody* plays Black Sabbath by mistake.'

'Okay, so she likes Black Sabbath. Your point?'

'It just . . . *jarred*. And then she kind of turned it around and started asking all these questions about our business and how we got involved in the case and who was actually employing us, seeing as how The Man in the White Suit wasn't saying anything, and part of me was thinking, She's just bored and a bit nosy, but there was a bit of me also thinking, She's a little too inquisitive – and doesn't she protest too much about being in the God squad and . . .'

'. . . maybe you're making a mountain out of . . .'

'And then I saw it.'

'Saw what?'

'Nicola was resting her cup on the arm of her chair and she knocked it over – I don't know, nerves, just an accident – but anyway, it was all over her jeans and she said they were new and she ran to the kitchen to sponge them before they got stained and I got up and had a look around. It's one of those houses where there's loads of framed photos on the wall and on every available surface, and there were lots of her and her husband Bobby at weddings and baptisms and on holiday all over the place. And then I was looking at one of their own wedding day and I was thinking how happy they looked and how awful it must be to lose a loved one and how wonderful it must be to have a wedding day, and I lifted it to get a better look at her dress and there was another photo right behind it, not hidden exactly, just blocked by the one I was holding and I just kind of half-noticed it at first, but then my eyes were drawn back to it, I don't know why, *intuition* maybe, but whatever it was I bent a little closer and I saw it was Nicola and Bobby raising their glasses at some dinner-party, but it wasn't them so much as who they were with.'

She looked at me and smiled and said, 'They were raising a glass and all chummy and smiles with Fergus O'Dromodery,

Bernard O'Dromodery and Sean O'Dromodery – in short, the Brothers Karamazov.'

I let it sit for several long moments. Then I said, 'And you gave her *my* business card?'

37

'Well,' Alison was saying, 'I couldn't get out of there quick enough. It gave me the heeby jeebies.'

'Why?' Jeff asked. 'One photo doesn't mean anything. I have a photo of myself with Seamus Heaney – it doesn't mean that I was somehow involved in his murder.'

'Has Seamus Heaney been *murdered*? When I was in hosp—?'

'No, Jesus! Famous Seamus is alive and kicking,' said Alison. 'And I'm not saying she's a murderer, I'm just saying I thought it was a wild coincidence, enough to make me go hunting for more info as soon as I got home, or as soon as I got home and fed Page and made supper for your mother and put the wash on and hoovered three carpets and washed two floors and took the wash out and tumble-dried what wasn't going to shrink and hung the rest on the radiators, which I had to bleed because they're so old and decrepit and then I had to iron what was tumbled and get your mum to bed and take her up her sherry and then put Page to bed and catch up on *EastEnders* because I have to have a little me time, but eventually I got round to searching for more info on her and her husband – and what did I discover?'

'I don't know,' I said, 'but I'm beginning to feel redundant.'

'I discovered that she didn't take her husband's name when she got married.'

'So? Why's that relevant?'

'Because it slowed down the search for him.'

'And why wouldn't she change her name?' Jeff asked.

'Because you spend half your life building a reputation based on your own name, then you get married and you have to start all over again.'

'Sounds like as good a reason as any not to get . . .' I started to say.

'Park it. What I *then* discovered on a building-trade website was a photograph of the O'Dromodery Brothers with the husband, full name Robert Preston. They were celebrating breaking ground at the site of their new shopping centre in West Belfast. He was the architect. The Preston Practice. He wasn't an employee, but judging from the website, which is still up, most of his work came through the O'Dromoderys.'

'Okay,' I said. 'Is that it?'

'Is it not plenty for half an hour's work with someone attached to my left nipple and biting hard the whole time?'

'I hope you're talking about Page.'

'No,' said Alison, 'I'm talking about DI Robinson.'

That was cruel. She knew how I felt about DI Robinson and the attentions he paid to her. I think she realised that. She punched me playfully in the arm. And then she laughed.

'There's no need to laugh,' I said.

'Yes, there is,' she said. 'In the old days, if I'd punched you in the arm you would have cried like a baby. But you just stood there and took it like a man.'

'The implication being that I wasn't a man before.'

'You have an amazing ability to suck the goodness out of any compliment, Mystery Man. I wonder, though, if the new you now has the ability to give a few compliments of your own, for example, for what I've just found out.'

'Well done,' I said.

'Once more,' said Alison, 'with feeling.'

'*Really* well done,' I said.

She sighed. 'Well, we can work on that. But seriously, Robert Preston.'

'I have him,' said Jeff.

We turned to discover that while we were bantering, Jeff had moved to the computer and typed in the late architect's name. Google had brought up a series of headlines from local newspapers about the hit and run death of what they all described as one of Northern Ireland's leading architects. He clicked on one page and we read over his shoulder an article from the *Irish News* which gave a few scant details of the incident and showed a small photograph of the man. He had been knocked down while out jogging half a mile from his home eight months previously. Police had appealed for witnesses.

I drummed my fingers on the counter.

Jeff said, 'The bodies are piling up.'

He wasn't wrong. Alison counted them off. 'In chronological order – Robert Preston, Fergus O'Dromodery, Fat Sam Mahood,

Francis Delaney and, most recently, Bernard O'Dromodery. Having anything to do with the Karamazovs, including being one of them, would seem to be extremely bad for your health.'

'There's nothing to say Robert Preston was murdered,' said Jeff. 'Hit and runs happen all the time.'

'It's too big a coincidence,' said Alison. She looked at me. 'Why so quiet?'

'Just marvelling at how my young apprentices have come on. Okay – there's definitely two camps here. Fergus and Bernard and Fat Sam, all with *defixios*, and then Francis Delaney and Bobby Preston without.'

'We don't know there isn't one for Preston,' said Alison.

'The pattern is that they're buried close to home or a place of work or, in Fat Sam's case, somewhere he was known to be a regular visitor. Delaney died in a brawl in Purdysburn, and I pretty much know it wasn't Gabriel who killed him.'

'How?'

'I just do. It wasn't premeditated, hence no *defixio*. And if you're going to deliberately run someone down in a car, you can't predict in advance exactly where they're going to be, or when they're going to step off the footpath or cross at a junction.' I avoided eye-contact with Alison while I said this. She didn't need to know that I had made several attempts on her life. 'If you were being true to your operating ethos you'd have to bury dozens of *defixios* to make sure they were in the right place at the right time. So two camps.'

'But connected.'

'Yes. Definitely. Somehow. So that brings us back to Nicola

Sheridan. Do-gooding Christian with a penchant for Satanic rock, who just happens to become a hospital visitor where Gabriel is being held *or* she's gone all Miss Marple on us.'

'Would that be a reference to the Miss Marple who first appeared in *The Murder in the Vicarage* in 1930?' Alison asked.

I beamed at her. She beamed back.

'You're coming along very well, my young Padawan,' I said, 'although it was actually in a short story four years earlier. But full marks.'

We were quite a team. I'd always said it.

'But what I'm saying basically,' said Alison, 'is that Nicola believes her husband was murdered, and because the police think it's just a normal hit and run, she has set about trying to track down the culprit herself.'

'Is that not a bit . . . far-fetched?' Jeff asked. 'You said she'd been visiting Gabriel for how long?'

I looked at Gabriel. 'Six months, was it?'

He did not respond.

'About that, yes,' I said.

'You really think she's going to pretend to be someone else, and visit that hospital – what, every week?' Jeff asked. 'Just on the off-chance that a deaf mute with a penchant for violence might either confess to her husband's murder or lead her to who really did it?'

'I can't believe you said *penchant*,' said Alison. 'And it's not *that* far-fetched. If you lost someone you loved, you'd clutch at whatever straws there were. In fact, if someone killed *you*,' and she pointed at me, 'I wouldn't rest until I'd tracked them down and exposed them and they were brought to justice, and then I'd write a book about it and sell the movie rights and retire to a life of leisure with someone new and less annoying.'

'I'm still available,' said Jeff.

'*Less* annoying, I said.'

I rubbed at my chin. Gabriel was still just staring into space. Alison and Jeff, on the other hand, were both looking at me, *to* me, their leader, to show them the way forward.

'Okay,' I said. 'We're stuck on the music. Sean O'Dromodery is shacked up with bodyguards and Martin Brady is staying behind closed doors, so they're both off-limits. We've spoken to the current staff at the All Star and been stonewalled there, we've spoken to the ex-staff and learned nothing relevant. We've interviewed Gloria Mahood and we briefly suspected her, but based on nothing really. At the moment, the only connection we have between Gabriel and Fat Sam is some CCTV footage which is circumstantial at best. If the O'Dromoderys sent Francis Delaney in to get at Gabriel, then we have to presume that Nicola Sheridan isn't working for them, but independently. They may be after the same thing, they may not. But if she has been going in to see him for the past few months, then we also have to presume that she thinks she's getting somewhere and will undoubtedly be feeling thwarted by Gabriel's escape. So what we're going to do is take Gabriel to see her, and between us all we're going to find out what they know about who did what to who.'

'*Whom*,' said Jeff.

'And I need you to look after the shop,' said I.

*   *   *

The surprising thing was that Jeff did not protest. I think perhaps that being half-strangled had made him realise that we were dealing with real danger. We had shared many previous adventures together, but he had never really been exposed to violence before. He was a sensitive guy. He had the soul, if not the talent, of a poet.

'Sure,' he said, 'I'll open up the shop. It'll give me the chance to get some more revision done.'

I did not rise to his bait.

'Thanks,' I said. 'I appreciate it.' His eyes narrowed, searching for a sarcasm that was not there. I turned to Alison and said, 'We're going to need the Mystery Machine.'

She produced her mobile phone. 'On it,' she said.

I nodded at Gabriel and said, 'This would all be a lot easier if you talked to us.' He did not look at me or otherwise respond.

Alison came off the phone, grinning. 'Your mother,' she said, 'takes me to the fair. She led DI Thompson on a wild-goose chase, and then parked on Bedford Street. She put a three-hour pay and display ticket on the window and then walked off with Page; she waited round the corner and watched as Thompson checked the time on it, and evidently decided he had better things to do for three hours and disappeared, at which point she got back in the machine. She'll be here in a minute.'

And she was. She arrived at the back door and I ignored her in favour of taking Page out of her arms to check for signs of abuse. When nothing was immediately apparent I held him up in the air and shook him gently and saw him smile and my heart pounded and I purred, 'And how are you, little man?'

And Mother snapped, 'He's four months old, he doesn't fucking talk yet.'

38

Alison came back down the driveway to my window and said, 'Well, she's a bit shocked and stunned, but she says to come on in and bring him with you.'

I looked up at the house. Nicola Sheridan stood in the doorway, in black jeans that were slightly too tight for her frame and a voluminous black T-shirt; her hair was indeed frizzy. Satanic rock was not blasting out. I had told Alison not to reveal anything other than the fact that we had Gabriel with us. I wanted to see the look on her face when I told her we'd rumbled her.

'Okay,' I said, 'I'll coax him out, but you keep an eye on her, make sure she doesn't try to phone anyone. I don't want Robinson scooting up here and surrounding us.'

As Alison returned to the house I slid open the back of the Mystery Machine. Gabriel was buckled into a fold-down seat, and surrounded by boxes of books which Jeff had not yet found the time to move to the shop and unpack, what with his revision, and exams, and poetry and an endless quest to save the world one political prisoner at a time.

I said, 'All right, fella? Just taking you to meet an old friend.'

I waited for what little traffic there was to pass before releasing his belt and guiding him down the step. I kept a hand on his arm as I walked him up the drive. As we approached the door Nicola beamed at him and said what a turn-up for the books this was and how she'd heard all about it on the news and she was really worried about him and she almost, almost put a hand to his face, but held back, and I wondered if he'd had a go at her at some point as well.

As we moved past her into the lounge Gabriel's eyes did not meet Nicola's or otherwise appear to take in his new surroundings. The lounge was as cluttered with photographs as Alison had described; there was a sofa and two armchairs – the design was a mock-Chippendale I knew from Mother's own poor taste in furniture. I stood Gabriel by one of the armchairs, and when he showed no inclination to sit, I gently lowered him into it. Nicola hovered over him for a moment and said, 'Poor wee soul,' and then asked if we wanted shortbread, she'd only made it that morning. I said no, and Alison said yes, and when Nicola went into the kitchen to get it I told Alison to go with her to make sure she didn't call anyone, and Alison hissed that I'd already told her that and she wasn't a child who needed constant reminding and I said I knew that.

There was small talk from the kitchen. I already knew Nicola to be an actress, but now I knew she was a liar as well. She had not made shortbread that morning; if she had, there would have been residual smells. I detected neither butter nor flour nor caster sugar, nor even just the oven smell. I am an expert on shortbread and have studied it, and made it, and promoted it. Shortbread was chosen as the United Kingdom's representative at Café Europe during the Austrian presidency of the European Union in 2006. I could have told Nicola Sheridan this but chose not to in case she thought I was weird. She would have been wrong. It is good to have a broad base of general knowledge. *Weird* would be to have only known about crime fiction and badgers.

While I waited for the shortbread and tea to appear I perused the many photographs on display and soon found the dinner-party shot that had so heebie-jeebied Alison. I noted that it showed a Nicola Sheridan who was at least two stones lighter and perhaps ten years younger. She was the only woman present. There was no Martin Brady and I supposed that it pre-dated him. Bernard O'Dromodery was the only brother who had married, and I wondered if in fact they were all gay; it was not uncommon for siblings to share traits and preferences, although they could, equally, go the other, opposite way, like my brother Mycroft. We had been shown directly into the lounge when we'd arrived; now I saw across the hall a room with crowded bookshelves and one leg of a piano. I presumed there were three other legs and that the rest was hidden by the half-open door.

I sat in the other armchair as Nicola came in with a pot of tea and three cups and saucers on a tray and Alison followed with a matching plate of shortbread. I could tell at a glance that they were Marks & Spencer All Butter Shortbread Fingers which currently retailed at £2.08 for a

210-gram packet. I also kept this information to myself. I said no to the tea and the shortbread. Nicola offered me Coke or Fanta or a glass of milk and I said no. I was gloriously caffeine-free and Alison helpfully pointed out that I was lactose intolerant, although I was no longer sure that I was. Gabriel was offered tea and shortbread, but did not respond.

Nicola sighed and said, 'Same as he ever was. I don't know how he keeps the weight on him – he never seems to eat.'

'They coach him through it in the hospital,' I said. 'Eventually he takes something.'

Nicola said, 'So, you're from No Alibis. I was telling your wife I've been past the shop and always meant to call in.'

'She's not my wife,' I said.

'Yes,' said Alison.

I said, 'Thank you for the tea and homemade shortbread, and for agreeing to see us and . . .' And I indicated Gabriel.

'We call him Gabriel,' said Alison.

'Gabriel,' Nicola repeated. 'One of God's angels.'

'Archangels,' I said.

'Yes, of course.'

'Do you mind me asking, have you had much success converting patients – you know, to God?'

'No, I don't mind, and no, I haven't. It's not about converting, it's about giving them a little peace of mind.'

I said, 'Can you recite the Ten Commandments?'

'The . . .?'

'Or indeed give me the names of the Twelve Disciples?'

'I . . .'

She looked to Alison for guidance, which was not

forthcoming. Alison was sitting back and looked quite content to allow me free rein.

'Thaddeus,' I said. 'Thaddeus is the one everyone always forgets, mostly because he didn't have any lines. If the New Testament was a movie, they'd be arguing over whether he was an actor or an extra. It makes a big difference in what they get paid.'

Nicola said, 'I'm sorry, I don't follow. Thaddeus?'

'He'll get there,' said Alison. 'Eventually.'

I nodded my appreciation of her and returned my attentions to Nicola.

I said, 'We know who you really are and what you're up to.'

'You . . .?'

'You are Bobby Preston's widow, and you have been masquerading as a hospital visitor in order to get close to Gabriel.'

'I . . .'

'You believe that he holds the key to the murder of your husband. I don't know why you think your husband was murdered, but clearly you and the police do not agree. It also seems to me that the O'Dromodery Brothers, who provided the bulk of your husband's income, also believe or believed that Gabriel could reveal who was responsible for your husband's murder, and progressively that of Fergus and Bernard O'Dromodery, but had been approaching it in a much more rigorous manner i.e. by employing Francis Delaney to enter Purdysburn masquerading as a mentally ill patient to force the issue with Gabriel. Now, am I right or am I right?'

She had stopped sipping her tea and set it down, chinking the cup off the saucer and spilling a little as she did. There were shortbread crumbs at the corners of her mouth. She said, 'My God,' and I did not deny it.

Alison said, 'We're not here to get you into trouble. If anything, we're here to help.'

Tears began to roll down Nicola's cheeks. She wiped at them. 'I wasn't trying to . . . I mean, I was . . .' Her hand moved to the side of the armchair cushion and delved down and she produced a rolled-up tissue and dabbed at her face. 'Honestly – this is such a *relief*. I felt terrible pretending to be someone I wasn't, but it was the only way I could think of. Everywhere I tried, they didn't want to know. I knew Bobby was murdered – I knew, I knew, I *knew* – but I couldn't prove anything. The police listened to me, they took statements from me, but they were just being kind; they've done nothing. I went to the O'Dromoderys and they were the same.'

'Even after Fergus supposedly committed suicide?'

'Yes! That's when I decided I had to do something myself. But I'm hopeless at it. I keep at it, just in case there's some tiny little thing he comes out with.' She gazed red-eyed across at Gabriel. 'The funny thing is, I went in there hating him, but he's grown on me.' She gave a sad kind of a smile. 'What more could a girl want, but a beautiful man who says nothing?'

'Perfect,' said Alison.

I ignored them and said, 'And now that you've studied him, do you *still* think he was involved in your husband's murder?'

'I don't know. Not directly, maybe, but somehow he's part of a bigger picture – he *has* to be. Look at him. What do they say – never judge a book by its cover? You'd know all about that. He seems so innocent and he does what he's told and there's no fuss and there's nothing but that music he keeps bashing out, and a huge part of me wants to believe he's innocent, but . . .' She gestured helplessly.

'Has he said *anything* at all?' I asked. She shook her head. 'Has he even reacted to anything, apart from when Francis Delaney tried to kill him?'

'No, and I can't even vouch for that. I was just told there was a struggle – but no, the only thing he ever did was sneeze once and I said, "Bless you" and for a moment, a fraction of a moment, I thought he was about to thank me, there was something in his eyes, but just as quickly it went away and there was just that terrible blankness again.'

'Okay,' I said, 'but why would you lie about the shortbread?'

'Excuse me?'

'Your shortbread, you said it was freshly baked. It wasn't, it's from Marks & Spencer.'

'I . . . just . . . what are you trying to say?'

'I just want to know that you're telling me the truth.'

'Forgive him,' said Alison, 'he doesn't get out much. Listen, Mystery Man, we *all* lie about the shortbread. That home-made lasagne you like so much? Homemade by Mr Tesco.'

'But then what are you doing in the kitchen all that time?'

'Drinking,' said Alison, 'and laughing. Now can we get on with this? Page will be wanting fed.'

I studied her. 'Do you *actually* breastfeed him?' I asked. Alison winked.

'Okay,' I said, 'to get back to business – forget the short-bread and the masquerading, and for the moment ignore the *why* – tell me *how* you think your husband was murdered?'

'*How*? Well, he ran the same route every morning, really early, and he said that the only thing that ever passed him was a milk-float. He didn't run that fast. The route was completely circular, just behind here; it's a big block of new apartments with two entrances, one on each side, and those are the only breaks in the path, and he wasn't knocked down anywhere near them. He had no reason whatsoever to step out onto the road, so whoever hit him would have had to deliberately mount the kerb and actually chase him onto the road and kill him.'

'Joy-riders lose control of their vehicles all the—'

'There were no cars reported stolen in Belfast either the night before or on that morning. I checked.'

'Okay, a drunk driver,' said Alison, 'maybe going home late. Your husband ran onto the road to try and avoid him, but too late . . .'

'There was glass on the road,' said Nicola. 'It came from the sidelight of a Porsche. The police had the evidence, they just wouldn't go and check it out.'

'I don't follow,' said Alison.

'Patience,' I said.

Nicola nodded her appreciation. She blew her nose into the tissue and then held it in her hands for a moment trying to decide where to put it before finally squashing it back down the side of the cushion. 'Yes, you see, I told the police everything I knew, that my Bobby had had a row in work with someone, and that he was really under pressure and felt like he was being watched, and I told them who he had a row with but they said they couldn't go accusing someone of *anything* without proper evidence and I said what about the glass from the Porsche and they said they'd look into it but I never heard another thing. They were just fobbing me off.'

'Who did he have a row with?' Alison asked.

'Fat Sam Mahood,' I said, 'and he drove a Porsche. It's still in Gloria's drive.'

Nicola nodded. 'My Bobby loved his work, he loved being his own boss and having all sorts of diverse clients, but when the recession bit, the work started to dry up and he ended up mostly working for the O'Dromoderys. He always said they were a bit creepy and stingy with the money, but it was steady work. I only met them once, some corporate dinner we had to attend a couple of years ago, and I didn't like them one bit. And that Sam Mahood even less. He was mean, and a bully, you could tell.'

'Do you know what they rowed about?'

'I really don't. I mean, he was working day and night on one project. They've been building a—'

'Shopping centre, West Belfast.'

'Yes, exactly, so I suppose it had something to do with that, but he never said what it was. I should have pressed him on it – it's the biggest regret of my life. I could see he was wound up but I just thought it was this bloody recession – everyone's on a short fuse, it would work itself out. I never for one moment thought it was that bad, but I suppose now that he kept the worst of it from me. And then that big bastard came to the house and they had their row . . .'

'This house, your house?'

'Yes! It happened a couple of nights before he was killed, and that's where I saw the Porsche, because I went outside to have a cigarette and tried to have a wee earwig at the window but I couldn't hear anything beyond raised voices because they were all smothered down by the double glazing.'

'But if you took the fact of the rows at work and then at home, and the police already had the glass from a Porsche, and Fat Sam Mahood was a well-known thug, surely they could make a connection?'

'Oh, I think they spoke to him – they knew him well enough – but he said they'd had a business discussion, that was all, and that the glass could have come from any Porsche. And because it was several weeks after the murder – well, if his car *was* damaged it was long since repaired and he wasn't likely to be caught with the paperwork to prove it. So he got off scot free.'

'Until you came along,' I said.

She began to nod, but then stopped and her eyes bore into me. 'What exactly are you suggesting?'

'Me?'

'Yes, you're insinuating . . .?'

'*Me*?'

'It's just the way of him,' said Alison. 'He has no people skills. He tries to sound normal, but it always sounds like he's making an accusation. Darling, it's almost as if you're accusing Nicola of murdering Fat Sam, or somehow orchestrating it.'

'No,' I said, 'I'm just drawing your attention to the confluence of circumstance.'

'Sorry – again, in English?' said Alison.

'Nicola here makes accusations about Fat Sam's involvement in her husband's murder, and shortly thereafter *he* is murdered. If you were that way minded, you could draw parallels and conclude that—'

'Oh pish and fish!' Nicola exploded. 'How could you even imagine I could be involved in . . . after my husband was killed!' The tears sprang again, and she jumped up and said, 'Sorry . . . sorry,' to Alison and disappeared into the kitchen.

'Excellent,' Alison hissed across. 'Well done.'

'I'm just trying to get a reaction,' I said. 'Everything is possible right now.'

'Oh, would you get a grip? She has the thighs of an elephant – can you even imagine her chasing Fat Sam around with a knife?'

'It wouldn't have to be her, acting alone. She could—'

'Can't you see she's distraught? Where's your compassion? Where's *your* intuition, Mystery Man? Did you leave it behind in Purdysburn?'

Alison jumped up and followed Nicola into the kitchen. In a few moments I heard soothing sounds, and more tears, and the kettle being refilled. I was pretty sure Alison wasn't serious. She was putting on an act for Nicola's benefit, getting to our shared goal by roundabout, or dare I say it, nefarious means. We were a good team.

I gave them a few minutes, and then I joined them. They were standing together, their backs to the sink, teacups clasped in their hands. As I entered, Nicola looked to the floor. Alison raised an eyebrow in my direction.

I said, 'I'm sorry, I didn't mean to upset you. When a

case is this complicated, sometimes you just have to throw things out there and see what sticks. I really don't think you killed Fat Sam. Or anyone else. And I admire your tenacity with Gabriel. He's hard work.' I turned to indicate him through the open door, which would have been fine if he'd still been sitting in the armchair. 'Gabriel?' I said, and stepped back into the empty lounge with Alison and Nicola right behind me.

'Where the—?' Alison began, but I held up a finger to shush her, so that we could better hear the familiar notes coming from Nicola's piano.

39

It was a much grander piano – without actually being a grand piano – than the one Gabriel had been playing in Purdysburn. This one had not been head-butted, covered in graffiti, vomited over and otherwise abused by mental patients, at least as far as I knew. It was polished and pristine and perfectly in tune.

'Do you play?' I asked.

'Not as well as him,' said Nicola.

As I have previously stated, he was not a great piano-player. He had long, thin fingers and fingernails long enough to turn my stomach.

'You don't happen to recognise the music?'

Nicola shook her head. 'Bobby was really the musical one,' she said.

'This is only the second time I've heard it,' said Alison, 'and the first time it was through a ceiling. I think I prefer it through a ceiling.'

311

I clicked my fingers and said, 'Phone.' Alison ignored me. I added, 'Please,' and she reluctantly handed it over.

'What're you up to?' she asked as I fiddled with it.

'Recording him, and then sending it to Jeff. He can e-mail it to my database, see if anyone recognises it.'

'You seem convinced that it's recognisable – what if he's just making it up?'

'It *sounds* like he's just making it up,' said Nicola.

'No,' I said. 'It's something already in existence.'

I was certain. As Gabriel played on I sent the recording to Jeff. It was only thirty seconds long, but enough, I thought. Within moments he texted back that he would do what he could, but he was revising. I texted back that it was a matter of life and death and he texted back *LOL:-)*.

Nicola said, 'What're we going to do now?'

'*We?*'

'We're in this together now, aren't we? Don't we have the same objectives? Come hell or high water, I am going to find out who murdered my husband, and as far as I can under-stand it, your main concern is to reveal this man's identity, and somehow through that, prove that he is innocent.'

'*Somehow*,' said Alison.

'But all I can really contribute to this is my relationship with Gabriel,' said Nicola. 'I'm not a professional detective like you.' Alison snorted. 'And apart from annoying the police, I've done nothing and don't really know what I *can* do except volunteer to look after Gabriel for you – to babysit him, if you will – and talk to him and see if I can get anything out of him. I think I have a connection with him. He seems more relaxed when he's with me. But I've only ever spent a maximum of about half an hour with him each time. I'm sure if I had longer, I could really get through to him.'

I studied Gabriel. My plan had been to observe him for an extended period, but I was already pretty convinced that there was little more I could ascertain by remaining in his company. It was seeming more and more likely that the music was the key to him, and we weren't going to crack that by merely listening to it; the annoyance factor alone was making it difficult to concentrate. Nicola was an amateur, for sure, but Gabriel was comfortable enough in her company, she had time on her hands, and her looking after him would allow me to pursue different avenues of investigation unencumbered by having to drag him around with me.

'Are you sure you're up for it?' I asked. 'In Purdysburn you were never more than a few feet away from security. Here, it'll just be you and him. I don't have to remind you that he's the chief suspect in two murders, although I just have.'

'Exactly,' said Alison. 'What if he turns on you? I don't like it. We have no proof that he's innocent. What if he's like – what do you call it? Like a . . . sleeper, is it?' She looked to me for guidance. I nodded. 'And he's just waiting for something to trigger him again. Maybe *he* was the one in the Porsche and, and . . . his mission isn't over yet. I mean, it'll just be you, and him.'

'It's a chance I'm prepared to take,' Nicola said firmly. 'For my Bobby.'

Alison put a hand on her arm and stroked it gently. 'Bobby is gone,' she said softly. 'You should be looking out for yourself.'

'No – don't you see? That's the point. He isn't gone. I *want* him to go – I *need* him to go. But I can't let him go until this is resolved. And I think this might just be the best way. Can we not be like a team – me with Gabriel and you two out there? We keep in touch, we compare what we find out and, you never know, we might just solve this together?'

'Absolutely,' I said, and asked for my business card back. Nicola asked why, but still handed it over. I gave her a replacement. 'This one includes Facebook and Twitter, you'll get me one way or another.'

Nicola grinned. She turned the card over in her fingers. 'This is great,' she said. 'We'll be just like The Three Musketeers.'

'Or Stooges,' said Alison.

'Tell you what,' Alison said, as we turned the corner in the Mystery Machine, 'she's game. There's no way I'd want to be left alone with a psycho like that.'

'I was once classified as a psycho like that,' I said.

Alison nodded. Then she said, 'You're much cuter.'

I tried not to glow too much, and instead concentrated on the traffic, and the radio news, which was telling us about an escaped lunatic and a civil war in the Middle East, in that order.

Alison said, 'So, what's the plan?'

'To do what I normally do.'

'Obsess, interfere and annoy?'

'Yes.'

'You didn't go for all that bull about us making a little team with her.'

'No, of course not.'

'You told her virtually nothing about our investigation. You did not mention the *defixios*.'

'Clearly.'

'Because although her heart might be in the right place, the less she knows, the less trouble she can get us in if she gets caught with Gabriel.'

'Something like that.'

'And also, you don't like to share the glory.'

'It's not the glory, it's the satisfaction.'

'And the glory. I should point out that you appear not to be driving me home to Page, who needs fed, or taking us to No Alibis, where Jeff needs supervision.'

'No,' I said. 'Detour.'

40

'Ah,' said Alison.

'Uhuh.'

We parked about thirty metres from the entrance to the site of the WestBel shopping centre, on the opposite side of the road. It was, as its name suggests, in West Belfast. It was not a part of the world I had ever had a fondness for. Too much history, too much violence, too much poverty, too many nuns. I became aware that I had said that out loud when Alison asked what on earth I had against nuns and I said, 'Mother always believed they hid guns in their habits.'

Alison shook her head.

Across the road, there were two security guards at the entrance to the building site. What we believed to be the shopping centre was hidden behind a wooden fence. We sat for about twenty minutes. There were lorries coming in and out of the site, and schoolgirls from St Mary's next door moving back and forth during their lunch-hour. The lorries entering

316

were stopped by the security guards so that their bona fides could be examined; the girls weren't stopped, but their bona fides were also studied.

Alison said, 'It's just a building site, and I've a child to be fed.'

'But it's all about the building site. It has to be.'

'Okay, never mind our child.'

'There are pretty hard and fast rules when it comes to the planning of and building of shopping centres. It's being built on land that was surplus to the school and sold off for profit. There were some protests about that. There was an initial refusal of planning permission, though mostly because of access problems. There was a Planning Appeal, which came down in favour of the Karamazovs, and full permission was granted eight months ago. That's all pretty standard.'

'So what're you thinking of? Fraud or something?'

'Maybe. If they were a public company, we could do some kind of forensic accounting check on them. But the O'Dromoderys have to tell nothing to no one.'

'Nothing to no one,' Alison repeated. 'Nice.'

'But then you would tend to think, Bobby was an architect not a quantity surveyor, was he going to have access to the finances anyway? Or there was some flaw in the design he discovered at a late stage and they wouldn't change it? Or they were using cheap materials, cutting corners, he was going to turn whistle-blower and . . . *what*?'

She was giving me the eyes.

'If you stare at schoolgirls for too long,' she said, 'you'll be arrested.'

'Why would I stare at schoolgirls?' I asked.

She laughed. 'Only you could ask that with a straight face.' She held up a finger to stop me from responding. 'Hush,' she said, 'do you hear that?'

I could hear traffic, and the chitter-chatter of schoolgirls above it.

'What?'

'The sound of my son crying out for his mother's milk.'

I ignored her, and got out of the Mystery Machine. She popped out the other side and asked me what I was doing and I told her I was going to take a closer look at the building site. She knew what I was like about observing things, and how long I liked to take, and her response was that she'd be reported to the Social Services for neglect and I observed that Page was with Mother, so they would probably do her for cruelty as well.

When a gap in the traffic didn't immediately present itself, we moved to a Zebra crossing twenty metres up. There were girls in purple uniforms crossing here too. They swore like troopers. When we got to the other side of the road Alison turned to walk on to the building-site entrance, while I turned towards St Mary's.

It took her a few moments to realise I was no longer by her side. She shouted, 'Oi! This way.' I ignored her, and entered the school grounds. When she caught up she asked what I was doing and I pointed. There was a newly built stone wall to our right, and running up to the school chapel and beyond. There was a small, ancient graveyard and then a short expanse of overgrown ground with enough of an elevation to give us a view over the wooden fence and into the building site next door.

Alison said, 'You can't just walk into a girls' school by yourself, this day and age.'

'I'm not by myself, you're with me.'

'*Now* I am.'

'It's fine then,' I said, and marched on with not inconsiderable vigour. My breath was not laboured, and my knees were not clicking. The air was crisp with a hint of cheap perfume. It felt good to be alive, words which had never previously entered my mind. As we walked, Alison slipped her hand into mine. I did not find it overly repellent.

As we passed through the graves, she said, 'Why would there be graves in a school?'

'Church school,' I said. 'The priests or nuns would live on site, and die on site, and be buried on site.'

'Creepy.'

'That's probably the point,' I said. 'Nothing like a few corpses to put the fear of God into the young ones.'

The grass around the graves had been tended, but the headstones were mostly all at odd angles, or had fallen over completely. Alison said, 'Look at the dates, they're hundreds of years old. The names are all faded. It's so sad.'

'If you say so,' I said.

We moved beyond the graveyard to the wilder ground and up the short elevation. We now had a good view over the fence into the building site, which extended back over several hundred metres. The buildings quite close to us were about half-finished. Further away, there were large areas where the foundations had been pegged out and trenches were being dug. There were bulldozers and excavators and at first glance, fifty-six builders.

Alison said, 'It's going to be big.'

'Massive,' I said.

'You wouldn't want anything to jeopardise it,' said Alison. 'Or anyone.'

We watched the builders at work. I was aware, out of the corner of my eye, of Alison attempting to surreptitiously look at her watch.

She saw that I was aware and shook her head. After a bit more observation she said, 'If something happened to me, would you track down my killers the way Nicola is trying to? Would you not rest until justice was done?'

'Probably,' I said. After a while I added, 'And if something happened to me?'

'I would probably give myself up.'

Three cars – two Land Cruisers front and back of a Jaguar – appeared at the entrance and were waved through. They pulled up in front of the Portakabin that was serving as the site office. Big men in dark clothes jumped out of the Land Cruisers and formed a guard of honour around the Jag. The rear door was opened by one of them, and a man in a blue suit whom I recognised as Sean O'Dromodery climbed out, briefly surveyed the area, and then mounted two steps and disappeared inside the office.

'Nice suit,' said Alison.

'Cashmere,' I said.

'At this distance?'

'You can always tell a suit of quality.'

'I mean, your eyesight is suddenly . . . like, incredible.'

'Are you complaining?'

'I haven't got you into bed yet, so the jury's still out.'

She squeezed my hand. I was thinking she could have had me there and then, but then I realised that she was no longer looking at me, but at the man approaching us through the gravestones; he was wearing a long black coat, with his hands thrust into the pockets. He was mostly bald with wisps of white hair above his ears. He did not look pleased to see us.

He said, with a smoker's rasp, 'Can I help you?'

I said, 'No, we're fine.'

He said, 'What I mean is, this is private property. Can I help you?'

'We were just taking a look at the graveyard,' said Alison. 'It's fascinating. Are you . . .?'

'I'm the Vice Principal. You can't just wander in without permission.'

'Absolutely,' said Alison, 'you're quite right. We didn't think. Sorry. I was just telling my husband here,' and she squeezed my arm, 'that my mum, God rest her soul, was a pupil here in the seventies and how she always said these gravestones gave her nightmares.'

The VP nodded warily. He said, 'Well, they're in a bit of a state, but we're going to tidy them up shortly. We're not open to visitors, not when school's in. And not when it's out either, for that matter.' He turned and pointed at the church. 'See what they've done there last year? The hellions stripped so much lead from the roof, it all but caved in during the Eucharist. Now if you don't mind I really . . .'

I said, 'Which came first, the church or the school?'

He gave me an exasperated look and said, 'The church. Two hundred years ago. The school celebrates its one

321

hundredth and twentieth anniversary next year. It's a lot bigger now, of course. Now if you don't mind . . .'

He tried to usher us along, but we remained sure and steadfast. I nodded towards the main school building; it was a big, red-brick establishment with a sixties look to it.

'The pupils aren't taught by priests or nuns any more, are they?'

'No . . . just regular teachers. Which is what I should be doing, teaching.' He withdrew a hand from his pocket and indicated the gates.

Alison pulled my sleeve gently. 'C'mon,' she said, 'we shouldn't be here.' She gave the Vice Principal the thumbs-up and said, 'Thanks. Sorry. Mum loved it here.'

'So did I,' I added.

As we passed through the graves, Alison said, 'What?'

'What *what*?'

'I thought you said something. Your lips were moving.'

'I was counting.'

'What were you counting?'

'Gravestones.'

'O*kay*. And why would you be doing that?'

'Because they're there to be counted.'

'Right,' she said. 'Not *completely* cured yet, then.'

I smiled. And I winked.

She said, 'I know that smug look. You've worked some-thing out.'

'I'm not there yet,' I said.

She gave me a smile, and I pulled her closer and she snuggled up against me as we proceeded to the school gates.

She even raised her lips to my cheek and kissed me. We were quite loved up, really.

'I've been around you long enough to know when to leave you alone,' she said. 'But for future reference – when you're counting, don't move your lips. It makes you look simple.'

'Okay,' I said.

41

I had a reasonably good idea of where I was going with it now – at least the first part of the mystery. I knew why Bobby Preston had been killed. I would need to back it up with research which might even include producing some proof, though I have never laid much store by actual evidence, because I am only ever trying to satisfy myself, not the views of twelve good men and true. The rest of the case was bubbling away, with hints and intimations and impressions hovering around the truth, just waiting to come into focus. I did not doubt that I would get there, and very soon, although not before we did something about the Land Cruiser that had slipped into our wake as we left the WestBel building site.

Never crossing the 29-miles-per-hour barrier of death allows one to become very attuned to one's surroundings; I am always aware of the make and model of the vehicles that precede me and follow me, and I am usually also very aware of the drivers, and their red faces, and the fists that they shake at me and the abuse that they mouth as they eventually pass me. In this case the Land Cruiser remained patiently in my wake. Alison might have noticed my eyes darting repeatedly to the mirrors, but paid no attention; she was well used to it. But when we did not proceed in the direction of home, or indeed No Alibis, I could sense her increasing irritation, and she finally snapped that if I was going off on another one of my tangents, could I please just dump her off here and she could make her own way back to the fruit of our loins. When I pulled into the side she gave me an incredulous look and said, 'You're really going to let me walk?'

'No,' I said, and a moment later there was a tap on my window and a bulky, baldy man in a zip-up Harrington jacket indicated for me to roll down the glass. I said I'd rather not and Alison said, 'Christ,' as another man in similar attire appeared at her window and demanded the same.

I said, 'What do you want?'

And my man said, 'My boss wants a word with you.' He indicated the car behind. 'Nothing to worry about, he just wants you to take a wee ride with him.'

'That's what they said to Rommel,' I observed, 'and that didn't end well.'

'Robble?' the man said.

Alison's man said, 'Open the doors,' and tried the handle, but Alison had taken the precaution of locking them. She could do that, from her side. I never did it in case we were in a pile-up with multiple vehicles and a petrol tanker and we couldn't get out because the doors were locked and then the tanker exploded, killing us badly, or in case we plunged off a suspension bridge and were drowning but could not swim to safety because the locking mechanism was jammed. Alison pointed out that there weren't any suspension bridges in Ireland. She also took my hand and said, 'What will we do?' as we stared out the windows at our prospective assailants.

I said, 'They work for Sean O'Dromodery, so it's probably okay. That said, he might be up to his neck in these killings and want to also kill us. Why don't you go and have a chat with him, and I'll go for help.'

She said, 'This is no time for joking.'

I did not dignify that with a response.

My window was tapped again.

I said, 'Okay. *I'll* go and talk to him. But as soon as I'm out, slip across and make your escape. If they have both of us, we're at their mercy; if they just have me then they can't do anything much.'

'You would do that?'

'You seem surprised.'

Tap, tap, tap, tap.

'Constantly,' said Alison. 'But if it's all the same to you, I'm going to stick here with you, for better and for worse.'

'No,' I said, 'you have Page to look after, and Mother's funeral to arrange. So go. I will deal with this.'

'You're really serious?'

'Always.' I took her hand. 'And it will be *fine*. Honestly. Just go.'

I reached for the door handle, but she held on to me, and pulled me close and said, 'I know it will. Love you.' I nodded.

She said, 'Love you.' I nodded again. She shook her head, and I made another attempt on the door, but not before she asked who Robble was and I resolved to get my sinuses checked if I survived my encounter with Sean O'Dromodery, the last of the Karamazovs.

They did not make any attempt to stop Alison from escaping. They just looked bemused as she dove behind the wheel, fired up the engine and sped away with tyres screeching.

I thought of Rommel again, and realised that actually all along I had been picturing James Mason in the 1951 film *The Desert Fox* instead of the Field Marshal himself. I am not greatly into war movies, but this one had stuck with me because I admired its director, Henry Hathaway, since he was also responsible for *Call Northside 777*, one of the finest of film noirs. It had received an Edgar Award from the Mystery Writers of America for Best Motion Picture Screenplay in 1949, and I was happy to remember that, because since I'd been electric-shocked and then failed to recognise Gabriel's theme tune I had begun to doubt my own vast knowledge of all things consequential and many things less so.

And then I thought that I had better focus on the situation at hand, which entailed me being escorted the few yards along to the open back door of the Land Cruiser and then being beckoned in by a gaunt-looking Sean O'Dromodery, albeit gaunt in cashmere. I stepped up and into the vehicle, and the door was closed behind me from outside and Sean O'Dromodery looked me up and down in much the same way that I looked him up and down and he said, 'So you're him,' and I said, 'Who?' and he said I was the one who'd been hired by his brother and been incarcerated in Purdysburn and then all over the news for fleeing, and I said, 'Uhm, yes, that would indeed be me.'

He said, 'You helped that lunatic escape.'

'He's no more a lunatic than I am,' I said.

He said, 'You mean he's not guilty?'

'That remains to be seen.'

'Then why in hell would you help him escape?'

'It seemed like a good idea at the time.'

'*It* . . .?' He stopped and gave me a funny look, then said, 'My brother said you were hard to read. He also said you get results.'

I nodded. 'You spotted us looking at your building site.'

'Yes,' he said. 'We have very good security anyway – it's a deprived area and if you don't literally nail things down they tend to disappear. But they've been extra-vigilant of late, for obvious reasons. However, I think you put yourself up there for a reason: you wanted to be seen, you wanted me to come after you.' He gave me what he supposed was a reassuring smile but it actually came out more like a grimace. 'I've been keen to talk to you for quite a while,' he said. 'I'm intrigued by what my brother saw in you. You own a bookshop, yes?'

'A mystery bookshop.'

'But you do your private investigations on the side.'

'Not so much on the side,' I said. 'The book business is in turmoil.'

'Tell me about it,' he said, though I soon found out that he didn't mean it literally. He raised a hand and I fell silent and then we sat there in the relative quiet for a bit, the Land Cruiser being well insulated against the sounds of passing traffic. There was no driver. I could see that the radio on the dash was tuned to BBC Radio 2, but the sound was turned down, which was the best way to listen to it.

After what felt like a long time he said, 'I bury Bernard tomorrow.' I nodded. 'I have lost two brothers, and although we fought like cats and dogs, they were my family, and I loved them. Do you have brothers?'

'Yes,' I said. 'Three.' I was going to add, *but not necessarily on this planet*, but did not.

'It is a terrible thing to lose a brother,' he said.

He lifted a leather bag from his feet. There were fasteners on the front like a primary-school satchel, which he struggled to open because his hands were shaking. When he got them free he delved inside and produced an object wrapped in an old tea-towel, and from the way he handled it I did not have to guess what it was.

As he unwrapped the *defixio* he said, 'This was found outside my home, buried under a pile of autumn leaves. It could only have been there for a couple of days. I know you've encountered these before. My brother told me about his, eventually, but I didn't really take it seriously. Now it's put the fear of God into me.'

He handed it to me. It had the same O'Dromodery curse, but was cleaner, with little soil or dirt engrained in the letters. Without having the other *defixios* all in a row, it was impossible to say if they had all been cut from the same piece of lead, but I thought it probable.

'Was there nothing on your security cameras?' I asked.

'How do you know I have cameras?'

'You are travelling with two carloads of bodyguards. I'm sure you've taken other precautions.'

'Yes, indeed – and yes, we found a fleeting glimpse of someone in a big coat, with their face masked, really nothing identifiable.'

'Male or female?'

'I would say from the way they moved, maybe female.'

'Big coat, or big person?'

'I would say – not a large person, and moving quickly.'

'And the date and time on the footage?'

'Tuesday the nineteenth, and I can't remember the time off-hand, but it was in the morning.'

'The early hours?'

'No. Day-time. Around eleven, I think.'

I nodded, and calculated.

He said, 'Do you know what this is about?'

'I'm getting there.'

'You have to tell me *something*. My house is crawling with security, but I don't know if I need security men for the security men, and security men for the security men for the security men. It's driving me mad. And now I know that psycho is out there, I'm expecting him to jump out of the woodwork any time and stab me the way he stabbed that other poor fella. If you know who is doing this or why, please tell me. I will pay you double whatever my brother was paying you.'

'Plus VAT,' I said.

He nodded warily. 'My brother said you were a cool one. Okay. Not a problem.'

'It'll be tomorrow before I have answers. Where's the funeral?'

'Roselawn. But we're keeping it small – family, friends and a few close business acquaintances. Would it help if you came along?'

'I can't,' I said. 'I'm barred.'

'From *Roselawn*?'

'Yes. But it doesn't matter. I'll see everyone back at the house.'

'The . . . Who told you we were . . .?'

'The killers did. Once they found out you were inviting mourners back home, instead of to some hotel or restaurant, that's when they decided to bury this *defixio*.'

'Jesus! I don't understand any of this! But why, why would they bury this . . . thing?'

'You *know* why. Your gathering is the perfect time to strike.'

'*Strike*?'

'Absolutely. At all other times you'll be surrounded by security, but with a house full of mourners they know that it might be their only opportunity.'

'I don't . . . You mean that one of my *relatives* or *friends* might try and . . . That's just not possible. *Is* it?'

''Tis,' I said.

42

Sean O'Dromodery dropped me off round the corner from No Alibis and quite close to the burned-out wreck of Jeff's mother's car. Employing me did not seem to have cheered him up much or reassured him in any way that his troubles were coming to an end. For some reason, I don't inspire confidence in people, even though my results are testament to my abilities.

I resolved, as I observed the shop from the sanctuary of Starbucks, to work on my motivational skills. I was, after all, a new man. My body was free of legal and illegal medications and potions, and if the voices in my head were not quite gone, then certainly their volume had been dialled down. There was a whole new world out there for me to conquer now that I was largely unencumbered by mental or physical illnesses, and I would do it with charm, panache and a new regard for the sanctity of life and appreciation for the eccentricities of human nature.

When I was satisfied that the shop was not under observation, and Jeff was not being held against his will, but rather playing with his phone, I lifted my Americano and approached my beloved premises. When I opened the door, Jeff grinned at me.

I said, 'Have we broken the £30 barrier for takings or something?'

'No,' he said. He came out from behind the counter, shut the door after me and turned the sign that said *Open* to *Closed*. 'Haven't sold sod all, but I *have* solved your little mystery.'

I did not like his condescending tone, or his smug face, and I very much doubted if he had solved anything. He may have *stumbled* upon something, the way peasants occasionally stumble upon landmines. I turned the sign from *Closed* to *Open*, for I have a business to run, and followed him back to the counter.

I said, 'Has no one been looking for me?'

'No,' said Jeff.

'I'm a fugitive, on the run,' I said.

'Apparently not,' said Jeff. 'They're still warning people not to approach The Man in the White Suit, but you don't get a mention. Incidentally, how is he? Attacked anyone of late?'

'No, Jeff. It must be something about you.'

I smiled. He smiled. His eye was much better now, but there was bruising around his throat.

Jeff said, 'Did you hear what happened to my mum's car?'

'No,' I said, 'it's not top of my list of—'

'Someone torched it. Local kids, most likely.'

'Oh. Well. Sorry to hear that.'

'Don't be. Mum is extremely happy.'

'Happy?'

'Absolutely, she's delighted. It's a complete write-off.'

'*So . . .?*'

'You didn't notice it was held together with bubble gum? It was condemned by the garage about six months ago, but she just drove on, but now the insurance company's going to be giving her a nice new one. She's delighted.'

'I'm pleased for her,' I said, 'but can we get back to crime-fighting?'

He was turning his phone over in his hands, and sticking with the smug look. He said, 'First, I want an acknowledgement of how important I am to your investigations.'

'You're important to my investigations, Jeff.'

'A sincere acknowledgement.'

'That was sincere. I can't help if it sounds sarcastic, it's the way of me.'

'Nevertheless.'

'Jeff, whatever you think you've solved, it remains to be seen. I'm not giving out compliments based on nothing much. Prove to me that you're worthy of sincere acknowledgement.'

'Then you'll have the solution, and I'll have nothing, and you'll tell me to catch myself on.'

'Jeff, I give you my word.'

'Your word is worth nothing. I know you.'

'Jeff, I've changed. You know I've changed. I was just thinking on the way here what a grand job you've been doing for me, and how it's great I can depend on you to man the barricades while I'm out on a case.'

'And also I want a pay rise.'

I managed not to snort. I said, 'Jeff, Kindle.' And opened my palms to him. Before he could respond I added, 'Tescos, iPads, smartphones. The book business is in *chassis* and our footfall is down thirty-six per cent year on year. For Godsake, Jeff, even James Patterson is virtually on the breadline! He only wrote thirty-six novels last year! How's anyone supposed to make a living from that? Never mind Amazon – the bloody Amazon rainforest is recovering because no one's buying books any more!'

'Do they even make books out of the rainfo—?'

'Jeff, my point is, a pay rise just isn't going to happen. Appreciation, *yes*. Spondulicks, no. Now, I am on the verge of cracking this case wide open, and yet you seem to care more about your mercenary demands. You haven't even asked how close I am to solving it.'

'Well, how close . . .?'

'Never mind that now. I have work to do, serious work. If you have a contribution to make, please make it now.'

'But I—'

'*Jeff!*'

He sighed. He showed me his phone. 'The music,' he said, 'I know what the music is.'

Jeff had, as instructed, posted the MP3 of Gabriel playing his party piece on the store website and also sent it as an attachment to every one of my Facebook friends, Twitter followers, Christmas Club members and other devotees of crime fiction in Belfast who had come to my attention and whom I had stalked relentlessly.

Not one of them had responded.

The fact that I bombard them every other day with offers, inducements and begging letters probably meant that they hadn't bothered to actually open the e-mail or listen to the music. Jeff, as I suspected, had stumbled upon the answer to the mystery by accident, and it was entirely to do with his short attention span and extreme laziness.

He said, 'Have you ever heard of the *Angry Birds*?'

'You mean, Jeff, *The Birds*, the 1963 movie by Alfred Hitchcock, based on the short story by Daphne DuMaurier.'

'No, I mean the *Angry Birds* – the app: it's the most popular in the world by far. These birds have to try and rescue their eggs which have been stolen by some hungry green pigs, and there's all these different levels.'

'Jeff, relevance?'

'Okay. *Angry Birds*. So what happens every time something is hugely successful?'

'Tescos discount it?'

'A million and one rival and usually crappier versions of it come out, right? Like when *The Da Vinci Code* was briefly more popular than *The Highway Code* and all those rubbish Vatican conspiracy thrillers you always rant about came out?'

'Yes, Jeff,' I said.

'*Well*, there's been a whole lot of different *Angry Bird*-type apps, most of them terrible, but there's one that manages to send it up and at the same time is actually quite good to play. It's a Scottish one called *Angry Lairds*.'

'*Angry* . . .?'

'*Lairds*. It's Scottish for—'

'I know what a Laird is, Jeff.'

'It's a Lord,' Jeff said authoritatively, 'and ranks below a Baron and above an Esquire.'

'Yes, Jeff,' I said. He wasn't showing an aptitude for investigation, he was showing it for Wikipedia.

'What I'm saying is, instead of birds you have crofters, and they have their possessions stolen by the Lairds, and the crofters try to get them back.'

'So why isn't it called *Angry Crofters?*'

'Because it isn't. That wouldn't make any sense, and it doesn't matter – what I'm saying is, I knew I recognised that tune he was playing but I couldn't quite get it, at least not until this morning, when I was just sitting here trying to do my revision but I couldn't get my head around it, so I went on to the *Angry Birds* but got a bit bored with it, and then I remembered about the *Angry Lairds* and thought I'd give it a go, and . . . listen.'

He pressed the touch screen and loaded the *Angry Lairds* app and immediately some rudimentary animations of little red-haired men in tartan kilts appeared and then some grander-looking creatures mocking them from ancient castles, but I did not pay any attention to either group because it was all taken up with the very simple, very repetitive *plinkity plink* of the soundtrack: electronic, with a hideous Casio backbeat – and also very familiar as Gabriel's theme tune.

If I'd been a more expressive individual, I might have jumped for joy; and, in fact, with my much improved knees, I literally could have done so without worrying about them collapsing under me. But as it was I just grinned at Jeff and said, 'This is wonderful, Jeff, well done.'

'Well, thank you,' Jeff replied, beaming. 'I'm thinking he's some kind of games designer, or he works on the sound-tracks for games, or maybe he's just fixated with *Angry Lairds*. Anyway, just before you came in I looked up the *Angry Lairds* website and read the credits and it says exactly who composed the music, and his name is Alexander Kh—'

'. . . orsikov,' I said.

'You *know* him?'

'No,' I said, 'but as soon as you said Alexander, it was exactly the prompt I needed. Alexander Khorsikov. Indeed.'

I drummed my fingers on the counter. The music continued to play. I smiled. Everything was falling nicely into place.

'Well?' Jeff asked. 'Is that who Gabriel is? This Alexander . . .'

'No,' I said. 'Alexander Khorsikov is dead.'

43

It was a long night, although in my world, all nights are long. Regular readers will know that I haven't had a good night's sleep since Mary Peters won the Pentathlon Gold at the 1972 Munich Olympics. She was a big country girl with hair like straw and throwing muscles that could make Finn Mac Cool weep. If the West German authorities had sent her in against Black September instead of relying on their own miserable sharpshooters, there might have been a very different outcome. I had thought about it often, since. But not this night. Nor was it one of tossing and turning and plotting and fantasising about matricide, patricide or suicide, it was one of research, locked and shuttered into my store, a night of poring over documents, and maps, and lifting the devil phone and talking to humans who were not much interested in talking to me at four in the morning but who soon changed their tune when I spoke to them of *defixios* and conspiracies, fraud, and many, many bodies, and bones.

I spoke to a bleary-voiced Dr Winter at the City, who again tried to join the Midnight Gardeners and was again rebuffed; but I used my charm to persuade him to consult Big H, the National Health Service's master computer, and then when he'd spent hours on that I ordered him round to Nicola's house to examine Gabriel. I spoke to the Vice Principal of St Mary's who had accosted us in the graveyard and invited him to the funeral, which confused him greatly, but I assured him that the future reputation of his beloved school depended on him attending, which was a lie, but he fell for it, because I am good. When I could not find them on the web, I persuaded the chief librarian at Belfast City Library to rise from her bed and travel downtown so that she could photograph old maps and documents and e-mail them to me. She was a great supporter of crime fiction, and we often exchanged views on the new trends; she hated the Scandinavians even more than I did. My Russian is not great, but was good enough to exchange e-mails with the Lavrentiy Beria Conservatory in Moscow. They were very relieved to hear from me, and most informative.

As dawn approached I consulted the on-line menus of the Milltown Road Catering Company and discovered what they would be offering to the mourners at the après funeral gathering at the home of Sean O'Dromodery, and found it to my liking, which was unusual, because my allergies normally stopped me from enjoying anything other than gruel or Starbucks, but now I was positively looking forward to a mushroom *vol-au-vent*. Indeed, in the middle of the night, and almost without thinking, I made myself a Nescafe coffee from the jar Jeff kept in the kitchen because I did not often stretch to buying Starbucks for him, and in drinking it realised that I had broken the Starbucks spell; it did not repel me, and my head did not swell to the size of a pumpkin.

The final thing I did, before slipping out of the back door and boarding the Mystery Machine, was to phone DI Robinson to invite him to the gathering at Sean O'Dromodery's, but my call went through to his voicemail and I left a message instead.

I drove at a leisurely pace. I always drive at a leisurely pace, but this driving at a leisurely pace was because I was calm, and content. It was a beautiful morning, with a sea mist lingering over the centre of town and birds chirruping in the trees and milk-floats on their way back to base and the Bank of England base lending rate increased by half a per cent which had to be good for small traders. I was going home to my partner and child and Mother, and I had solved the most complex of cases by way of research, observation, intuition and nous. I was on top of my game, and I was abuzz already but not pharmaceutically with adrenaline for the coming day. I would, once again, take centre stage and reveal all. I would have remained in the shop, honing my presentation, but Alison had texted me to hurry home because she wanted to 'give me one for Ulster', which, roughly translated, meant that she wanted the sex, and seeing as how it had been an extraordinarily long time, I was happy to oblige. It was also good to notice, as I approached the house, that my erectile dysfunction was a thing of the past, and I could only hope that nobody else noticed, between car door and front door, or I would be arrested.

I bounded up the steps and put the key in the door and stood in the hallway and it felt good to be home. I could smell bacon, and it did not make me ill, but ravenous, and I had to decide whether to give in to the ravening or insist on the ravishing, and the latter won because there would always be pigs, and so I called Alison's name and she said she was 'in here' which meant the kitchen, and I pounded forward quite happy to have her on the table or the hob, but instead I found her leaning against the sink with a mug of tea in her hand, and wearing a dressing-gown stained with milk and spaghetti hoops and smiling at me but fleetingly with it, because there was someone else there who did not often make anyone smile – not Mother, but DI Robinson sitting with his back to me and not even bothering to turn round but nodding and saying, 'Welcome home,' and I knew then that he had influenced Alison to send her text and I should have guessed that, she being a lady, she would not have offered to give me one for Ulster or any other small but optimistic province, but I had allowed myself to be carried away by my own extreme state of horniness which had now, thankfully, instantly dissipated because DI Robinson, even naked in a Babygro, does not do it for me, not that he was.

I stood in the doorway and said, 'You made him bacon?' because I could now see the plate before him, and a rind, and some evidence of egg.

'Well,' said Alison, 'he's been here most of the night, and we were both hungry.'

DI Robinson finally turned in his chair and looked me up and down and said, 'Don't get your knickers in a twist. I've been here trying to give her the Three Degrees but she hasn't given me anything. But I'm not too stressed about that. I know how you work, how you like to put on a show, and besides, the bacon was lovely. She makes a mean fry.'

He turned back to the table, and I joined Alison at the sink. She took hold of the bottom of my sleeve. 'Sorry,' she said. 'I had no choice. He was going to take me in for questioning, and I couldn't leave Page with Mother.'

'Why? I thought she was God's gift to babies.'

'I may have misjudged her parenting abilities. I caught her giving whiskey to him.'

I gave her a reassuring smile. 'It's an old wives' thing, a wee dab of whiskey on the tip of your finger, to help him sleep.'

'This wasn't a dab, it was a shot. That's why Page has been so placid in her company. I thought they were bonding, but she was getting our baby pissed so he wouldn't cry so much.'

'More ammunition,' said DI Robinson. 'I'm going to have all of you locked up, including the baby for underage drinking.'

I said, 'What do you want? Why are you here?'

He sat back in his chair and folded his hands in his lap. 'Take a wild guess. You break someone out of a not very secure mental institution, and half the police in Belfast are out looking for him. You interfere repeatedly in a murder investigation, and you expose your wife and child to extreme danger which might have resulted in their untimely deaths if I hadn't been hanging around keeping an eye out for you.'

'What're you talking about?'

Alison chewed on her lip. Her eyes flitted up from the linoleum and back down. 'Someone tried to break in,' she said, 'in the early hours.'

'The house? Did they touch . . .?'

'They had the outer door open,' said DI Robinson, 'before I chased them away. I thought they were just a couple of kids in fright masks on a burglary and didn't go after them, but then your girl here found something, once I'd roused her.'

'Did you not notice on the way in?' Alison asked. 'The new plant pot in the front? I bought it in B and Q yesterday. To replace the one you destroyed?'

'Yes,' I said, though in truth, I had not.

'Well, once DI Robinson *roused* me,' she gave me a wink, and my stomach lurched, 'and bearing in mind what has gone before, I checked out the pot, and lo and behold . . .'

She turned to the oven, which was on, and picked up a pair of oven gloves draped over the handle. She opened the door, and I could see on the top shelf a plate stacked with bacon and eggs and sausages and potato bread and soda bread and black pudding, a Belfast Deathpak for Mother, but for which she would have to wait until I examined what was on the bottom shelf, which was very clearly a *defixio*. Alison reached in and retrieved it. 'I was drying it out,' she said.

She set it on the draining board. DI Robinson, who had clearly already examined it, did not move from his seat at the table. 'And before you ask,' he said, 'she had it all washed smooth before I knew what she was playing at, otherwise I would have had Forensics all over it.'

'It's just force of habit,' said Alison. 'We never have recourse to fingerprints and DNA. We rely on Superbrain,' and she indicated me.

I did not glow (a) because it was the truth, and (b) because I was too busy trying to hide my pleasure at reading the inscription, which was a mild variation of the O'Dromodery curse:

> *This curse on the house of Anthony Boucher*
> *Let them suffer, let them boil*
> *Bring fear and death down upon*
> *The forever cursed house of Anthony Boucher.*

Alison peered over my shoulder and said, 'I don't get it. Who the hell is Anthony Boucher? And why are you grinning like a loon?'

44

A cold hard rain had enveloped the mourners at the burial of Bernard O'Dromodery at Roselawn Cemetery, and they had not dried off sufficiently before stepping into the cranked-up central heating of Sean O'Dromodery's house on Balmoral Avenue so that they were, literally, steaming. I watched from the top of the stairs as Sean, under the firm gaze of his security guards, welcomed them one by one, with a firm handshake, and quickly directed them towards the young staff from the Milltown Road Catering Company, on hand to dispense glasses of Bucks Fizz, and then on into the main lounge, which was large and wood-panelled, and for the purposes of the day had been largely emptied of comfortable furniture and set out with folding chairs. Their entrance was to the little-known Fourth Concerto by Alexander Khorsikov. It wasn't loud enough to be truly distracting, but you couldn't help but notice it. This was deliberate. I desired an unsettling ambience.

I did not attend the funeral service or the burial afterwards, but instead sent Jeff. He was one of the last to arrive back at the house, and joined me on the stairs, dripping. He said, 'That was a miserable experience. Why does it always rain at funerals?'

'Does it, Jeff, or have you been watching too many movies?'

He said, 'Good point. But still, I'm drenched. But happy to report that the internment passed without incident.'

I smiled and said, 'Really?'

And he said, 'What?'

'Internment, Jeff? Were they detained without trial?' He looked at me blankly. 'Interment, Jeff. *Interment.*'

'Same difference,' he said, and he was probably close enough to the truth.

Alison was busy setting up my laptop and a small projector in the lounge. The mourners milling around her probably thought they were going to be treated to a celebration of Bernard O'Dromodery's life, rather than a PowerPoint demonstration of who did what to whom and why.

A woman with short dark hair arrived at the door, looking rather overawed by the size of the house, and during the pleasantries it became clear she was Sonya Delaney. Martin Brady came next; there was a handshake with Sean, but I could see that there was no love lost.

Jeff said, 'I overheard him talking at the service. It seems Bernard's house was owned by the O'Dromodery Brothers building company rather than Bernard himself. Sean's given him six weeks to get out.'

I saw through the landing window a yellow Lexus pull

through the gates, and a few moments later Fat Sam's widow Gloria dripped into the porch and gave Sean a hug. The next to arrive was Gary Drennan, the manager of the All Star Health Club; he was wearing a tracksuit, and clearly had no idea why everyone else was in suits and black ties. All he knew was that he had been summoned by who he thought was the owner of the Health Club. Sean solemnly shook his hand, while at the same time glancing up the stairs for my approval that a man so incongruously dressed be allowed in. He repeated the same routine for Dr Winter, and for Rory Quinn, the Vice Principal of St Mary's.

DI Robinson was one of the last to arrive. He was wearing a beige trenchcoat which showed up the rain; his hair was plastered across his head. He had interviewed Sean several times during his investigation. As he shook his hand he looked up the staris at me and raised an eyebrow. I gave him a condescending nod. I always enjoyed showing DI Robinson how to do his job.

When it appeared that all the mourners had arrived, I nudged Jeff and said, 'Okay, you better go and get them.'

He looked out at the rain and sighed. 'Why do I always have to do the donkey work?' he asked, without immediately realising that he had just answered his own question. But he saw the look on my face and said, 'Oh, *very* funny.'

I accompanied him down the stairs and then stopped with Sean by the front door. We watched as Jeff hurried across the pooling tarmac to the Mystery Machine.

Sean said, 'I hope you know what you're doing.'

'I am brimming with confidence,' I said, 'though there is

always the chance that something will go catastrophically wrong.'

He said, 'That is not very reassuring.' We stared at the teeming rain for several moments. He took a deep breath. 'I can't believe this,' he said. 'I've just shaken all those hands, but one of them may have wielded the knife that killed my brother. The rest of them are going to think I've taken leave of my senses, allowing you to just . . . take over.'

I had already explained to him that this was how I worked, that statements and interview rooms and solicitors protecting one's rights were not for me, that the important thing was not being able to *literally* prove someone's guilt, it was sufficient for me to demonstrate conclusively in the room, in front of witnesses, that a person or persons was or were guilty of the crime; nobody leaving his home today would be in any doubt. That was my job. Actually hauling them before a court – that was DI Robinson's.

I said, 'This way you will know the truth, in yourself. That's why you're paying me the big bucks. Which, incidentally . . .' I raised an eyebrow.

He said, 'You want paying now? At my brother's funeral?'
'Absolutely.'
'You don't pay for a meal before you've eaten it,' he said.
'In this restaurant, you do.'
'And what if I don't like the meal?'
'That's the chance you have to take. The chef has put a lot of work into preparing the meal, including the use of some combustible ingredients. He should be paid. In cash. Plus VAT.'

Sean O'Dromodery reached into his pocket and took out

an envelope. He pressed it into my hand. As I went to take it, he held onto it, and looked hard into my eyes. 'I knew you were a bit of an operator. We built our business the same way, cash in hand. So it's all there. Take it. But I'm telling you now: if this all turns to shit, if you embarrass me in front of my family and friends, I will take every penny back, and I'll break your legs into the bargain.'

I gave him an equally hard look back. I was getting better at it. One day I might even be able to stare down Alison. I didn't mind the threat. It kind of went with the territory. It didn't make him a bad or guilty man. Worse things happened in the book trade.

Sean let go of the envelope, and I slipped it into my inside jacket pocket. He said, 'Okay, do what you have to do. But can you do me one favour? Will you turn that fucking music off?'

DI Robinson stepped up to the table with my laptop on it and called for order, and aked if everyone would take a seat. Two staff from the Milltown Road Catering Company, in the act of distributing mushroom *vols-au-vent*, didn't quite know whether to stand where they were or quietly exit, but I whispered to them that this wouldn't take long and they should take a seat. In passing I took one of the *vols-au-vent* and placed it whole in my mouth. It seemed as good a time as any to discover if I was allergic to them, and it was pleasing to discover that I was not, although this one tasted like a warm slug encased in cardboard.

The mourners were still chatting amongst themselves as they took their seats, and weren't paying huge amounts of attention to DI Robinson as he held up his warrant card and thanked them and then said that we weren't about to pay tribute to the recently deceased builder, that that had all been done at the service. 'No,' he said, 'I am a detective. I am investigating a series of murders, including that of Bernard O'Dromodery. I have reason to believe that his killers are in this room. I should warn you that all of the exits have been sealed.'

That got them.

Martin Brady said, 'What the fuck?'

Gloria Mahood let out a cackle and said, 'Priceless.'

Malachy Quinn stood up and said, 'What on earth has this got to do with Saint Mary's?'

Gary Drennan unzipped his All Star tracksuit top all the way to the bottom and then brought it right back up to the top.

Sean O'Dromodery nodded around them, studying their reactions for clues.

Everyone, at some point, looked to the lounge door. DI Robinson had used some dramatic licence – there was only one exit, and that was being guarded from the other side by Alison, holding a poker. If anyone tried to make a break for it, she would attempt to take them down. The security guards, who might have been called upon to prevent an escape, had themselves been herded into the room and warned by Sean O'Dromodery not to interfere unless instructed to by DI Robinson. Nobody but I had any idea if they themselves were involved in the conspiracy.

DI Robinson ignored the rumpus, and waited for everyone to calm down before he went on: 'Some of you I know, many of you I don't. Bernard O'Dromodery's death is one of nearly half a dozen which I believe are related, but as to exactly *how* they are related, I just don't know. However, there is one man who does believe he has not only established that relationship, but also discovered who is responsible for those deaths, and he is . . . this bloke.'

He pointed at me, sitting in the front row. I nodded around them as I stood up, and drank in the confusion, and the concern, and the bewilderment.

'He runs a fucking bookshop,' said Martin Brady.

'A mystery bookshop,' I corrected, 'and this is a mystery.'

'And watch your language,' DI Robinson added. 'This is still a funeral. All I'm asking you to do is indulge him. If he's right, then we may unmask a murderer. If he's wrong, he will be returned to the mental institution from which he escaped.'

Several laughed, as if it was a joke. Nevertheless, I stepped forward to the accompaniment of increased rumblings and took my place beside DI Robinson. He whispered, 'You better know what the hell you're doing.'

'More or less,' I said.

He shook his head, and moved through the chairs to the back, where he took up position just to the left of the door.

The room was lit by a series of small spotlights on a long strip. I had taken the trouble before the mourners arrived to align these so that three of them beamed down exactly where I was standing, and the other six shone slightly more intensely onto a spot on the carpet I had marked with a small red grape I had liberated from a bunch in the kitchen. I now bent and lifted this grape, which had been tramped flat, and replaced it with a chair. I had thus, under the watchful eyes of intrigued people, established my court.

I said, 'Thank you, and hopefully I won't detain you for too long, apart from the guilty parties amongst you, who might find themselves detained indefinitely.' It was a joke, and I thought, quite a smart play on words, but nobody seemed to agree.

The door at the back opened and Alison slipped in. She gave me a wink. I did not wink back, in case it made me look unbalanced.

'I came to this case through an old friend who asked me merely to help identify a young man who had been arrested on suspicion of murdering a notorious hard man called Sam Mahood . . .' I glanced at Gloria. 'Or Fat Sam Mahood, as he was more widely known.'

'That's what they called him,' said Gloria.

I moved to my laptop and pressed a button, and on the plain white wall behind me the first of a series of photographs appeared. 'These,' I said, 'are the Faces of the Dead.'

Fat Sam's picture was, clearly, a mugshot. It had been carried in all the papers.

'The man they arrested was identified on CCTV footage at the murder location, the All Star Health Club in East Belfast, but arrested about a mile away, fast asleep, having broken into a house. The All Star Health Club itself was and is managed by Gary Drennan,' I indicated him and he shifted uneasily in his chair, 'and built by the O'Dromodery Brothers, of whom we are obviously all very well aware, and of whom Sean here is the only surviving member.'

Sympathetic eyes were turned upon him. He studied the carpet.

'It is indeed a terrible thing to lose a brother,' I said, 'and how much worse to lose two?' The second picture appeared. 'Fergus O'Dromodery fell to his death from the O'Dromodery Brothers' headquarters eight months ago. The police, in their wisdom, treated it as a suicide. We now know better. Fergus O'Dromodery was thrown from that roof.'

There were gasps and cries. I did not, in fact, know this to be true. But all the evidence indicated that it was. It was like the Higgs boson – you didn't have to actually see it to be able to prove that it existed, but if it *didn't*, the laws of physics would be rendered a bit shit.

I raised my hand for calm, while continuing to fan their unsettlement. I like to keep my audience on edge. I showed a photograph of Bernard O'Dromodery. 'Yes, indeed,' I said, 'two brothers murdered. Fat Sam, murdered.' I clicked onto the fourth picture. 'This is Francis Delaney. A builder who also worked for Fat Sam in the ahm . . . enforcement busi-ness . . .' I raised an eye towards Sonya, and she gave a bit of a shrug '. . . and therefore indirectly for the O'Dromoderys – also murdered.' I moved to the fifth photograph, which Nicola had supplied. 'And this is the fifth victim, the architect Bobby Preston, whose main clients were the O'Dromoderys.'

I stood and looked at the five pictures, now resting side by side, and my audience did the same. I said gravely. 'This is, without doubt, a murder spree intrinsically connected not just to the O'Dromodery company but, as we shall see, to their development of a shopping centre in West Belfast.'

Sean O'Dromodery, sitting barely a few feet away from

me in the front row, visibly stiffened, and his knuckles whitened where his hands gripped his knees. I caught Alison's eye. She turned and opened the door and slipped out, leaving it just wide enough for me to see into the hallway behind her.

'But I'm getting ahead of myself,' I said. 'I was, as I have mentioned, brought into this case to try and identify the man who was arrested shortly after Fat Sam's murder – a man who, because of his inability, or perhaps refusal to communicate with anyone, and the clothes he was found in and continues to favour, has become known as The Man in the White Suit. Because of his perceived mental condition, this man was not held in prison, but rather in Purdysburn Hospital. Without doubt you will have heard on the news that The Man in the White Suit yesterday made a daring escape from this so-called secure facility and has been on the run ever since. There have been many dire warnings not to approach him because he is so dangerous; he has in fact become public enemy number one. No wonder Sean O'Dromodery is mortally afraid for his life, and has had no option but to surround himself with so many bodyguards.

'Well, Sean . . .' and I nodded kindly at him, and then around my audience, 'you no longer have to be worried. The Man in the White Suit is on the run no more. He's in your vestibule eating a Crunchie.'

45

The rumpus died down, eventually, and I beckoned Gabriel forward from the door where he had been hovering at Nicola Sheridan's side. She led him between the chairs, followed by Jeff, who was carrying a small musical keyboard, and another man, a tall, distinguished-looking gentleman in a tweedy suit and with his glasses perched on the end of his nose.

I said, 'Ladies and gentlemen, please do not be alarmed. Gabriel – for that is the name we have given him, because it gets very annoying endlessly having to say "The Man in the White Suit" – Gabriel is perfectly placid, and apart from one episode of extreme violence has not been at all difficult since I broke him out of Purdysburn.'

'You actually *admit* breaking him out?' said Sonya Delaney. 'He *killed* my husband!'

'Well,' I said, 'that remains to be seen.'

She pointed down the room at DI Robinson. 'Why aren't you arresting him? He stabbed my Francis to death!'

She had plenty of support in the room.

DI Robinson raised a hand for calm. 'Let's just see what he has to say.'

'He's a deaf mute,' said Gloria Mahood. 'What's he going to say?'

Nicola guided Gabriel into his seat in the front row and sat beside him. She gently patted his hand. Gabriel stared straight ahead, which happened to be directly at me, without giving any indication that he was actually seeing me, or that he was remotely aware that so many eyes were transfixed by him. Because they were all so busy sizing up Gabriel, they didn't pay much attention to Jeff setting up the keyboard, with a small amp, nor to the distinguished gentleman in the suit, who quietly took a seat beside Nicola.

As things settled down again, I thanked DI Robinson for his support and the audience for their indulgence, and introduced Nicola, resplendent in the same green ensemble that had given her the appearance of a Sunday School teacher on her visit to Gabriel in the hospital, explaining that she was the wife of the late Bobby Preston. I said that far from believing that Gabriel was somehow connected to her husband's death, she was now so convinced of his innocence that she had put her own safety at risk by agreeing to shelter him following his escape from Purdysburn, and that she appeared to be none the worse for it. That got them murmuring anew.

Jeff finished his set-up and scurried away.

'Nicola,' I said, 'if you would kindly bring Gabriel forward to the keyboard?'

Nicola eased Gabriel out of his seat and guided him to the

keyboard. It was in fact a small synthesizer belonging to Jeff. I had been vaguely aware that he harboured ambitions not only as a poet, but also as a singer-songwriter, but had never been sufficiently interested to actually ask him about it. *This*, I suspected, would be his greatest contribution to music.

Gabriel sat, and without being asked raised his hands to the keys and began to play. *Silently.* I gave Jeff a filthy look and switched on the machine. Immediately a version of his theme tune with the backing of an angelic choir began to roll out of the amp, at least until I pushed a button which returned it to the basic piano sound.

My audience may or may not have been familiar with the piece already, as it had been playing in the background upon their arrival at Sean's house, but without the distraction of small talk they were now directly exposed to it, and it did not take more than thirty seconds before I could see the annoyance creeping onto their faces.

'Gabriel,' I said, 'has been playing this music, almost non-stop, since he was taken to Purdysburn and given access to a piano six months ago. Imagine, six months of this . . . but the question in my mind was always, why this music, what is the significance of it? When I began to observe Gabriel playing it, I knew immediately that he was not a natural-born pianist – it is a difficult piece, and he makes mistakes. He is, at best, a talented amateur when it comes to the piano. And yet . . . note the side of his neck *here* . . .'

I stepped closer to him, and indicated an area of scarring on his left-hand side as my audience looked at him. 'I concluded that this was not as a result of some injury, but rather through the wear and tear that comes with using another musical instrument entirely – a violin. I have not however, had the opportunity to prove this theory, at least until now.'

I held up my hand and clicked my fingers, and Alison duly appeared in the doorway and moved down the aisle between the seats with a violin case in her hand. She reached the front and placed the case on Gabriel's vacated seat, opened it, and then handed the instrument and bow to me. I showed it to the audience and said, 'This Stentor Elysia violin has been sponsored and tuned by Matchetts Music of Wellington Place, Belfast, for all your musical needs.'

My audience looked suitably confused. I held the violin and bow in my right hand and moved beside Gabriel. I placed my left hand on his left hand to stop him playing, and he did not resist. I then raised his hand and placed the neck of the violin in it, and his fingers immediately closed around it and sought out the strings. He held out his other hand automatically, seeking the bow. When he had grasped it he moved the instrument up is until it nestled between his shoulder and neck, pressing directly into the scarred area.

I stepped back and held my breath.

But not for long, because he began to play almost immediately.

The same music – but utterly transformed.

It soared. It swayed.

His fingers moved with a fluidity which had been totally absent from his piano-playing. There was a total and utter concentration on his face which belied the ease with which he was playing. I was also aware of something else – for the first time he was showing an emotion – an emotion of pure, unadulterated joy. And it wasn't just him. My audience was transfixed right through to the flourish at the end. There even threatened to be an outbreak of applause, mostly from Alison, but her hands never quite met once she saw the look on my face. I wrapped my hand around the neck of the violin to prevent Gabriel launching into it again, and his eyes seemed to focus on me for the first time. I tried to take the instrument from him, but he resisted, and I thought it better to let him hold onto it.

I nodded around at my audience, who appeared intrigued.

'Astonishing,' I said, 'truly astonishing. And now, ladies and gentlemen, I am going to call my first witness. Professor . . .?'

Immediately Martin Brady spoiled the atmosphere I had so carefully cultivated by cutting in with, '*Witness*? This isn't a court, it's a charade. Why are we even putting up with this?'

Sean O'Dromodery leaned forward and glared along the front row at him. 'Why don't you shut up, and let him get on with it?'

'It's my husband's funeral,' Martin snapped back, flapping his hand first in my direction, and then towards Gabriel, 'and I don't see why we should be subjected to this . . . circus.'

I could see the pulse hammering in the side of his head. If pushed to it, Martin Brady could probably have broken me in two. Nevertheless, it is good to goad.

'Maybe you're complaining too much,' I said. 'Perhaps you know more about all this than you're letting on?'

'Are you accusing *me* of—?'

'Just saying . . .'

'Jesus Christ! This really is pathetic! Good God, everyone knows me here.' He looked around him. Many nodded. Several looked away. 'That you could even—'

'You were in the SAS,' I said. 'You must know a hundred and one ways to kill a man.'

'Yes, I was – and yes, I do!' He stopped and pressed his fingers into his brow. He understood that he wasn't doing himself any favours. When he spoke again, his voice was lower, more restrained, but no less intimidating. 'I have killed *many* men – but *always* in the defence of our country, our way of life. But I also saw enough violence, enough *carnage* in my time in Afghanistan not to want to *ever* indulge in it again. Bernard was my oasis of peace and tranquillity. If you seriously think . . .'

'As it happens,' I said, 'I don't.'

'Then why the hell did you . . .?!'

'I'm just showing you, showing you *all* how easy it is to accuse someone of something, and once the mud sticks, it's very difficult to remove, even with new, high-powered Omo, which, incidentally, is no longer available in the United Kingdom.' They looked at me. 'So many of you have precon-ceived notions about Gabriel's guilt, which has been fanned by recent newspaper headlines and police warnings – but I intend, if you will give me the opportunity, to prove that he is in fact innocent. So may I proceed?'

Martin took a deep breath, and sat back. Sean did not take his eyes off him.

'Professor,' I said, 'if you would please have a seat?' I indicated the chair in the spotlight, and he quickly took it. He smiled benignly at me and flattened out a crease in his trousers. 'Will you please give us your name, and your profession, your position?'

'I am Joseph Sikorsky, and I am Professor of Music at the Beria Conservatory in Moscow.' His accent was identifiably Russian, but his English was very good. 'I am also the conductor of the Beria Conservatory Orchestra and Touring Ensemble.'

'Thank you, Professor. And you flew in for this today?' He nodded. 'Could you tell us something about the Conservatory?'

'Yes, indeed. The Conservatory was named after its original founder and sponsor, Lavrentiy Beria, the Georgian politician and state security administrator, chief of the Soviet security and secret police apparatus (NKVD) under Joseph Stalin during World War Two, and Deputy Premier in the post-war years. Beria was fiercely proud of his roots and particularly so of the works of his fellow Georgian, the composer Alexander Korsakov. When Beria was at the height of his powers he was able to support the founding of the Conservatory to help preserve, restore and promote Korsakov's music, which had fallen, as you say, off the radar, during the years of the glorious revolution, civil war and war.'

'Excuse me,' Gloria Mahood said, 'this is all very interesting, but what does it have to do with the price of fish?'

'Please,' I said, 'bear with us.' I returned my attention to the witness. 'Do you recognise this piece of music that Gabriel has been playing, Professor Sikorsky?'

'Yes, of course. It is from Alexander Korsakov's Fourth Concerto – it is a familiar piece to many Georgians but it is not well-known in the West.'

'More importantly, Professor, do you also recognise the man who has been playing it for us, this man, Gabriel, also known as The Man in the White Suit?'

'Yes, I do. His real name is Sergei Litvinov, and until earlier this year he was principal violinist with the Conservatory Orchestra. He is thirty-two years old, he is married to Ivana, and he has a young son, Sasha. They both miss him very much.'

I said, 'Sergei Litvinov. And can you tell us why he is no longer principal violinist?'

'He is no longer with the orchestra because he went . . . I believe the phrase is AWOL? Yes, he went AWOL during our most recent European tour, simply disappeared while we were in Vienna. He walked out of our hotel one night, and vanished. And despite our greatest efforts, that is the last we knew of him until I received an e-mail from you yesterday, after which I immediately jumped on a plane.'

'And you met him for the first time since, barely half an hour ago?'

'That is correct.'

'I have previously explained to you, and to our audience that Sergei has for all intents and purposes been a deaf-mute since his arrest, and perhaps prior to that. We now know that he is Georgian. Since you have arrived, have you been able to communicate with him in your native tongue?'

'No, nor in English, in which he is, or was, fluent.'

'You obviously knew him quite well – did he show any indication that he recognised you?'

'None.'

'And how did you find his general appearance, condition, et cetera since you last saw him?'

'He has lost much weight, but otherwise he is the Sergei I remember.'

'Was he in the habit on tour of wearing a white suit?'

'Yes. It was – how would you say, his trademark.'

'Yes, trademark indeed. Can you think of any reason why he should have disappeared in Vienna? Were there any particular pressures upon him, perhaps of a political nature or outside pressures?'

'I think not. There is no Cold War, he did not *defect*. If he wanted to leave the orchestra, if he wanted to come here to Ireland, that was entirely his choice. But he did have the pressure that comes with being a lead violinist, the pressure which comes with being away from your family for extended periods. He . . . how shall I say? He has . . . breakdown nervous, once before, and then too he disappeared, but in Moscow and he came home after a few days. This was different. I very much feared for his life. He is a fine violinist, and more, a fine man. It makes me very sad to see him here, in this . . . situation.'

'Thank you, Professor,' I said. 'You may retake your seat.'

Professor Sikorsky stood, but instead of crossing directly to his chair he stepped up to Gabriel, to *Sergei*, who was still cradling his violin. The Professor put a hand on his shoulder and gave it a gentle squeeze and his former colleague a benevolent smile before finally re-taking his seat.

Sergei's eyes followed him.

Whether he was confused by the deception or it was some kind of magical response to finally playing the Korsakov concerto on the instrument for which it was intended, I could not tell, but *something* had definitely changed: there was a light in his eyes that hadn't been there before and he was finally reacting to outside stimuli. I nodded gratefully towards Professor Sikorsky, or as I preferred to think of him, Brendan Coyle. He was not only an acclaimed writer, but also a rather good actor, or charlatan, depending on your point of view.

46

There was *obviously* no way for the real Professor Sikorsky to have travelled from Moscow in the few hours since we had exchanged e-mails and in time for the funeral; not only was it not feasible, there was no need for it. I was only seeking a way to communicate the information I had learned from him about Sergei to my audience without boring them to death. I was presenting a drama, after all, and it was vital to engage their interest in case they switched over to another channel.

The PowerPoint presentation of *The Faces of the Dead* had, I felt, not excited them as much as it had excited me. It did not matter that I had lied to them. I was not a lawyer, and Sean's front lounge was not a court of law. I was interested in getting to the truth by fair meals or foul. Brendan Coyle, though not everyone's cup of tea, was not particularly foul.

I took several moments to check the next projections on

my laptop while allowing the audience to exchange whispered views on the preceding evidence, then turned back to them and called Malachy Quinn to the witness chair. He came forward from the fourth row and took his seat. He sat stiffly, with his hands on his knees. He cleared his throat several times.

I said, 'Are you okay?'

'Yes, fine,' he replied, 'just a little discombobulated.'

'There is no need,' I said, 'to feel discombobulated. You're not on trial.'

He nodded but did not appear any more relaxed. It didn't much matter. I had only responded so that I could say 'discombobulated' out loud. One didn't often get the opportunity. It was even rarer to be able to say that one was combobulated. Or even bobulated. Alison, from somewhere, cleared her own throat, and I realised that I had said this out loud, and was managing to discombobulate my entire audience, while remaining bobulated myself.

I said, 'Mr Quinn, will you please tell the jury, ahm, everyone present, what you do for a living?'

'I am the Vice Principal of Saint Mary's Grammar School on the Falls Road.'

'And how long have you been at the school?'

'Twenty-five years, the last five as Vice Principal.'

I clicked up a photograph of the school. It was one of the most boring photographs ever taken.

I said, 'This was originally a church school?'

'There's been a church on the site for two hundred years; the school followed nearly a hundred and twenty years ago.'

'So would I be right in thinking that it started as

quite a small school, and gradually built to its current size? You have, what, about eight hundred and twenty-five pupils.'

'Yes, eight hundred and twenty-five exactly,' he said.

I knew that. I said, 'We can see the school here, and the church, and to one side there's a small graveyard, then there's a wall, and beyond that there's the site of the new shopping centre the O'Dromodery Brothers are building.'

'Yes.'

'This is being created on land that formerly belonged to the school?'

'Yes. It was deemed surplus to our requirements, and was sold about five years ago, when property was worth considerably more than it is now. We were very fortunate with the timing, and the school has benefited greatly as a result. We have managed to modernise the entire—'

'Mr Quinn,' I said, 'too much information. Let me ask you about *this*, the graveyard, which is kind of unusual to find in school grounds, is it not?'

'Well,' he replied, 'in a modern school yes, of course, but Saint Mary's has such a long history. With a church school, the priest and nuns would have been living on site, so back then it was only natural for them to be buried there. As I understand it, when the new school was built in the 1960s, it was felt important to maintain the graveyard within the school grounds.'

'How many graves are there?'

'I'm not entirely sure.'

'Simple enough to count the headstones, and from the photo, we can see perhaps twenty-five, would you agree?'

'Ahm, yes, probably.' Mr Quinn shifted in his seat. He said, 'I don't understand how this is relevant.'

'It is relevant because this was never a public graveyard – it was not for parishioners but was reserved for the priests and nuns who served in the church or worked at the school. It is relevant because twenty-five into two hundred simply does not compute. For the maths to work, it would mean that for every year the church has been in existence, only point one-eighth of a body could have been buried.'

He said, '*What?*'

I looked to my audience. 'Yes, indeed, one-eighth.'

From their lack of reaction, I quickly surmised that they had no idea what I was on about. So I clarified.

'Mr Quinn, there aren't enough bodies. I've been through the parish records. The school started small, but it built up quickly enough. Through all of those years there would have been many nuns teaching in the school, many priests, and this was in the days when life expectancy was low. There is no escaping the fact that there should be more graves. Many more.'

'Well, I see what . . . but, of course, priests retire, nuns often go home to their families, they move parishes, they—'

'And they are replaced. Mr Quinn, your school, your church – it's missing some corpses.'

'No, that's imp—'

'Not if you look at this.' I pushed a button. It brought up a Google street map of St Mary's. 'This is the school with its grounds as it is today. *This*, on the other hand,' I said, and pushed for the next picture, 'is one from the 1960s, when the new school had just been constructed. Note the line along the edge of the graveyard and compare it with this,' I brought up a third, 'from around a hundred years ago, showing the church, a much smaller school and the original living accommodation, which has long since been demolished. Note *this* line along *here*,' I said, approaching the wall and running my finger along the oldest of the images, 'which shows what was the original wall surrounding the graveyard. If you use the scale, and you can take my word for this, it clearly demonstrates that the area covered by the graveyard in the 1960s is much smaller than that on the older map.'

'I don't quite understand what you're getting at.'

'What I'm *getting at*, Mr Quinn, what I can *prove*, in fact, is that at some point during the construction of what was then the new school, the old wall around the gravestones was knocked down, and when it was rebuilt, it was rebuilt in the wrong place. It left a number of the graves outside the wall.'

'That's just ridiculous!'

'Mr Quinn, you told me yourself that the graveyard had fallen into disrepair, and we saw in the photo that even some of the comparatively recent gravestones have fallen over. You don't think it's possible that those much older graves, which perhaps only had simple markers, might have become overgrown, and then accidentally forgotten?'

'Well, I suppose . . .'

'My point being, Mr Quinn, that when Saint Mary's chose to sell part of its grounds to the O'Dromodery Brothers, it did not realise that it was also passing on to them land which contained the remains of some of its former staff.' I turned and looked directly at Sean O'Dromodery. 'Remains which began turning up once ground was broken on the WestBel shopping centre.'

I moved from my position at the wall to stand before the last of the Karamazovs. The adrenaline was pumping. Free of my previous ailments, I was able to enjoy it without worrying about a stroke. I looked down at him, and he looked up, and neither of us blinked.

'Remains which,' I went on, 'were their existence to become known, would not only lead to all building work being stopped, but might possibly threaten the entire project and conceivably lead to the collapse of your family business.' I nodded at Sean, and then extended it to the entire audience, who were, I was gratified and encouraged to see, absolutely enthralled.

'Yes, these skeletons could indeed have meant the end of the O'Dromodery Brothers' business, a building company which was already facing extinction because of the recession. They had *everything* riding on WestBel, and now it was being thrown into very serious doubt by these dusty, broken bones. What were these tough builders, who dragged themselves up from the bogs of Donegal by their fingernails, who built their empire through their own blood and sweat and tears, going to do? Run to the planning authorities with what they had unearthed and beg not to be shut down? Just lie down and take it? Or were they going to hold on to their last great hope by whatever nefarious means they could?'

I jabbed a finger at Sean O'Dromodery. 'In fact – by *murder*!'

47

'That's bollocks,' said Sean O'Dromodery, before rejecting my invitation to sit in the witness chair. He glanced back at his security guards, and must have been contemplating having me thrown out, but then DI Robinson moved along the side wall towards the front, and stopped against it without actually saying anything. This reminder of his presence was enough for Sean to stay his hand; he must also have been aware that all eyes were upon him, and that that scrutiny demanded a defence other than 'that's bollocks'. But he was not about to wilt under the expectation. He said, 'I invite you into my own house, on the day of my brother's funeral, and you disrespect him, and my family and me?'

'Yes,' I said. 'And I told you – you pays your money and you takes your chances.' I was in a confident mood. I liked being off all my drugs.

'If you – if *any* of you – think I'm somehow involved in

murder, I . . . Christ, I've never heard of anything so ridiculous. Bones? Bodies? Show me them. Show me the evidence!'

I indicated the wall-screen. 'I *have*.'

'No, you've shown a few maps and photographs. Where are these bones? Show me the *skeletons*.'

'Sean. Mr O'Dromodery. I don't need to. It's all there, it's in the paperwork. It brought Al Capone down, and it'll bring you down too.'

'I'm not Al bloody Capone! Christ! What is this?' He turned to DI Robinson. 'You're *allowing* this?'

DI Robinson gave a little shrug. 'You have to admit,' he said, 'it is kind of interesting. Usually he throws out a lot of dots, and then you wait and see him pick a pattern out of them. Really, you should stick with it – he can be very entertaining.'

'I don't believe I'm hearing this. I don't have to sit here and—'

'Well, actually, you pretty much do,' said DI Robinson. 'Alternatively, you can sit with me down at the station, where the food isn't as good and I can have you kept for as long as I want, what with all the murders we're trying to clear off our books before the inspectors come in.'

'Inspectors? What are you . . .?'

'Oh yes, we're going for one of those kitemark things – you know, to show we deliver a quality service? Bagging the likes of you would be the icing on the cake. So that's your choice: deal with it here, see where it goes, or take a trip downtown with me.'

Sean sat back and folded his arms. 'Right, *fine*,' he hissed, 'but I don't get it. I just don't get it. There is no fucking evidence. No bones!'

'There is no other logical explanation,' I said. 'Between the numbers of staff that passed through Saint Mary's and died in harness over the course of two hundred years and the number of graves, and the size of the current graveyard and the size of the original, one cannot draw any other conclusion.' I decided to return to my earlier analogy. 'It's like the once elusive Higgs bosun particle, Sean. Nobody has ever seen it, but still—'

'What the hell are you talking about? Higgs who?'

I looked to my audience and found that most of them looked as confused as he did. I had failed to take into account the fact that the O'Dromoderys really had emerged from the Donegal boglands, and while they undoubtedly knew how to throw a building together, they had probably not been well educated, and the same probably went for many of their relatives and friends present in the room. It was a rare lapse on my part. But I persevered with the analogy by attempting to explain it. It was, after all, part of the reason for my presence on this planet to educate. Granted, this usually revolved around mystery fiction, but I was far from a one-trick pony.

I said, 'Have you ever heard of the Large Hadron Collider?'

'No,' said Sean.

'Anyone?'

A scattering of hands went up.

'It's in Switzerland,' said one of the relatives.

'Underground,' said another. 'It's like a big tunnel. It goes round in a circle. They shoot things around it, really fast.'

'Like Corgi Rockets?' asked one.

'You mean Hot Wheels,' said another. 'I don't think they were made by Corgi . . .'

'It was Mattel,' I said, because I knew *exactly* what they were talking about. I had never been allowed toy cars or their race tracks, but at Christmas Mother would give me a wrapped Kays Catalogue so that I could at least look at the presents I wasn't getting. 'But more to the point, I'm actually referring to the world's largest particle accelerator as built by the European Organisation for Nuclear Research. It allows physicists to test the predictions of different theories of particle physics and high-energy physics, and particularly to test for the existence of the hypothesised Higgs boson, the so-called God particle. The Higgs is a hypothetical elementary particle that is predicted to exist by the Standard Model of particle physics . . .'

I only stopped when I caught sight of Alison, back by the door, making a cutting motion across her throat, and Jeff, covering his face with his hands. I looked instead to DI Robinson.

He said, 'Some bones would certainly help.'

I said, 'There are no bones.'

'Then stop this with this bullshit!' Sean erupted.

'No bones,' I said, 'but I do have a coffin.'

And that stopped him. I looked across the room to my trusted assistant, and said, 'Jeff – bring forth the *defixios*.'

They were all craning their necks as I lined them up on a table which had previously held tea and coffee urns and which Alison and Jeff hurried to remove; I didn't lend a hand because it was beneath me. Alison smoothed down the tablecloth and Jeff pulled the *defixios* one by one out of a Nike sports bag and set them down. I put three of them side by side, then the fourth a little to the right, leaving a space between it and the others. I then projected pre-loaded images of the tablets onto the wall. I stood back and gave my audience a little time to study the images and the inscriptions, and exchange whispered views with their nearest and dearest.

Then I said, 'These, ladies and gentlemen, are what are known as *defixios*. They are curse tablets, and were once common in the Graeco-Roman world. Basically they ask the ancient gods to do harm to others. Each of these four *defixios* was discovered either at one of our murder scenes, or at a place where murder was intended. These first three were found at the homes of each of the O'Dromodery Brothers, including just outside this very house, though fortunately Sean is not yet dead. This fourth one was found at my own house, where I believe an attempt was made to murder me, though luckily only my girlfriend was in. The assassins were foiled by the intervention of Detective Inspector Robinson . . .'

I nodded my appreciation at him, and I kind of meant it. Before I could continue, Sonya Delaney said, 'Was there not one for my Francis?'

'No, Mrs Delaney. Nor was there one for Bobby Preston.'

'What about my Sam?' Gloria Mahood asked.

'Well, as it happens . . .' I picked out the All Star Health Club's manager in the fourth row back. 'Gary, did you bring the *defixio* you discovered after Fat Sam's murder like I asked you?'

Gary Drennan nodded, and reached down to a Tesco bag

at his feet. I waved him forward. As he approached I said, 'Ladies and gentlemen, if my theory is correct, this *defixio* will fit neatly into the gap I have left here for it.'

Gary handed me the bag and I carefully lifted out the fifth *defixio* and took it to the table, where I moved the other tablets slightly to make room for it.

'You see that they fit together perfectly? This proves that they were cut from the same strip of lead.'

'So what?' Gloria asked. 'What's it got to do with my—?'

'Mrs Mahood – Gloria – please note the length of the strip. Please note the shape. And finally please note . . .' I moved back to the table and turned over the *defixio* that had come from the All Star; I pointed to the image on the wall '. . . this mark, and this number, engraved in very small numbers on the reverse.'

'I still don't get it.'

'This strip formed an interior base to a coffin. Lead was used to stop the essence of a corpse leaking out through the wood both for spiritual and practical reasons. *This* is its maker's mark, and this number identifies which undertaking establishment it was sold to. With this number, which Gary read to me last night over the phone . . .'

'I didn't know it was you,' said Gary. 'You said you were one of the directors of the club.'

'Yes,' I said. 'I lied. But there's nothing wrong with lying in pursuit of the truth. So with this number I was able to track down the coffin's manufacturer in England, which was and still is part of an undertaking business with several funeral homes across the country. They were able to tell me that this coffin was built in 1938 and sold in the following year for the transportation of an Irish priest who had been killed in a road accident while attending an ecclesiastical conference in Derby. We can see from *this* copy of the under-taker's original invoice that it was paid for by Saint Mary's Church and School in Belfast, for the burial of Patrick Duncan, who was, I understand . . .'

'Father Duncan!' Vice Principal Quinn suddenly piped up. 'He was Headmaster before the war! His picture hangs in our reception!'

'But he's not in your graveyard as it currently stands?'

Quinn rubbed at his chin. 'Do you know, I've been there quite a few years and I've never seen his grave. And yet, now that I think about it, he must have been buried there. I've seen photographs of the service in our archives.'

'Which again suggests,' I said, 'that when the wall was rebuilt, he and many others found themselves on the wrong side of it, and more recently, part of the foundations of the WestBel.' I turned to face Sean. 'What do you say to that? Is that bollocks too?'

'Yes, it still sounds like—'

'And the fact that these *defixios* were cut from this coffin and inscribed with ancient curses suggests that someone on your side of the fence knew about its discovery. Someone who wouldn't shut up about it and threatened to go to the authorities, so something had to be done about him – and who better to sort him out for good than your very own employee Fat Sam Mahood? What do you say to that, Sean? Is *that* bollocks too?'

'Yes, it is.'

I laughed. A bit stagey, but apt.

'You *really* don't think this means anything?'

'I *really* don't.' He stood up and looked around the mourners. 'And I *really* think this has gone on long enough. My friends, I apologise for making you sit through this. I thought we were here not only to say a final farewell to my brother, but also to unmask whoever was trying to kill me. But so far all I've heard are some vague accusations against my late brothers and me which seem to be based on some frankly barking logic and even more dubious history. Whatever you may say, sir,' he said, sticking a finger in my direction, 'this is most certainly *not* what I've paid you for.' He thumbed towards the door. 'So I say to you, either shit or get off the pot.'

People can be very impatient. I had set this up in a particular way, but now he was threatening to drop the curtains and close the show before I was fully into the third act. But I was a showman, and the show had to go on even if it meant rewriting on the hoof. I let out a sigh and threw my hands up in mock exaggeration.

'Okay,' I said. 'You want whoever is responsible for trying to kill you? And your brothers? Right now? On a plate? Okay, if it's *that* important to you, have it your way.' I spun to my left – I can do that, these days – and pointed along the front row. 'Nicola Sheridan,' I said, *'j'accuse*!'

48

Nicola did not seem unduly surprised by my accusation, which was in itself not a surprise. I knew her to be calculating, and quite the actress. She sat quite still, her eyes fixed on me, but unreadable, and then slowly she reached up and checked her green hat was sitting properly. She smoothed down the creases in her skirt, and then stood and crossed to the witness chair. She sat with her back straight and her thickset legs at a slight angle. It was, I thought, a confident pose, and I supposed that this meant that she had some surprise of her own up her sleeve. I observed that Sean O'Dromodery was trying to catch her eye. When he finally did he mouthed her name and then shook his head and looked at me.

'Nicola,' he began, 'is . . .'

'Overweight, yes,' I said.

'I didn't mean . . .'

'No, but we're all thinking it: how could a big girl who

hasn't seen the top side of a vaulting horse for many a year possibly throw herself about sufficiently to stab one brother, throw another from a roof and rip the guts out of Fat Sam Mahood?'

I turned to Nicola. 'Do you want to tell him or should I?'

'Tell him *what*?' Nicola asked. 'I've no idea what you're talking about. The very notion of *me* killing anyone! I thought we were working together to try and clear this poor man's name, but now suddenly you're accusing me of murder.'

'Yes,' I said.

'Well then, you are a sad and twisted individual. But for the record – and *that's* a laugh, though I do hope someone *is* recording this, because it will be *very* sad when it goes on YouTube – but for the record, yes, I very much believe my husband was murdered.'

'And who do you think was responsible?'

'You know this already.' I indicated the audience, and she let out an exasperated sigh. 'Okay. All *right*. I became convinced that Fat Sam Mahood was responsible.'

'And what did you do about that?'

'I appealed to the O'Dromodery Brothers to help me prove it, but they very understandably wanted to leave the investigations to the forces of law and order. Look – I very much believe that the Lord moves in mysterious ways, and that when Fat Sam was killed, that was Him doing some of that moving. And that's about as much as I know about this whole sordid business. Sean? I'm sorry for your loss, and the only reason I'm here is that I've come to believe that . . . Sergei . . . isn't guilty of anything – and that's where I hoped all this was leading. But no, all we're getting are the state-sponsored ravings of a lunatic.'

She made a point of looking at DI Robinson and then allowed her gaze to settle back on me.

I said, 'They're not state sponsored.'

'State indulged,' said DI Robinson, 'but there *is* a limit to the state's patience.' He gave me the eyes.

I don't take many of my cues from James Patterson, but brevity now seemed the way to go. I said, 'Nicola, nobody is accusing you of actually physically killing anyone, but you did, without doubt, orchestrate the deaths of Fat Sam and the O'Dromodery Brothers and you organised the attempt on my own life.'

'What about my Francis?' Sonya Delaney demanded.

'No,' I said, without taking my eyes off Nicola. 'But I'll come to that. Nicola, your husband Bobby was the architect of the WestBel project. He worked closely with the O'Dromodery Brothers and was often on site.' I turned to my left. 'Is that right, Sean?' He nodded. I turned back. 'You have told me yourself that he was unhappy about something in work, and that Fat Sam came to see him, and they had an argument, and the following day, Bobby was knocked down and killed. You say your husband never discussed with you the nature of the problem at work?'

'No, he didn't.'

'These *defixios*,' and I indicated the screen, 'are without doubt inscribed with Latin curses. Nicola, would you mind identifying this next photograph?'

I clicked it up and she looked at it, and there was a moment of incomprehension, followed by a moment of comprehension.

It showed two rows of young people, somewhat formally posed, and looking studiously at the camera. Judging by the hairstyles and fashions, it was at least twenty years old.

'Nicola?'

She said, 'It's my year at Queen's.'

'Yes, indeed. You are well remembered in the History Department, and one phone call brought me to this picture. You are – as we look at it – back left, two from the end of the row.' There were a few whispered comments from the audience, no doubt alluding to the fact that since then she'd put on a lot of weight. 'And your late husband?'

'Yes, in the front row, right in the middle. With the glasses.'

'I see. Yes. Bobby Preston. But, Nicola – this is more than just your year group. This is a club within the university, isn't it? Will you tell us what that club is?'

'It's the History Society.'

'Be more specific.'

'It's the Latin Club, within the History Society.'

Murmurs.

'You and your husband were both passionate about Latin.'

'*Yes*. It isn't a crime.'

'Well, that remains to be seen.'

There was a ripple of appreciation for that. I felt a little surge of adrenaline.

For the first time, Nicola looked a little piqued. 'So I know Latin. I also speak German, but I am not guilty of war crimes.'

'Well, that remains to be seen.'

She did not like that, but my audience loved it. There were beads of sweat on her brow. The lights were helping, which was intentional.

383

I said, 'Nicola – I have great sympathy for you. I do believe your husband was murdered by Fat Sam Mahood. We know that they argued on the night before Bobby was killed. That argument must have been about the bodies found on the building site, but there would have been no need for it unless Bobby had some evidence he could show to the authorities. And this is what I believe he had.' I indicated the table with the *defixios*. 'And this is what Fat Sam wanted – the return of the coffin, which your husband somehow smuggled out. Are you with me on this?' Nicola nodded warily. 'You'll agree, he must have been under tremendous pressure.'

'Yes – yes, he was.'

'And he may have been torn – the need to keep working in these difficult times versus perhaps his conviction that these bodies, these remains, should not end up under some shopping centre, but that they should be acknowledged and treated with the respect they deserved.'

She moved position, this time sitting straight up and gripping the arms of her chair. As she did so, her hat began to fall; she plucked out a longish hatpin, fiddled with it for a moment, and then changed her mind and took the hat fully off and placed it in her lap. 'He *was* a nervous wreck,' she said, 'but I didn't know why. If only I'd—'

'He was chariman of the Latin Club?'

'What? Yes, yes. Captain, we called it.'

'So he was passionate about it.'

'Oh yes, he lived and breathed it. He could have been an academic, but he said he didn't want to ruin his love for Latin by teaching it. He just enjoyed the language.'

'Nicola, do you think it's reasonable to suggest that perhaps

Bobby was a little bit . . . thrown, maybe even unbalanced by the pressure that was being applied to him? He knew all about *defixios* through his love of Latin, didn't he? Is it possible, do you think, that *he* wrote these inscriptions? That *he* planted them at the homes of those who were putting him under this pressure? Is it possible, Nicola, that your husband predicted his own demise, and decided to organise his revenge in advance?'

Her mouth dropped open a little, and her eyes flitted from me to DI Robinson and back. 'I . . . don't know.'

I moved closer. I put my finger to my lips and stared at the projection above her as if I was just then working it out in my head.

I said, 'Nicola – your husband was a middle-aged man, an architect, a Latin scholar, he was not a man of action. But he had worked in the building trade for a long time. It is an industry full of unsavoury types prepared to do things for cash, no questions asked. He suspected he was going to be killed so he set a plan in motion for what would happen if he was. He cut these *defixios* from the lead base of the coffin, inscribed them in his favourite language and ordered that they be planted, one by one, over a period of time so as not to arouse enough suspicion that the entire plan would be compromised, and once they were in place, then the killers he hired would strike, and take his revenge in the most bloody manner imaginable.'

I nodded around the audience. They were transfixed.

Nicola said, 'I don't know. That's not very plausible. My Bobby – he did have this real sense of right and wrong, and also . . . also . . . he never really got angry – although he never forgot when someone hurt him, in life, or in business. He never forgot, so I suppose . . . I mean – could he have done that? Could he really?'

I spread my hands before her. 'I think he could.'

'*My* Bobby?'

'Your Bobby.'

'No, no – wait a minute,' It was Sean O'Dromodery, on his feet. 'That doesn't make sense. My *defixio* was only planted a few days ago.'

'True,' I nodded, 'but as I said, he knew if he planted them all at the same time, people would become suspicious.'

'Okay – but what about the one at your house?' Sean demanded. 'He could not possibly have predicted that my brother would hire you to look into this! He was dead long before you got involved.'

I made it look as if I was thinking about this. I rubbed at my jaw.

'Well, perhaps he gave the killers free rein to take whatever measures they had to, to protect the master-plan. Perhaps they had access to the remaining lead from the coffin and created their own *defixio*. Engraving is easy enough.'

Sean was trying to work it out in his head, without much apparent success. He could build things, he just couldn't take them apart and analyse them the way I could.

I said, 'It's as unlikely as it is complicated. But it is *possible* that Bobby Preston set this all up in advance. He was an architect, he made plans for a living, he designed extremely complicated things which had to work. That's what this is and was – an architect's revenge. In fact, almost the perfect crime.'

Sean stood there, shaking his head. 'We were never anything other than good to him,' he said, before dropping back into his seat. He raised his hands so that they covered his mouth and nose, almost in prayer. 'He planned it all? He killed my brothers?'

'No.'

It was not I. Nor was it Nicola, making a last desperate attempt to save the reputation of her late husband. It was not even DI Robinson applying his jaundiced eye to my theory.

It was Sergei, sitting forgotten at the keyboard, with the violin and bow cradled in his lap. He had said it so quietly that at first only Nicola and I, being closest, heard him.

Nicola began to get up. 'No . . .'

'No!' Sergei said louder. 'It was not him!'

And this time he got everyone's attention.

It was all going absolutely to plan.

49

I was certainly not alone in recognising that we had reached a tipping point. Sergei was involved in the murder of Fat Sam Mahood; he was definitely involved in the death of Francis Delaney; and if he was not physically involved in the killing of the O'Dromodery Brothers, he was at least connected to them, because they were connected to each other. He knew things, he *had* to know things, and whether it was his stay with Nicola, being reunited with his precious instrument or even having the memories dredged up by my skilful interrogation of the fake Professor Sikorsky that had prompted his interruption – well, it didn't matter. The fact was that he was out of it and apparently ready to talk.

When the hubbub had died down sufficiently, I asked Nicola to vacate the witness chair and she did so without further comment. She lifted her hat and made her way – somewhat shakily, I might add – back to her seat, which was just two up from Sean O'Dromodery, who now appeared as buzzed as everyone else in the room. She avoided eye-contact with Sergei, who studied her every step of the way.

'Sergei,' I said, 'will you please take the witness chair.'

He set the violin and the bow onto his seat and moved slowly but deliberately across to sit in the witness chair. He looked at the ground for several long moments, as if he was psyching himself up, and then his eyes ranged across the audience. They only settled on me when I said, 'Over here.'

And he said, 'Hello.'

'So – you are Sergei, Sergei Litvinov, and you were principal violinist with the Beria Conservatory Orchestra, until you went missing in Vienna?'

'Yes.'

'Good. And are you . . . feeling better now?'

'Better?'

'You have been unwell.'

His hand moved to his side and he said, vaguely: 'Unwell, yes.'

'In fact, you were seriously ill. Physically *and* mentally.'

'I . . .'

'You suffered a nervous breakdown once before, and another, more serious one while on tour with your orchestra. It came upon you so suddenly that there was no time to tell anyone; you just walked out of your hotel in Vienna and disappeared.'

'Yes, I think so.'

'Christ,' said Martin Brady, 'he's like a nodding dog – he says yes to everything.'

I ignored him. 'And then you turned up here, Sergei. What brought you to Ireland?'

'A ferry,' he said.

'I mean, why Ireland?'

He shrugged. 'I do not know. I was in many countries, I think. I drink a lot of vodka. And the more I drink, the less money I have, and the cheaper vodka I buy. I . . . how you say . . .?' He raised his arm and mimicked playing his violin, and then held his hand out in front of him, palm open.

'You begged.'

'Yes – no. I . . .?' He kept his hand out.

'Busked,' said Jeff, from the back.

Sergei nodded. 'Busked, yes.'

'This was in Belfast?'

'Yes, a very lovely people. But then they attacked me. Beat me. I do not know why. Many people, with feet.'

'You were kicked, you mean?'

'Many times. Yes. And then I woke up in hospital. I was not well.'

'No, you were not.' I moved to the laptop and pressed the button and the next image was thrown up on the wall. I allowed my gaze to wander over my audience until I found who I was looking for. 'Dr Winter?' He raised his hand. 'Dr Winter, you work in the City?' He nodded. 'Do you recognise these medical records?'

'No, I've never seen them before, and if I had it would be unethical and illegal for me to display them in this manner.'

'Absolutely. But can you at least tell us what they show?'

'Yes. They show that a male by the name of Joe Soap was admitted to the Belfast City Hospital, suffering from a catalogue of injuries. Head trauma, spleen, ribs, other internal damage.'

'Fairly serious.'

'*Very* serious. Life-threatening, I would say.'

'And the name, Joe Soap?'

'That's like a generic name that would be used if a patient is brought in without indentification. In America they use John Doe – here no set name is used, so it could be a John Smith or a Fred Bloggs or in this case, Joe Soap.'

'And what does the second document show?'

'That would be a surgical record, which indicates that the patient underwent a double kidney transplant. Double transplants are extremely rare.'

'Would I be correct in thinking that a single kidney transplant – the donor could be a relative, or a friend, or someone who has passed away?'

'Yes, of course. It all depends on getting the right match.'

'But a double kidney transplant would necessarily have to come from someone who has very recently died.'

'Almost certainly.'

'Dr Winter – you have examined the witness, have you not?'

'Yes, you know I have – you asked me to.' I gave him a look. 'Yes, I have.'

'And can you confirm without us asking him to take his top off, if there is indeed a scar that would suggest that he has fairly recently had an operation in his kidney region.'

'Yes, he has.'

'And the third document I'm putting up now – it shows the name of the donor of these kidneys, does it not?' He nodded. 'Would you please read out that name?'

The audience was there way ahead of him. But he said it anyway.

'Robert Preston,' said Dr Winter.

*   *   *

Everyone *jumped*.

But not because of the revelations, but because the girl from the catering company had dropped her tray, and the metallic clatter sent a shockwave through them. As displaced vols-au-vent rolled under chairs, the embarrassed young thing was torn between apologising and retrieving them.

'For God's sake, leave them!' snapped Sean.

The girl seemed to wilt under his gaze. She slowly eased herself back up onto her seat. Her colleague was both more subtle and less intimidated. The young man lowered himself from his chair, which was at the end of a row, into a crouching position which allowed him to move in behind the front row and out of the eye-line of his employer to feel about for the spilled pastries.

This is what I was going to do next: I was going to get Dr Winter to explain the next set of documents, which showed that Bobby Preston had been filleted like a kipper and his body parts transplanted in no less than seven individuals in need of a heart, a liver, lungs, pancreas, intestine and thymus. I was going to jokingly ask what had killed him, because all his bits and pieces seemed to be in fine working order. I was going to then return to Sergei and ask how he had first come to meet Nicola Sheridan, and I expected that he would tell me that she had sought him out and in his weakened physical and mental state convinced him that the only reason he was alive was because of her husband, that he owed him a blood debt and that the only way to repay that debt was to exact vengeance, an eye for an eye and a murder for a double kidney. She had directed him to the All Star Health Club where he hid himself away at the end of the night and waited

The Prisoner of Brenda

for Fat Sam. I did not quite know what he would say after that: whether he had been involved in the actual stabbing or whether it had been left to the others.

Yes, the *others*, who had definitely carried out the murders, who had gutted Fat Sam and thrown Fergus, and zapped Martin Brady before stabbing his husband, who had made an attempt to enter my house and whose final act of violence was to be today, on Sean O'Dromodery, and which I and DI Robinson had been anticipating all morning. That was why we had armed officers strategically placed around Sean, that was why when they made their attempt, they were ready for it.

Jackie McQuiston, the erstwhile All Star employee, now working for the catering company, took her seat as ordered and was replaced by Peter McDaid, another ex-All Star employee, who shuffled along the floor looking for lost vols-au-vent until he was right behind the last of the O'Dromoderys. He then produced his knife and rose up ready to slash Sean across the throat, only for the police officers to pounce upon him and drag him down as the audience screamed and threw themselves away from the mayhem.

DI Robinson hurled himself into the thick of it, while other officers piled upon Jackie McQuiston even though she was crying and shaking like an orphan in a snow storm. And I couldn't help but clap my hands together joyfully because I had correctly identified Sergei and exposed the killers. Alison was smiling broadly at me and Jeff was giving me the thumbs-up.

Sergei was inspired to pick up his violin again and he began to play his damned theme tune once more. And in all of the shouting and screaming and reading of rights and playing of music, nobody noticed that Sean hadn't moved a muscle and it only became clear why when I saw that he was stone cold dead, with a hatpin through his eye and into his brain, and Nicola was standing there as triumphant as I had been, but in a hell of a lot more trouble.

50

It was definitely the most exciting funeral gathering anyone had been to in years.

Depending on whom you spoke to it was, variously, a shambles, a triumph or a horror show. Everyone seemed to have an opinion on it with the notable exception of Sean O'Dromodery, who no longer had an opinion on anything. Because nobody had actually seen Nicola insert the hatpin in his eyeball, they had to leave Sean where he was while they calculated angles and positions and tried to second-guess the arguments that the experts called in by her defence team would make about opportunity, and her being left-handed when the pin could only have been stabbed into him with the right and other such proofy-type nonsense. They didn't yet know that I had it all on a crisp digital recording, which I could later use to bargain my way out of any charges DI Robinson might choose to hang on me for busting Sergei out of Purdysburn.

Nicola was as guilty as sin. She sat on a chair in the hallway, handcuffed to a WPC; her head was slumped down on her chest, and there was a dried-out riverbed of tears on her cheeks, which was replenished every few minutes by a little flash flood. I did not know how much she had wept over the death of her husband, but I suspected she had kept most of it bottled up while she was consumed by planning her revenge. Two of her accomplices were outside, in separate police cars. I was sure that they would tell all. Their arrest had seemed to break whatever spell Nicola had over them, and the words and the justifications and even the apologies came spilling out of them as they were led away. Soon enough their solicitors would order them to clam up, but for the moment the most obvious emotion coming from them was one of relief. My first impression from listening to them was that they were a bit stupid, and therefore easily swayed and manipulated by someone who was used to swaying and manipulating, like a schoolteacher. Sergei, meanwhile, was left sitting in the front room, playing his violin, while DI Robinson tried to puzzle out what to do with him. I suggested something to him, and he seemed to find it reasonable, so I said I would set it up and went outside to make the call.

Alison found me there.

She said, 'It's raining.'

I said, 'Is it raining? I hadn't noticed.'

She snorted and said, *'Four Weddings and a Funeral.'*

I said, 'I have no idea what you're talking about.'

I put the phone away. She hooked her arm through mine. 'You okay?'

I said, 'So-so.'

'You don't like to lose a client.'

'Yes.'

'And you think you could have saved him.'

'Yes. I should have guessed about the pin, the way she was playing with the hat the whole time. She might as well have been twirling a gun around in her hand.'

'There were police all around him, they should have protected him.'

'Yes, and no. Part of me thinks she always intended to use those kids as a diversionary tactic. The other part thinks she just seized her opportunity. Either way, he was my client and I set this all up. If I hadn't put on the show trial, he would still be alive.'

'Perhaps. But if you hadn't put on the show trial, they'd still be out there, plotting, and they've been tenacious and efficient up to now, so he was on borrowed time anyway.'

I said, 'I suppose. It's just unsatisfactory.'

'Because you weren't carried shoulder-high from the court, with people cheering and yelling bravo? You wanted your Atticus Finch moment.'

'Of course. But more than that. I . . . made a mistake. He should not be dead.'

'Hey – you're only human. Humans make mistakes.'

'You mean you agree I made a mistake?'

Her eyes narrowed.

We began to walk around the outside of the house. The rain was not heavy, nor was it particularly cold. She said, 'How did you know it was Nicola? And when?'

'Uhm. I suspected, as soon as I knew she was putting on

an act for her hospital visits. But I only knew for sure when the *defixio* turned up at my house.'

'Our house,' said Alison.

'Legally . . .' I began. She gave me the eye. *'Okay.* Our house. The inscription – the curse on the family of Anthony Boucher.'

'Who's he? I thought you were going to call him as a witness.'

'If only, but he's been dead for years. Anthony Boucher was a renowned American mystery writer, editor and critic. You've heard me talk about Bouchercon before? It's where writers and devotees meet every year . . .'

'Like Comic-Con.'

'Yes, but interesting. Well, it's named after him. The awards given out there are called the Anthony's, after him.'

'And the relevance to *this* is . . .?'

'None, apart from the fact that when we left Nicola's house, you remember I swapped one business card for another?'

'I do. I remember thinking you were being a bit anal about it, but then that's you. The *old* you, I might add.'

I gave her a squeeze and told her that I'd printed the card out on the morning of my escape from Purdysburn, and substituted my real name for that of the late mystery writer. 'It was just a shot in the dark. But I think our little visit spooked her enough to set the dogs on us. She couldn't just scare us off, she had to create a *defixio* for us. It was all part of her justification for what she was doing. And being so focused on her master-plan, she hadn't registered my name when you gave her my card the first time round. She found the second card, copied the name onto the *defixio* and that was enough to trap her: nobody else in the world knew about the card, so it had to be her.'

'Sometimes,' Alison said, 'I wonder what your brain would look like under a microscope.'

'Well,' I said, 'I hope you never get the opportunity to find out.'

It was a big house. Round the back, out of sight of the police and the few remaining mourners, Alison grabbed me and gave me a snog. I did not resist. A taxi was just pulling up when we arrived back in front. The rear door opened and Nurse Brenda climbed out. She was glowing. She came straight across and threw her arms around me and said, 'Thank you, thank you. You did it, you did it.'

Her bosoms were enormous. When she let me go I saw that Alison was grinning.

'Sergei,' Nurse Brenda said. 'His name is Sergei!'

I had updated her on the phone. I said, 'He could still be charged with murder.'

'I know that. I always knew that. But I also know he's innocent. You can tell. Oh look – here he comes!'

We turned. DI Robinson was just emerging with Sergei, who was still carrying his violin. He was not handcuffed, which pretty much summed up the inspector's thoughts on how dangerous he was or how likely he was to make a run for it without me there to encourage him. I had told him about Patrick confessing to the murder of Francis Delaney and he'd said it would be difficult to prove that anyone was guilty of it, given that they were all a bunch of nuts.

They came down the steps, and Nurse Brenda went forward

and put her arms around Sergei and hugged him – and I could see over her shoulder his eyes widening and I could tell that he did not recognise or remember her at all.

DI Robinson cleared his throat, and then once again, until Nurse Brenda released Sergei. He nodded at the taxi and said, 'I'll ride to Purdysburn with you, just to make sure you all arrive safe and sound, and then we'll take a look at everything once all this calms down.'

'I'm sure we'll be fine by ourselves,' said Nurse Brenda.

'I'll ride with you to Purdysburn,' DI Robinson repeated.

Nurse Brenda was too happy to put up an argument, or to use her eyes on him. It was a pity that I was no longer controlling the agenda, because I would like to have seen how she coped with *my* eyes now that I was free of my drugs; I reckoned I could have held my own. I would like to have told her that Sergei had a wife and family and that they would be coming to see him and perhaps claiming him back and taking him away, but I did not. Everyone should have a little happiness, no matter how fleeting, and I was looking forward to mine, one day.

Nurse Brenda guided her charge towards the cab and he climbed in and sat back and then turned his stubbled, hollowed face towards me. I nodded at him and he nodded back and slowly, slowly he began to disappear as his breath misted up the window.

Nurse Brenda squeezed in beside him from the other side. DI Robinson intended to move in after her, but hesitated when he saw how little room there now was; then he moved to the front passenger door and opened it, but before he climbed in he winked at Alison, which I didn't like, and then jabbed a finger at me and said, 'I'll be seeing you,' and I said, 'Not if I see you first.' He gave a shake of his head and got in and slammed the door.

As the driver started the engine I took a last look at Sergei, but his face was almost entirely hidden by the misting up – except for where he was moving his finger across the glass and making shapes, and then I saw that they weren't shapes, but numbers, and written in reverse so that they were easy for me to read.

Alison, holding on to me, felt me tense, and said, 'What is it?'

I kept staring at the window, at the figures, until Sergei put his full palm against the glass and smoothed it across, removing them. The car began to pull away, and he did not look towards me then or back at me as they departed.

I said, 'One hundred and forty-eight point five.'

And Alison said, '*Wah*?'

And I said, 'It's the square root of twenty-two thousand and fifty-six.'

And Alison said, 'So *what*?'

Epilogue

I was back where I belonged, and yet I was no longer sure if I really did. I love No Alibis and I love my books, but I was unsettled. In the absence of anything resembling a customer, with Jeff off taking another exam, I had spent several hours on Mother's Kindle, trying to distract myself, and much to my surprise I found that I did not hate the machine as much as I had imagined, and in fact it got me thinking about the possibilities, and wondering if there was a way to exploit them. I daydreamed about selling e-books through the store, or the website. Perhaps I could get neglected Irish crime classics digitised and act as their publisher, taking a cut and passing at least some of the profits on to the authors or their literary estates. And then I thought, why stick to Irish classics? There were thousands of pulp titles that had never been properly published or which had fallen out of print. Maybe I could get the rights to them and aim at the world market.

Or perhaps – now that my head was clear and my body clean – I could do what I had always secretly thought of doing, but had never dared say out loud: I could write my own novel. What was to stop me? I had read every crime-fiction title worth reading and many others besides, I had the experience of tackling real crime and I had listened to enough of Brendan Coyle's crappy creative writing classes to know I was at least on a par with his best students, and probably much, much better. I knew the template for writing crime fiction, and that the key was to write something new and original but to remember not to mess with that template too much. Give the public what it was used to, but with a twist. I could write an Irish crime classic. No – why limit myself? I would write a classic, for the whole world, and for all time, and make a mint in the process. I would transform myself from bookseller to a book *seller*.

I put the Kindle down and sighed. I could not get Sergei and his square root out of my head. He might well just have dragged it up from his subconscious – or he had been perfectly aware that I was in that Purdysburn cell with him and that I had tossed the number out to him as a challenge which had seemed not to register. Was his muteness an act all along, and if so, what did that say about him, and his contribution to the murder of Fat Sam Mahood? What frustrated me was that I might *never* know. I like things to be in black and white, but like Sergei's only suit, they were increasingly grey.

Alison phoned to see if I was coming home for lunch and when I said no she said good, because there was nothing in and she was about to go to Tescos and I said, 'I'd like to go to Tescos.'

She snorted. She said, 'You never go to Tescos.'

'Nevertheless.'

'But you never go shopping with me!'

'That's true. And I don't want to now. I want to go shopping *for* you.'

'*What?*'

'It's not fair that it's all left up to you. I'm sure you have a million and one other things you have to be doing.'

'Are you serious?'

'Completely.'

'This is brilliant! I love the new you! When you get home I'm going to ride your brains out!'

'Okay,' I said.

She did have other things to do. She had to take Page to try out a nursery, and Mother had a doctor's appointment. So she gave me a list of groceries we needed but said that they weren't prescriptive.

'Feel free to improvise,' she said.

I drove to Tesco. I chose the one off the Newtownards Road. From the car park, I had a view of the All Star Health Club. I knew there were hoods in there, working out and popping steroids. I would never know what Fat Sam's connection to them really was, or how much involved the manager was, or if he had thrown me out to protect himself or because I was very, very nosy. Sergei had been caught on security camera inside. He had been the only one not wearing a mask. He told DI Robinson that when he fully realised the consequence of what was about to happen, he tore off his mask and tried to warn Fat Sam, but was beaten to it by his accomplices, whose faces he had never seen. DI Robinson said he was guilty by association and intent, but was unsure if he could get a conviction. Something was worked out with the Russian Embassy and he was released into their custody until he could be picked up by his family and escorted home.

When I called the hospital and asked to speak to Nurse Brenda, they told me she was on sick leave. Perhaps she had her heart broken. Perhaps she found that once Sergei opened his mouth and mind, she didn't like him quite as much.

I pushed a trolley around the shopping centre. I had only completed one aisle and it was almost full. I realised that taking one of everything wasn't the way to do it. I would have to pick and choose. There was a whole new world out there, and I was determined to sample all of it. But I needed to take my time, otherwise I would never make it out of the fruit department.

After ninety minutes I joined a queue at one of the check-outs, more or less satisfied with my selection, which evenly covered all of the major food groups.

When my turn came and the groceries passed along the conveyor belt, the woman behind the cash register said, 'Would you like some help in bagging your items?' and I said no, and I began to bag them myself. I found it quite therapeutic. I organised the fruit, and meat and the vege-tables into separate bags. When the woman had totted up the final amount she said, 'We have a special offer on today – if you spend another 14p you get £5 off your next shop.'

I said, 'What do you have for 14p?'

She said, 'Well, probably not very much, but that's the minimum amount you have to spend to qualify for the offer.' She called out to a supervisor who was beside the next till, delivering more plastic bags. 'May – could you get this gentleman something for 14p plus to make it up to the money-off offer?'

May said, 'No problem. Anything in particular you would like, sir?'

'No,' I said, because for the moment I had purchased everything I really wanted.

'Well,' she said, 'we have a number of special offers just over here.' She indicated a display at the foot of the nearest aisle. 'I can give you a Twix, or a packet of Starburst, or a crème egg or there's a small box of Tesco paracetamol.'

'Give me the paracetamol,' I said.

When I got out to the car park, I put the groceries in the back of the Mystery Machine, with the exception of a can of warm Pepsi Max and the paracetamol. I sat behind the wheel, opened the drink, and swallowed all twelve of the pills. It seemed like the right thing to do.

I drove home. Alison was not back yet.

I brought the groceries in and divided them into their respective cupboards, drawers, the fridge and the freezer. Then I began to retrieve the pills and potions that I had hidden in strategic places. Alison thought she had discovered all of my stashes, but in fact she had only found those which I had intended her to find. I am not an idiot. I know how to hide things. I swallowed and I mixed and I imbibed. It had been a long time, too long, and it was good.

Half an hour passed pleasantly. When they had still not returned I wandered upstairs. I found myself in Alison's makeshift study. I looked at her paintings and sketches of Page as an alien or demonic baby, and found that I liked them even less than before. So I took them down, and gathered them up, and took them into Mother's room, which smelled of sherry and cigarettes. Mother liked a coal fire in her room and it rarely ever went completely out. I tore up Alison's work and fed it into the embers of the fire, and it soon revived. It took a while to get through them, but I did not mind. I had all the time in the world.

When it was done, and with nothing better to do, I looked through Mother's cupboards, and at the dresses she had worn in my younger years. I took one of them out, a yellow number with little flowers on it. I remembered her wearing it to collect me from school, before she went bad. I tried it on. It fit quite well. I admired it in the mirror.

I went back downstairs and into the kitchen. I extracted a pair of red Marigolds from beneath the sink and pulled them on. I moved into the corridor leading to our small utility, and opened the electricity meter box, above which there was a shelf on which I kept handy household items like bulbs, and fuse wire, and screwdrivers and hammers. I selected a hammer. I weighed it in my rubber hand. And it was good.

I took a stool from the kitchen and moved it along the hall towards the front door. I sat on it, hammer in hand, and waited.

After twenty minutes I heard footsteps outside, and the doorbell was rung, and I thought maybe that Alison had forgotten her key, but then I saw from the outlines in the glass that it wasn't her, so I got off the stool and answered the door and there were two well-scrubbed young men there in brown suits. They had plenty of teeth and were using them. They did not appear unduly surprised to see me in a dress. In their line, they were probably used to all sorts, and were just happy that I had not immediately shut the door in their faces. They were not aware of the hammer, which was behind my back.

'Good afternoon,' one said. He had to be in his mid-twenties, with a good tan. 'We're from the Church of Jesus Christ of the Latter-day Saints. We're visiting houses in the area and we were wondering if we could come in and have a chat with you about our missionary work and God's good news?'

I stepped aside and said, 'Be my guest,' and they looked heartened and hopeful as they passed by me, into my house, and I closed the door after them.